"I want ...

Marry him? T... ...ulcrous, so
incongruous, so impossible that Cora could only
stare at Rafael, her brain unable to coordinate with
her vocal chords or inform her feet to get her the heck
out of there. Forget the Spanish Mafia, Rafael
Martinez was obviously nuts. Loop-the-loop. A few
bricks, a bucket of cement and a shedload of mortar
short of a wall.

Then anger rushed in on a tide of outrage. "Is this
your idea of a joke?" Some kind of mad reality TV
show where billionaires humiliate the aristocracy?

"Of course it isn't a joke." There was that near
amusement in the rich treacle of his voice.

Curiosity broke through and surfaced the haze of
anger. "Why? Why would you even suggest something so insane?"

"Because I think marrying you will change Don
Carlos's mind."

"I told you that I am not for sale. Nor is my title. End
of." Finally her body caught up with events and she
pushed her chair back and rose to her feet. Tried to
ignore the stew of hurt that bubbled under the broth
of rage. There was no need for hurt. Why should she
care that Rafael Martinez was only after her title?
She'd... ...ea he

RAFAEL'S CONTRACT BRIDE

BY
NINA MILNE

MILLS & BOON

First Published in Great Britain 2016
By Mills & Boon, an imprint of HarperCollins*Publishers*
1 London Bridge Street, London, SE1 9GF

© 2016 Nina Milne

ISBN: 978-0-263-91985-1

23-0516

Our policy is to use papers that are natural, renewable and recyclable products and made from wood grown in sustainable forests. The logging and manufacturing processes conform to the legal environmental regulations of the country of origin.

Printed and bound in Spain
by

Nina Milne has always dreamed of writing for Mills & Boon—ever since as a child she played library with her mother's stacks of Mills & Boon romances. On her way to this dream, Nina acquired an English degree, a hero of her own, three gorgeous children and (somehow) an accountancy qualification. She lives in Brighton and has filled her house with stacks of books—her very own real library.

To all the wonderful Dog Rescue charities
and organisations who work so hard
to find loving homes for dogs
(like those included in this book!)

CHAPTER ONE

CORA BROOKES LEANT down to ruffle the Border Collie's head, and flopped down on the park bench. She adored Flash, just as she adored all the dogs she walked, but piled onto her day job, and on top of the extra accounts work, it meant exhaustion stretched her every muscle—physical and mental.

Still, she should look on the bright side—she had landed an excellent day job—an administrative position at Caversham Castle Hotel, part of Caversham Worldwide Holidays, and Ethan and Ruby Caversham were generous employers. So with her salary and all the extras one day she *would* be able to pay off the enormous debt that burdened her soul.

Determination banded her chest—she knew that repaying her parents wouldn't buy their love, or even their affection, but it would make Cora feel a whole lot better about how badly she had let her family down.

Don't go there, Cora.

Flash's sharp bark was a welcome relief from her thoughts and she squinted through the light spring mizzle at the tall, lean figure headed purposefully towards her.

Relief made a rapid exit as her forehead scrunched into disbelief. That couldn't *possibly* be Rafael Martinez. What would a billionaire Spanish-vineyard-owning playboy be doing in a park in the depths of Cornwall on a drizzly Saturday evening?

For a stupid second her heart skipped the smallest of beats. Hardly surprising—Rafael Martinez no doubt had that effect on the entire female population. Though in her case it wasn't attraction that caused the skitter effect—it was nerves. Logic told her that he wouldn't remember her—he'd shown no glimmer of recognition in the handful of times he'd seen her at the Cavershams'. Hadn't once indicated that he recognised Cora Brookes, Administrative Manager, as being Lady Cora Derwent, daughter of one of aristocracy's premier families.

And why should he? Cora had never been in the public eye. She had left that to her charismatic siblings, with their good looks and charm. She had kept her carroty-red hair, non-descript features and gaucheness out of the spotlight. Her only claim to distinction was the turquoise-blue of her eyes, and that hardly made her memorable. Plus, she and Rafael hadn't even been introduced at that one party years ago.

And yet she hunched down on the bench, busied herself with Flash, and prayed he would walk on by.

No such luck. Out of the corner of her eye she espied a pair of denim-clad muscular legs.

'Cora.'

The deep voice that always seemed laced with a tinge of amusement sent a shiver over her skin. Bracing herself, she straightened and looked up. Midnight-black hair. An aquiline face with eyes dark with a depth you could drown in. The jut of his nose spoke of determination and his jaw said the same thing. His lips charmed and allured, but his aura was one of danger.

This was a man who knew what he wanted and would take it. Not by force, but that only made him all the more dangerous—because what came with beauty was charm

and arrogance. Her family demonstrated that in spades—
and in clubs, diamond and hearts—the belief that they
could succeed at anything because it was their God-given
right.

'Rafael.'

'Evelyn told me I would find you here.'

Mentally Cora cursed Ethan's PA, but she could hardly
blame her. Rafael Martinez was Ethan Caversham's business partner and friend, after all, plus Cora had little doubt
that Rafael had charmed the information out of her. The
question was why? Even if there was some admin work
to be done on the Caversham-Martinez Venture surely it
could wait until office hours.

'Is there a problem?' she asked. 'I assume you know
Ethan isn't here?'

'I do. I understand he has whisked Ruby off to Paris.'

His deep tone was neutral, but the lines of baffled disdain on his face stoked her irritation further.

'It's very romantic.'

A shrug denoted indifference and caused her eyes to
glance off the breadth of his shoulders.

'I'll bow to your greater knowledge. I thought it a bit
of a cliché myself. But I'd be the first to admit romance
isn't my forte.'

No, but dalliance is. Cora bit back the words, though
she couldn't eradicate her frown—there was nothing cli-
chéd about Ethan and Ruby's palpable joy in each other.

'Paris is the romantic capital of the world and I'm sure
they're having a fantastic time.'

Heaven knew why she had turned into a romance cheer-
leader—her experience on that particular playing field
was nil.

'Anyway, romance is not what I came here to discuss.'

Of course it wasn't. The idea of a romance between
them was laughable.

'So what *did* you come here to discuss?'

Irritation fluttered inside her; she was not on the Caversham clock right now. Annoyance escalated as she caught herself in the act of smoothing her hands down her jeans, aware of a desire to smooth down her frizzed-by-drizzle hair.

'How can I help? I assume it must be urgent to bring you here in person?'

Wariness made her neck prickle. This didn't make any sort of sense.

His lips twisted in a sudden wry moue as he lowered himself to the bench next to her. 'You could say that.'

To Cora's surprise Flash sat up and put his chin on Rafael's knee.

'Flash—down.'

'It's fine.' Rafael patted the black and white dog; his strong fingers kneaded the exact spot the dog liked best. 'Is he yours?'

'No.'

The thought of her own beloved dogs rekindled the tug of missing them. But she'd had no choice but to leave Poppy and Prue behind on the Derwent estate—it wouldn't have been fair to bring them with her.

'I'm a dog-walker in my spare time. Flash is a rescue dog and he needs a lot of attention. His owner is working long hours on a freelance assignment so I'm walking him. He doesn't usually like strangers.' Her tone was snippy but she couldn't help herself.

'Dogs like me.'

Of course they did. In a moment of silence, as Rafael focused his attention on the dog, Cora realised that she appeared to be mesmerised by the movements of his fingers. The small growls of pleasure Flash emitted pulled her attention away and she shifted apart from Rafael, suddenly all too aware of him—the strength of his body, the way he filled the space with an aura of…of…something she had no wish to analyse too closely.

'So, as I said, how can I help?'

'Ethan mentioned he is about to send you on secondment to another Caversham enterprise.'

Cora nodded. 'He and Ruby want to focus on Caversham Castle, so he thought I would be better deployed elsewhere.'

'How about the Caversham-Martinez venture? Working directly for me?'

'You?' Her jaw dropped kneewards.

'You sound surprised.'

'I am. Or rather I'm confused.' She was an excellent administrator—it might not be the job of her heart and dreams, but she was darn good at it—but… 'Why not just email me and set up an interview? Turning up in person seems extreme.'

'I think it's eminently sensible. I like the element of surprise and this way what I see is what I get.'

His dark eyes rested on her face and Cora resisted the urge to squirm in her seat. The prolonged scrutiny made her uncomfortable—too aware that compared to his usual eye candy she wasn't anywhere near to measuring up. Especially kitted out in mud-spattered jeans, hiking boots and an oversized hoodie, with her red hair scraped back into a frizzy ponytail. But she forced herself to maintain eye contact, to keep her back straight and her gaze cooler than iced water.

'Or don't get,' she pointed out.

'So you wouldn't be interested in working for me?'

Cora tried to think, swallowed the instinctive *no* that had leapt to her vocal cords. Surely by now she had learned not to blurt out the first thing that came into her mind? How many times had her mother sighed and wrinkled her face in lines of distaste at her younger daughter's lack of social grace?

The constant refrain of her childhood had been, *'Why can't you be more like your sister?'* Why, indeed? Cora had always wondered. What cruel fate had decreed that her twin should be so beautiful, vibrant and perfect and that she, Cora, should be so different? So average, so invisible—Kaitlin's pale shadow.

As if in reminder, she tugged at a strand of her hair and looked at it. Carroty-red whereas Kaitlin's hair was a beautiful red-gold that caught the light with magical hues. If Kaitlin were here she'd lean forward, enthral Rafael Martinez with her smile, her throaty voice and a hint of cleavage. She'd lead him on to tell her more, and then decline in a way that somehow robbed her refusal of all sting.

Well, Kaitlin wasn't here, and Cora didn't want to work for Rafael. Every instinct told her that Rafael Martinez was every bit as lethal as her very own family. Well, she couldn't choose her family—but she could choose who to work for.

'I appreciate the offer, but I don't think that is the right move for me.'

'Why not? I haven't even told you about the role I have in mind for you.'

'It doesn't matter. Really, I don't want to waste your valuable time.'

Please don't let her have put a sarcastic inflexion on 'valuable'.

'It's *my* valuable time to waste.'

His eyebrows rose, though his black eyes held more amusement than chagrin. And then he smiled—a smile that had no doubt brought more women than she could count to their knees. Heaven help her, she could see why— but she knew the exact value of such smiles. What she *did* wonder was why Rafael Martinez was wasting one on her.

A flicker of curiosity ignited—one that she suppressed. No doubt Rafael expected her to roll over and beg to work for him. *Tough*.

'I appreciate that, but it would also be a waste of *my* valuable time.' A smile of saccharine-sweetness sugared her tone as she rose to her feet. 'I'm sorry, but I'm not interested.'

The man simply sat there, made no move to stand. 'Trust me, Cora. What I have in mind you will want to hear.'

The easy assurance in his voice flicked her on the raw.

'Hear me out. I accept that your time is valuable—I'll pay you well for it.'

Cora stared at him—heard the steel under the silk of his voice, saw the sculpted line of his jaw harden. Curiosity surged, despite all resolution, instinct and common sense. This was important to Rafael Martinez, but for the life of her she didn't know why. Administrative staff were ten a penny. Yet Rafael Martinez was willing to pay for her time...

Her brain emitted a reminder flare of her need for cash. 'No strings. I hear you out and then if I don't want the job I say no.'

'Deal.'

That worked for her—in truth there would be satisfaction in saying no. In pulling down his arrogance a notch or two.

'Fine. Five hundred for an hour of my time.' It was outrageous, but Cora didn't care—she would almost be relieved if he got up and walked away. *Almost*.

'I'll give you five thousand for a day.'

'A *day*?' Once again drop-jaw-itis had arrived.

'Yup. I'll pick you up from Cavershams at nine tomorrow morning.' In one lithe movement he rose to his feet—clearly her consent was a token he didn't need. 'See you then.'

Part of her itched to tell him to forget it, but common sense yelled at her that five thousand pounds was a windfall she couldn't afford to refuse. Suspicion whispered that he had orchestrated this entire encounter. And then there was a part of her that she didn't want to acknowledge—the one that fizzed with a stupid sense of anticipation.

He turned. 'And don't forget your passport.'

Rafael Martinez parked on the gravelled drive of the renovated Caversham Castle Hotel and for a scant second wondered if he had run mad—whether this whole enterprise qualified him for bedlam.

No. Resolve tightened his gut and clenched his hands around the steering wheel. This was the best way forward—the only way to persuade Don Carlos de Guzman, Duque de Aiza, to sell his vineyard.

Correction. The only way to persuade Don Carlos to sell his vineyard *to Rafael Martinez*. Because Don Carlos despised Rafael without even knowing his true identity.

Anger burned as the voice of Don Carlos echoed in his brain and raked his soul. *'Men like you, Rafael, are not the kind of men I like to deal with.'*

Well, they'd soon see about that. *Soon, Grandpapa. Soon.* The taste of anticipated revenge was one to savour, but actual revenge would be better yet. Full-bodied and fiery and with a hint of spice—like the Rioja the Martinez vineyards produced.

But first things first—right now he had to persuade Cora to join his scheme. It was more than clear that Cora disliked him—and the only reason he could think of was the fact she too disapproved of his background. To Lady Cora Derwent, as to Don Carlos, he must appear the epitome of jumped-up new money and bad blood.

That new money might be despised but it would be the key—he was sure of that. The previous evening Cora had obviously wanted to tell him to take a hike, but the idea of filthy lucre had prevented her.

A glance out of the car window demonstrated that Cora herself was headed towards the car through the light smattering of rain. She was dressed in a dark blue trouser suit expressly designed, it seemed to him, to minimise her assets, and sensible blue pumps. She looked…muted.

He swung the door of the sleek silver two-seater up and climbed out of the car; stroked the roof of his pride and joy—the glorious creation that was proof he'd left his childhood in the dust.

Not that Cora looked impressed—in fact her lips had thinned into a line of disapproval that Don Carlos himself would have applauded.

'Good morning.'

'Good morning.'

Up close, Rafael could see that her ensemble didn't just mute her: it almost rendered her invisible. Her red hair was pulled back in a severe bun, her posture was slightly slouched, her face ducked down. Perhaps it was a bid not to be recognised. Though *why* Lady Cora Derwent was masquerading as Cora Brookes was a mystery he fully intended to solve.

True, she had always kept out of the limelight, whilst the rest of her family played social media and celebrity rags for all they were worth. Nothing sold a paper like aristocracy, after all, and the Derwents were as aristocratic as they came—a family that traced its bloodline back to Tudor times.

The thought of bloodlines served as a reminder of his own and he felt the familiar pulse of anger. An anger he crystallised into purpose.

'You ready to go?'

'I am.'

Rafael walked round and swung the passenger door up,

waited whilst Cora slid inside the low-slung car, censure radiating from every pore. Perhaps she felt the car to be a vulgar show of wealth.

Yet he caught her slight exhalation of appreciation as she nestled back on the sumptuous carbon fibre seat.

As he revved the engine he shifted to face her. 'Cora, say hello to Lucille.' Another push of the accelerator elicited a throaty purr. 'See—I think she likes you.'

A very small smile tilted her mouth, and for a second his gaze snagged on her lips. Unadorned with lipstick, they were full and generous, and when she smiled he wondered why she didn't do so more often.

'You can't fool me. Or Lucille. You *are* impressed.'

A decisive shake of her head emphatically denied the statement. 'Nope. Not impressed.' Then, as if relenting, she reached out to stroke the dashboard. 'But you *can* tell Lucille that I prefer a British sports car to an Italian or German one any day. I like it that a UK designer came up with the idea, and I love it that it can compete with those European giants and come out the winner. Apparently Lucille is based on the "Blackbird" spy plane, and—'

She broke off and Rafael blinked. Genuine enthusiasm had illuminated her face and totally eradicated the dowdy image.

'You're a car buff!'

'No. My brother is, so I know a bit about it.'

Her brother. Gabriel Derwent. Super-charismatic, super-intelligent, currently abroad and off the radar for a while, following a public break-up with Lady Isobel Petersen. There had been a harvest of rumours along the celebrity grapevine of a family rift, but these had been countered by the Derwent publicity machine with assurances that the Derwent heir was involved in an exciting, new project, details yet to be revealed.

Cora frowned—perhaps in regret at the mention of her

brother, given the identity charade she wished to maintain. Then her lips snapped back into a thin line and she folded her arms across her chest.

'That doesn't mean I understand why anyone would spend such an exorbitant amount of money on a car. For the sake of a status symbol.'

'I can't answer for "anyone", but *I* bought Lucille because of the immense pleasure it brings me to drive her.'

Cora shrugged. 'I'll stick to chocolate. Cheaper.'

'But if you had the money…?'

Her expression clouded. 'I'd buy more expensive chocolate. Anyway, what you do with your money is your business. I wish you and Lucille well. In the meantime, what's the plan for the day?'

'We're on our way to Newquay airport. Then we fly to Spain.'

Shock etched her features. 'You're kidding, right?'

'Nope. We're going to one of the Martinez vineyards in La Rioja.'

'But why?'

So that I can propose to you.

Somehow he couldn't see that answer flying. 'So I can outline the job I have in mind.'

'So let me get this straight. You are paying me five grand to spend a day at a Spanish vineyard with you so that you can outline a job offer. What's the catch?'

'Hold on.' This conversation needed his full attention. 'I'll find a place to stop.'

Minutes later he'd pulled into a layby and shifted his body to face her.

'There is no catch.'

Her blue eyes focused on his face as her shoulders lifted. 'There is *always* a catch.'

'Not this time. I told you—all I want is for you to hear me out, and if you're not interested so be it.'

Cora shook her head. 'You seem mighty sure that I will be.'

'And you seem mighty sure that you won't. It's a risk I'm willing to take. It's a day of my life—if you refuse, so be it.'

'So no catch? Nothing nefarious? Everything above board?'

'No, no and yes.'

Rafael allowed his most reassuring smile to come to the fore but to no avail. Instead of bringing reassurance, his legendary charm seemed to have made her even jumpier.

'It just seems a little OTT.'

Not given the enormity of his plan.

'That's not your worry. Loosen up. Life is full of opportunities. Take this one.'

'I'm not keen on opportunity.'

The hint of bitterness in her voice didn't elude him, and a small stab of unexpected sympathy jabbed him even as he filed the information away.

'You don't *have* to take the opportunity,' he pointed out. 'You only need to consider it. What have you got to lose? Worst-case scenario: I tell you the job, you say no, and you've benefited from a trip to Spain and lunch with me.'

'Yay...'

Despite the sarcastic inflexion he was sure there was a smidgeon of a smile in her voice.

'Come on. Enjoy the day. When's the last time you took a day off?'

A long time if the slightly peaky look of her skin and the smudges under her eyes were clues.

'The temperature in La Rioja is twenty-two degrees. Plus it is an incredibly soothing place to be. Snow-capped mountains, leafy vineyards, vast blue skies, medieval villages...'

Enough, already.

An exhalation puffed from her lips and she relaxed back

in the seat. 'OK. I'm sold. But just so we're clear upfront, this won't make me swoon at your feet. Or make me want to work for you.'

'Understood.' He winked at her as he started Lucille. 'I love a challenge.'

And this one was a doozy.

CHAPTER TWO

'You hired a private jet?' Cora gazed around the interior of the plane as further misgivings heaped up. This was a bad idea. There was no way that Rafael Martinez would go to these lengths to hire her as an administrator. That was fact.

Mad thoughts filtered through her mind—maybe he was part of a drug-smuggling gang and this was an attempt to dazzle her with his wealth as part of a recruitment drive. Maybe the whole holiday venture was a cover-up. Maybe he was part of the Spanish mafia.

Maybe she should curb her over-active imagination.

'Is that a problem?'

'Yes, it is!'

Though higher in the problem stakes was the whirl of emotion that unfortunately wasn't only to do with the sheer insanity of proceedings. Ever since she'd set eyes on Rafael Martinez the previous day she'd been restless—edgy, even. The couple of hours she'd spent researching him probably hadn't helped either. Had only ensured that his image had haunted her dreams.

'Nobody hires a private jet for something like this.'

'Well, I do. Otherwise it would have taken us all day to get to La Rioja.'

Oh, no fair. The way he said the Spanish syllables evoked a strange sensation inside her and she had to force her feet to adhere to the floor of the jet. So he spoke fluent

Spanish? No big deal. The man owned a Spanish vineyard, and for all she knew he *was* Spanish.

Her research hadn't been clear on that point—it had simply told her what the world already knew: Rafael Martinez had been a teenage phenomenon, a millionaire by the time he was twenty, and he had developed a technological app that had taken the business world by storm. But right now that wasn't the point.

'But the expense…to say nothing of the carbon footprint…'

'I don't use a private jet every day. I do understand about the carbon footprint, but I also understand about the pilots who work for this company, the beauty of this aircraft, the mechanics who work on it. And I enjoy the luxury of not having to queue up at the airport, change flights and hire a car. I like the idea of not being spotted by some celebrity-spotter who then announces my destination on social media.'

The words arrested her—come to that, *she* wouldn't be too keen on recognition either. Her family knew she was safe, but they didn't know where she was or what she was doing—and right now she wanted to keep it that way. Wanted time and space to lick her wounds. More than that, there was her pride to consider. Next time she saw her parents she wanted to be in a position to hand over at least a fraction of the money she owed them.

Rafael Martinez was giving her five thousand pounds towards that goal, so maybe she should stop carping at his use of a private jet. Especially when in reality it suited her.

'Fine. I just feel bad that you're expending all this money on a losing prospect.'

As the roar of the engines signalled their departure he sat down on a chocolate-coloured leather chair that yelled luxury. 'Why are you so adamant that you don't want to work for me?'

It was a fair question, she supposed—and not easy to answer.

You're too good-looking, too arrogant, too successful, too dangerous...

Whilst true, that all sounded stupid. Then there were the fast cars, the private jets, and worst of all that aura that unsettled her more and more with every passing second.

'I have got to know the Caversham brand very well and I like working for Ethan and Ruby. I only have contacts in the company, and there is also the fact that I know nothing about wine.'

Her eyes narrowed as he shook his head at her. 'Very good, Cora. Top marks for politeness. Now tell me the real reasons. Tell you what…' He pulled his laptop towards him. 'How about I transfer your fee for today into your account now? Then you can feel free to say whatever you like to my face.'

A flush touched her cheeks. 'That's not necessary.'

'Then tell me the truth. Unvarnished. I can take it.'

There was that smile again—the tilt of his lips that somehow indicated that he knew he would win her over.

He tipped his palms upward. 'How can I hope to persuade you to work for me if I don't know what I'm up against?'

'Fine.'

If he wanted straight shooting she'd give it to him. After all, right now she didn't have to be a lady, and he'd given her carte blanche to be honest. Better for him to understand that her desire not to work for him was genuine and absolute. This was a man who went for what he wanted, and for unfathomable reasons he wanted her—Cora Brookes. Not Lady Cora Derwent.

For a second the idea held a fascination and, yes, a lure all of its own…

Time for a mental shakedown. The words *fascination* and *lure* were not apposite, and it was time to prove to Rafael and herself that she had no intention of calling him her boss. *Ever.* All her life she'd been surrounded by people like him, and for the past few years she'd worked for her parents—she knew what it was like.

'I don't like the way you think your wealth and your looks entitle you to—' She broke off at the sudden flash of something that crossed his face.

'Entitle me to what?' he asked, his voice smooth as silk.

'Entitle you to whatever you want—glamorous women, fast cars, private jets, endless favours…I don't like the sense of superiority…'

'My wealth entitles me to whatever I can afford, as long as I'm not hurting anyone or doing anything illegal.' There was no sign of a smile now, no hint of charm or allure.

'It doesn't entitle you to feel superior.'

Any more than *her* family's bloodline entitled them to do that.

'I don't feel superior.'

'But you *do* feel entitled.'

'To what? To buy a sports car? To hire a private jet? Yes.'

'What about the women?' Because, in all honesty, that was what stuck in her craw the most. 'They are flesh and blood—not carbon fibre or titanium.'

'I know that, and I'm thankful for it.'

The amusement in the tilt of his arrogant lips made her palm itch.

'I get that—but you still see them on a par with the car and the jet. As accessories.'

How many pictures had she seen of Rafael with a different model, actress or celebrity on his arm?

Rafael opened his mouth and then closed it again; a flush touched the angle of his cheekbones. 'I don't see women as accessories.'

Aha! 'Do I sense a touch of defensiveness there?'

'No.' A scowl shadowed his face and his dark eyes positively blazed. 'I don't accessorise myself with women. I don't collect them and I make it very clear upfront that my maximum relationship span is a few days and that I don't believe in love.'

Although the heat had simmered down in his eyes every instinct told her she'd hit a nerve.

'But you do admit these women all have to look good?'

'I admit I have to be attracted to them.'

For a second she saw the smallest hint of discomfort flash across his expression.

'But that would be true regardless of my wealth.'

'I think you'd find that without your wealth and looks you would have to lower your standards.'

'In which case the women I date are as shallow as I am.'

'And you don't have a problem with that?'

'Nope. I see no need to apologise for dating beautiful women.'

'What about the fact you *only* go out with beautiful women?'

'I don't *force* them to go out with me, and I make them no promises.'

'But even you admit it's shallow?'

'It's called *having fun*, Cora. I believe in fun. As long as no one gets hurt. I've earned my money fair and square and if I choose to spend it on living life to the full then I won't apologise for it.'

'So the whole fast cars, beautiful women, party lifestyle is all you want from life?'

Why did it matter so much to her?

Because she wanted to shout, *What about women like me? Don't we rate a look-in? What about those less endowed with natural charm and grace? People like me, who knock things over, say the wrong thing or—worse—say nothing at all. The ones who haven't been touched by the brush of success. What about us?*

'Not *all* I want, no.' His lips were set to grim and a clenching of his fist on the mahogany tabletop suddenly made him appear oceans apart from shallow playboy.

'What else do you want?'

'I want to make Martinez Wines a success, I want to run the London Marathon, to climb Ben Nevis, travel the world with a backpack, sail the oceans... I want to live life to the full and set the world to rights.'

Cora stared at him, unsure whether he meant it or was mocking her.

'What do *you* want, Cora?'

The question was smooth, but laced with a sting.

What *did* she want right now? A vast amount of money—enough to repay her parents for the loss of the Derwent diamonds, stolen thanks to her naïve stupidity.

What did she want from life? She wanted the impossible—approval, love, acceptance from her parents, who had shown nothing but indifference to the child they perceived as surplus to requirements.

For an instant she envied Rafael Martinez his brash desire to live his life as he wanted, by his own rules. He wanted to live life to the full and she wanted...

'I want...I want...' Her voice trailed off. 'I want to get on with my life. Be happy.'

But as she stared at him, so handsome, so arrogant, smouldering, for an instant she wanted him—wanted to be one of those gorgeous women he was attracted to. She wanted, coveted, *yearned* for Kaitlin's looks and her presence—that elusive 'It' factor her sister possessed in abundance. How shallow was that? Clearly the atmosphere was affecting her and it was time to get a grip.

'Are you happy now?' he asked. 'Do you enjoy being an administrator?'

'It's what I need to do.'

It had been a cry for approval. Another step on her

quest to be a useful daughter. She had slogged through a business studies degree and offered to help manage the Derwent estate. Had been doing just that when she had messed up—big-time. Following the diamond heist her parents had told her they could no longer trust her to carry out her job 'with any level of competence'. The memory of the ice-cold disdain in her mother's tone brought back a rush of humiliation and guilt. Reminded her of her imperative need to repay her debt.

'It pays the bills.'

Her minimal bills. For an instant the depressing contents of her weekly supermarket shop paraded before her eyes. Every spare penny put aside.

For a second a look of puzzlement crossed his face as he surveyed her. 'Well, the role I have on offer will definitely help with that. *If* you can get over your prejudice.'

'What prejudice?'

'The "I can't work for you because I disapprove of your lifestyle" prejudice.'

'It's not a prejudice. It's a principle.'

'No it's not. A principle is when you don't do something for moral reasons. Working for me wouldn't be immoral. So...' His voice was deep, serious, seductive. 'Promise you'll hear me out.'

'I'll hear you out,' she heard herself say, even as cautionary bells clamoured in her ears. *Fool.* Last time she'd heard someone out it had ended in disaster. A pseudo-journalist who had turned out to be a conman extraordinaire and had stolen the Derwent diamonds.

Turning, she stared out of the window as the turquoise sky and the scud of white clouds receded and the airport loomed.

Rafael led the way out of the small airport, glanced round and spotted Tomás and his pick-up truck. 'There's our ride.'

Cora's blue eyes widened in exaggerated surprise. 'And here was me expecting nothing less than a limo.'

'Tomás loves that truck like a child. In fact, according to his wife María he loves it *more* than he loves his children. Tomás is a great guy—he has worked at the vineyard his whole life, as his father did before him. I was lucky he and María agreed to stay on when I bought it.'

It had been touch and go—Tomás had deeply disapproved of the sale and hadn't believed Rafael was serious. Yet he had given him a chance to prove himself.

'He brings knowledge better than the most cutting edge technology and most importantly he loves the grapes, the soil, the very essence of the wine.' Rafael set off towards the truck. 'He is, however, the embodiment of the word taciturn, and doesn't speak much English, so don't be offended by him and try and remember he is a valued Martinez employee.'

Cora frowned. 'What do you think I'll do?'

Fair question. He bit back the answer that sprang to his lips. In truth he had been worried that she would look down her haughty, aristocratic nose at the hired help. Only Cora's nose was more retroussé style and…and maybe he was at risk of being a touch stereotypical. Aristocratic did not have to equal Don Carlos.

'Hey, boss.' Tomás's grizzled face relaxed into a fraction of a smile as they reached the car.

'Tomás. This is Cora. Cora—Tomás.'

Cora stepped forward and touched the bonnet of the truck, then bestowed a friendly smile on Tomás. Rafael's eyes snagged right on her lips and a funny little awareness fluttered—he'd like Cora to smile at *him* like that.

'This is wonderful,' she said, and turned to Rafael. 'Could you tell him that I'm truly impressed? It's better than a limo—this is a classic. I didn't know there were any pick-ups this age on the road any more. And it's immaculate.'

Rafael translated, and blinked as the old man's weather-beaten face cracked a genuine smile. One forty-five-minute journey later and, despite the language barrier, it was clear that Tomás and Cora had struck up a definite rapport. Tomás even went so far as to smile again in farewell as he entered the white villa he and María shared on the outskirts of the vineyard he loved.

'So.' Rafael gestured around, filled with a familiar sense of pride. 'How about a tour?'

As she stood there in the shapeless blue suit, her face tipped up to the sun, Rafael could almost see its rays and the sultry Spanish air spin its magic.

'Sounds great.' Cora inhaled deeply. 'It's incredible. It smells like…sun-kissed melons mingled with a slice of fresh green apple and—' She broke off and gave a delicious gurgle of laughter. 'Listen to me! The vines have gone to my head. Honestly, I could almost get tipsy on the smell alone. But they don't smell like grapes.'

Rafael glanced down at her face and a strange little jab of emotion kicked at his ribcage. Cora looked genuinely entranced—the most relaxed he'd ever seen her. Almost as if she'd decided to lay aside her burdens and the prickle of suspicion for a few moments. The sun glinted off the colour of her hair. It was a hue he'd never seen anywhere, as if woven by fairies.

He blinked. *What? As if what by what?* There clearly was a spell in the air.

Focus on the vines, Rafael.

'I think of it as the scent of anticipation and wonder… the whole vineyard is on the brink of what will eventually lead to this year's harvest.'

'So how does it work? I always imagine a vineyard looking as it does just before harvest.'

'Most people do, but this is a special time too. Bloom time.' Rafael halted. 'It's when the developing grape clusters actually flower, get fertilised. Look.'

He pushed aside a saucer-sized vine leaf and beckoned Cora closer to see the thumb's-length yellow-green nub, wreathed with a crown of cream-coloured threadlike petals. A step brought her right next to him and she leant forward to smell the cluster.

His throat tightened and his lungs squeezed at her nearness, at her scent—a heady mix of vanilla with a blueberry overtone. Her bowed head was so close he felt an insane urge to stroke the sure-to-be-silky strands of hair. The drone of a bumblebee, the heat of the sun on the back of his neck seemed intensified—and then she stepped back and the spell broke. Reality interceded. There was no room for attraction here.

The whole moment had been an illusion, a strange misfiring of his synapses—no more. Maybe brought on by the importance of his mission.

Her face flushed as she looked up at him. 'The smell is…intoxicating. You should work out a way to sell it. So tell me—what happens next?'

He wanted to pull her into his arms and kiss her.

The unexpected thought made him step away. Fast. 'You really want to know?'

'Yes.'

Fifteen minutes later Rafael broke off—at this rate he'd bore her comatose. Which would *not* further his plan at all. Yet Cora's interest seemed genuine—the questions she asked were pertinent and proof of that.

'Sorry. I get a bit carried away.'

She shook her head, the crease in her forehead in contrast to the small smile on her lips. 'It's fascinating. I didn't realise that you were so passionate about the whole process.'

'How can I not be? The whole process is magical. Though I've made sure we have the best technology too. I truly believe that the mix of the traditional and the new works. It took me a while to convince Tomás, but I've even brought him round. So it's a combination of his eye and modern technology that picks the grapes.'

'So you're involved the whole time?'

'Absolutely.'

'To be honest, I assumed it was a hobby for you. You know…kind of like most people buy a bottle of wine you bought a vineyard. But it sounds like you care.'

'Of course I do. These vineyards are people's livelihoods, and they have been here for years—in some cases for centuries. But it's more than that—this is a job I love.'

'More than you loved being a global CEO? More than you love your lifestyle?'

'Yes. The whole CEO gig wasn't me. Too much time spent in boardrooms. It was restrictive. I mean, I loved it that I invented an app that took the world by storm, but after a while it was all about marketing and shares and advertising and I knew it was time to sell.'

'So why do you think the wine business will be any different?'

'Maybe it won't be.'

'So if times get tough or you get bored you'll just move on?'

Cora's lips were pursed in what looked to be yet more disapproval, yet he'd swear there was a hint of wistfulness in her voice. He shrugged. 'Why not? Life is too short.'

'But surely some things are worth sticking around for?'

If so he hadn't found them yet, and he'd make no apology for the way he lived his life.

His mother's life had been wasted—years of apathy and might-have-beens because she had never got over his father's betrayal. At his father's behest Ramon de Guzman of the house of Aiza had deceived and then abandoned Rafael's mother, and Emma Martinez had never recovered—hadn't been able to live her life as it should have been lived. Until it had been too late—when the diagnosis of terminal illness had jolted her into a fervent desire to pack years of life into her last remaining months.

The thought darkened his mood, and it was only lightened by the idea of winning restitution in his mother's name.

Once Don Carlos sold him the vineyard, Rafael would tell him the truth. That he had sold his precious Aiza land to his own illegitimate grandson, whom he had once named the tainted son of a whore. Don Carlos and his son Ramon would seethe with humiliation and Rafael would watch with pleasure.

'Come on. Lunch should be ready.'

Time to get this show on the road.

CHAPTER THREE

As Cora walked through the beauty of the flowering vines curiosity swirled with anticipation. Over lunch presumably Rafael would outline the role he had in mind for her, and she had to concede he'd played his hand well.

The vineyard had enticed her with its scents and its atmosphere, and in the glorious heat of the Spanish sun it would be hard to refuse whatever he offered. But she would—because she knew with deep-seated certainty that whatever Rafael offered there would be a catch—a veritable tangle of strings attached. As the saying went, there was no such thing as a free lunch—let alone a lunch you were being paid thousands to eat.

Plus—she might as well be honest—it wasn't only the vineyard that exerted heady temptation. It was Rafael himself. Her prejudices against Rafael Martinez seemed to be in the process of disintegration. After her harangue on the plane about his lifestyle the very last thing she had expected was what she'd seen on the vineyard tour.

Rafael took his wine seriously—he'd spoken of the grapes with passion and a deep knowledge—and it was also clear that he had ethics and environmental morals she couldn't fault.

But, be that as it might, it didn't alter the fact that Rafael Martinez was dangerous. Because there had been moments when her heart had skipped a beat and his proximity had made her shiver despite the heat of the Mediterranean sun. Made her believe that all those beautiful glamorous women might well count themselves lucky.

The thought made her blood simmer. How could she, of all people, be at even the smallest risk of attraction? Rafael was like both her siblings—he only dallied with the beautiful and all he touched turned to gold. Cora was ordinary and average and went pink in the sunshine. Plus, she disapproved of his lifestyle, for heaven's sake.

As they approached the cool white villa a small plump woman bustled towards them, a beaming smile on her face as she surveyed Cora, and burst into a stream of voluble Spanish.

'This is María—Tomás's wife,' Rafael said.

Cora returned the smile, though a sudden hint of wariness made her hackles rise as María continued to speak, gestured to Cora, and then wagged her finger at Rafael, whose tautened jaw surely indicated a smidgeon of tension?

'Is everything OK?' Cora asked.

'Yes. María seems to feel that you are probably a bit hot and uncomfortable in a suit and is giving me a hard time for not telling you I was bringing you to Spain. She would like to give you a dress.'

Another torrent of Spanish.

'María says you mustn't worry. It is not *her* clothes she is offering.'

María chuckled and waved her hands.

'She says once she was as slim as you, but that the years have not been good to her.'

Cora shook her head. 'Tell her I am more scrawny than slim, and that if I look half as good as her in twenty years I will be a happy woman.'

'Her daughter owns a clothes store in Laguardia and

there is some of her stock here. María insists you change so you can eat the lunch she has prepared in comfort.'

'Um…' Cora looked down at her suit. 'It feels a bit unprofessional to change, but I don't want María to think I don't appreciate her kindness.'

And she *was* hot, and it would be a relief to clear her head of all foolish thoughts of attraction and temptation.

'Come, come.'

The plump woman gestured and Cora followed her into the welcome cool of the whitewashed villa.

María smiled at her, a smile that took away the disapproval indicated by a wag of her finger as she gestured at Cora's suit. 'Not right,' she said. *'Un dia especial.'*

Cora frowned. A special day? Was that what María meant?

The question was forgotten as María led her into a small bedroom, opened a large wardrobe and pulled out a brand-new dress. *'Perfecto,'* she announced, in a tone that brooked no denial.

Though denial flooded Cora's system. The T-shirt-style dress was vividly patterned with a butterfly motif. Bright, bold and eye-catching, it represented everything Cora avoided in her wardrobe.

'Um…'

María beamed. *'Perfecto,'* she repeated. 'Rafael. He love.'

The thumbs-up sign that accompanied the words did little to assuage Cora's sense of panic. Clearly María had grasped the wrong end of the stick. But how could she vault the language barrier and explain that really Rafael's opinion of the dress meant less than nothing? That she was here on a strictly professional footing?

What really mattered right now was the fact that she could not wear the dress. It was the sort of dress that Kaitlin would pull off, no problem—but Kaitlin would look good in a bin bag. The point was the dress did *not* constitute 'professional'.

But as she looked at María's beaming face Cora managed to manufacture a smile and nodded. 'Thank you.'

No need to panic, she told herself as María left the room. How bad could it be?

Ten minutes later Cora had the answer. Pretty darn bad. Self-consciousness swamped her, along with a dose of discomfort in the knowledge that there was way more of her on show than she felt the world deserved to see.

The door opened and María bustled in. *'Bella!'* She handed over a pair of jewelled flip-flops and a sun hat and gestured for Cora to follow her.

Minutes later they approached a paved mosaic courtyard, dappled with sun and shadow and awash with the smell of flowering grapes, the aromatic smell of spices and the tang of olives.

Cora's legs gave a sudden wobble as Rafael rose from a wooden chair and any last vestige of confidence soared away. No man had the right to look so good. His rolled up shirtsleeves exposed tanned forearms that made the breath hitch in her throat, and as her gaze travelled up his body her eyes drank in the breadth of his chest, the column of his throat, and the sheer arrogant strength of his features.

María said something and then turned to walk away. From somewhere Cora found her voice and a smile and said, *'Gracias,'* before turning back to Rafael. From somewhere she found the courage to stand tall, not to tug the hem of the wretched dress down.

Something flashed across his dark eyes: surprise and a flicker of heat that made her heart thud against her ribcage.

'That looks way more comfortable,' he said eventually.

Comfortable? She must have imagined that flicker—

of course she had. She was not Rafael's type and best she remembered that she didn't even *want* to be.

'It is,' she said coolly, and headed to the table—at least once she was sitting down the dress would be less obvious.

But before she could take a seat her gaze alighted on the table and she came to a halt. Crystal glasses gleamed, and a cut-glass vase of beautifully arranged flowers sat next to a silver wine cooler amidst an array of dishes that smelt to die for. This didn't look like a business lunch—and it didn't *feel* like a business lunch.

But what else could it be? Maybe this was the billionaire version. But María's words echoed in her brain. *'Un dia especial.'*

'This looks incredible.'

'I asked María to produce some regional specialities. We have *piquillo* peppers, wood-roasted and then dipped in batter and fried. Plus the same peppers stuffed with lamb. And white asparagus, whose shoots never see sunlight—which makes them incredibly tender. And one of my favourites—*patatas riojanas*—cooked with chorizo and smoky paprika. And *chuletas a la riojana*—perfectly grilled lamb chops over vine cuttings.'

A special meal for a special day?

'Is this how you usually entertain your business guests?'

'No. I don't usually give my business guests lunch here.'

'So who *do* you entertain here?'

'No one. I don't bring my dates here either.'

'So why me? Why have you brought me here?'

Wrapping one arm round her waist, she tried to subdue the prickle of apprehension as she awaited his answer.

Crunch time, and a small droplet of moisture beaded his neck as he surveyed Cora's body language. Doubt whispered as he considered his own. He had not anticipated an attraction factor. In all the times he'd seen Cora at Caver-shams he'd noticed her, been intrigued by the itch of memory that told him he'd seen her before, but there hadn't been any hint of attraction.

Instead he'd written her off as cold, aloof, and set on avoiding him. And once he'd figured out her identity he had assumed she didn't like him because of her social position—that she was a snob.

But now… Well, now for some bizarre reason his body was more than aware of her. Because it turned out that Cora Derwent wasn't cold or aloof or a snob. There was a feistiness to her, countered by the sense of her vulnerability, and he'd felt a tug of attraction even when she'd been hidden beneath that hideous blue trouser suit.

Now that she was clothed in a dress that showed off long legs and curves in all the right places his libido was paying close attention. Which was *not* good.

Especially as she was waiting for an answer to the million-dollar question.

'Well, why don't you sit down and I can explain. Have an olive. And a glass of wine.'

For a moment he wasn't sure that she'd comply, and before she sat her eyes narrowed. 'OK. But eating your food does not mean I will agree to anything.'

'Understood.'

He poured the pale golden wine for them and then settled back on the wooden chair. 'OK. Here goes.'

Cora speared an olive. 'I'm all ears.'

'So, I've explained how the wine business sucked me in—and I now own four vineyards across Rioja. You also know that Ethan and I have set up a Martinez-Caversham venture which will offer vineyard holidays. As part of that venture I want to buy another vineyard, which is owned by Don Carlos de Guzman, the fifteenth Duque de Aiza—it would link my vineyards beautifully and it is for sale. I arranged a meeting, but…'

His skin grew clammy as he recalled the churning of hope, anger and anticipation. He had even wondered if the old man would somehow recognise him—even though he'd known it would have been impossible for his grandfather to have kept tabs on him. His mother had changed their surnames and gone to ground.

'Unfortunately the Duque is…' *A stubborn old man and my paternal grandfather—although he doesn't know it. Yet.* 'Unwilling to sell it to the likes of me.'

Rafael kept his voice even, though it was hard. Each word stuck in his craw. But he didn't want Cora to garner even a glimmer of the truth. Though really there was no risk of that. Who would believe that Rafael Martinez was the illegitimate grandson of the Duque de Aiza? He'd had difficulty believing it himself. But there had been no disputing the facts in the letter his mother had left with a solicitor, to be given to him on his thirtieth birthday. The phrases were etched on his brain as if his mother had been alive to read them to him herself.

Cora frowned, confusion evident in the crease on her brow and the expression in her bright blue eyes. 'I don't understand…'

Careful, Martinez. Stick to facts and keep emotions off the table.

'Don Carlos doesn't approve of my background or my lifestyle, so I need to change his mind.'

And he was pretty sure his marriage into the *crème de la crème* of British aristocracy would do exactly that.

He sipped his wine, savoured its silkiness. 'That's where you come in.'

'Me? I don't see how I can help.'

There was a faint hint of trepidation in her voice and he saw her hand tighten round the stem of the glass.

'I'm an administrator.'

'You're more than that, Cora.' Rafael kept his voice even, gentle—he didn't know why Cora was hiding her identity, and he didn't want to spook her, but… 'You're Lady Cora Derwent.'

Her turquoise eyes widened and the sudden vulnerability in them smote him. For a second he thought she'd push her chair back and run, but instead she sat immobile.

'How long have you known?' she asked eventually.

'You looked vaguely familiar—I've got a good memory for faces.'

Probably because he had spent so many years studying them—always wondering if *that* person was his father, or related to him in some way. He'd constructed so many fantasies as a child, each more farfetched than the last, and yet none had been as out there as the truth.

'Then, when I was trying to figure out a way to persuade Don Carlos to reconsider my credentials, something clicked in my brain and I remembered that I had seen you years ago at some party. I knew exactly who you were. After that it was easy to make sure.'

Cora inhaled a deep breath. Her face was still leeched of colour but she managed a shrug. 'OK. Fine. I'm Lady Cora Derwent.'

Her voice was tight, but he could hear the supressed hurt mixed with a tangible anger.

'I still don't see how that helps you. I'm a lady, not a magician. I can't convince Don Carlos that your lifestyle is moral and upright. It wouldn't wash—the Duque de Aiza won't listen to *me*. I don't even get why you would want him to. Why not tell him to shove his stupid hidebound ideas? I wouldn't have the nerve, but I'm pretty sure that you do.'

'An enticing option, but that wouldn't get me the vineyard.'

'Surely there are other vineyards?'

'True. But not that many are for sale—plus, the Duque de Aiza made it more than clear that he would consider selling to the *right* sort of person.' With the right sort of blood. The supreme irony had nearly made him laugh out loud. 'Let's say this is the optimum vineyard, and therefore I am prepared to go the extra mile to get it.'

'Well, I'm not.' The scrape of her chair on the terracotta mosaic indicated that as far as she was concerned this lunch was over.

'Wait. You haven't even heard what I want you to do. Or what the salary is.'

Her blue eyes narrowed. 'I'm not for sale, Rafael, and neither is my title.'

'Do you agree with Don Carlos?'

For a second he thought she would fling the wine at him.

'Of course I don't. In fact I can't stand the man.'

'So you know him?'

'My family knows him. I went to his grandson's wedding a year or two back. Alvaro.'

Rafael froze—it took every ounce of his iron control to keep his face neutral, to keep the questions from spewing forth. Cora had met Alvaro—his half-brother—and Juanita his half-sister. She might have spoken with Ramon. *His father.* No—the heir to a Spanish dukedom wasn't his father in any way that counted. The man had abandoned him without mercy.

He blinked, suddenly aware of Cora's eyes on him, a look of assessment in their turquoise depths.

Cool it, Rafael. Focus on Cora.

'So if you can't stand him why won't you help me? Help the Martinez-Caversham venture? This vineyard is important.'

'I really don't see what I could do even if I wanted to help. Truly, he won't listen to me.'

Rafael inhaled deeply and said the words he had never in his wildest dreams thought he would utter. 'I want you to marry me.'

CHAPTER FOUR

MARRY RAFAEL? THE IDEA was so ludicrous, so incongruous, so impossible that Cora could only stare at him, her brain unable to co-ordinate with her vocal cords or inform her feet to get her the heck out of there. Forget the Spanish mafia—Rafael Martinez was obviously nuts. Loop the loop. A few bricks, a bucket of cement and shedload of mortar short of a wall.

Then anger rushed in on a tide of outrage. 'Is this your idea of a joke?' Or some kind of mad reality TV show in which billionaires humiliated the aristocracy.

'Of course it isn't a joke. I'd be up the creek without a paddle if you agreed.'

There was near amusement in the rich treacle of his voice.

'There is no danger of that because of *course* I'm not going to agree. I mean…I—' Curiosity broke through and surfaced through the haze of anger. 'Why? *Why* would you even suggest something so insane?'

'Because I think marrying you will change Don Carlos's mind.'

'I told you that I am not for sale. Nor is my title. End of.'

Finally her body caught up with events and she pushed her chair back and rose to her feet. Tried to ignore the stew of hurt that bubbled under the broth of rage. There was no need for hurt. Why should she care that Rafael Martinez was only after her title? But somehow the idea he would *marry* her for it made her feel…*icky*.

'Wait.'

The word was a command.

'Please.'

The second word was a concession that didn't so much as make her pause.

'The answer is no.'

'I will pay you a substantial salary.'

Without hesitation he named an amount of money that boggled her mind. Shame trickled through her veins as the words resonated in her brain and flooded her with temptation. The figure of her debt flashed in neon colours—and the yoke of guilt relaxed its hold on her for a heartbeat. The salary he proposed would nearly wipe out the amount she owed her parents. Could be put towards the flood repairs on Derwent Manor. Then pride stiffened her spine. There was no universe in any parallel existence where this marriage could take place.

'Still no. The whole idea is ludicrous.'

To say nothing of stupid. And yet Rafael Martinez was many things…unscrupulous, arrogant…but he wasn't stupid.

'Wrong. This idea is an opportunity. For both of us.' He leant back and looked up at her, seemingly at ease with their positions. 'If I marry you Don Carlos will see that I have changed my lifestyle. He will also, I think, be happy to sell his vineyard to Lady Cora Derwent's husband. After all, the Derwent blood is as noble as his.'

Cora frowned at the note of bitterness in the honey of his voice. 'You want a vineyard so much that you are willing to get married? Doesn't that strike you as a little over the top?'

'No. And I am not proposing we stay married. Once the knot is tied I will move full speed ahead to secure the deal.'

'Won't that look a little odd?'

'Not if I handle it right. I don't want to risk Don Carlos selling it to someone else. This would be a very temporary marriage of convenience. The whole charade should only last a month, tops. Hopefully way less.'

'There would be nothing *convenient* about us being married.' This she knew.

'What about the money? Most people would agree that is a pretty convenient amount to have in the bank. Plus you'll be able to enjoy a few weeks of luxury.'

Cora closed her eyes, grasped the back of the wooden chair and tried to fend off temptation. An image of her parents' faces when she repaid them the worth of the Derwent diamonds seeped into her retina—surely that would win her a modicum of approval, a way back into the fold?

The price to pay: a temporary marriage. A few weeks, *'tops'*, with Rafael Martinez.

Opening her eyes, she regarded him, saw the incipient victory in his dark ironic gaze. 'And where would *you* be whilst I lolled about in the hypothetical lap of luxury?'

Perhaps sarcasm would hide the fact that she was still standing there, a participant in a conversation she should have closed down long ago.

'Lolling right alongside you. This marriage would have to look real. The world will have to believe that we were swept off our feet in a romantic storm.'

For reasons she did not want to look into a small shiver ran through her whole body at his words. *Absurd.* The need to hang on to reality was imperative.

'As if anyone would believe *that*.' *Good.* That had been exactly the right mix of scoffing and disdain.

One dark eyebrow rose. 'Why wouldn't they? It's plausible enough—we met at Cavershams in the line of business and *bam*.'

The snort that escaped her lips might not have been

ladylike, but it was way more ladylike than the words on the tip of her tongue. 'Get real! You've admitted yourself that you don't do romance—you do *fun*.' With women so different from her it was laughable.

'So you're saying marriage can't be fun?'

The question stopped her in her tracks. Her parents' marriage was one of duty, not fun. Their commitment to the Derwent estate and the family name was unquestionable, and that was what their life revolved around. Fun wasn't part of the programme.

Rafael's lips curved up into a smile that turned all her thoughts into a fluffy white cotton ball. 'I promise you as much fun as you like in *our* marriage.'

Irritation permeated the after-effects of the Martinez smile. How could he sit there as if the whole idea of a fake temporary marriage was commonplace? Was he flirting with her, mocking her, or just having a good old laugh at her expense?

'No one in their right mind will believe the "romantic storm" theory.'

'*Everyone* will believe it. I promise.'

And suddenly the heat that surrounded her was nothing to do with the Spanish sun. Because Rafael rose, stepped around the table to within touching distance, where he halted.

'The world will believe that I have eyes only for my wife. That I am head over heels in love.'

The words were like molten chocolate—the expensive type...the type that tempted you to believe you could eat it by the bucketful and it would be positively good for you.

*No. C*hocolate—expensive or otherwise—was only good for you in moderation, and it seemed clear that this man didn't do moderation. Whereas 'Moderate' was Cora's middle name.

'It won't work.'

Thud, thud, thud. Any minute now her heart would leave her ribcage as he took another infinitesimal step towards her, his eyes resting on her face with a look so intense it took all her backbone to stay upright and not ooze into a puddle at his feet.

'Care to bet?' he drawled.

Right that second it was hard to care about anything but his proximity, the citrus clean scent of him, the sheer beauty of his lips and the look in his eyes as they darkened to jet-black pools of desire. Her lips parted and she released the back of the chair to bring her hand upwards—and then reality, mortification and the prospect of humiliation had her stepping backwards.

What was she thinking? *Acting. The man is acting, Cora.*

Something flashed across his face and was gone. 'We can pull this off.'

His words were a shade jerky and Cora forced her breathing to normal levels, prayed he couldn't sense the accelerated rate of her pulse.

'Your choice. Marry me…help me persuade Don Carlos it's a real union. In return you get a shedload of cash'

Cora tried to think. 'Then what happens? A few weeks after a massive high-profile wedding we announce our divorce?'

'Yup. We can make it an amicable split—say that we rushed into marriage and realised we weren't compatible. There will probably be a tabloid furore, but they usually die down.'

The idea made her insides curl in anticipated humiliation. As if anyone would believe the incompatibility story—the world would think that she hadn't measured up, hadn't been able to hold the attention of a man like Rafael Martinez. She would be able to add 'failed wife' to the résumé that already charted her failure as a daughter.

His dark eyes surveyed her with a hint of impatience and she shrugged. 'My tabloid experience is nil, so I'll bow to your better knowledge.' For that fee she could withstand a few days of paparazzi attention—the pay-off in parental approval would be worth it.

'Good. After that you could afford a career break, but if you'd rather return to work I'm sure the Caversham-Martinez venture could use an administrator when it launches.'

'That won't be necessary.' Because if all went to plan she would win back her job at Derwent Manor.

'Or, if you preferred, I'm equally sure Ethan will take you back.'

Her ahead awhirl with the surrealness of the situation, Cora tried to think. 'Hold on. *Ethan.* I can't leave Ethan and Ruby in the lurch. They took a risk taking me on in the first place, and…and they don't even know I'm Lady Cora Derwent… He and Ruby think I am plain Cora Brookes.'

'Once Ethan and Ruby are back we can explain our engagement and tell them who you really are. You can finish up this week in Cornwall and after that Ethan was going to send you on secondment elsewhere anyway. So you aren't deserting the Caversham ship. They'll understand. After all, their courtship was pretty whirlwind itself.'

'Can't we tell them the truth?'

'No.' Some reporter might get hold of them and Ruby couldn't lie her way out of a paper bag. 'Plus, the fewer people to know the truth the better.'

'OK.'

'So, any more questions?'

'What if it doesn't work? What if Don Carlos still won't sell you the vineyard?'

'You still get your money.'

As her thoughts seethed and whirled she studied his expression, the tension to his jaw, the haunted look in the dark depths of his eyes that spoke of a fierce need. This meant a lot more to Rafael than a mere business deal. Because no matter how reasonably he was spinning this idea—so much so that for a moment Cora had been caught up in the threads of the tale—it did not make sense.

'This is about more than a vineyard.'

'This is *all* about the vineyard. But my motivations are irrelevant—I am offering you a job, an opportunity. The question is, do you want it?'

For a long moment she stared at him, felt the sun soak her skin with warmth, and somewhere deep down inside her soul a remnant of the old Cora surfaced—the impulsive Cora, who still believed it was possible to even out the playing field with her siblings and win some love from her parents.

'Yes,' she said, and pulled out the chair, her tummy tumbling with a flotilla of acrobatic butterflies.

Tension seeped from Rafael's shoulders as victory coursed through his veins. The plan had paid off. Every woman had a price, after all, and he'd known money was Cora's Achilles' heel.

He pushed aside the small frisson of doubt. Turned out Cora was no different from those shallow women she'd dissed—cash and the promise of some luxurious living had been too much for her principles. Not that he would be fool enough to point that out. Yes, she had sat down, but she was still perched on the edge of the wooden slatted seat as if poised for flight.

She chewed her lip, and there came another wave of doubt as his gaze snagged on that luscious bow. *Again.* Only minutes before the desire to kiss her, *really* kiss her, had nigh on overwhelmed him. Rafael blinked. It had been an aberration brought on by adrenalin, by the knowledge that he was on the brink of success. Nothing to do with Cora and her absurdly kissable lips at all.

Focus.

He topped up her wine and lifted his own glass. 'To us,' he declared.

There was a moment of hesitation before she raised her glass and then replaced it on the table with a *thunk*.

'So how will this work? Exactly?'

'We announce our engagement; we organise a wedding. *Pronto.* We get married, I approach Don Carlos, secure the vineyard—marriage over. We move on to pastures new.'

'Define "pronto".'

'Two to three weeks.'

The potato she had just speared fell from her fork. 'We can't organise a wedding in that time. And anyway Don Carlos may not be able to make it at such short notice.'

Rafael shook his head. 'I can guarantee *everyone* will clear their diary for this. Lady Cora Derwent, from the highest echelons of English society, and Rafael Martinez, billionaire playboy from the gutters of London, get married after a romantic whirlwind courtship? I need the wedding to be soon—before Don Carlos sells the vineyard to someone else. Plus, a wedding shouts real commitment.'

A troubled look entered her turquoise eyes and a small frown creased her brow—almost spelt out the word *qualm*. 'Whereas this one's shout-out should be "great big lie".'

Ah. Her principles were obviously making another play for a win.

'Yes, it is a lie.'

There was no disputing that and he wouldn't try. But he didn't give a damn—he understood her scruples, but when it came to immorality the Aiza clan had graduated *cum sum laude* and Rafael didn't feel even a sliver of conscience at the way his moral compass pointed.

'That doesn't bother you?'

She'd tipped her head to one side and for a second the judgement in her gaze flicked at him.

'I totally disagree with Don Carlos's principles, but it is his vineyard to sell to whomever he wants. This plan is a con.'

The troubled look in her eyes intensified to one of distaste.

No. This plan is my birthright. This is my retribution.

The night he and his mother had left Spain was a blurred memory, seen through the eyes of a five-year-old, but he could still taste the fear—his mother's and his own. Through all the tears and the pleas had been the presence of a man who had come to see 'the whore' with his own eyes. Of course then the word had meant nothing to him, but he'd sensed the man's venom, had witnessed his delight in brutality and humiliation. Had watched those goons he'd brought terrorise his mother as they trashed her belongings.

But until recently he hadn't known the identity of the man he had dreamt about for long after their ignominious return to the London housing estate his mother had grown up on. Now, though, he *did* know—beyond the shadow of a doubt—and when he'd seen Don Carlos there had been a jolt of recognition so strong it had taken all his control to keep his hands unclenched.

'Rafael?'

He scrubbed his palm down his face and focused on Cora, whose troubled blue eyes studied him with concern. For a second of insanity he was almost lured into telling her the truth. An impulse he squashed without hesitation. To confide in Cora would be madness—the very last thing he wanted was for this news to go public. He didn't want Don Carlos to get a heads-up and the lawyers in.

All Rafael wanted was the personal satisfaction of getting some Aiza land and then telling his grandfather exactly who he was. Maybe that moment would in some way compensate for the way the de Guzman family had ruined his mother's life. Maybe the ownership of Aiza land would give him some satisfaction—he would produce Martinez wine from Aiza grapes and dedicate the wine to his mother.

'I will pay a fair price to Don Carlos, and if he makes the decision to sell based on the fact I have married a lady that is his look-out. We will be legally married. I will have changed my lifestyle. If you have a moral issue with that then now is the time to pull out, so I can find someone else. If you are on board I need you to be on board a hundred per cent.'

Her delicate features were scrunched into a frown, and the swirl of bright colours on her dress intensified the hue of her hair, emphasised the curves of her body. Cora looked miles away from the cool, aloof woman who had climbed into his car a few hours earlier.

He found himself holding his breath as he waited her response.

'So,' he said. *'Are* you on board?'

CHAPTER FIVE

WAS SHE ON board with the idea of marrying Rafael Martinez? Faking a marriage for money and a vineyard? It was a con of gigantic proportions and as such it should fill her with disgust. After all, she herself had suffered hugely at the hands of a con artist. Yet it didn't feel wrong. Instinct told her that whatever Rafael Martinez was he wasn't immoral—this was more than a business deal to him, for sure, but she knew his hidden purpose wouldn't be sinister.

Stop it, Cora. Why was she kidding herself? Her instincts had let her down before and she *knew* nothing. Everyone had an agenda. Including herself. The point here was that Rafael would give Don Carlos a fair price for his land. If the Duque de Aiza chose to sell just because of their marriage that was his look-out, and she would win her way back to the Derwent fold.

'I'm in.'

The words filled her with apprehension, and yet exhilaration zinged through her body as he lifted his glass and this time she raised her own, and clinked it against his. The sunlight glinted off the cut crystal and the sound echoed in her ears like an omen.

'So what now?'

'We get engaged. I thought we could do it here. I've got a ring.'

As he reached into his pocket a small thread of sadness tugged at her heart. True, she'd written off the idea of romance in her life, had accepted that men only wanted her for her title or as a conduit to gain access to her infinitely more desirable sister. But the cool, clinical nature of this engagement made her swallow down a stupid regret that it wasn't real.

'Is there a problem?' His words were said with a surprising gentleness. 'We can do it somewhere else if you prefer.'

'No. You've put a lot of thought into this.'

A sweep of her hand encompassed the beauty of their surroundings, the tang of the food, the smooth burst of the wine on her tastebuds. She glanced round, inhaled the glorious scents, heard the lazy drone of bees, let the sun warm her skin. Every sensation was suddenly heightened. The only necessity lacking was love; the irony was bittersweet.

'It's the perfect setting for a proposal. Are you sure you want to waste it on a fake engagement?'

'It's not a waste. Believe me, I have no intention of ever doing this for real.'

'How can you be so sure? Maybe there is an ideal woman for you out there.' After all, surely a man who had put so much thought into a fake proposal must have a romantic side to him—however deep it was buried.

'I'm sure. If I ever met my "ideal woman" I'd sprint a marathon in the opposite direction.'

'Why?'

'Because I can't see the point of setting myself up for disillusionment.'

'Maybe you won't be disillusioned. Look at Ethan and Ruby.' Cora thought about her boss and his wife—their love was tangible. 'They are ideal for each other.'

Rafael hitched his broad shoulders. 'For now. I wish them well, but at some point real life will get in the way of their foolish dreams of happy-ever-after.'

'I'm sure they'll have their ups and downs, but I believe they will sort out any problems they encounter.'

'I figure why have problems in the first place?'

'Because they're worth it for all the happy times?'

Rafael raised his eyebrows, his dark eyes wicked with amusement. 'But my way I'll still have plenty of happy times.'

'What about when you're old?' She would not let herself be put off or distracted by the teasing glint in his eyes. 'Will you still want interchangeable women then?'

'I can't see why not—I hope to be capable of "happy times" into my old age. What about you? I take it *you* hope to grow old with your ideal soulmate?'

Despite the mockery of his tone there was no underlying harshness—more a 'to each their own' vibe. 'It's not a hope I expect to achieve.' The words fell from her lips before she could stop them.

'Why not?'

'Because my ideal man is—' she broke off. 'It doesn't matter.'

'Sure it does. Tell me—it may help me play my role of perfect husband better.'

Cora shook her head 'No. It won't. It truly would be beyond your acting abilities. You are *nothing* like my fairytale hero.'

For an instant she would have sworn a look of chagrin crossed his face, though to his credit it vanished so fast she couldn't be sure.

'Hard to believe?' she asked. Of course it was. Men like Rafael were of her family's ilk—they thought they were irresistible, and to be fair to them woman and mankind had given them no reason to disbelieve that theory.

'Not at all,' he said easily. 'But I'll admit I'm curious.'

Why not tell him? Maybe it would be good for him to

know there was at least one woman in the world immune to him.

'My ideal man is someone ordinary.' Cora took another sip of her wine and allowed her dream Mr Right to float to the forefront of her brain. 'Someone average, gentle, endearing and kind.' As unlike the Derwents as it was possible to be. 'Someone restful—someone I can trust, and someone who loves me just for me. He wouldn't have lots of money or be upper class or have Hollywood good looks. He'd have a normal job—maybe as an osteopath or a teacher—and we'd live in a lovely normal terraced house, and he'd support my job aspirations and...'

And she'd got a whole lot carried away. Placing her wine glass back on the table, Cora decided Rafael had probably got the point—her ideal man was as far from Rafael Martinez as the moon from the sun. Unless, of course, you counted the treacherous way her body was betraying her dream man with its acute awareness of Rafael's.

'So you crave an ordinary life with an ordinary man? Why?'

Because she had been surrounded by *extra*ordinary people all her life and always been found wanting.

'It's not a question of craving. *I* am ordinary, and I am good with that, and I'd like to find a man who is ordinary too. Traits like kindness and generosity can be worth as much as extraordinary feats or beauty or talent.' She had to believe that—had made herself believe that over the years when her parents' indifference had made her feel less than worthless. 'Ordinary people have worth.' Just not in the land of the Derwents.

'You have no argument from me. Joe Average sounds harmless enough. So what's the problem? You said you had no hope of growing old with your ideal man.'

'Derwents don't marry the Joe Averages of this world. Derwents make alliances worthy of their name.'

Her breath caught in her throat at his expression—distaste mingled with anger darkened his features and sent a shiver of foreboding down her spine.

'So how will your parents react to our engagement?'

'I think they will appreciate that it's a business deal that—' *That will benefit them.* Cora stopped—she didn't want Rafael to know why she wanted the money, didn't want to relive the humiliation of the con.

'No.' The force in his voice was discordant in the lazy sun-filled air. 'As far as everyone is concerned, friends and family alike, this is a love match.'

Cora shook her head. 'My family won't buy that.' It would be inconceivable to her parents that anyone would fall in love with the daughter they considered inferior in every way *and* unlovable. The old familiar ache for parental love twisted her tummy.

'Then we will have to convince them. Will they have an issue with me not being "worthy" of the Derwent name?'

Discomfort touched her insides. 'They might…' No way would they let Kaitlin marry Rafael, however much money he had, but it was possible they might not care so much when it came to her.

'But the idea of my money might compensate.'

'Yes.' There was little point in denying it. 'But I really don't think they will care whether it's a love match or not. They have an immense belief in the worth of the Derwent name—they will totally get that you want a slice of it and that you're willing to pay for it. I told you—they will understand it's an alliance.'

'I can't risk anyone suspecting the real reason for this "alliance", or working out that this marriage is a fake. Especially given your family is connected to the Duque de Aiza.'

'But fake and convenient are two different things. Trust me—the de Guzmans don't do love matches. I'm pretty sure that Alvaro does not love his wife. I'm not even sure he wanted to marry her.' Both bride and groom had projected intense reluctance at the wedding, despite the camouflage of ducal splendour.

There was that expression again—pain, and a cold anger that made her realise Rafael Martinez had a dangerous streak.

'This is part of the deal, Cora. The world—including Don Carlos—*will* believe this is a love match. I will *not* risk this going wrong. If your parents have an issue remind them that I'll be footing the bill for the wedding. That seems only fair after all.'

There was no glimmer of potential compromise. Cora hadn't the foggiest idea why he was so insistent on the love match idea, but… 'OK. I'll do my best. Any other stipulations for the deal?'

'Yes. Whilst we are supposedly together you will only have eyes for me. It may be a marriage of convenience, but I require fidelity. No liaisons—however discreet.'

Well, seeing as 'liaisons'—discreet or otherwise—didn't figure in her life, that wasn't exactly a tough proposition. But for Rafael…? 'What about you? Will you be bound by the same rules?'

His eyebrows rose. 'Of course.'

'I suppose it would hardly show Don Carlos that you have changed your lifestyle if the minute the knot is tied you start playing away.'

To her surprise a flash of anger crossed his face. 'That is not why I will remain faithful. I may not wish for a long-term relationship but I do not seek to hurt anyone. You may not be hurt by my betrayal, but you *would* be hurt by the media headlines. I won't do that to you.'

'OK.' *Thank you.* She bit back the words before they could fall from her lips. *Sheesh.* What exactly was she thanking him for? An agreement to remain celibate for a few weeks? 'Anything else?'

'Yes.' A line creased his forehead. His expression was shadowed by annoyance. 'I should have mentioned this earlier. I will pay you the agreed fee in instalments, and I will pay you the full amount regardless of whether I get the vineyard or not. On top of that, whilst we are together you will enjoy a lifestyle suitable for my fiancée and my wife. But don't get used to it—this marriage is temporary. And the fee is not negotiable.'

All her inclination towards gratitude evaporated in a puff of angry smoke. Anger stranded with hurt inside her. He didn't trust her. Yet why should he? Rafael Martinez was a man used to dating women who were after his money—to him Cora must seem cut from the same cloth.

'I get it. This is a business deal—my title for your money, for a limited period of time.' Another man after her title… But at least he had been upfront about it and had something to offer in return. Plus, the lack of trust should maybe go both ways. 'I fully accept the amount is my full and final fee, and when it comes to the time to sign the divorce papers I will do so without any problem. But I think we should have a contract drawn up—after all, how do I know you won't renege on my final payment?'

If she'd hoped to annoy him her shot went wide—instead the frown dropped from his brow, as if he were relieved to have the situation back on a business footing.

'I'll make sure the prenup covers you for the final payment.'

'How does your being head over heels in love tie in with a prenup?'

'No matter how in love I was I would have a watertight prenup, because I'd be a fool not to realise that however much I loved someone they might not love me back.'

The harsh note in his voice mirrored the grim twist of

his lips. Rafael Martinez was clearly not big on trust or love, let alone a combination.

He gave his head a small shake, almost as if to rid himself from the darkness of a memory. 'So now that's sorted do you have any other questions?'

'Only about a million. I mean, where will we live? What happens now? How…?'

'Once we're married we'll live in Spain. I have an apartment in Madrid and a villa here in La Rioja. As for what happens now—I'll give you this ring and we'd better organise the wedding. I assume it's customary for a Derwent bride to get married on the Derwent estate?'

'Yes.' His words made her realise exactly what she had agreed to, and she couldn't help but wonder whether she had lost her mind.

'We'll also need to spend this next week practising.'

'Practising?' The hairs on her arms stood to attention as at an announcement of doom. 'Practising what?'

'How to pull off a convincing double act. Even with a whirlwind romance there is some information we will be expected to know about each other.'

The tension seeped from her body—that made sense. That was manageable. 'Sure. I can come up with a table or a spreadsheet for us both to fill in, and…'

Without so much as a blink of acknowledgement he continued, 'And then, of course, there is our body language.'

'We can't practise body language.' Oh, heck—that sounded so…*inappropriate*. But panic had started to unfurl at a rate of knots. Because her head was totally on board with Rafael Martinez as anti-hero. Unfortunately her body had clearly missed the train.

'Yes, we can,' he stated.

Was it her imagination, or was there a hint of strain in the depths of his tone?

'We have to make this look real, so we need to show we are attracted to each other.'

'If you think I'm going to plaster myself all over you, you can think again.' The very thought was enough to bring a sheen of moisture to her neck and heat her cheeks.

'I am quite sure Lady Cora Derwent wouldn't do anything so crass. We need to go for the subtle approach. The occasional look of adoration…holding hands as though it comes naturally.'

'I'm not sure I'm comfortable with that.' The very words were making her inwardly wriggle with a tangle of embarrassment.

'Then you'll have to learn. Come on. Let's go for a walk. Hand in hand. And instead of filling in a spreadsheet maybe we could talk. How about we go and visit the local town? It's historic, beautiful, and it has the kind of atmosphere that pulls life into perspective.'

He'd lost her after 'hand in hand'. *Hand in hand. Hand in hand.* The syllables careened around her brain with unnatural force. *Get real.* It wasn't that big a deal. Yet she couldn't remember the last time she had held hands with anyone—a telling point about her life. Or lack of it…

Breathe—and quit the overreaction.

'Unless there's something else you'd like to practise…?' he drawled.

Great. Now he was laughing at her. Yet instead of annoyance she almost liked the teasing caress of his voice, the glint of laughter in his dark eyes. Her gaze snagged on his lips and she gulped.

'Nope. I'm good, thanks. I'm just not a touchy-feely kind of gal.' Her parents weren't tactile—had avoided any contact with her—so maybe it was a button that had never been pressed. 'I'm better with animals.'

'Pretend I'm a large shaggy dog and you'll be fine.'

'Ha-ha!'

Though his words coaxed a smile they didn't solve the problem. The problem being that whilst her ideal man was comparable to a big shaggy dog, Rafael wasn't. Her brand-new fiancé was more lion, tiger and wolf rolled into one sleek, dangerous package. *Fiancé.* Hysterics loomed, and for once she was grateful that a lifetime of etiquette lessons allowed her to fend off panic and hide behind a mask of neutrality.

'Let's go. The village sounds beautiful.'

'First we need to get engaged.'

Cora pressed her lips together before an insane giggle bubbled from them. 'Of course.' Forcing her feet to adhere to the mosaic paving stones, she watched as he tugged a dark blue jeweller's box from his pocket and flicked it open.

It was hard to keep her eyes open when the diamond cluster glittered with almost cruel intensity in the Spanish sunlight.

Diamonds…her very own worst enemy.

CHAPTER SIX

RAFAEL GLANCED AROUND at the cobbled timeless beauty of the town but for once the ambience failed to captivate him. His mind was focused on Cora Derwent instead.

There wasn't another woman of his acquaintance who would have been so cool at the sight of that ring. A ring he had believed would impress any woman. The diamond cluster discreetly conveyed incredible wealth and untold elegance. Yet for a second he had been sure Cora was almost repelled by it, although she had slipped it onto her finger without demur.

Then, to his surprise, she had insisted that they clear the table, load the dishes and wash up before leaving.

Even María, full of excited congratulations and clucks of approval at their engagement, had been unable to dissuade her, so the three of them had made swift work of the clean-up.

'This is amazing,' Cora murmured beside him, turquoise eyes wide as she surveyed the ancient stone walls that surrounded the village. 'You can almost see what it must have been like in medieval times.'

'It is an incredible part of Spain. I'd like you to see the cathedral. It was originally built in the tenth century and it's definitely worth a look.'

'Sounds good.'

'And whilst we walk we can start to get to know each other.'

Despite extensive research he hadn't unearthed much about Cora at all. Every search ended in a fanfare on Kaitlin, Gabriel and the Duke and Duchess, but a dearth of information on the elusive Cora Derwent.

'Tell me something about you.'

'Such as…?'

'Whatever you like.'

'Um…I have a degree in business studies, I worked on the Derwent estate, then moved to Cavershams.'

'Why? And why incognito?'

Cora stilled for a second and then continued walking, although he could sense the tension whispering in her body.

'I thought a change would give me a more rounded perspective. As for being Cora Brookes instead of Lady Cora Derwent—I wanted to see what it felt like.'

Rafael looked at her. There was definitely more to it than that. 'I don't get it. Why would you want to be someone other than who you are?' It didn't make sense. Hell, he'd spent most of his life not knowing who he was and it had sucked—though now that he knew the truth he wasn't so sure it was much better.

'This is a fake engagement—I don't have to reveal personal stuff.'

'You do if it is relevant. If you are in some sort of trouble then tell me.' Maybe there was a more sinister reason for her need for money than he had suspected. 'Come on—this is about trust-building as well.'

'Fine.' Stopping on the cobbled street, she folded her arms and glared at him. 'How about you go first? Show that *you* trust *me*. Tell me something personal.'

Maybe he should have seen that coming, but right now all he could think about was how pretty Cora was. The dress skimmed her body, showcased all the right bits, but it was more than that. It was the character written on her face, the glint of fire in the turquoise of her eyes. Had he got so used to women whose aim in life was to please him that he'd forgotten what it felt like to be challenged?

The silence had clearly stretched too long, and Cora dropped her arms to her sides and shrugged. 'There you go. We clearly aren't ready to do personal.'

There was definite relief in her stance, and Rafael realised that he *wanted* to know something personal about her—something more than what was on her resumé.

'Not so fast. I'm in. What do you want to know?'

'Um…' Surprise scrunched her features. 'Something about your childhood?'

Reluctance tugged at him as he pushed his hands into his pockets and trawled his memories. The first five years were hazy—he and his mother had lived in Spain in a place much like this sleepy town. Emma had been happy—their tiny house had been filled with laughter and love. Sometimes there had been visits from a smiling dark-haired man who had picked him up and twirled him round and brought him sweets and toys. A man he now knew to have been Ramon de Guzman.

But then one tragic night all that had come to an abrupt and brutal end that had culminated in a trip to the grey shores of England and the harsh lines of a London housing estate, with a mother who no longer laughed, a mother who had been crushed and broken and betrayed.

Sometimes it felt as though his childhood had ended that night.

But he had no inclination to share any of that. Instead he found a different type of memory—bittersweet, but one of his most cherished.

'My fourteenth birthday. My mum and I went to the funfair—we went on all the rides and ate hot dogs and candy floss and we laughed. A lot.' It had been a magical day—one of his last precious memories before his mother's untimely death.

Aware of Cora's scrutiny, he manufactured a smile. Realised that to Cora the memory he had shared must seem meagre at best. How could Cora understand its precious value? His mother had spent years of her life mourning the end of her relationship, waiting for his father to return. She hadn't lived or laughed until those final months of her life, when the knowledge that she had so little time had spurred her to make the most of every second. Yet the look Cora gave him now was full of an emotion he would have classed as empathy if that were possible. Which it wasn't. Cora had a childhood full of wonderful memories—the same memories that her sister Kaitlin had described in numerous celebrity magazines: horse-riding, family banquets and the like.

'Your turn. Tell me... Tell me what you wanted to be when you grew up.'

'I wanted to work with animals. Preferably dogs. When we were children we were always desperate for a dog, and finally my parents gave in. Kaitlin and Gabe chose pedigree puppies, but I wanted a rescue dog. My parents were appalled, but they'd publicly promised we could all choose so they let me have Rusty. He was the scruffiest dog you've ever seen, and he was a scamp, but I loved him to pieces. I felt so terrible about all the other dogs I couldn't rescue—some of them had such horrific backgrounds—that I cried for days. I decided that one I day I wanted to be someone who helped animals.'

'So what happened?'

Her expression was closed off, her lips pressed together. 'I grew up and realised I needed to do something that would support the family.'

Needed—not wanted. And that still didn't explain why

she had stopped working for her parents and moved to Cavershams. But he sensed she wouldn't answer that question, so he led the way to the unassuming exterior of the cathedral.

'Building started at some time in the tenth century, but over the next couple of hundred years it was repaired and rebuilt.'

Anticipation built inside him as he pushed open the heavy door and was rewarded by her intake of breath.

'This is incredible.' Cora stood stock-still as she stared at the huge wooden panelled interior door.

The intricate carvings were indeed spectacular, with minute attention to detail in the beauty of the depicted figures—the Madonna, the apostles... But again it was Cora who captured his attention as delight and awe danced over her features.

'It's like a secret treasure trove,' she declared.

'And there are more treasures within.'

The magnificent altar and the ancient baptismal font to name but two.

Half an hour later Cora turned to him and smiled. 'Thank you for bringing me here. There is something intensely awe-inspiring about its history and the different contributions over the centuries.'

'Surely you must be used to that? Derwent Manor dates back centuries.'

'Yes...I do love it, and the family history is fascinating—I used to spend hours making up stories about the adventures of past Derwents. But occasionally I wonder what life would be like if we didn't live in a show house that eats money. What it would be like not to be aristocracy—if we were just a normal family. Whether life would be different.'

Her voice held a wistful note that puzzled him.

'Different how? Surely the important thing is that you

have a family, you have a background, and you have never lacked for money. You've never lacked for anything.'

Nor had to subsist on hand-outs from reluctant relatives. His mother's family had extracted and expected maximum grovelling and gratitude for allowing them to share their roof on their arrival in London and he'd loathed every minute. It was a loathing that had made his words come out more harshly than he'd meant.

'There are types of want and need other than food and a roof over your head.' Her words were said with an intensity that matched his.

'Such as…?'

Cora grimaced. 'Such as nothing. You're right. I know there are many people in the world with so much less, and I'm coming across like a spoilt brat. I'm sorry.'

With that she turned to face the altar, but her stricken look touched him with surprise.

'Hey…' He moved towards her. 'Look at me. I'm sorry.' Without thought he captured her hands in his. 'I didn't live your life and I don't know how it feels to bear the weight of a title.'

'I…um…' She glanced down at their intertwined hands and then back up to his face. 'When you're a lady all people see is your title. It's who you are.'

'No.' Rafael shook his head. 'It's a *part* of who you are. Part of what makes you the person you are. Embrace it. It's an asset. Use it.'

'Like I am now—by selling it to you?' There was bitterness in her voice and she tried to pull her hands away.

Increasing his grip, he refused to let her. 'Yes. Exactly like this. There is nothing wrong with our deal.'

'My title for your money. At least you're upfront about it, I suppose,' she said.

Ah. The implication was there that someone or maybe more people hadn't been. 'Yes, I am. '

Her gaze had dropped to their hands again and he smiled. 'See—holding hands. It's not that bad.'

'No,' she agreed. 'It's not.'

And just like that something shifted—awareness entered and heightened the atmosphere with its heady sensory overload. All he could focus on was the feel of her skin against his, her closeness, her warmth, the tendril of red hair against the curve of her cheekbone.

Whoa! Attraction was not part of the deal. This was a fake engagement. As his father's proposal to his mother had been fake. *No.* Anger clawed his soul. There could be no comparison. He wasn't lying, deceiving or taking advantage of Cora. Cora understood the score—knew this marriage was going to be fake.

Emma Martinez had believed that the heir to a Spanish dukedom had loved her enough to flout his parents and society. Turned out her belief had been mistaken, and she had paid for that mistake dearly. But now it was the Duque de Aiza's turn to pay—Rafael had a plan to gain retribution in his mother's memory and he would not let that plan be sidelined due to an unforeseen and unwanted attraction.

Realising he still held Cora's hands, he dropped them and forced a smile.

'We'd better go. I want to get back to Cornwall tonight.'

One week later

Cora leant back on the luxurious leather seat as the chauffeur-driven car Rafael had sent to bring her from Cornwall to his London apartment glided to a halt. Their original plan had been to travel back together, but he'd decided to return a day early and Cora hadn't been sure whether to be relieved or offended.

That was the whole problem with Rafael—around him she felt unsettled, edgy, and unlike herself. But right now she couldn't afford to be any of those things. Because here she was, outside the swishest apartment block she'd ever seen, in the heart of South West London, where property sold for the type of sum that boggled the mind.

And the charade was about to take off in earnest. Because she and Rafael were off to dinner with her family in a five-star restaurant. Joyful reunion? Cora thought not—and her heart plummeted in her chest at the idea.

The car door swung open and there was Rafael.

'Hi.'

Cora climbed out and her poor confused heart stopped its downward surge and did a strange little pitter-pat. The man looked divine—suited and booted and utterly gorgeous. Familiar feelings of inadequacy trickled through Cora's veins—Rafael would fit right in with her family, leaving her the perennial misfit.

'Hi.'

His gaze raked over her and she forced herself to meet his eyes, steeled herself against the assessment in his. There was no way *his* heart was pounding in the breadth of his chest at *her* appearance.

'Come on in.'

'Um…' It felt like the equivalent of Daniel and the lions' den—Rafael's home versus a family dinner. Talk about a 'between a rock and a hard place' scenario. 'Maybe we should go straight to the restaurant.'

'We've got time. Anyway, I have something for you.'

'Oh…' His expression was neutral, and as she followed him into the marble lobby she felt that same sense of being wrongfooted again. What did he have for her? Why? Did he think she was like his usual type of women, who expected lavish gifts?

Then all such thoughts were taken over by the sheer wow factor as she took in the extent of his London home. Lavish didn't cover it—the apartment was *huge*. The lounge made her eyes widen as she took in the floor-to-ceiling windows that looked out on a London panorama. And yet the interior design was simple, minimal, with a home-like feel.

'It's beautiful.'

'Thank you. I don't spend a lot of time here, but when I *am* here I like to feel comfortable and uncluttered.'

Envy touched her for a second. The words summed him up—he lived his life free of clutter, whereas sometimes *her* life felt like an accumulation of emotional debris.

He pushed upon a door and stepped back to usher her in. 'This will be your bedroom whilst we are in London.'

Again space and light gave the room a feeling of luxury without being too overbearingly opulent. The enormous king-size bed looked so comfortable that Cora had a sudden desire to go and live in it. She would pull the duvet over her head and block out the world. Inhale the scent of the freshly cut flowers on the dresser…imagine that entry into the cavernous wardrobe would lead to a fantasy land.

'I bought you this for tonight.'

He gestured to the bed and Cora moved across the plush carpet.

There on the snow-white duvet was a dress—and not any old dress. This dress looked as if it had been spun from gold into a garment that epitomised elegant sophistication. It was exactly the type of dress that would be expected of a girlfriend of Rafael Martinez.

Turning, she saw the look of expectation on his face—clearly the norm here would be girlish cries of appreciation and who knew what other displays of gratitude?

Anger began a slow, deep burn. *Deep breath, Cora.* The man might be misguided but he had given her a gift, and the level of her rage was perhaps a touch out of proportion.

'Thank you very much, but actually I would rather stick with what I'm wearing.' The look of surprise on his face should have caused her amusement—instead it stirred hurt into the broth of her emotions. 'Unless you have a problem with that?'

His dark eyes looked over the dress she had decided on as appropriate. It was nothing like the golden concoction that seemed to call and lure from the bed, but it was good quality—a dark grey, mid-calf-length, demure collared garment. It whispered discretion and that rendered it perfect.

'I don't have a problem as such—but that dress does *zilch* for you. In fact it almost mutes you. You would look a hundred times better in the other one.'

He was probably right. But… 'That isn't the point. I will not dress to fit your criteria or to measure up to what you expect of your eye candy.'

'It is nothing to do with my criteria.' The words were said with more than a suggestion of gritted teeth. 'Part of our deal is that you will play the role of happy fiancée and wife *convincingly.*'

'So you're saying that no one will believe you would marry someone who looks like *this*?' As she gestured downwards with a sweep of her hand she focused on the anger and pushed away the hurt.

'No!' Rafael stepped forward, inhaled a deep breath and rubbed the back of his neck.

She could almost see the thought cloud forming above his head. *Give me patience.*

'No. That's not what I meant at all.' For a long moment his dark eyes rested on her in a scrutiny she schooled herself to meet. 'I bought the dress because this is the evening we will announce our engagement. I got the impression you were a bit nervous about this dinner, and pulling the whole act off, and I thought a fantastic dress might help.'

'Oh…' The anger fizzled out—Rafael was trying to help. The idea produced a funny little pit of warmth in her tummy. But she still couldn't wear the dress. The memory of six years ago still burned—the searing humiliation was still fresh. Those words still rang in her ears, made worse because they'd been said with gentleness: *'However hard you try you can't ever be anything but a pale shadow of your sister.'*

Blinking away the memory, she stared at the dress on the bed and for a crazy second imagined herself in it. A sense of anticipation caught her by surprise. A strange, feminine desire for Rafael to approve—no, to be awe-struck, to see the socks fall from his feet.

Whoa. Careful, Cora.

For a start she didn't or at least shouldn't care what Rafael thought, and secondly the heavy knowledge weighed her down that the moment they entered the restaurant and saw Kaitlin she would fade away no matter what dress she wore. Better not to compete—the playing field was way too uneven. Better to melt away, be her own person, and if that person was 'muted' so be it.

Turning away from the shimmer of gold, she faced him. 'I appreciate this. Really. But I can't wear it.' Heaven knew that sounded inane and she braced herself for his argument.

'Hey...'

Before she could do more than register the unexpected compassion in his voice he had stepped forward and his hands cupped her jaw with a gentleness that caught her breath.

'It's OK. Don't look so sad. That was not my intent. I don't get it, but if you prefer your dress that's fine with me. But would you do me a favour?'

'What?' The word was a whisper. Her whole being was wrapped up in his touch, the feel of his roughened finger-tips against her skin.

'Keep the dress for another occasion—another time

when you do feel comfortable in it. Because you will wow the world and the man you wear it for.'

Cora gulped down the sudden urge to cry as she nodded.

'And one more favour?' he added.

Gathering herself together, she managed a tremulous smile. 'Depends what it is.'

'Will you wear your hair loose tonight?'

Cora stilled. 'Why?'

'Because you have beautiful hair and I think the world should see it.'

As she stared up into the dark pools of his eyes all ability to think vanished. There was sincerity in his gaze—sincerity and a blaze that made her head whirl.

'I...I...'

'Let me.'

Then his fingers were in her hair, gently and deftly removing the plethora of pins that kept the heavy mass under control and as invisible as possible.

'There.'

The satisfaction in his voice stroked her skin and made protest impossible. Instead she gave her head a little shake and felt the locks tumble to her shoulders. She looked back up at him—and, heaven help her, she wanted him to kiss her.

CHAPTER SEVEN

RAFAEL STARED DOWN into Cora's face—she was beautiful. The realisation pounded in his brain and jolted him to awareness. *Rein it in.* Kissing Cora was not an option—because if he did it wouldn't be pretence, it would be for real. And it wouldn't stop at one fake practice kiss. This was not part of the plan.

Inhaling deeply, he released her gently and took a step back. 'We'd better get going.' The words sounded strained, but for the life of him he couldn't help it.

'Yes…' It seemed that Cora was in the same predicament, because that was all she said before she followed him towards the bedroom door.

The silence reigned, ruled and dictated as the limo glided along the London streets en route to the restaurant chosen by the Duke and Duchess. Annoyance at his own stupid irresponsibility churned in his gut. This dinner was important, and like a fool he had taken his eye off the main chance—blindsided by the unexpected jolt of desire—and had spooked Cora.

Glancing across at her, he absorbed the expressive cast of her face, saw the nervous smoothing of her dress and cursed himself anew. The last thing he needed was for this dinner to go awry—their engagement announcement had to look real.

'So, let's go through our plan of action for tonight.'

As she turned from the window to face him he could see her pallor in the shine of the streetlights that illuminated the London pavements.

'You don't need to worry,' she said. 'I understand what you expect of me at dinner and I'll do the job you are paying me for. I've agreed to play the role of loving fiancée and I will.'

'How about some last-minute tips on how to impress your family?' Somehow he needed to activate conversation, to recapture the more relaxed attitude they had achieved in Cornwall.

'You don't need any tips.'

Rafael frowned at the hint of bitterness that infused her words.

'You are perfectly capable of charming my family—especially as they are perfectly happy to be charmed.'

That knowledge still niggled him—he'd expected the Duke and Duchess to put up some resistance. 'So you still have no idea why they accepted our engagement so readily?'

'No.'

The answer was too quick and his disquiet intensified.

'But does it matter? The important thing is that they did, and they will now orchestrate this engagement so that everyone including Don Carlos will believe in it. The press will be all over it after dinner.'

'Are you worried about that?' Frustration touched him anew that she had refused the dress. 'I know you've always shunned the limelight.' He just didn't know why.

'The public eye and I don't have the best relationship.'

The tightness in her voice spoke of memories she would rather not relive, and curiosity and sympathy mingled in him.

'So I figure it's best to leave it to my family. That's why I don't need to worry about tonight—I can hide behind the rest of you.'

'You don't need to hide. Especially not tonight. Tonight *you're* the star of the show.'

Her look said *As if*, even as she nodded her head. 'I told you not to worry. I'll make sure I wave the engagement ring at the cameras—I'm sure that will dazzle every reporter into a shedload of belief in our engagement. I understand my role.'

'OK. Then let's make doubly sure I understand mine.' The press announcement would go better if dinner was a success—in which case he couldn't rock the unexpected boat of his acceptance into the Derwent clan. 'Your parents and Kaitlin will be there tonight, but Gabriel won't?'

'Correct. Actually, it's probably best if you don't mention Gabe at all.'

'Why not?'

A troubled look crossed her face. 'Because I don't really know what is going on with him.'

'You can trust me with this. Whatever you tell me about Gabe stops here. The more I know, the less likely I am to upset the apple cart at dinner.'

'I can't tell you what I don't know myself. A few months ago Gabe suddenly broke up with his girlfriend and upped sticks to go abroad.There was some pretty unsavoury press around the split which my parents stamped on but I don't know any more than that. I was working at Cavershams and I wasn't at home when it all went down.'

'And you haven't heard from him since?'

'Nope. We aren't that close, though he and Kaitlin are. But if she knows she isn't telling.'

'Not even her twin?'

'No.'

The clipped note raised another flag of concern; the last thing he wanted was some sort of family row at the table tonight.

'But you and Kaitlin are close?'

Cora shifted on the leather seat and slipped her hands under her thighs. 'Of course.'

'Is it true that twins have a special link?'

'When we were younger we did. There were times when I sensed Kaitlin's feelings, or was worried about her even though we weren't in the same place. But as we grew older that happened less and less. The last time I felt it it turned out to be a false alarm. I guess we've grown apart.'

There was sadness in her voice, along with resignation, an acceptance he couldn't comprehend.

As if she heard it too, she shook her head. 'In fact you probably see her more than I do.'

'I do see Kaitlin. But I don't really *know* her.'

Before she could respond the limo glided to a stop at the back entrance to the restaurant and she smoothed her hands down her dress.

'You'll do fine,' he said.

Within minutes they were ushered inside, and before he could do more than register the dazzling interior, red-olent of fame, celebrity and an expert interior designer, Kaitlin swept up. 'Cora. Darling. And Rafael—you dark horse.'

She looked incredible. Kaitlin Derwent was rhapsodised over in the press for her looks, her poise and her sophistication. Rumours abounded about her love-life, but always in the most tasteful of ways—never tainted by scandal. Kaitlin had never so much as fallen out of a single night-club even a touch inebriated. Yet somehow she didn't come across as a goody-two-shoes. Kaitlin was the poster girl for the aristocracy, and the smile she bestowed on them was generous and genuine—it lit up her classically beautiful face with its sculpted cheekbones and emerald-green eyes. Yet her smile didn't warm Rafael the way Cora's more hard won one did.

Next to him Cora stiffened slightly, then stepped forward into her sister's embrace, hugged her and stepped back. 'You look fantastic, Kait. Love the new hairstyle. The fringe suits you.'

'Thank you, hun. And I'm glad to see your hair loose for once as well.'

Now Cora froze, and whilst he had no idea why, he instinctively stepped closer to her and wrapped his arm round her waist to pull her close. 'Kaitlin, it's good to see you again.'

'I cannot believe you two have kept this under wraps. Cora, why didn't you tell me?'

Rafael frowned—given Cora's disclosure that the sisters had grown apart, Kaitlin's words seemed disingenuous, spoken because they were the 'correct' words to use.

'Your sister is wonderful, but stubborn—she refused to believe that I meant every word I said about how I feel about her.'

Kaitlin smiled, laid a perfectly manicured hand on his arm. 'Well, I am very happy to help you convince her. Now, why don't you both come over to the table? My parents are so looking forward to meeting you.'

Somehow he doubted that, but it appeared that Kaitlin spoke the truth. As dinner progressed the table rang with laughter and chat—the Duke and Duchess were full of charm and had ordered a wonderful meal. Course followed course, and Rafael could almost see the bonhomie oozing over the pristine white damask tablecloth.

So what was bothering him?

For a moment he let the music, the voices and smiles wash into the background of his mind and tried to pinpoint what his instinct was blaring. He knew instinct should never be underrated—his gut feelings had allowed him to fathom his mother's moods and work out the best ways and times to bring some cheer into her life. Instinct had made him his first million and subsequently added the magic touch to ensure his investment portfolio was the envy of many.

So… Now he knew that Cora wasn't happy. Oh, to outward appearances she looked the part of happy fiancée… but her turquoise eyes lacked the sparkle that denoted her real smile. The smile she bestowed indiscriminately on all her canine friends, whom he had met in the previous week—Flash and Ruffles et al. Border collie, terrier, or mastiff cross, Cora loved them all. The same smile she had occasionally graced Rafael with. But the smile she offered now was just an upturn of her lips, not the real McCoy.

Plus, she was too quiet—or rather the words she spoke were anodyne. They went with the flow of the conversation, echoes of whatever her family had just said. But it was as if she had to concentrate and consider each syllable before she uttered it.

Then there had been the trip to the ladies' room with her mother—it had been over-long, and when Cora had come back he had sensed her withdrawal, seen the shuttered look on her face. Yet the Duchess had been smiling the serene, gracious smile she was so well known for.

'It's lovely to see my daughter so happy,' she'd said, and as if in obedience to an unwritten command Cora had shifted her chair closer to his and laid her hand on his forearm.

And then there had been the Duke's jovial greeting. 'So you want to marry my daughter, hey? Sure you've got the right one?' Then a guffaw that indicated it had been a joke. 'Well, it's good for you that you picked Cora. We have higher hopes in mind for Kaitlin.'

Which brought him to Kaitlin—in truth he couldn't tell whether she was for real or not. Everything she said was either clever or funny. The idea of her putting even a little toe out of place was an impossibility, and it was clear her parents doted on her. True, they had filled the conversation with family anecdotes, but somehow, although Cora was mentioned, it was always Kaitlin who was at their centre. Gabriel seemed to have been whitewashed from the family annals completely.

'What do you think, Rafael?' The Duchess's melodious tone broke his reverie. 'Dear boy, you haven't been listening to a word, have you? Not to worry. We were saying that we're sure you won't mind if we whisk Cora away from you tonight until the wedding. There is so much to prepare in such a short time.'

Rafael raised his eyebrows. 'I understand there is a lot to do, but I'm sure Cora and I can manage some time together.'

Now the Duchess's smile held a hint of steel. 'We'll see what we can carve out. But if you want a whirlwind wedding, worthy of high society, then I'm afraid I will need Cora near me at all times.'

Rafael knew he should agree—after all it was the perfect solution. It would take the pressure off them having to play the part of happy couple, and he wouldn't have to get involved in the wedding preparations. Win-win. It wasn't as if he *wanted* to spend time with Cora after all—this was a business deal. Whatever the familial undercurrents were, if any, they were nothing to do with him. Cora was in this for the money—for all he knew it had been her idea.

And yet… Maybe it was a simple dislike of being railroaded that made him turn to Cora. 'What do you think, darling? How about you come home with me tonight and then I'll deliver you home tomorrow?'

'Um…' A quick glance at her mother and then Cora nodded. 'That works for me.'

'Good.' Rafael raised his glass. 'To the wedding,' he said.

A delicious concoction of strawberries, meringue and cream, a swarm of photographers and a limo ride later,

Cora was perched on the edge of a sumptuously cushioned, gloriously comfortable armchair in Rafael's lounge and staring out over the brightly lit London streets.

'You have got such a glorious view.'

'Yes,' he said, with a slight edge to his voice.

Glancing across, she saw that he was looking at her with an impenetrable expression.

'Whisky?' he offered.

Why not? She hadn't touched a drop of alcohol all evening and Rafael had drunk only sparingly, his dark eyes in constant assessment mode even though he had played the role of suave fiancé and prospective son-in-law to perfection.

'For lower class he scrubs up well—not as vulgar as I'd expected.' That had been the Duchess's grudging verdict, delivered in their extended stay in the restrooms.

'Yes, please.'

Accepting the cut crystal tumbler, she looked into the peaty depths and then took a sip. 'Beautiful. Fifteen-year-old?'

'A whisky buff as well? I'm impressed.'

'So am I—you may have missed your vocation. You delivered an award-worthy performance tonight.'

'You'd have been up on the podium right next to me.'

'Yeah, right. All I managed was a smile at the photographers.'

'That wasn't really your fault, though. Your parents did a lot of the talking, and Kaitlin played sister of the bride to perfection.'

His glance was way more discerning than Cora liked.

'Anyone would think the two of you are super-close.'

'It's important to present a united front.'

Time for a subject-change—she'd had more than enough of her family's dynamics for one evening.

'Just like it was important we portray ourselves as a

couple. I assume that's why you suggested I come back here tonight?'

'Partly. And partly because I wanted to make sure that you were OK with the arrangements.' Picking up his glass, he crossed the polished wooden floor and sat in the armchair opposite her, leant back with a frown. 'I sensed a vibe at the table—something not quite right.'

Now she really *was* impressed—she had thought the 'happy families' tableau had been deployed with conviction by her parents. So much so that in the first heady moments even Cora had almost believed it. Until the trip to the Ladies', where her mother had made the situation more than clear, and explained exactly how the family felt about the engagement. Not that she had any intention of sharing *that*.

'It all seemed fine to me.'

'Then why the need to separate us until the wedding?'

The true reason made her insides squish in mortification. 'You heard what my mother said. It's not easy to organise a wedding of this magnitude in two weeks!'

'Sure. But an actual embargo on our seeing each other at all seems a bit extreme.' Suspicion lingered in the frown line that creased his forehead. 'Come on, Cora. Tell me the real reason. I don't like being kept in the dark.' His eyes hardened and he put his glass on the marble-topped side table with a decisive *thunk*. 'Did you tell them that our engagement is fake?'

'No!' Affront scratched in her voice. 'Of course I didn't. You asked me not to.' His expression didn't change, and the idea that he didn't believe her hurt more than it should. 'Look, the truth is they *aren't* happy with the idea of a Derwent marrying someone of your background.'

'Then why were they so welcoming?'

'Because they don't believe our marriage will last.' Humiliation seethed inside her. 'They think once you spend time with me you will change your mind.'

Her mother's words rang in her head. *'I have no idea how you managed to catch him, but there is no way you'll be able to keep him. Not with your looks and personality. So we'd best keep you away from him before he sees beyond the title to the real you.'*

'They don't want that to happen before the wedding because they want to use the wedding to generate income and publicity.'

Though she suspected there was more to it than that. Her mother's emerald eyes had held a gleam of calculation that told of some sort of additional scheme.

She forced herself to meet his gaze. After all, why cringe at the truth? A woman like her *wouldn't* be able to hold Rafael Martinez's attention for long. 'Don't look so surprised. They have a point. You don't exactly have a track record of long-term relationships. You can have any woman in the world. If this engagement *were* real any minute now the infatuation would fade and you'd move on.'

'So they don't mind marrying their daughter to a heartless bastard?' His lips twisted in a grimace and he took a gulp of whisky, as if to cleanse his mouth of a bitter taste.

'No. They stand to make money which they can put towards Derwent Manor.' Cora hesitated. 'I know how mercenary it sounds, but for my parents there is nothing more sacred than the manor and keeping it in the family.'

'Not even their daughter's happiness?'

'They don't think my happiness is at stake—after all, I have told them I want to marry you. They think keeping us apart will help with that. They want to keep you out of Kaitlin's orbit as well, in case you try to swap sisters.'

How she wished the words unsaid, but all through dinner her mother's words had resonated. *'We can't afford for him to transfer his affections to Kaitlin either—and that's inevitable. Not even the slightest taint of scandal can at-*

*tach itself to her right now—not when we have our sights
set on royalty for her.'*

'Swap sisters?' Confusion swept his face. 'Why would
I do that? I'm engaged to *you.*'

'I know. I guess it would just have made more sense
for you to have tried to hook up with Kaitlin. You already
knew her, she is way more your type, she's beautiful and
sophisticated and she would probably have charmed the
vineyard out of Don Carlos by now.'

Cora pressed her lips together. What was she trying to
do? Convince him he'd done a dud deal? But she was on
a roll and couldn't seem to find the brakes.

'Plus she is far better in the public eye than I am.'

Cora and the public eye really didn't have the best of relationships—right from babyhood she had given off what
the Duchess referred to as 'the wrong image'. Once she
had heard her mother tell a photographer to hide her behind a potted plant because she looked 'too sickly, ugly
and pale'. The words had flayed her seven-year-old soul.

'I mean, why *didn't* you try her first? Or someone else?
Why me?'

A flash of discomfort crossed his face and her eyes
narrowed.

'You were right there. We worked together. It made
sense.'

'It was more than that, though, wasn't it? Tell me. You
asked me for the truth earlier and I gave it to you.'

Rafael sighed. 'At the time I thought you were cold,
aloof, and not my type at all. I figured that would make
it easier to be married to you. I didn't want attraction to
be a problem.'

A cold churning of humiliation swirled inside her. Of
course—he had chosen her because he *wasn't* attracted
to her.

'Makes sense,' she managed, drawing deep for poise.

After all it wasn't the first time a man hadn't rated her charms.

Seeking comfort, she took a sip of the whisky—welcomed the burn as the peaty liquid trickled down her throat, horrified that she could feel a tear prickle the back of one eyelid.

'Hey. Cora. Sweetheart… Don't cry.'

'I am *not* crying.'

This was ridiculous—her reaction extreme. It did not matter to her *at all* whether Rafael found her attractive or not.

'Oh, hell,' he muttered.

And then he was next to her. His hands cupped her jaw and he leant forward and brushed his lips against hers. The featherlight touch sent a jolt of sensation straight through her.

Not enough! her senses screamed, and as if in response he deepened the kiss. Without thought she wriggled closer to the muscular warmth of his body. Raised her arms and placed one hand on his shoulder and one on the nape of his neck, where a tendril of hair curled. She heard his intake of breath, wondered if he could hear the pounding of her heart as her lips parted beneath his. Then all rational thought vanished and she lost herself to the incredible vortex of desire, to the feel of his fingers against her skin, the surge of need and anticipation and sheer want as she eased backwards on the sofa, pulling him down with her.

Then the sensation of pleasure was ripped away, leaving her bereft and exposed.

Cora sat in near shock as she registered that Rafael had pulled away and risen to his feet in one lithe movement. As she gazed up at him, perplexed, he scrubbed a hand down his face.

'Hell. Cora, I'm sorry… That was a mistake and…'

Mortification hit her in a tsunami—what had she been

thinking? Rafael had chosen her as his fake bride because she was *not* attractive. The only reason he'd kissed her was *pity*, because she'd been on the verge of tears like some sort of idiot. And she'd reacted like a sex-starved groupie and kissed him as if her whole life depended on it.

Given her experience of kissing was on the limited side, restricted to a few teenage fumbles and one disastrous short-lived relationship, she had little doubt that she had humiliated herself with her gaucheness. If he hadn't stopped—no doubt in horror—she would have offered herself up.

The idea brought her to her feet as her skin crawled with revulsion. She scraped the back of her hand against her lips.

'I need to go.'

For a second she registered shock on his face, intermingled with a flash of anger. Then she turned and headed for the door.

CHAPTER EIGHT

HER WEDDING DAY. Wedding day. Wedding day.

The words careened around her brain, but no matter how hard she tried Cora couldn't translate them into reality. The past two weeks had seemed like a surreal dream of wedding dress fittings and press coverage, and in a daze she'd smiled and posed and allowed her mother and sister to dictate every detail of the planned extravaganza.

Through it all had been interspersed flash images of that kiss, overlaid with the burn of embarrassment. How *could* she have kissed him like that? When he had made it plain he didn't find her attractive? Even worse was the intensity, the riot of sensation the kiss had wrought. There was *zip* doubt that she would have slept with him. Joined that string of shallow, candy floss women, accepted a pity sha—

'Earth to Cora.'

Her sister's face swam into focus and she blinked and reached for a glass of water. And now she had no choice but to face him as she walked down the aisle. Her throat constricted.

'Nope, little sis.' Kaitlin's voice jerked her out of her reverie. 'You can't risk your lipstick smudging so much as a jot. You are a work of art.'

More like a counterfeit.

Cora summoned a smile. 'You look gorgeous, Kaitlin.'

It was a wedding where the bridesmaid had been groomed to outshine the bride. In the past fortnight it had become clear exactly why her parents were so keen on the wedding. They wanted to use it to ensnare royalty into Kaitlin's train. Prince Frederick of Lycander, one of Europe's wealthiest principalities, had been invited to stay at Derwent Manor in the run-up to the festivities and photographers and publicists had been primed to orchestrate a subtle bridesmaid's coup.

'Thank you. But this is *your* day.'

'Do you really believe that?'

Cora regretted the words as soon as they left her mouth—they hadn't discussed the Duchess's plan and it would be better to keep it that way. She and Kaitlin had always had a tacit consent not to discuss their parents' differing attitudes to each twin. Had known that to do so would ruin the relationship they had managed to salvage—one of civility.

Even in childhood Kaitlin had been compliant—whilst she had never mocked Cora or been mean to her, neither had she defended her to her parents. Yet the bond of twinship *did* exist, and there had been times when Cora had found herself calling Kaitlin, and vice versa, just to check if her sister was all right.

Kaitlin sighed. 'I believe it should be. But what I hope most of all is that you and Rafael are happy together. Mum and Dad don't have to be right, you know—if you and Rafael love each other this marriage *will* work.'

Cora frowned. Was that a tear? 'Kait? You OK?'

'Of course I am. I'm just glad for you. Be happy, little sis.'

If only. Cora couldn't see so much as a glimmer of happiness in her near future. She had no idea how Rafael would be, but anger would be somewhere in the mix. Given she had ignored his two attempts to get in contact and had kept herself behind the barricade of wedding preparations. Childish, yes, but she simply hadn't wanted to face him or her actions.

But now—now there would be no escape.

Her tummy churned and she could feel the colour leech from her skin, so no doubt she was paler than the creamy tulle and lace of her gown. If only she could locate a pause button and stop events. Better yet fast forward to when the marriage was over.

Pride stiffened her spine—if it killed her she would act as though that kiss hadn't happened. Perhaps if she tried hard enough she could kid herself that it hadn't.

'Let's go.'

All she had to do was follow her mother's instructions.

All you need do is smile, Cora. That and be gracious. Try to remember that, hard though it is to believe, you are a Derwent. Do not let your name down again.'

So Cora smiled and posed and waved from the splendid gilded horse-drawn carriage that bowled her along the gravelled pathways of Derwent Manor. The sun had decided to co-operate and it glinted on the green-leaved oaks that edged the driveway as the church bells rang out to join the clip-clop of the horses' hooves and the light jingle of their bells. Cora smiled until her muscles ached, even as the words *fake, fake, fake* tolled through her brain.

She alighted from the carriage and posed with her father in front of the ancient sandstone church that had stood for centuries and seen the nuptials of generations of Derwents. Her father beamed down at her, one arm across her bare shoulders. The irony struck her so hard her knees nearly buckled. *Everything* about this day was fraudulent—her father had never once hugged her, and now he was playing to the camera for all he was worth.

The impulse to shove him away, to spin on her couture heel and abandon the pretence, nigh on overwhelmed her.

But as her body tensed and turned she glimpsed the tall form of Rafael through the imposing arch of the church doors. Flight was not possible—she had made a promise, struck a deal, and she wouldn't—couldn't—renege on that.

Instead she kept her heels grounded and smiled even harder as Kaitlin and the Duchess stepped forward under the pretext of rearranging her veil. Cora sensed the shifting of attention to Kaitlin with relief, took the moment to regroup and try to soothe her ever-mounting panic at the magnitude of her actions.

Then she took her father's proffered arm and entered the church to begin the portentous walk down the aisle. The deep notes from the organ reverberated around the cavernous interior, bounced off the sunlit blues and reds of the stained glass and mingled with the delicate scent of the pew-end posies of sweet peas and stocks redolent of spring.

The simple beauty of the church weighted her soul and her feet in equal measure as she approached the altar and the man who had haunted her dreams. Her heart twisted, pounded and cartwheeled, but from deep down she channelled cool, tried to be aloof. Not by so much as a hair on her head would she reveal the sorry state she was in.

Instead she focused on her remit, sought out people, smiled at the aquiline profile of Don Carlos Aiza, nodded at Prince Frederick. She witnessed how few people Rafael had asked—a handful of business associates, but no family at all. She caught a glimpse of Ethan and Ruby, hand in hand, smiles on their faces, and a lump formed in her throat. Their vows had been meaningful. Hers would be worthless and the idea hurt.

The last few paces and the music swirled around her, the guests merged into an anonymous mass and there was only Rafael. Her emotions were in a tailspin as she absorbed his aura, sensed the leashed tension in his powerful body, glimpsed the ice in his dark eyes that belied the smile on his lips as he stepped forward.

Their surroundings diminished as the vicar took them through the ceremony; Rafael's deep voice was clear, confident, almost triumphant. Then it was done. They were pronounced man and wife and Rafael lifted the gauzy silk of her veil and took her hands in his. Cora looked down at their clasped hands and a host of sensations stampeded along her synapses. There was a thrill of unwanted desire alongside a disconcerting sense of safety.

'You may kiss the bride,' the vicar declared.

Rafael stared down into Cora's wide turquoise eyes and saw the hint of vulnerability in their depths. The slow burn of anger that had wrapped his chest for a fortnight dissolved in a strange ache of confusion. *Bad idea.* He needed to hang on to anger.

Anger with himself for the folly that had put this whole enterprise at risk. Kissing Cora had been foolhardy, but he'd wanted to *show* her how attractive she was—that he'd got it wrong in his belief that she was cold and aloof. One gentle brush of the lips—that had been his intent. Instead he'd released a tidal wave of desire and passion that he'd been nigh on helpless to withstand. It had taken every atom of will power to pull away from the brink.

But then he had seen her reaction, and the revulsion on her face had sucker-punched him in the gut. He had seen the savagery of her swipe against her lips, as if she had sullied herself in some way. It had dawned on him then that Cora was no better than the rest of her family, than the de Guzmans, in her inherent feelings of superiority.

Focus. Or it would be him who blew this pretence to smithereens.

Gently he tipped her chin up, dipped his head and touched his lips to hers. Against his will he let his lips linger, fascinated anew by the lush softness, the taste of mint with a hint of strawberry, the texture of her hair against his fingers, the slight intake of her breath. Something shimmered—a connection that bound them together.

Get a grip. They were connected in a business sense—temporarily. That was all. For better or for worse they had committed to this charade and they needed to see it through. Cora wanted money and he wanted retribution.

He broke the kiss and scanned the church until he found the erect figure of Don Carlos. His hands threatened to fist and he allowed an image of his mother to fill his brain, her heart and body broken by the Duque de Aiza's betrayal. Whilst he had been unable to protect her.

That was when he'd vowed to become strong—and he had. But no amount of strength had been able to heal his mother's sense of loss, nor had his strength been able to save her from the illness that had taken her. But now—now he could at least avenge her memory.

The thought carried him through the interminable photographs, helped to steel him against the Cora effect—her scent, her grace, despite the over-fussiness of her dress. It was an ivory and lace confection that she wore with a self-consciousness he sensed beneath her outer poise. He frowned—it wasn't the dress *he* would have picked for her—though he could see its beauty, the design was too lacy, too frilly for Cora.

'It's a wrap,' the photographer said.

The Duchess stepped forward. 'I'd like one final picture of Kaitlin and Cora together.'

Instinct nudged Rafael as he saw Cora's face etched with an almost stoic pain, clocked Kaitlin's expression of near refusal.

'Come on, girls—I think it's a picture the world will appreciate.'

Whatever the sisters really thought they nodded in unison, and for a fleeting second Rafael saw evidence of their twins' connection in the swift glance they exchanged. They moved close together for the photo and Rafael's frown deepened. Something niggled, but he couldn't put his finger on what it was.

Moments later the Duchess bestowed upon the group her trademark serene smile. 'On to the Manor for the reception. Now, I thought you two newlyweds would like a few moments' privacy, so we've put you in the limo and we'll commandeer the horse and carriage.'

Rafael studied the Duchess's expression and wondered if only he could see the glint of steel behind the smile. For a second he considered a counter-command but then decided against it. After all, he'd appreciate a private chat with Cora—she could hardly pull a disappearing act in a limo.

'Great idea,' he said easily. 'Have at it.'

Once inside the cool interior of the limo he turned to Cora, who had moved as close to the window and as far away from him as possible, given the sheer volume of her wedding dress.

'Are you and your parents hiding me away from the masses?'

Her lips twisted in a small grimace. 'You heard my mother—she's giving us privacy.'

Not a denial, he noted, but now wasn't the time to press the point even though the idea made his molars grind. The important thing now was the reception and making sure they pulled it off.

'Why didn't you return my calls? We needed to talk about the other night.'

Twisting her hands in her lap, she shifted to face him. 'No, we didn't. There is nothing to talk about. As far as I'm concerned it never happened and all I want to do is forget it.'

There it was again—her expression held a distaste that packed a powerful punch and chagrin hit him low in the gut. It was as though the thought of that kiss made her feel sick. His fingers clenched round his knees and he forced himself to relax. It didn't matter—all that mattered was the vineyard.

'As you wish. But don't let your feelings affect how you perform.' Anger and hurt weighted him down. 'This is our wedding reception and you need to play the part of loved-up bride.'

Her hands clenched into the froth of lace and she gave a small almost bitter laugh as the limo guided to a stop. 'Don't worry, Rafael. A deal is a deal. I'll smile my way through this.'

Cora's head pounded. Almost as if a thunderous hip-hop beat the air rather than the tasteful strains of classical music from an elite string quartet. But still she smiled at the parade of people who walked the receiving line where she stood next to Rafael, flanked by her parents and Kaitlin.

Behind them the famed Derwent Gardens were in bloom, a riot of spring colours and scents, forming the backdrop for the enormous marquees erected on the lush lawns. Muffled by the canvas walls, champagne corks popped amidst the tinkle of laughter and the chink of glasses.

Tuxedoed waiters circled with platters of canapés— skewered tiger prawns, *foie gras*, caviar-topped crackers, tiny herby croutons topped with shavings of smoked beef and parmesan.

All garnered murmurs of appreciation. It was the perfect fairytale wedding. And all Cora could feel was muted horror at the fraudulence of it all—after the clinical coldness of the past fortnight of wedding preparations. It was a wedding designed to dupe Don Carlos and entice Prince Frederick. And she was as guilty as anyone in the deception. Here she was—perma-smile in place as platitudes poured from her tongue in torrents.

What was Rafael thinking? What was he feeling? Impossible to know. A sudden regret assaulted her that she hadn't taken him up on his offer to talk. But no—there could be no benefit to an analysis of her humiliation.

Next to her, he tensed, and she glanced up at him and bit back a gasp. For a second his dark eyes had been pools of fury and pain. She followed his gaze and saw the approach of Don Carlos and his granddaughter Juanita. Without thought she shifted closer to him and upped the wattage of her smile as she faced the Duque de Aiza.

The silver-haired man returned her smile, though there was no warmth in the upturn of his thin lips or his eyes. 'Congratulations to both of you. I apologise that the rest of my family were unable to attend. Juanita—you remember Cora from Alvaro's wedding, don't you?'

The sultry dark-haired young woman shot her grandfather a look that denoted sulkiness but then nodded.

Cora stepped into the breach. 'I certainly remember *you*, Juanita—you looked so very beautiful in traditional Spanish costume, and your flamenco dancing was incredible.'

It was the right thing to have said. All trace of sullenness vanished and Juanita's face lit up. 'Thank you. I love to dance.' Her tone held the weight of defiance. 'If I could I would make it my career.'

The old man's face hardened and Cora almost flinched.

Then Don Carlos smiled. 'But you can't, Juanita. I have told you that.'

He turned to Rafael, and it was only then that Cora registered how rigid her husband's body was. She slipped her hand into his to give it a warning squeeze.

'Rafael,' the Duque said. 'How interesting to see you

again. I'm surprised you didn't mention Cora at our business meeting.'

Rafael had recovered now, his expression polite, his body relaxed. 'As you say, our meeting was business and this is personal.'

'Sometimes the two can connect.'

'Indeed.'

And with that the Duque de Aiza moved along the line.

Rafael glanced down at their entwined fingers, an unreadable expression on his face before he acknowledged congratulations from the next guest.

Then they moved forward to mingle and sample the delicacies. Cora heard Prince Frederick's amazement at the inclusion of pickled herring, a favourite of his, and her mother's melodious laugh as she informed the Prince that Kaitlin had suggested the dish.

Rafael was borne away by Ethan, and Cora felt an irrational emptiness—somehow his proximity made the part of bride easier to play...perhaps because his very aura diminished others and made them less scary.

Juanita approached her and Cora breathed a sigh of relief—she liked the young Spanish girl.

'Thank you for what you said earlier. About the dance at Alvaro's wedding. Grandfather didn't know I was going to do it and he was furious.' Her look darkened. 'Truly angry. But for once my father stood up to him—he said I have amazing talent. But he won't stand up to him further—make him agree to let me dance as a career. Just because my grandfather believes that it's beneath a noblewoman. Well, he is wrong—and I *will* fulfil my ambition. Sometimes when something is wrong and you want it very much you should disobey and rebel. Don't you think?'

Envy touched Cora for an instant as she looked at Juanita's vital, determined face. It had never occurred to her to disobey her parents or rebel—all she had ever wanted was their love, or even just a morsel of affection.

'I think people *should* pursue their dreams,' Juanita continued loudly, her eyes gleaming with defiance as Don Carlos came up.

'Off you go, Juanita. I would like a word with Cora.'

He would? Panic swirled in Cora's tummy as she glanced around for Rafael. The last thing she wanted was to mess up this vineyard deal by saying the wrong thing— a speciality of hers.

Smiles and platitudes.

'I think my granddaughter likes you.'

'I like her too.'

'Good. Then perhaps you can persuade her to follow your example.'

'In what way?' Apprehension tickled the base of her spine, and the heaviness of her wedding dress seemed suddenly magnified.

'I want you to advise her to marry money. I wouldn't want her to marry riff-raff, as you have, but the principle is sound. I have found an extremely affluent suitor of good birth for Juanita, but she is proving to be stubborn.'

Disbelief at his words vied with a surge of anger. *Riff-raff?* Was he for real? 'I don't consider Rafael to be "riff-raff".'

'Cora. You are a Derwent—one of the aristocracy. You can trace your heritage back for centuries of blue blood. Who is Rafael Martinez? I can tell you. He is of low birth, and his ancestors were no doubt louts and criminals. But he has money.'

Her palm itched with an urge to slap him, or better yet ram her stiletto into his shin. 'I am not marrying Rafael for his money.'

Don Carlos shook his head. 'I see why the "love-match" story is better publicity, but in reality you *are* marrying him for his money—and please don't think I blame you. You are guaranteed a luxurious lifestyle and you will help your family. I am aware of the pressures of running a vast estate in today's world, believe me. I am sure your father is proud of you.'

Self-loathing ran through her veins—how she wished she could truthfully tell this man he was wrong. But he was right—she was standing there in an elaborate, flower-filled marquee, surrounded by women dripping diamonds, emeralds and titles, clad in a frivolous lace dress that she loathed, for *money*. But that didn't give Don Carlos the right to insult Rafael or to make these arrogant assumptions. Yet she shouldn't be surprised—after all he had insulted Rafael to his face, refused to sully his land by selling it to a man of Rafael's low birth.

Anger flared and surged in her at the derisive look on the Duque's face, along with a lightning bolt of understanding that made her heart ache. Did Rafael want Don Carlos to believe this was a love-match to *prove* that a titled person could love a person lower down the social strata? The idea was strange—Rafael's aura of self-confidence was so impermeable—but somehow Cora knew she was right, and an urge to defend him swept over her. Much the same way she felt the need to adopt every stray dog.

'Actually, I don't feel I *am* marrying beneath me—I admire what Rafael has achieved, his work ethic and the way he has made such an incredible success of his life through his own efforts. As for my title—I did nothing to earn it. I simply inherited it.'

Cora came to a sudden stop; she was supposed to help charm this man into giving up a vineyard. *Smiles and platitudes, remember?*

But Don Carlos simply looked amused. 'But it's what comes *with* the title, Cora. It is the heritage, your pedigree, your background—those are things you cannot renounce.

I'm sure Martinez will be more than happy that his children's veins will run with Derwent blood to dilute his own.'

Before she could respond, annoyance swept the aquiline cast of his face.

'I had better go and find Juanita. It looks like she is in conversation with a member of the string quartet. Any minute now she will persuade them to play some song she can dance to.'

As he departed Cora narrowed her eyes. 'Good luck to her,' she muttered, and then spun round at the approach of her mother.

Her heart sank at the annoyance in the Duchess's emerald eyes. It belied the mother-of-the-bride smile on her coral-pink lips.

'Did you upset Don Carlos?' she demanded in a low tone. 'I *told* you, Cora—this wedding is designed to show Prince Frederick and the whole Lycander family the worth of the Derwents, and that our connection with the Duque de Aiza counterweights our new *association*—' the word dripped contempt '—with Rafael Martinez. So you need to charm Don Carlos—or at least not alienate him.'

'I…'

The icy light of disappointment in her mother's eyes had the age-old effect of turning Cora's insides to a mush of misery and blanking her brain. *Think of the future, Cora.* Soon her marriage would be over and she would hand over a considerable sum of money to her parents. Then her mother's eyes would hold warmth and approval.

For once the fantasy that soothed her didn't work its usual magic.

'Is everything all right?'

Ah, that would explain it—her senses had clearly been distracted by the approach of Rafael. The deep timbre of his voice warmed her skin and brought back a sudden vivid image of their clinch.

'Everything is fine,' the Duchess averred. 'Just a little mother-daughter chat.' Her gaze swept the room. 'Excuse me. I must find Kaitlin.'

For another 'mother-daughter chat', no doubt. Prince Frederick was surrounded by a bevy of beauties and Kaitlin was conspicuous only by her absence.

Rafael's expression was unreadable—although his gaze was intense, as if he weighed her soul—and she summoned yet another smile. 'We'd better circulate.'

Not that it mattered now. The knot was tied and this reception was now geared to showcase Kaitlin and promote her ascent to royalty. Hence the profusion of flowers that garlanded the marquee, the beautiful centrepieces that decked the snowy-white linen tablecloths. Hence the colour scheme picked to complement the Titian of Kaitlin's hair, the seating arrangements that somehow sidelined the bride and groom and shone a spotlight on the chief bridesmaid, inviting Prince Frederick to observe Kaitlin's eminent suitability as a Lycander bride.

The speeches were met with laughter, and perhaps it was only Cora who noted the imbalance of her father's speech, tipped towards Kaitlin, his older daughter by five minutes. Most of the anecdotes he recalled centred round Kaitlin, with the occasional 'and Cora' tacked on. The rest of them were of necessity pure fallacy, seeing as in truth her parents had avoided Cora's company whenever possible.

As for the message the Duke read from Gabriel, that wished his little sister 'all the best' and expressed his deep sorrow that he couldn't attend her nuptials…as she listened Cora knew it was all hooey. True, she and Gabriel weren't close—her brother had always been distant—but the message smacked of something her parents would concoct.

Perhaps Gabriel had asked them to do it because he disapproved of her marriage. But that didn't sound like him either. Anxiety whispered, only to be dismissed—Gabriel was too assured, too handsome, too golden to be in trouble.

Now Ethan had taken the stage, and as best man he did a gallant job—despite Cora's conviction that the man had his own doubts. On the Cavershams' return from Paris she and Rafael had announced their engagement, and she had witnessed first-hand the surprise on the couple's faces. Some of their surprise had no doubt been due to the revelation that Cora was a member of the aristocracy, but she suspected most of it was down to utter bafflement at the romantic whirlwind scenario.

True, their perplexity had been succeeded by congratulations, champagne, and the assurance that Cora was free to leave work with no hard feelings whatsoever and would be welcome back any time, but Cora knew Ethan and Ruby held reservations as to the validity of their sudden engagement. Guilt touched her that she had avoided all Ruby's attempts to make contact—too worried that she would break down and confess the truth to this woman she liked so much. Then the proverbial fat and fire would be conjoined—Ruby would march up to Rafael and pull the whole deal apart.

And she didn't want that.

The realisation shocked her in its intensity. Despite the falseness of this whole wedding, despite her mortification, she didn't want to cancel the deal. Because she needed the money. Nothing to do with the growing knowledge that this deal meant more than business to Rafael.

Because as the day spun out into evening she knew that there was no way a man like Rafael would go through all this without some stronger motivation than business.

'Now the dancing shall begin. Will the bride and groom take the floor?'

The strains of a familiar melody started.

'I didn't choose this.' Indignation strummed inside her.

'No. I did. I thought it suited our supposed courtship.'

And it did—its melody haunted the air with the tale of a whirlwind love and a happy-ever-after. Words of happiness and joy and hopes of a bright new start in life.

The sheer hypocrisy suddenly made her rage inside that he had chosen it in cold blood. The rage a relief, because it carried her to the dance floor in front of the sea of watchers. Its fire blocked out the sheer knee-trembling proximity of him—until the scent of him infused the air around them and pulled her back willy-nilly to *that night*. Until his hands spanned her waist as he pulled her close and she rested her check against the breadth of his chest. Until for a heartbeat she allowed herself to relax, to float on a dream where this was true—where the lyrics echoed their feelings.

Stop it. This is a pretence.

The song was fake, the wedding was false, and if she remained plastered all over him he would think she wanted a replay of their kiss and more. She tensed against him, straightened up and kept the fake smile in place.

Smiles and platitudes—she was awash on an ocean of them as the evening progressed. Champagne flowed, more nibbles appeared—miniature fish and chips, mini bangers in dollops of mash, tiny exquisite tartlets—and her head whirled. Then finally, when she thought her face might disintegrate under the weight of her smile, when her tongue cleaved to the roof of her mouth and tasted the coating of platitudes, it was time to leave.

Kaitlin extracted her and bore her away to change into her going-away dress—a trouser suit that was just a touch the wrong shade of pink for her. Not that she cared—her need to flee was too urgent. Until she clocked the stress on her sister's face under the smile.

'Kait, what's wrong?'

'Just don't throw the bouquet to me. Please, sis.'

'But…' But the Duchess had been very specific in her instructions and… And *what*? If Kaitlin didn't want the bouquet would it be so bad not to chuck it at her? Yes, Cora would face her mother's wrath and, yes, she would disappoint her parents yet again.

She could almost hear the Duchess's voice so clearly. *We should have known Cora wouldn't be able to manage something even as simple as that.* But it would be one more barb amongst many, and soon all those barbs would be wiped out by approval, once she handed the money over. Plus this was her *sister*.

'OK. Consider it done.'

'Thank you. Truly.'

So when it came to it Cora aimed the bouquet as far away from Kaitlin as possible and turned to see it fall into the grasp of Juanita, who looked absolutely horrified and batted it away.

Cora gave a small chuckle.

'Why is that funny?' Rafael's low voice was surprisingly intense.

'Don Carlos wants to marry Juanita off and she's having none of it.'

There was a portent to the following silence, and when she turned Rafael's haunted expression sent a hum of concern through her.

'What's wrong? Do you know Juanita?' she asked.

'Nothing and no.' His voice was brusque. 'Let's get the last bit of this charade over with and get out of here.'

It was only then that it occurred to Cora that they were about to embark on their honeymoon. The idea was enough to send her hurtling back to the dance floor—smile in place, platitudes at the ready.

CHAPTER NINE

RAFAEL LOOKED AROUND the supposed honeymoon suite of the country hotel and frowned in consternation as the shabbiness of its décor permeated the cloud of confused thoughts that fuzzed his brain.

Of course he had known about Alvaro and Juanita, but he had written them off, blocked them out, never considered them as real people. His whole focus was on Don Carlos and revenge. But now he'd met Juanita and emotion twisted his gut at the idea of Don Carlos marrying her off.

Yet his surroundings were impossible to ignore. The lobby had been a precursor of things to come, with its peeling wallpaper and faint smell of must and damp. As for this honeymoon suite—its sheer dowdiness brought irritation and confirmed the disquiet that the wedding had perpetrated within him. Because there had been a vibe about the day that made his skin prickle, and this shunt into a honeymoon that smacked of being 'good enough for the likes of you' cemented the icing on the proverbial wedding cake.

The champagne was warm, the flowers drooped and his frown deepened as he swept the withered petals off the dresser.

'Why did you choose here?' he asked as Cora emerged from the bathroom, where she'd vanished the second they had arrived.

All signs of Cora the bride had been eradicated—her hair hung loose round her face in damp tendrils, her face held not so much as a vestige of make-up, and the pink trouser ensemble had been replaced by jeans and an over-sized sweatshirt with 'Dogs Rule' on it in faded letters.

'I didn't choose it. Veronica, my parents' PA, organised it.'

Cora's voice was clipped with exhaustion, and for a second compassion touched his chest as he took in the smudges under her eyes. It was a compassion he shrugged off—this was a woman who was revolted by his touch, who was in this for the money.

'The owners offered it for free in return for a bit of publicity.'

'I can only hope they didn't specify what sort of publicity. This is a joke.'

A sigh escaped her as she sank gingerly onto a sagging chair. 'Does it matter? This is a fake honeymoon. You've got what you wanted—a wedding that Don Carlos and the world believe to be real.'

'Yes. But I need Don Carlos to continue to believe in our marriage, and this is *not* a realistic honeymoon destination. You should have realised that.'

'*You* could have checked it out—I'm sure Veronica kept you informed.'

'Yes, she did. Right from the morning after you ran out on me, when she emailed to introduce herself. She told me that she was the Derwent PA and you had asked her to keep me up to date with the wedding preparations because you thought it would be *romantic* for us not to be in touch directly until "the big day". Veronica told me that she had arranged a luxury hotel in the beautiful depths of the English countryside for our honeymoon and that you had approved it.'

A flush tinted her cheeks. 'OK. So I should have

checked it. But to be honest I didn't really care. And I *didn't* run out on you.'

Was she for real?

'What would you call it? You left at speed, in the middle of the night. I was worried about you.'

'You were worried about our charade being blown. I was careful. I got a cab to the train station and I lay low until the first train home. I don't get what you're so mad about.'

There was little point in denying he was angry. The way he was pacing the room and yelling was a bit of a giveaway. Hauling in a calming breath, he halted. 'I may not be the King of Relationships but I don't tend to flee the scene after the event.'

'Well, bully for you.' Rising to her feet, she slammed her hands on the curves of her hips. 'I was embarrassed—OK?'

'I got that.' *Loud and clear.* 'I got it that you felt sullied by slumming it with a commoner like me.'

'Sullied?' For a second confusion reigned supreme on her face, and then she rocked backwards as if in shock.

His jaw jabbed with tension. *Keep calm.* 'By someone of my lowly birth. Isn't that what Don Carlos said to you?'

'You…you think that I…agree with Don Carlos? You think that I feel ashamed of kissing you because of your background? How *dare* you believe that of me? If you overheard my conversation with Don Carlos then you must have heard me defend you and refute his ideas.'

'I did—and I applauded your role-playing skills.'

'Well, you wasted your appreciation. I meant every word I said. I *don't* hold my title in reverence and I *do* admire your achievements. That is the truth. As for that night—I do not believe I was "sullied" in any way at all.'

She took another step forward; her gaze was fearless and open as their eyes met and suddenly he was all too aware of her proximity, the fresh smell of soap and sham-

poo and pure Cora. Warmth touched him that she had defended him—he couldn't remember the last time anyone
had. His head whirled and he forced himself to focus—
words were just words…not proof of anything. His mother
had placed blind, foolish trust in words and love, and it
had made her weak and vulnerable and led to her ruin.

'Then why did you run like that? What were you embarrassed about?'

All of a sudden the anger melted from her face and her
gaze skittered away from him as she shifted from one bare
foot to another.

'Look, let's just forget it. It's over and done with.'

'No. Clearly there is some misconception here and I
want to clear it up.'

If there was anything worse than secrets it was miscon-
ceptions. Throughout his childhood he'd been fed a diet of
fallacy and it had left him spinning in a quagmire of confusion. One minute his mother would tell him his father's
identity 'didn't matter', the next day she'd tell him his father had been a soldier, the next month a diplomat, and so
on and so forth. The only constant had been her dreamy-
eyed look—and the description of the love they had shared,
her conviction that one day he'd find her.

He shook the memories off and stepped towards Cora.
'We need to sort this out. I don't deal well with misread
situations.'

She hesitated, and then huffed out a sigh that spelled
resignation. 'Fine. I can't bear for you to believe that I am
tainted by Don Carlos's ideas. I felt mortified by my behaviour, but not for the reasons you think.' She glanced
down, as if to gain courage from the shabby carpet, before straightening up. 'You said it yourself. The reason you
asked *me* to marry you, rather than someone like Kaitlin,
was because you weren't attracted to me.'

'I did say that, but—'

'Then you felt sorry for me, and I threw myself at you, and you were rightly horrified—'

'Whoa! Hold it right there. Pity was *not* at the party.'

'*Tchaa.*'

It was amazing how much scoff she put into the noise.

'Look, I have as much self-esteem as the next person.'

A statement he doubted was true.

'But I *know* the type of woman you are usually attracted to and I am not in their league.'

'There is no "league". I agree, you are different from the women I usually date, but that is *zip* to do with attraction. I date women who want the same things I want from an association. You don't fit that criteria—you want a happy-ever-after with Joe Average.' *All the more reason he should never have kissed her.* 'Plus, I will not let attraction blur our marriage lines—our marriage is a business deal. Nothing more. But the attraction was real and you have no reason to be embarrassed by your behaviour.'

Her head dipped in acknowledgement but he couldn't shake the idea that she hadn't fully bought into his words. His eyes assessed her expression, wondered what could have knocked her self-esteem so badly. The urge to reassure her washed over him. *Enough.* It had been the urge to reassure her that had landed them in this mess of a conversation in the first place.

'Thank you,' she murmured. 'Now, I'm going to turn in.' Her lips twisted in a small grimace. 'Would you prefer the bedroom? I'm quite happy to have the sofa.'

They both contemplated the lumpy, seen-better-days excuse for a sofa.

Rafael sighed. 'I'll be fine out here.' No one could accuse Rafael Martinez of being unchivalrous.

Cora opened her eyes and decided to abandon any idea of sleep as frivolous. The mattress was way past its use-by

date, but she couldn't blame its state for the scratchy feel
of her tired eyes. How could she sleep when confusion
fuzzed her brain?

The conversation with Rafael had not been the talk
she'd expected, and had triggered a conflict of emotions
inside her. A dangerous temptation to believe the attraction was real alongside an anger and a funny little ache
in her heart at his belief that she'd thought she'd lowered
herself by kissing him.

The drumming of rain against the window distracted
her and she sighed as she clambered out of bed. English
spring at its best—and yet in truth the weather suited her
mood, and the drab surroundings and grey vista illus-
trated the fact that her use to her parents was over. The
wedding had been for Kaitlin's benefit and now Cora had
been shuffled off-stage and returned to shabby storage.

But not for long—once this marriage was over she
would repay her debt and regain her life. So she would
not stew in self-pity. Time for a shower and then she would
while the day away with a book, avoiding any more conversation with Rafael. A business marriage did *not* require chit-chat.

Fifteen minutes later she pushed the bedroom door
open, entered the adjoining living area and paused. Rafael sat at the flimsy wooden table, laptop open in front
of him, his dark hair shower-damp, presumably post-visit
to the hotel gym, dressed in a long-sleeved grey tee and
jeans. *Be still, her beating heart.*

'Good morning.'

He looked up and the frown on his face made her prickle
her with foreboding.

'Morning. We have a problem.'

'What sort of problem?'

'This.' Rising, he gestured to his laptop. 'You'd better
read these articles on our wedding.'

Bride is pretty, groom is gorgeous, but maid of honour steals the limelight and the eye of Prince Charming!

There can be no doubt that Lady Kaitlin Derwent stole the show from her less well known sister. Though the bride's dress was lavish frilly froth, as ever Kaitlin showed that the 'It' factor cannot be bought, and her simple charm and elegance bewitched Prince Frederick of Lycander...

It was one article of many. Cora scanned a few more headlines: *Kaitlin Derwent rocks it while her sister rolls to second place... Outclassed bride still enjoys celebrations...*

She pushed the computer away. It shouldn't hurt but it did, and each comparison was a jab at an age-old wound. But pride allowed her to shrug.

'It's no big deal. No one has said they don't believe in our relationship.'

His eyes narrowed. 'It's a big deal to me.'

Of course it was. Rafael Martinez would not like to be portrayed as a man who had won the booby prize.

'I don't like the idea of people reading this any more than I like this ridiculous choice of a honeymoon venue.' His strides ate up the worn, faded carpet. 'I'm going to do something about it.'

'No!' Consternation overtook hurt. 'You can't.' Her parents would have an indigo fit if their careful plots and manoeuvres were impeded.

'Yes, I can. This *matters*. I will not have my wife reduced to a second-class bride and do nothing.'

It really did matter to him. He was looking at her, but she had a feeling he was seeing something or someone from his past. More to the point, Rafael had *paid* for the wedding. Guilt touched her and she clenched her nails into her palms—she owed him the truth. However hard her tummy twisted at the thought, she couldn't hide behind a wall of lies.

'Rafael. I need to tell you something. The wedding… Kaitlin upstaging me—it was deliberate.'

There was a long moment of silence. 'Explain.'

'My parents saw the wedding as a chance to promote a marriage between Kaitlin and Prince Frederick. The idea was to present Kaitlin as the perfect candidate for royalty, and if that meant sidelining the bride then so be it.'

No need to supply Rafael with the exact words. *'Kaitlin outclasses you anyway, Cora—we may as well take advantage of it.'*

'It wasn't a big deal—they just designed the wedding to impress Frederick and show off Kaitlin.'

They had chosen Cora a dress she'd loathed—all frills and fuss so that Kaitlin's classic beauty would stand out—picked a colour scheme that suited Kaitlin, made sure the photographer knew the score, and Bob was your uncle… or Frederick was your son-in-law.

'At your expense?'

'Yes. But it really doesn't matter. It wasn't a real wedding, and I knew a wedding designed to impress the House of Lycander would also impress Don Carlos.'

'So you don't mind this?' He gestured at the computer.

'No. I have long since accepted that Kaitlin is more beautiful than I am, as well as more…more *everything*. The point is no matter what dress I wore Kaitlin's natural grace and beauty would have put me in the shade. So why not let some good come of it? It doesn't bother me.'

Because she wouldn't let it—she had come to terms and made her peace with her family's dynamic.

'I'm not sure I believe that. Comments like this are hurtful—and besides, Kaitlin isn't *"more everything"* than you. Your appearance was deliberately sabotaged by your parents. I don't see how you *can* be OK with it. Either way—I'm not. Regardless of your parents' agenda I will *not* let you be sidelined, nor allow your parents to display their true belief as to my worth. Or yours.'

There was a hint of compassion in his voice that made her wince; she could not bear to be an object of pity yet again.

'Well, you'd better believe it. I am completely on board with their plan and those articles do *not* bother me.'

CHAPTER TEN

RAFAEL LOOKED AT CORA, seated at the rickety table, her turquoise eyes narrowed as she gazed at him. For a moment curiosity displaced the cold burn of anger at the Derwents' behaviour. His mother had been a tragic victim of aristocratic arrogance and he didn't like the echo of that in the here and now. But *why* was Cora content to accept these malicious comments in the press? *Why* had she agreed to a deliberate portrayal of herself as second best?

'OK.' He pulled out a chair and sat down opposite her. 'Convince me.'

Cora scrunched her forehead as if in internal debate, placed her elbows on the table and rested her chin on her cupped hands.

'I don't mind the headlines and I didn't mind the wedding because I've accepted reality. For years I strove to be more like Kaitlin—more beautiful, more clever, more serene, more graceful, more—' She broke off. 'More everything, I guess.'

'Why not be happy being you?'

'That's easy to say, but when your twin sister represents perfection that's what you aspire to, right? Kaitlin was immensely popular, cool and beautiful. People were only interested in me as a gateway to her.'

'That must have been tough.'

Her eyes narrowed. 'I am not looking for sympathy—I

just want to explain how I *am* perfectly OK with the situation.'

'OK.' He raised a hand. 'No more interruptions.'

'When I was twenty-one I met Rupert. I'd given up on romance because I was fed up with being simply a conduit to Kaitlin or only desired for my title. But I thought Rupert was different. He seemed different—interested in *me* as a person. We spent time together and I fell for him. Big-time. He made me believe it was possible for someone to prefer me to Kaitlin. One night I decided to go to party I knew he'd be at. I dressed up to the nines and decided to bare my soul—and a whole lot else.'

For a moment Rafael could almost see her, standing on the edge of the party, hair loose, giving a quick swipe of her hand to the skirt of her dress to smooth it, her turquoise eyes wide and oh, so vulnerable.

'What happened?'

'I did my throwing myself at him routine and he... Well, he rejected me. Poor man was mortified—he was lovely and kind, but he explained that it was Kaitlin he loved. He knew he didn't have a chance with her, and he wasn't using me to get to her, but being with me made him feel closer to her. I felt like such a fool.'

Of course she had. Rafael's gut twisted at her humiliation. 'I'm sor—'

'No interruptions,' she reminded him. 'I saw that Rupert had done me a favour. He told me that I was—and I quote— "a pale imitation of Kaitlin...a shadow." And I realised he was right. That no matter what I did, how I dressed, how hard I studied, how much I tried, I would never be on a par with Kaitlin. That's when I came to terms with it—decided to accept that I am who I am and that is OK. That's why things like those headlines don't matter any more.'

It all made sense—Cora had given up trying to be like

her sister. Which was great. Except he could spot the flaw. She'd given up full-stop—still believed she was inferior to Kaitlin, a pale shadow of her twin. The only difference was that she'd decided to accept it. That was why she'd rejected the gold dress he'd bought her to wear for dinner with her family, why she wore clothes that muted her, worked at a job that didn't inspire her. Cora had built herself protective armour—told herself that if she didn't try she wouldn't feel a failure.

She frowned. 'What are you thinking?'

'I'm thinking that Rupert was wrong. You aren't a pale shadow of Kaitlin. You are you, and you need to work out who Cora Derwent is and feel good about it.'

He wasn't sure why she felt as she did, but sensed that Rupert had been the tip of the iceberg—the culmination of a stream of events that had knocked her self-esteem out of the ball park and way beyond.

'What is *that* supposed to mean?' Indignation sparked in the turquoise of her eyes. 'I know exactly who I am and I am happy with that person. *Very* happy. That was the whole point of me telling you all that. To prove it.'

'I…' Rafael pressed his lips together.

Best to leave well alone—Cora believed she had it all sorted and maybe she did. Maybe he was reading way more into the situation than there was on the page. Lady Cora Derwent had money, family, and was quite capable of living her own life without his input. They were *business* partners and it was business he needed to consider now.

So… 'Good,' he said. 'I'm glad you're OK with this mess. But I'm not, and if you think we're going to languish here in this godforsaken hotel you can think again.'

'What are we going to do?'

'We are going to honeymoon in style and make sure the press knows about it. You'll have to swallow your principles and board another private jet.'

'To where?'

'To Granada.'

It made sense for them to be in Spain, to make a bit of a splash in the Spanish press…remind Don Carlos of his existence.

A few hours later Cora looked around the interior of the private jet and felt a sense of *déjà-vu* descend. And yet there was a difference to this trip. This time she and Rafael were man and wife—an outcome she would never have foretold in a million years a few weeks before.

A glance at him now showed a man at ease as he leafed through a magazine. Yet over the past few hours he had arranged this trip with lightning speed and an assurance Cora could only envy—maybe it was because Rafael Martinez knew exactly who he was and what he wanted and felt *excellent* about it.

Her thoughts went back to his words. *'You need to work out who Cora Derwent is and feel good about it.'*

That was exactly what she'd done, for goodness' sake. Accepted who she was and got on with her life. Decided that as she could never be Kaitlin she would win her parents' love via a different route—proving her use to them. That was a good thing, right? So there was no need to let Rafael's words niggle at her like this. The man had known her a scant few weeks—his opinion was hardly valid.

But still his words haunted her—he'd uttered them so thoughtfully, as if he knew he was right. As if he could see something she couldn't.

So when he glanced up her mouth opened and she said, 'Do you really think that I don't know who I am?'

Opposite her Rafael blinked, but didn't miss a beat. 'I think you have been so busy comparing yourself to Kaitlin you don't realise your own assets—your looks, your abilities, your potential.'

There was no judgement in that simple statement.

'In what way?'

He shrugged. 'Over the past weeks you've told me what you want from life. To be happy. To be ordinary. To live happily ever after with Joe Average. To work with dogs. Yet you aren't doing *any* of those things.'

'It's not that easy.'

'Yes, it is.' He tipped his palms in the air. 'Do it. Set up Derwent's Dogs. Advertise and start walking dogs. Set up a kennel. You might meet Joe A or you might end up with franchises all over the world. You can do anything you want to. Or you can at least try.'

His words seemed to emphasise the differences between them—Rafael thought universally *big*. How boring she must seem to him—pedestrian, almost. 'That's not my choice. I'm not like you—I want *ordinary*, remember?'

'Then start small and stay small. Or study to be a vet. The possibilities are endless. But whatever you do make sure it's what you *want* to do. You aren't a pale imitation of Kaitlin and you don't have to live in her shadow. It's *your* life. Live it.'

The words were said with an intensity that sent a shiver to her very soul, gave her the belief that he meant every one.

But words were easy and, whilst she deemed his sincerity to be real, she needed to hang on to reality. That reality dictated family obligation and the importance of *her* goal. Rafael might have hidden depths, but right now they had been thrown together by a business deal. Within days she would pall for him, and once this marriage was over he would forget her within minutes and move on. So she needed to hold on to the rules that governed her lifestyle and not be beguiled by his.

'I do plan to live it. I know what I want from life.' Her

parents' love and approval…the chance to prove she was a true Derwent.

Before he could reply his phone rang, and within seconds there was an exchange of dialogue, the words uttered in rapid-fire Spanish. Could it be Don Carlos? Already? The thought gave her pause—hope mixed with an inexplicable trickle of disappointment. At the thought of missing out on Granada, *obviously*.

'Is everything OK?' she asked once he'd ended the conversation.

'That was a Spanish gossip magazine reporter I left a message for earlier—Cristina Herrera. She's agreed to meet us tomorrow for a honeymoon interview. That should help make it clear that our honeymoon is not a second-class event. I know you don't like the limelight, but I think this is important. With a bit of luck Don Carlos may even read it.'

'No problem.' Cora tried to inject confidence into her voice. In truth the whole idea left her frozen, but she could see his point of view. 'I faked an entire wedding—this will be a doddle.'

Only it didn't feel that way—this time the spotlight would be focused solely on her and Rafael. No Kaitlin, no Duke and Duchess, and no array of glittering celebrities for the paps to focus on. Just her. A frisson of nerves rippled through her.

'I'll even let them dress me up so I look a bit more Kaitlinesque.'

What? Where had that come from?

Rafael looked as though he were wondering the same thing. Cora could almost see his mental eye-roll.

'That's not what you need to do at all. You don't *need* to look "Kaitlinesque". You need to look *Cora*-esque. Wear whatever makes you feel good without comparing yourself to Kaitlin.'

'No problem. Easy-peasy.' Had she really said that? 'I'll stick to my own wardrobe, then.'

To her own irritation she could hear the mixture of defiance and defensiveness in her voice. Which was mad. There was nothing to defy *or* defend. Surely she could find something in her suitcase that would make her feel good? Yet as she mentally reviewed the medley of dark, over-sized garments that made up her wardrobe doubts began to creep in. This was ridiculous—it didn't *matter* what she wore. Clothes were just bits of material, necessary to maintain decency and keep you warm.

Her navy blue sundress would be fine. An image of the dress floated to the forefront of her mind. Loose-fitting. Buttoned-up neck. Puffy sleeves. Now the doubts began to stockpile. Had she *really* chosen her clothes to deliberately mask any hint of femininity? Had she *actually* decided to become invisible rather than a pale shadow of Kaitlin?

Suddenly aware of the slightly sardonic gleam in Rafael's eyes, she narrowed her own.

'Easy-peasy, lemon-squeezy,' she stated as she picked up a magazine.

Enough. These thoughts were a product of being around someone like Rafael Martinez, with his Hollywood looks and charisma and his larger than life persona. She could only hope this honeymoon was as short-lived as possible.

CHAPTER ELEVEN

RAFAEL SCOOPED COFFEE into the cafetière and gazed out of the wooden-framed kitchen window. The early-morning Spanish sunshine shed its dappled rays on the pavement as he inhaled the familiar aroma of Granada—a heady mix of exotic spice mingled with the glorious smell of orange blossom and a waft of tea leaves.

'Good morning.'

He turned at the sound of Cora's soft voice and leant against the marble-topped counter. 'Morning…' Her glorious hair was piled on top of her head and a few tendrils fell loose round her face; her expression was a mix of uncertainty and a flicker of defiance, as if she was daring him to comment.

Presumably on her choice of dress…Rafael schooled his features to remain neutral at the sight of the sheer staidness of the navy blue sundress and swallowed a sigh. How Cora dressed was irrelevant—if that was what made her feel good, so be it. Yet the idea that she lived her life in her sister's shadow sent a twinge of frustration through him.

Life really was too short—he knew that. His mother's final months had been weighted with regret that she had lived a decade in the shadow cast by his father's betrayal. That knowledge was woven into the fabric of his identity—a reminder as to why he and Cora were in this apartment in

Granada. Their purpose was to fake a honeymoon—there was no item on the agenda that declared a need to help Lady Cora Derwent with her emotional baggage. Heaven knew that was hardly his forte, and yet for reasons he couldn't fathom he wanted to make her see herself as she truly was.

'The reporter will be here in an hour. We'd best get ready.'

'I *am* ready.' Shoulders back, she narrowed her eyes. 'You told me to dress in a Cora-esque fashion. This is it.'

'I meant we need to move our clothes and so on into the same bedroom, just in case she does a journalistic sneak peek whilst pretending to use the bathroom.'

Cora stilled, an expression of pain sweeping her features, and he blinked. He filtered his words on a rerun but was none the wiser.

'I'm not suggesting you actually move in to my bedroom,' he clarified. And then wished he hadn't as, unbidden, the idea of sharing a bed and a whole lot more with her sent a reel of images through his brain. The memory of her lips against his…the soft, sweet passion of their kiss…the texture of her skin beneath his fingers…the press of her body against his…

Whoa. Don't go there.

'I understand that.' Her voice low, with a huskiness that sent his senses into overdrive. 'Let's get a move on.'

Half an hour later, as she smoothed the duvet on her bed, he glanced round to ensure there was no stray evidence of her occupancy. 'Looks good,' he said, just as the doorbell chimed. 'You ready?'

'As I'll ever be.'

Rafael frowned as her lips turned up into the smile he recognised as wholly fake. His mind whirred—no reporter worth their salt would be taken in. Not in a private interview. However well he and Cora had rehearsed their words. The wild idea of kissing her entered his head—he knew that would ignite a spark and summon a genuine smile to their faces. But that way spelt danger, and the risk of blurring a line he would not allow himself even to smudge.

Instead he asked, 'What do you feed an invisible cat?'

The smile dropped from her lips as her forehead scrunched into lines of confusion. 'Huh?'

'It's a joke.'

'You're telling me a joke *now*?'

'Yup. Come on—this one is hilarious.' Jokes had been one of the few things that had made his mother laugh, and so as a child he had spent hours conning every joke book he could lay his hands on.

'Um…I don't know.'

'Evaporated milk.'

Cora stared at him, turquoise eyes wide with disbelief, and then a gurgle of laughter fell from her lips. 'That is the most ridiculous joke I've ever heard.'

'Try this one. What does a philosophical dolphin think about?'

'No idea.'

'Have I got a porpoise?'

To his own surprise the joke he had thought long since forgotten brought a smile to his own lips as she shook her head in mock sorrow. 'Where on earth did you get those from?'

'It doesn't matter.' And it didn't—right now the important thing was that Cora looked genuinely more relaxed and happy, in time for the reporter. 'There are plenty more where they came from, though.'

'I can't wait.'

'OK. Now, let's let Cristina in.'

'Let's do it.'

'So…' Cristina began, once she was seated on the leather sofa in the lounge. 'First, thank you for seeing me—I was surprised, given it's the first day of your honeymoon.'

Rafael smiled. 'It wasn't part of our honeymoon plan, but after the press coverage of our wedding I wanted to make it very clear to all those readers out there that I don't in any way feel I got the "second-best" sister. I want the world to know that Cora Derwent is the woman I…the woman for me.'

His lips were unable to use the word *love* even in pretence, and he could only hope Cristina hadn't clocked his infinitesimal stumble. Love was a word to be eschewed and dreaded; it led the way to allowing someone else power over you.

'And how do *you* feel about the comments on your wedding?' Cristina asked as she turned to Cora.

Cora smoothed the blue cotton of her sundress down. 'To be honest, Cristina, they bothered Rafael more than me. I had a wonderful day because I married Rafael— nothing can take away from that memory. Now I want to get on with our life, beginning with this wonderful surprise honeymoon. I have always wanted to see Granada and now I can.'

'So that's your plan whilst you're here—to soak up the sights?'

'Absolutely,' Rafael interjected. 'I am looking forward to sharing Granada with Cora. The Basilica de San Juan de Dios—I'm sure you'll agree the altar of gold needs to be seen to be believed. And I'd also like to take Cora to the Alhambra de Granada…'

'How does that sound to you, Cora?'

'Wonderful. Although actually there is one other thing I'd like to do whilst I'm here, though I haven't had a chance to discuss this with Rafael yet.'

Rafael blinked. OK—Cora had clearly decided to deviate from the script.

She leant forward a little and animation illuminated her features. 'I'm hoping to look up a friend of mine—Sally

Anne Gregory. Sally Anne set up a dog rescue charity here in Granada a couple of years ago and I took on one of her first rescues. A gorgeous Spanish Shepherd dog called Prue. But there are still a horrendous number of abandoned dogs here. A lot of puppies bought and then, when they grow bigger, simply left somewhere so they roam the streets, scavenge from bins and sleep in doorways and shop fronts. It's incredibly sad—if you could see some of these animals…it's criminal.'

Rafael could hear the passion and compassion in her voice, sense how much she cared from the tilt of her body and the jut of her chin, and it touched him.

'Anyway, now that I'm here I would like to meet Sally Anne and let her know in person how much I admire what she's doing. Oh, and show her loads of photos of Prue.'

'Do you have any other dogs?'

'Just one. Another rescue called Poppy. I'd love more, but it's not practical.'

'After the honeymoon presumably you'll bring your dogs to live with you? Will that be here or in London?'

'Um…I… We…'

Next to him Cora stiffened and he could almost see Cristina's reporter antennae twitch.

Rafael's mind whirred. 'At the moment Cora and I are in discussions about the best place for us to live. But wherever we go of course Prue and Poppy will be with us.'

Rising to his feet, he decided to head off any conversation about the intricacies of their future. After all it would be a waste of breath, because there would be no cosy, white picket fence future and he had no wish to envisage any such nightmare. He doubted his ability to pretend with even a modicum of conviction.

'Now, would you like a tour and a few quick photographs?'

Once the reporter had left Cora turned to him and

tipped her palms in the air. 'Sorry. I didn't mean to mention the dogs or Sally Anne. It just suddenly occurred to me what great publicity it would be for Sally Anne and I blurted it out. I know it threw us into the deep end and I shouldn't have done it, but…'

'Whoa. It's OK, Cora. No harm, no foul.'

'Really?'

'Really. Could even be a good tactic—the amount you care about the plight of those dogs was obvious and *real*. It was very Cora Derwent and a far cry from Kaitlin. Cristina's article will be about *you*—and that was the aim. Plus, it took the focus off our romance which was a relief—I found it hard to pretend to believe in happy-ever-after.'

After all he knew it didn't exist, and he knew the folly of believing that it did.

Cora shook her head. 'But there's proof. There are gazillions of happily married couples in the world.'

'There are lots of *married* couples in the world,' he corrected.

'Don't you think that's a bit cynical?'

'No. Think about it. How many of those couples stay together for the children, or for tax reasons, or because they're scared to be alone? How many of them set aside their dreams for the sake of their marriage?'

Cora lifted her hands as if she wanted to cover her ears, and then dropped them to her sides. 'Even if some of that is true there are lots of people out there who stay together because they love each other.'

'Maybe. But love can cause untold hurt. Why take the risk?'

'Because you trust the other person.'

'Trust?' It wasn't possible for him to put sufficient scorn into the word. 'Trust is pointless. Because people can deceive you. Or, worse, you can deceive yourself.' Her wince showed he'd hit home. 'Do you *really* believe it's possible to place absolute trust in someone else?'

'I...I don't know.'

'Exactly. So why take the risk? When the only benefit you'd get is the doubtful possibility of a happy*ish* marriage. And you'd risk the very distinct probability of the dwindling and disappearance of love. The near certainty of loss. There is no such thing as a happy-ever-after. Life dictates that there must be some unhappiness.'

'Enough, already. I get your point, and I'm not sure I can logically combat any of your arguments, but I think it's a risk worth taking with the right person.'

Rafael shrugged. 'Well, I hope one day you find that person.' The average, ordinary guy she craved. For some reason the idea of the mythical Joe Average sent a skitter of irritation down his nerves. 'But right now how about we go explore Granada? I have tickets for the Alhambra.'

Cora soaked in the ambience of Granada. The hustle and bustle, the glorious smells, the sheer vibrancy seeped into her bones. The stress of the wedding and her interview nerves faded away, impossible to maintain as Rafael spoke about Granada, his love of the place clear in his every deep-timbred word, his knowledge of its history impressive.

She listened spellbound to the story of how Granada had risen over the centuries to become one of the most prosperous medieval cities in Europe, until the fifteenth century when civil and religious wars devastated the countryside and finally resulted in the siege of Granada itself.

'Followed by the triumphant entry of Isabel and Fernando, the conquering Catholic Monarchs, who entered the city garbed in ceremonial Muslim dress.'

'Tell me more.'

Rafael shook his head. 'Later. You need to look around, see the Granada of today.'

He was right, and there was so much to take in. Music permeated the air, and the clack of maracas as street dancers torqued and swayed mingled with the sound of an accordion and the quick-fire riff of spoken Spanish. As for the food—Cora couldn't decide what she craved most as she looked at the luscious fruits on display.

'They smell like *real* strawberries,' she stated.

'As opposed to imaginary ones?'

His smile made her toes tingle. 'Ha-ha! I mean they smell like strawberries should smell, but supermarket ones never do. Even the pineapples look more…pineapply.'

'It's a shame it's not autumn—you'd love the seasonal fruit then. There's *cherimoya*, also known as a custard apple, persimmons, quince and *azuifaifa*.'

'What's *azuifaifa*?'

'It looks like an acorn and tastes like an apple. I think the English translation is Chinese date.'

Curiosity surfaced. 'How do you know so much about Spain?'

A rueful smile tipped his lips. 'Have I been boring you?'

'No! You've made Granada past and present come alive for me.' She shrugged. 'I just wondered whether your family lived in Spain and that's why you speak the language and love it so much.'

It was the wrong question to have asked—the relaxed stance of his body morphed into tension and the smile vanished from his lips as if it had never been.

'Something like that.' He glanced at his watch. 'We'd better grab lunch if we want to get to the Alhambra by two.'

His withdrawal was palpable as they walked to a small restaurant. When would she learn to think before she spoke? It had been a stupid question—after all, Rafael had invited no family members at all to the wedding…evidence enough that his family was a topic to avoid.

As they sat outside at a white plastic table, under the shade of a canopy, Cora scanned the menu. But she couldn't focus on the black italics.

'I'm really sorry—I didn't mean to pry. Truly. Your family circumstances are none of my business.'

For a moment she thought he'd simply agree, and she wished *again* that she'd kept her big mouth shut. Why was she so gauche?

'I don't want to make this awkward. I was really enjoying our conversation and I love Granada. I don't want to spoil it with my big mouth.'

He studied her expression for a long moment and then he shrugged. 'It was a fair question. I grew up not knowing who my father was. The one fact I did have was that he was Spanish, so I became an expert on all things Spanish. You could say I was a touch obsessed. Hence my knowledge.' The words were said with a casualness that belied their importance. 'You may as well make the most of it,' he continued. 'I can translate the menu for you.'

Cora hauled in a deep breath. Clearly Rafael did not want to discuss this. He had only imparted the information in a defensive attempt to pretend it was no big deal.

'Better yet, why don't you order for us?' she suggested as a waiter approached.

'Sure.'

Once done, Rafael leant back, and she watched the play of light and shadow cast by the early-afternoon rays dapple his features.

'So what are we having?'

'I've ordered some typical dishes. There's *patatas a lo pobre*, which literally means potatoes of the poor. The potatoes are slowly fried in olive oil with green peppers and onion. And *plato alpujarreño*—you can't come to Granada and not try it. It's dried pork sausage with a fried egg. Then

I thought we'd finish with bread and *queso curado*—I'm not sure how they cure the cheese, but it's a unique taste.'

'That sounds perfect.'

And the food, when it arrived, was incredible. The earthy tastes lingered on her tastebuds as she savoured the spice of the meat and the flavour of the potatoes. But even as she enjoyed each mouthful her mind dwelled on a small, dark-haired Rafael genning up on all things Spanish in order to create some sort of link with a man he'd never known. A man who had given him the colour of his hair and the Mediterranean hue of his skin. A man who had presumably abandoned him.

'Penny for them?' Rafael asked.

Her brain scuttled for a platitude and gave up. 'I'm sorry about your dad. I understand that you don't want to talk about it, but I want you to know that.'

'There is no need to be sorry. I've done fine without him. The only reason I don't want to talk about him is that he isn't worth the time or breath.' He pushed his plate away with a decisive gesture. 'So, if you're finished, let's go to the Alhambra.'

Cora studied his expression and gained zilch—there was a tension to his jaw, but little else to suggest that the topic under discussion was of more importance than the weather. The man quite clearly did not wish for sympathy or comment.

'Let's go,' she said.

As they walked the avenue lined with an ancient canopy of gnarled trees Rafael questioned why on earth he'd mentioned his father at all. It must have been the mix of utter contrition and self-reproach on Cora's face, the sense he'd had that she was used to censure for blurting out something supposedly inappropriate. Still, whatever his reason it had been foolhardy, and he could only be relieved that she had spared him an in-depth analysis.

As if suddenly aware of the silence Cora looked up at him, and her prettiness struck him anew.

'What?' Her hand flew up to her chin. 'Have I got egg yolk on my face?'

'No. I was thinking how pretty you are.'

Her face tinted. 'Really?'

'Really.'

'Um…then, thank you, I guess. I mean—' Breaking off, she grimaced. 'Anyway. Clearly I'm not good with compliments so I'll shut up. Let's talk about the Alhambra instead.'

A good plan—what was wrong with him? Cora might not be good with compliments but he had no business handing them out—they were *business* partners.

Yet a sneaking suspicion crept in that somehow Cora was getting under his skin, and it made said skin prickle with foreboding. The phrase made him think of Ethan's description of falling for Ruby.

'It's hard to explain, mate,' his friend had said. 'One minute I knew I was immune to love, the next somehow Ruby had permeated that immunity and love took seed and grew and flourished.'

Well, that wasn't happening to Rafael—the only apposite thing about Ethan's analogy was the idea that love was a disease—one *he* would not succumb to by so much as one tiny germ.

Time to morph into a tour guide.

'You'll love the Alhambra.'

Part palace, part fort, it was a place of Moorish beauty mixed with Christian influence and splendour that never failed to bring him a measure of awe-filled peace. The glory of the architecture, the sound of the fountains and the rustle of leaves, the noise of the nightingales and the scents of wildflower and myrtle.

'Moorish poets called it "a pearl set in emeralds" because of the colour of the buildings and the surrounding woods.'

As they made their way through the Nasrid palaces he spouted forth information on the Nasrid dynasty. He tried to ignore the funny little tug to his heartstrings at the intent look of awe and wonder on Cora's face as she absorbed the glory of their surroundings.

'It all started with Mohammed ben Al-Hamar, in the thirteenth century, who established a royal residency here. The palaces grew from there. It was Yusuf I and Mohammed V who did most of what we can see today...including this—the Patio de los Leones.'

'Yet even the Nasrid family tree ended, didn't it?' Cora said as they entered the Patio. 'They had to give the Alhambra up.'

'The last "King" of Granada was Boabdil. He negotiated a surrender with Ferdinand and Isabella and was granted a fiefdom. It is said that once he departed Granada he stopped about twelve kilometres from the city, looked back at what he had lost—his heritage in all its splendour—and understandably he sighed. His mother said, "You do well to weep like a woman for what you could not defend like a man."'

Cora gave a small laugh that held more than a hint of bitterness and no mirth whatsoever. 'That may have happened centuries ago, but if my brother lost Derwent Manor now I can imagine my mother saying much the same.'

'At least no one will battle him for the Manor, so he can't really lose it. Unless he decides to pass it on to a heritage trust.'

'He won't. He will do as my parents have—devote his

life to raising enough funds to maintain the Manor. Do whatever it takes to keep the Manor.'

'*Whatever* it takes? What if it was morally wrong?'

The crease of her forehead denoted frustration. 'I don't know where Gabe stands on morals. My parents believe anything is justifiable to keep Derwent Manor in the family's hands, that there is no sacrifice too big, that wrong is right. They believe in the bloodline and in the importance of Derwent property being handed on intact from father to son.'

The same beliefs held by the Duques de Aiza—the belief that had dictated Ramon Aiza's betrayal, his cruel discard of Emma and Rafael.

'What about you? What do *you* believe?'

'I'd like to believe that right and wrong are more important—that individual wants and needs should be taken into account. That if Gabe doesn't want to uphold the Derwent heritage he shouldn't have to. But it's not that easy. I guess the point is a true Derwent would want to uphold the heritage and there is no choice involved—it's a given.'

'Because duty to your heritage is more important than anything else?'

Ramon had presumably felt *his* duty to his bloodline had been more important than his duty to the woman who loved him and his son.

Cora shrugged. 'You feel you have a duty to the people who work on your vineyard, but not to the land itself. You could walk away without a care. Don Carlos...my parents—they feel a connection with the soil and the bricks and mortar, because it has been in their family for centuries. If you passed your vineyard on in a few hundred years it would become Martinez land and your descendants would feel a duty to it.'

For an insane moment the idea held an appeal—an appeal he rejected out of hand. His ethos was to live for the moment, not for centuries ahead. 'Not going to happen. Because I won't be passing the vineyard on to any child.'

Curiosity alongside bafflement sparked in her eyes. 'So you don't have any desire to have kids?'

'I've thought about it. But it doesn't compute. I have no wish to commit to one woman for the rest of my life, but if I had a child I would want to be a proper part of that child's life.'

There was no way he would ever bring a baby into the world knowing he couldn't be there for him or her every single day.

Rafael huffed out a sigh. How did he end up in these conversations with Cora? No other woman would question him on his lifestyle choices. It was probably because they were too busy enjoying all the perks of said lifestyle.

'Anyway, we'd better move on. There's a lot to see.' Definitely time to resume the tour guide role. 'This is the Patio de los Leones.'

He gestured to the centrepiece of the courtyard—a fountain made of twelve lions topped by a dodecagon-shaped basin. Water sparkled as it fell from the mouths of the white marble creatures who symbolised strength, power, and sovereignty.

'It's one of the most important examples of Muslim sculpture—and it's certainly one of the most beautiful and the most scientific. There is a poem by Ibn Zamrak, a four-teenth-century poet, carved on the basin. He describes the fountain something like this. "Melted silver flows through the pearls, which it resembles in its pure dawn beauty."'

Next to him Cora caught her breath as she gazed at the fountain, seemingly oblivious to the crowds of tourists that milled around the floor. 'That's beautiful.'

'It is, but he ends the poem wishing that the peace of God will go with the reader and says *May your life be*

*long and unscathed, multiplying your feasts and torment-
ing your enemies.'*"

Cora looked up at him. 'You say that with way too
much feeling. Do you agree that your enemy should be
tormented?'

'Yes.' His answer was unequivocal. After all that was
the whole reason for this marriage deal—a means to torment Don Carlos, Duque de Aiza. Yet the look in her eyes
sent a strange defensive twinge through him. 'I take it
you don't?'

'I think it depends on the circumstances, but I guess
I'm not a great believer in tormenting anyone. I know it
depends on why you're enemies, but surely it's better to
try and sort the situation out rather than escalate it? I suppose it's a bit like facing an aggressive dog: the solution
isn't to be aggressive back.'

At the thought of sorting *anything* out with Don Carlos
he felt black thoughts grounding his feet as Cora moved
away to explore the rest of the courtyard. Yet as he watched
her warmth spread in his chest and dissipated the darkness, chased away the thoughts of revenge.

Suddenly aware of the way his gaze tracked her as she
walked around the marble columns, her features touched
with wonder, no doubt counting the damn things, he
scrubbed a hand down his face. What was wrong with
him? Revenge was exactly what he needed to be focused
on—this honeymoon was merely a necessary interlude
until he could realistically contact Don Carlos. Of course
he wanted Cora to seize the moment and have fun, but that
was a fringe benefit in the true purpose of this marriage.

And he had no intention of forgetting it.

CHAPTER TWELVE

CORA GAZED AT the contents of the sleek dark wardrobe and tried to decide what to do.

The obvious choice for dinner in a flamenco restaurant was the same dress she had worn when she'd gone out for dinner with Rafael and her family. The problem was she didn't *want* to wear that dress. She wanted to wear the other dress. The one Rafael had given her. The one that had tempted her gaze with its shimmer of gold.

And what sort of message would *that* send out?

Rafael's words echoed in her brain. *'Keep the dress for another occasion, another time when you do feel comfortable in it. Because you will wow the world or the man you wear it for.'*

Just flipping great. So now she wanted to *wow* Rafael Martinez—what had happened to her?

He had happened to her. The past two days in Granada had shown her a side to him she could never have imagined in a 'shallow playboy'. The day before, with its visit to the Alhambra, had demonstrated his deep knowledge and his love of history and culture. After the Nasrid palace they'd roamed the rest of the magnificent buildings and then visited the gardens, with their blossoming orange trees, seen the grandeur of the thousand-year-old cypress trees and gazed on the rose and myrtle bushes.

But it had been today that had constricted her lungs and

twisted her heartstrings. Because Rafael had insisted on accompanying her to the dog rescue centre, and once there he had shown a mixture of sensitivity, outrage, pragmatism and generosity that had astounded her. He'd listened to the plight of each animal and visited the kennels with her, approached every dog.

Cora's hand hovered over the gold dress and then she pulled it back. *Hang on.* Had she lost the plot and every single brain cell? Yes, Rafael had cared about the rescue dogs, but there was no correlation between that fact and her need to wear a dress with the wow factor. After all, any time she'd ever made an effort to impress before it had backfired horrendously and seared her soul.

There had been the disastrous boyfriend at university, who had courted and wooed her until she had finally succumbed and slept with him. After that he had refused all contact with her and she'd discovered that it had been done as part of an initiation dare—he had been given the challenge of adding a member of the aristocracy to the notches on his bedpost.

Then, of course, there had been Rupert. Most recently there had been the con artist posing as a journalist. There might not have been romance at stake, but she'd lost the Derwent diamonds as well as whatever small credibility she'd gained with her parents. So all in all a dismal record.

But Rafael was different.

'Tchaah.'

The snort dropped from her lips and shook her back to reality. That wasn't the point. The point was there was *no* point in wowing Rafael Martinez. The man had made it clear he did not wish to act on any attraction between them, and come to that neither did Cora. Rafael was dangerous—he had also made it abundantly clear relationships weren't his bag, and that even if they were, any relationship with Rafael had the potential to destroy her. There would be a terrifying constant drive to live up to his extraordinarily high expectations accompanied by a wait for the inevitable time when he would move on to the next opportunity.

The thought made her shudder and prompted her to reach for the trusted grey dress.

Yet she felt a fizzle of disappointment as she entered the lounge, was aware of a foolish feeling of cowardice and an inability to meet his gaze. Instead she focused on the sleek leather lines of the furniture, on the cool sun-scented breeze that flew in through the open window from the dusky Granada night, along with the faint notes of a jazz trombone that lingered in the air and touched her with regret that she had chosen the path of safety.

'All ready.'

The falsetto brightness of her voice caused her to wince as she turned towards the door. She halted as a broad body blocked her path, her vision filled with the breadth of his chest, the triangle of tanned bare skin, the black silk of his shirt. Heaven help her, he smelled so good her head whirled.

Digging deep, she pulled up a smile, reminded herself that she was in *Granada*, for Pete's sake, about to see a flamenco show and eat gorgeous food. There really was nothing to regret or rue.

'Let's go! I'm really looking forward to dinner.'

'Good. I thought you'd enjoy it more than a swanky restaurant.'

'You thought right.'

As they walked through the bright tableau of Granada by night a warmth touched her at the fact that he had thought of her—she had little doubt that his usual dates would prefer an award-winning restaurant, a place to be seen and papped. That would be as important to them as the quality of the food.

'Here we are.'

Rafael came to a halt and Cora gazed at the unpretentious building. A small crowd of people was entering—a mix of all ages, some dressed up to the nines, others more casual, some old, some young. A pretty good representation of life.

As they entered the building they were led down a flight of twisting stairs lit by candles that flickered from cavities in the stone walls. Down, down, down into what looked as though it had originally been a cave. The domed stone ceiling curved above brightly laid tables packed together in rows in front of the stage. Once they were seated, drinks appeared as if by magic.

Cora sipped the red liquid and grinned. 'Sangria. Isn't that an abomination to vintners?'

He returned the smile as he raised his glass. 'It all depends on the wine. In fact I supply the wine here, so even though it's diluted with orange juice, filled with chopped oranges and limes and then chilled, that fact makes it more bearable.'

The words were a reminder that for all his playboy enjoyment of life he also ran a savvy business in an area that he loved.

'To Martinez wine.' She clinked her glass against his. 'And your next venture. I hope it works out.'

'So do I.'

'Why is it so important to you?' The words flew out before she could stop them, pulled out by the haunted look in his dark eyes.

For a moment she thought he might answer with the truth. Then music beat a tune from the stage and he leant back in his chair as if in relief.

'I told you, Cora. It's business.'

Frustration gripped her as she gazed at the neutrality of his features, the sudden remoteness in his stance.

Chill, Cora. It's nothing to do with you.

Yet she wanted to know—not out of idle curiosity but because she could sense his pain and she wanted to help. In the same way that every time she entered a dog rescue centre she sensed the hurt the animals had been through.

Get a grip. Was she really comparing Rafael to a rescue dog? Rafael Martinez did not need her help. Didn't need anything from her.

Time to focus on the stage.

It wasn't exactly a hardship. For the next hour the dancers and the music held her enthralled. The two female dancers, in their figure-hugging, flounced ankle-length dresses vibrant with polka dots, mesmerised her, their high heels clacking in time to the tempo and the words of the song as though they, the singer and the guitarist had some sort of inner connection. Cora's breath caught as the guitarist's fingers blurred, the lyrics of the song vibrated in the air and the dancers shimmied—the whole fusing into a crescendo of pure emotion.

To her own shock she realised that along with everyone else her feet were pounding the floor as she called out *'Ole!'* Every feeling was intensified. Her heart pulsed, and a giddy, heady sense of intense freedom filled her as the final notes lingered in the air. And then there was silence, a quietness of profound depth, almost spiritual, before applause broke out.

'That was…I can't come up with any words,' she said when the final cheer had died away and the performers had quit the stage. Around them the heightened atmosphere relaxed into an excited murmur of voices and the clink of glasses. 'I can't believe I got so carried away.' A chuckle fell from her lips. 'So un-English and so unladylike. My mother would be horrified.'

'Well, I'm not.' His voice whispered over her already sensitive skin and his dark eyes roamed over her face with appreciation and heat. 'I feel privileged to have seen you let go.'

Again.

The unspoken word was louder than if it had been yelled from the rooftops. A memory of how much she had let go during their kiss sent a cascade of heat through her whole body.

'I…I've had a great time. The whole day has been fantastic. I've had *fun*.' The idea almost novel.

'That's the idea.'

Suddenly the room felt overheated, and the temptation to reach out and touch him caused her to push her chair back. 'Please excuse me for a minute. Bathroom break. I'll be right back.'

Rafael watched as Cora made her way back to the table—she was so damned pretty that even the grey dress no longer had the power to mute her. Truth be told she looked a different person from the Cora who had been at the Derwent family dinner. The sun had given her face a touch of colour, her blue eyes held a sparkle and she walked with a confidence that her family seemed to suck from her. As for the way she had lost herself in the flamenco… It had shown him that Lady Cora Derwent had a fun-loving, decadent side to her that she seldom allowed to be on display.

It was a side she seemed to have walled off now. As she sat down he sensed her withdrawal as she picked up the menu and stared into the plastic pages as if it were the Holy Grail.

'What would you like?'

'I know it's a bit of a cliché, but I really want to try a proper authentic paella.'

'Sounds good to me.'

Once the food was ordered she cleared her throat, sipped her wine and then glanced across at him. 'I wanted to thank you for today…at the dog rescue centre.'

'You've already thanked me. And I've already told you there was no need. I'm happy if I've helped.'

The whole visit had been an eye-opener, in more ways than one. He'd admired Sally Anne Gregory, a petite Scottish dynamo who had a passion for animals in need that matched Cora's. And Cora had been transformed before his eyes as she went into action.

She had sat down, rolled up her sleeves and sorted out the admin backlog, had come up with innovative yet doable strategies for raising awareness, updated social media accounts. Then they had visited the kennels. Anger and compassion threaded in his guts now as he thought about the dogs in care.

'This is just a drop in the ocean,' Cora had explained. 'But at least these dogs have hope.'

Cora had visited every dog, and to Rafael it had been a revelation. It was as though she had an uncanny link, an empathy, a lack of fear and a love for each of those dogs. Rafael had been truly shocked at the condition of some of the animals, and even more shocked to be presented with the statistics. He'd made some phone calls, transferred some money, and desperately tried to ignore the gaze of a dog called Dottie. An enormous Spanish Mastin-Shepherd cross, Dottie had been the only dog who'd seemed to zero in on him rather than Cora, her soulful brown eyes following his progress in mute appeal.

'I can't get Dottie out of my head,' he admitted now. 'I mean they were all worthy causes, but Dottie—for some reason she haunts me. She was so gentle, and to see her still being able to behold humans with kindness and affection after what she went through was humbling.'

'Dogs are intrinsically forgiving. That's why I like them

so much. And Dottie is on the right track—I think she can sense that to take revenge on all humans for what one person did would be wrong.'

'What about revenge on that one person? I would very much like the opportunity to spend some time alone with *him*.' When he thought about how Dottie had been hurt, neglected and abandoned his blood simmered.

Cora's turquoise eyes held sadness now. 'I don't understand how anyone can do what Dottie's owner did to her. And I wish there could be some sort of justice rather than vengeance. The two things are different. I think justice would be better served by showing him the truth of what he's done, making him understand and feel genuine remorse.'

'With people like that it's not possible. Sometimes vengeance is the only way to gain justice.'

'I don't want to believe that. Surely everyone is capable of change?' As she pulled her wine glass towards her she gave her head a little shake, her red hair glinting in the twinkling lights of the restaurant. 'Anyway, maybe you should consider taking Dottie. She connected with you too. I could see it.'

An image came of the large sandy-coloured dog pawing at his leg as her brown eyes beseeched him before she sank down and rolled over for a tummy-rub. *For heaven's sake, Martinez.* That was all she wanted—any human touch, not his in particular.

'It wouldn't be fair on her. I don't have the sort of lifestyle that could accommodate a dog. I travel too much, I move around too much, I...' He was making too many excuses, and his defensiveness was on display in the rigidity of his body. 'I've never owned a dog before and I'm not about to start now.'

'Well, it's a shame—because you are definitely a dog person. Even Flash liked you. Remember?'

Flash. The dog Cora had been walking in the Cornish park at the outset of this fake marriage plan. It seemed a long time ago. Another time. Another place. The Cora who sat opposite him now was a far cry from the cold, aloof woman hunched on a park bench. The thought evoked a mix of emotion in his gut—the predominant one being an irrational wish that she had maintained that ice and distance.

Nuts. Just because Cora had turned out to be a warm person with hidden depths of character it made no odds to him.

Unbidden, his thoughts flew to his mother and her description of falling for Ramon, written in her bold, curved script in her final letter to Rafael.

When I first met him I didn't know who he was—couldn't have imagined his rank and wealth. When he told me I felt awed, but then I saw the person, the man beneath. And so love crept up on me, and made me believe that a happy-ever-after was possible. With a man who fascinated me, a man who made me laugh and made me care.

A man who had ultimately gone on to betray her—something she had once believed to be an impossibility.

'Rafael?'

A small frown creased Cora's forehead, and there was a question in her eye. He forced his expression to neutral, refocused on the conversation. 'I remember Flash. A Border Collie.'

'Flash doesn't like anyone much. You're a dog person.'

'That's as may be. But I can't commit to a dog. It wouldn't be fair to the dog.' So it was ludicrous for him to imagine Dottie huffing out a mournful sigh. For a start she couldn't hear him, and secondly she didn't understand

English because she was a *dog*, for Pete's sake. It was even more ridiculous to feel a sudden defensiveness at his apparent inability to commit to anything. There was nothing wrong with a desire to keep his life free and uncluttered, unfettered by ties.

'Why not?' Cora's tone was non-belligerent—eminently reasonable, in fact.

'Because a dog is an enormous commitment.'

'I get that, but if Dottie would bring you happiness and vice versa I think you could do it.' She leant forward, her features illuminated by the candlelight. 'I mean I know you live in both Spain and London, but you could bring Dottie to and fro. There are certain pet travel rules but they aren't that complicated. Dottie would have a passport, and she'd need to have up-to-date vaccinations. I wouldn't recommend travel by plane, but by ferry it should be OK. With your kind of money I'm sure you could do it in style. And for short trips you could afford to hire the best, most empathetic dog-sitter in the world. There are answers to everything—the point is that you could have Dottie if you really wanted to.'

As he listened to her for a fraction of a second the idea almost took hold. *Almost.* Before sanity prevailed. 'I prefer to keep my life uncomplicated and that sounds way too complicated for me. I like my life exactly as it is.'

'Then I won't say another word. You've already helped all those dogs so much with that bank transfer, to say nothing of the money you persuaded others to give. You should only give Dottie a home if it's what you really want, and if it's too big a commitment then so be it.'

Her sheer reasonableness brought him a strange wave of discomfort, alongside a funny sensation of loss, and it was a relief when the paella arrived—before he could let himself regret his own inability to give on a personal level as well as a monetary one.

'What about you?' he asked once the waiter had wished them *buen provecho* and moved away.

'What *about* me?'

'We've established that I can't have Dottie, but…'

'I can't either.' Sadness touched her face. 'I already have Prue and Poppy, and anyway right now it wouldn't be practical. I wish I could take them all in—or at least help find them all a home.'

'Why don't you? If you don't want to set up on your own you could go into partnership with Sally Anne.'

'Don't start that again.' A sweep of her hand at the heaped paella indicated her desire to change the subject. 'This looks delicious.'

Perhaps she was right—he should let it go. But he couldn't—not now he'd witnessed her in action. 'It does. And, yes, the food here is pretty authentic. The chef uses locally sourced ingredients. So it's not the best paella you can get in Spain but it's pretty high up there.'

He spooned a generous portion onto her plate and then onto his.

'So that closes the subject of food. As for the wine— it's from my vineyards, so I can vouch for an aromatic spicy taste that complements the flavour of the food. So that's that. *Why* won't you do what you want to do with your life?'

'I *am* doing what I want to do with my life.'

Rafael shook his head. 'I saw you with Sally Anne. I saw you with the dogs. I saw the way you tackled the administrative side of things *and* the ideas side. That's why I asked you to speak to people and ask for donations.'

'No, it wasn't. You thought they were more likely to donate if a lady asked them.'

'Partly. But I promise you—they may have listened because of your title, but they donated because of what you said. I'll lay you odds that they wouldn't have given a fraction of the amount to Kaitlin.'

Cora stilled, her fork in mid-air, en route to her lips. 'Don't be silly.'

'I'm not. They could hear your passion for this cause. You care about it. So, seriously, why not set up with Sally Anne? Or set up a rescue place of your own? Use the money you earn from this marriage. Make a difference.'

A look of wistfulness crossed her face, then she placed her fork down and shook her head. 'I can't.'

'Why not?'

'I have other obligations. To Derwent Manor. To my family. My parents wouldn't buy in to a dog rescue scheme. In fact they would be horrified. The one time I wanted to do a sponsored walk for a dogs' charity they were rendered almost speechless. They pointed out that any fundraising I did should benefit Derwent Manor.'

'And you agree with that? You won't put money *you've* earnt, fair and square through this marriage, into a dog rescue centre because your parents wouldn't approve?'

'It's not that. Actually, I need the money for something else.' Her gaze skittered from his, and her foot tapped the floor in patent discomfort.

Rafael frowned. When they had embarked on this deal he had known she needed money. He had assumed that, like any other woman of his acquaintance, she wanted it for clothes, jewellery, a luxury lifestyle. Now that idea seemed absurd. Yet maybe it wasn't—maybe he'd misread Cora completely and she *did* want the money to spend and enjoy and just didn't want to admit it. And who was he to judge that?

'It's your money—if you want to blow the lot on a yacht you can.'

Her eyes narrowed. 'I am not going to blow the money on anything. I need it to…'

She pressed her lips together, and he felt curiosity over-rule the idea that it was none of his business.

'To what?'

CHAPTER THIRTEEN

CORA STARED AT Rafael across the table and tried to apply the brakes to her vocal cords. It didn't matter what Rafael thought. Only it did.

Cora winced as discomfort tangled in her tummy. She loathed the idea that Rafael might even *think* she would rather spend the money on herself than use it for good. Especially when she remembered the size of the donation he'd made to Sally Anne.

'I need the money to pay a debt.'

As the words flew from her lips regret struck as surprise simultaneously raised his eyebrows.

'I didn't have you down as the type to get into debt.'

'I'm *not*. I've never been so much as overdrawn before—and, no, I don't have a chequered career as a serial gambler either.'

His frown deepened and she could almost see disbelief dawning in his eyes.

'It's OK, Cora. It's your money. You don't have to justify how you spend it to me.'

The problem was she would rather expose her stupidity than have him think she was like the shallow women he dated. Plus, perhaps she needed a jolt of reality—because for a few minutes she had almost believed it was possible to change her life's trajectory. So...

'A few months ago I was approached by a journalist. He

said he was called Tom Elkins and that he was new in the business and hoping to break into one of the magazines. He wanted to do a "Lady in the Limelight" piece about me, putting the unknown sister under the spotlight. It was a great fee, and I thought it would be a great opportunity to show my family that I could bring Derwent Manor some positive publicity. That I'd outgrown my tendency to mess up on important occasions.'

Pathetic—that was what it had been—her neediness, her patent delight in the attention, her selfishness in wanting to show everyone. Well, she'd got her comeuppance, all right.

'Long story short: he persuaded me to show him round the Manor, even the parts we don't open to the public, so he could get a proper overall feel of what being a Derwent means. Then he brought in Lucy Gerald, supposedly his photographer. A week later there was a break-in at the Manor and amongst other heirlooms the Derwent diamonds were stolen. Funnily enough I never heard from Tom again, and it turns out from his description and fingerprints that he is an expert thief.'

The memory of that discovery, the cold, hard stone of reality, the aching, stabbing guilt, the pain of her parents' shock, horror and disparagement, still made her blood run cold.

'Weren't they insured?'

'Not the diamonds. The insurance was too costly and Mum and Dad were confident that security was tight enough.'

'It's still foolish not to have insurance unless you are willing to accept the risk of loss.'

'It was my fault.'

Her parents had been in total agreement on that score, for sure.

'In hundreds of years no one has ever stolen anything from the Manor. Not so much as a teaspoon. Then I come along and with true Cora Derwent panache I pretty much unlock the safe for a pair of well-known thieves and con artists. Not surprisingly, my parents weren't very happy.'

Rafael didn't look that happy himself; his jaw was set hard. 'You made an innocent mistake—they took a calculated risk.'

'And I screwed up the odds with my stupidity.' Cora tilted her chin. 'I can't blame them for being disappointed. So when they made it clear they no longer wanted me to continue to work at Derwent Manor I knew what I had to do. Earn their trust back by repaying my debt.'

'But that would have taken you years.' Bafflement infused his tone.

'Yes. But so be it. I figured once I got together a good sum hopefully they would at least forgive me.'

'Then I came along with my proposal?'

'Yes. Now I can pay them back in full.' The words sent a wave of relief through her—the feeling of a weight being lifted. 'I know that is the right thing to do.'

Rafael pushed his empty plate away from him and picked up his wine, cradled the glass in his large hands. 'I can see that. I don't understand why your parents were so harsh, but I can see why you feel the need to give them the money. But then what?'

Cora frowned. 'What do you mean?'

'After that. When you have repaid the debt, what will you do then?'

'Hopefully they will give me my job back and life can return to normal.' The plan that had filled her with such hope just days before seemed suddenly a little flat, and annoyance skittered through her. Somehow Rafael had messed with her head.

To her relief the waiter materialised and engaged in conversation in rapid Spanish with Rafael as he cleared the plates. Thank goodness—now they would leave the restaurant and this conversation behind, and it was undoubtedly time to resume the 'smiles and platitudes' strategy.

'Please, can you tell the waiter that the food was delicious and I have had a lovely evening?'

'Actually, the evening isn't over. Juan has explained that the chef would like us to have dessert on the house. A speciality, Lagrimas de Boabdil—the tears of Boabdil.'

Just flipping great.

Rafael studied Cora's expression as she dug her spoon into the honey and raspberry dessert. It seemed clear that she would like to terminate the conversation and instinct told him she was right. Her life choices were *zip* to do with him. But curiosity alongside frustration begged a question.

'Why do you want everything to revert to normal? Why not stay here and work with Sally Anne? Or get a job with an animal charity? Surely your parents would prefer you to do something that makes you happy rather than spend your life in a role that doesn't fulfil you.'

But even as he said the words he knew it didn't work like that—this was a family who had sabotaged their daughter's wedding day...had let her marry a man they believed would discard her...

'The Derwent family don't rock and roll like that. It's a family business. You are born into it and you work for it. That's how it is and I can't buck the trend.'

'Why not? You can't spend your life doing something you don't want to do.' Especially for a family Rafael was beginning to believe were on a par with the de Guzmans.

Leaning forward he tried to convey the importance of his words. 'You said it yourself yesterday. You believe in the right of the individual. You don't *have* to do what every Derwent has done since time immemorial. You can stand up for what you want. Your parents would come round.'

Her lips parted and he thought she would perhaps

vouchsafe the truth—a real explanation. Instead she smiled a smile that seemed expressly designed to humour him.

'Maybe you're right. Maybe one day.'

'No.' His fork dropped to his plate with a clatter as he exhaled a sigh heavy with frustration. 'Because one day may never come.'

How could he make her understand that she mustn't give up on her own life? He didn't want this new Cora, vibrant and passionate, to morph back to that cool, aloof, muted Cora, burdened by familial obligation.

'I *know* this. My mother was diagnosed with advanced cancer before she was forty—her chance to live her life was snatched from her.'

It felt strange to say the words—words he hadn't uttered for so very long, words that brought his mother's face into focus, reminding him of the gut-wrenching sheer panic and misery and the fear that had assailed him when she'd broken the news.

Cora reached across the table and covered his hand with both of hers. The warmth of her touch gave him a comfort he shouldn't want, and yet it consoled him.

'I'm sorry. *So* sorry. How old were you?'

'Fourteen.'

'So that memory you have—that happy memory of you and her at the fairground…?'

'Is from the final months of her life—she knew it would be the last birthday she'd spend with me. But she made sure it was a memorable one. We had a wonderful day— and it's how I like to remember her.' Blonde hair flying in the breeze, her face creased with laughter—having fun, full of life.

Cora blinked and he could see a tear quiver on the end of her lashes.

'So what happened to you?' she asked. 'Did you have family to take you in?'

'I had family, but they didn't want to take me in and I didn't want to go to them. They didn't like my mother—thought she was above herself. So the upshot was that I went into care.'

'Oh!'

'Don't look so aghast. It was for the best. I was already on the slippery slope to screwing up my life. I'd been bunking off school, had got involved in petty crime to make money, so that I could make Mum's last months at least a bit luxurious.' He shook his head as regret bit at him. 'A box of chocolates, a bottle of cheap perfume... Nothing compared to what I could have given her if she'd lived. But she was so appreciative of each and every gift.'

Cora's fingers squeezed his hand.

'I wanted to make good. I'd promised her I would get my life back on track and live it to the full. That was made easier by my carers. They were good people—experienced foster carers. I went back to school, I caught up, and I got into technology. And then I invented that gizmo that made me millions.'

'Your mum would have been so proud of you. And I believe—I really do—that somehow she knows that you did good. And not because you made bucketloads of money. Because you kept your promise to her to get your life on track and live your life to the full. Thank you for telling me, Rafael.'

'I told you because I want you to see the importance of seizing the day. You need to make your dreams happen *now*. Promise you'll think about it.'

'I promise.'

Rafael exhaled a breath and realised that Cora's hands were still wrapped around his. Realised that he had shared way more than he had intended, and that this dinner had veered into a dangerous area. He should have terminated this conversation long ago. No more. Time to remind Cora *and* himself that this was a business marriage and a business honeymoon.

'Good.' Pulling his hand gently away, he turned to look for the waiter. 'It may be an idea to think quickly. My plan is to put out a feeler to Don Carlos tomorrow and see if he is now willing to negotiate.'

An expression flitted across her face—a disappointment that she masked so fast he couldn't be sure it had even existed.

'Won't he think it's strange that you're thinking about business on your honeymoon?' Her eyes focused on her plate as she pushed the last crumbs into a small heap with her fork.

'No. He'll understand that, honeymoon or not, I won't want to lose out on the vineyard.'

Relief surged over him that he'd got his plan back on track. Yet that relief was lined with a sense of impending loss, a shadow of the way he had felt when he had realised he would lose his mother. A danger warning sounded and was heeded—never again would he open himself up to that level of pain.

CHAPTER FOURTEEN

CORA SHIFTED ON the sofa, stretched her legs down over the leather surface, stared at the pages of her book and wished that she could focus on the characters. But she couldn't—she had tried and failed for the past two days to lose herself amongst the pages.

Two days during which she'd barely seen Rafael. Ever since their dinner in the flamenco restaurant he had withdrawn, spent most of his time engrossed in work—presumably on the vineyard deal. There had been no more sightseeing—he had pointed out that real honeymooners would enjoy staying in. But the words had been uttered dispassionately, with no hint of the attraction or the closeness that had characterised their first two days. And she, fool that she was, missed both the attraction and the closeness.

The thought filled her with an urge to hurl the book across the room in sheer irritation.

Just then the door opened and Rafael entered. *Breathe.* Cora concentrated on her novel, refused to look up. Until ignorance was impossible to simulate anymore because he stood right next to her, the muscular length of denim-clad leg tantalising her gaze.

'Sorry to interrupt. I just wanted to let you know I've heard from Don Carlos's man of business—I've set up a meeting with Don Carlos tomorrow in Madrid to sign the paperwork for the vineyard.'

Despite the fact that she had expected some progress the words hit her with shocking impact, and she swung her legs over the leather seat. *Too soon.* The thought reverberated through her brain. *Too soon.*

Somehow she pulled a smile to her face. 'That's fantastic!' Because it was—*of course it was.* She surveyed his set expression—she could see no sign of triumph or even a smidgeon of happiness. 'Isn't it…?'

'Yes. But I won't fully believe it until the title deeds are in my hands.' He scrubbed a hand down his face. 'Anyway, whatever happens with the vineyard tomorrow, this marriage charade can end. I'll transfer the balance of your fee and you can pay your parents back.'

The idea should have her cartwheeling around the room, but still the words *too soon* tolled in her head. *Madness.*

'That's wonderful.' Squashing down the urge to leave it at that, she dug down and located a modicum of courage. 'And it seems like a good time to tell you that I *did* keep my promise and I *have* thought deeply about my future and the idea of a dog rescue centre. I've decided against it.'

His dark eyes bored into her as if they could read her inner soul and he sat down opposite her. 'Can I ask why?'

Damn. She'd hoped that he would just accept her decision, but she'd known that if he asked she owed him the truth. Rafael deserved that—he cared about her future because of the demons of his own past, and she wanted him to know why she couldn't change her life.

'Because I need to follow my ultimate dream. I need to prove to my parents, to myself, that I am a proper Derwent. All my life that's what I've striven for and I've never achieved it.'

'I don't get it. You seem like model daughter material.'

'If only! I've never managed that…' His dark gaze was focused solely on her, and somehow the words came easily. 'Not even as a baby. Mum didn't find out she was expecting twins until late on in the pregnancy and the whole idea freaked her out. Maybe if she'd delivered two Kaitlins or if I'd been a boy it would have been OK. But I was another girl, and I was a sickly, ugly scrap—whereas Kaitlin was bonny and beautiful. Kaitlin fed easily and never cried. To my parents it must have seemed that Kaitlin had got all the good and I'd got all the bad.'

How many times had she pictured the revulsion on her parents' face? Sometimes she wondered if it were a latent memory.

'They couldn't bond with me. I've always known that and I don't blame them. The Derwents set a lot of store in perfection, you see—looks, intelligence…it's all part of our breeding. I'm the ugly duckling who remained an ugly duckling.'

'No.' He shook his head. 'You were not an ugly duckling. You were a baby. And as a baby, as a child, as their daughter, you deserved your parents' love.'

'I think they used all their love up on Kaitlin and Gabriel—they were golden children and I was an unwanted spare. But they did at least do their duty by me.'

'That isn't enough.'

'Maybe. But that isn't the point. The point is I can't just go off and set up a dog rescue charity, or a dog-walking company. All that would do is prove to them that they were right about me all along. I *will* show them that I am a true Derwent, I *will* win their approval, and I *will* change their minds. And the best way for me to do that is to work for the Derwent estate.'

'Stop!' The word sounded as if it were torn from his throat. 'Don't, Cora. Don't waste your life trying to change them. People don't change.'

'You don't know that.'

'Yes, I do. My mother spent a decade in limbo, grieving for the love of her life—my father—a man who abandoned and betrayed her. Always hoping he'd come back, hoping he'd change. Well, he didn't—and she wasted her life hoping for something that was never going to happen.'

Cora could almost taste his frustration and doubt touched her. The image of his mother, waiting for a love that never materialised, chilled her with sadness. But...

'I can't let myself believe that.' How could she when this was what she had striven for all her life? 'Maybe there are facts that you don't know, Rafael. About your father. Maybe your mother was right to wait for him. Maybe...'

'Maybe he was a weak, cowardly bastard.'

'You don't know that.'

'Yes, I do.'

He rose to his feet, as if the very idea of his father forced some sort of movement, and paced the carpet to stand by the marble mantelpiece.

'My mother left a letter with a solicitor to be given to me when I was thirty. In it she revealed my father's identity. I traced him and I found out that he left us to marry someone else. But he didn't have the guts to tell her face to face—he left that job to someone else. Sent that someone to make sure my mother didn't cause trouble. He turned up with a bunch of goons and terrorised her. Hurt her. Vandalised all her belongings and threw us onto the street with nothing. I was five, and all I can remember is the feeling of sheer helplessness, my inability to defend her.'

Horror stole Cora's breath. 'That...that's awful.'

'Yes. Yet my mother persisted in her belief in him and wasted so many years.' He took in a deep breath. 'Don't let that happen to you with your parents. Don't see good where there is none to see.'

Right now all she could see was a vision of the five-year-old Rafael, forced to watch as his mother was beaten and hurt, and it tore at her heartstrings. Without thought she stood and moved towards him. Closed the gap and put her arms around him, her hands against the strength of his back. His body remained rigid, so she put her cheek against his chest, felt the pounding of his heart, heard his exhalation before he allowed his body to relax.

'I'm sorry for what you and your mum went through. It sucks. Big-time.'

It could have been seconds they stood there, it could have been minutes, but slowly an awareness of how close they were, of the breadth of his chest, the accelerated beat of his heart, the woodsy scent of him, pervaded her being. It filled her with a longing so intense it almost hurt. Not almost. It *did* hurt, and the knowledge gave her the strength to move backwards.

But now she could see him—see the awareness that mirrored hers, the heat in his dark eyes as he looked at her. And the whisper of an idea slipped into her brain, urged her to live in the here and now and take the opportunity to grasp what she wanted.

Madness. Say something, anything, before you do something stupid.

'How about I make us a farewell dinner tonight? I'll sort it out. I can pop out and get some food, no problem, and then...' *Put some distance between us.*

But distance wasn't what she wanted. If only she could read his mind. Did he regret what he'd shared? Or was he too caught in this web of misplaced awareness and the knowledge that after tomorrow they would most likely never see each other again.

The idea banded her chest in sudden panic.

'OK. That sounds great,' he said after an almost imperceptible pause.

'Great. I'll head to the shops, then.'

Did she dare? The question swirled and tapped and danced around her as she left the apartment and stepped onto sun-dappled pavement, inhaling the now familiar scents of Granada. Orange blossom, mingled with the mouthwatering scent of fried *churros* that triggered the remembered tang of melted chocolate and pastry on her tongue.

Did she dare? As she purchased a selection of pâté, cheese, olives and bread the idea of seduction cast its magical spell. *Could she do it?* The knowledge that this was her last chance urged her to throw caution to the wind, to risk certain heartbreak and seize this opportunity. Would she be strong enough to play by his rules? Strong enough to say goodbye with dignity and no regrets? After all, she knew Rafael wasn't for her—he was as far from Joe Average as it was possible to be. And she knew she wasn't for him.

There was no way in hell, heaven or earth that a woman like herself could keep Rafael for more than a brief interlude. A woman like her could never be more than an opportunity to him—but maybe in the here and now that was enough.

So this time as she got ready for dinner there was no hesitation as she pulled the shimmering gold dress from the wardrobe and laid it on the bed. She washed her hair and left it loose.

Half an hour later she gazed at her reflection—it was hard not to see an imaginary Kaitlin standing next to her, in the same dress, looking more…

Not this time.

Cora scrunched her eyes shut, reopened them and glared at her reflection, remembering Rafael's words.

'You aren't a pale imitation of Kaitlin and you don't have to live in her shadow. It's your life. Live it. Keep the dress for another occasion, another time when you do feel comfortable in it. Because you will wow the world or the man you wear it for.'

So 'comfortable' might be pushing it, and she didn't

care about the world, but the desire to wow Rafael was bone-deep.

Before she could change her mind she headed through to the dining area. Desperate shyness twisted in her tummy, along with the ice-cold realisation that Rafael might not even remember the dress.

He was immersed in a document, scanning it with ferocious concentration.

'Hey.' Her voice was too high-pitched as she stood there.

He looked up—and his double-take, the way he scrambled to his feet, his jaw ever so slightly dropped as he gazed at her, filled her with a fizz of anticipation.

'You look even better in that dress than I imagined you would.'

His voice was slow and appreciative, reminiscent of expensive chocolate and malt whisky, and she knew the dress spoke for itself.

'And I was right about the wow factor. You look spectacular.'

Pure feminine triumph streamed through her veins, filling her with heady power.

'Thank you. I'll bring the food through in a minute, but I wanted to talk first.'

'OK.' A few strides brought him towards her. 'Shoot.'

'I…'

As she looked up at him, absorbed the aquiline features, the jut of his jaw, the clear dark gaze that blazed with desire, saw the tiny, barely noticeable scar by his left eyebrow, the breath-stealing glory of him, her carefully rehearsed speech faded away.

Stepping forward, she rested her palms on his chest, stood on tiptoe, slid her hands up onto his shoulders and pressed her lips against his. She revelled in the sensation, in the tang of coffee, the sheer buzz that rocketed through her pulse.

His hands encircled her waist as he deepened the kiss and she gave herself up to the vortex of pleasure, soaring free from all her worries and fears and existing purely in the moment.

She only came down to earth when she realised he'd ended the kiss, though he still held her body close to his.

'Cora, are you sure…?' he began, his breathing ragged, his deep voice strained.

'More sure than I've ever been.' She held his gaze, even though her legs threatened weakness at the heat in his eyes—a heat that promised untold pleasures to come. 'I had a whole speech prepared, but what it comes down to is that I want to seize this moment, this opportunity. This is *it*, Rafael. After tomorrow we will go our separate ways—and I would always regret not doing this. If that's what you want too?'

'Yes. It is what I want too.'

His deep voice sent a shiver down her spine all the way to the tips of her toes, and then she gave a sudden squeak as in one deft movement he scooped her up into his arms.

CHAPTER FIFTEEN

RAFAEL OPENED HIS eyes and stared up at the pristine white ceiling of his bedroom. In that instant of waking, he felt drowsy contentment wrap around him like a blanket. Cora's head rested on his chest, and the silky smoothness of her hair tempted his fingers. He gently entwined them in the sun-kissed red strands.

She opened her eyes and he smiled. 'Morning.'

'Morning,' she murmured, and for a sleepy heartbeat she snuggled into him with a languorous smile.

Then reality smote him. Morning brought with it his meeting with Don Carlos. The night was over—and there would be no more like it.

His thoughts were mirrored in her expression, in the sudden withdrawal in her eyes, in her abrupt movement to sit up, the sheet clutched to her chest.

'Right,' she said. 'You need to get to the airport. I'll get coffee on the go.'

For an insane moment near reluctance kept him still. What was *wrong* with him? This was what he had worked toward for over two and a half decades. The idea of revenge had fuelled him, and now it was so nearly in his grasp.

'That sounds good. Thank you.'

Half an hour later Cora handed him a coffee and looked him over. 'You look great,' she said. 'Good luck.'

A moment's hesitation and she stood on tiptoe and

kissed his cheek. The so familiar scent of her made him close his eyes for a heartbeat, in a sudden unlooked-for ache. *Enough.* Right now he needed to be focused. Don Carlos was not to be trusted and he needed to be in complete command of the situation.

He should be savouring this moment. Yet throughout the plane journey images of Cora pervaded his mind. The soft gurgle of her laugh. The passion they'd shared. Skin against skin. The texture of her lips. The silken smoothness of her red hair.

As the private jet began its descent Rafael pulled his thoughts to order. *Enough.* Cora didn't belong here, no longer had a place in his life. Steel determination banded his chest—today he would finally get the revenge he'd sworn to achieve all those years ago.

The chauffeured car negotiated Madrid's traffic-laden streets, headed towards the city's business district, epitomised by the soaring four-tower skyscrapers that dominated the skyline.

Once there he alighted and a cold burning filled him—a sudden desire to forget this civilised vengeance and simply storm the Duque de Aiza's bastion, grab Don Carlos by the throat. *No.* That would not gain him what he wanted—he wanted to see the humiliation on Don Carlos's face when he realised he'd been duped, that he'd handed his land over to the 'illegitimate, tainted son of a whore' he'd terrorised twenty-five years before.

It was almost a surprise to see how calm his features were in the chrome-edged mirror of the elevator that carried him to Don Carlos's lair. And then there he was again, in the inner sanctum where he'd been months ago.

'Rafael. We meet again.' The elderly Spaniard remained seated in his ornate wooden chair behind a dark mahogany desk.

'We do. I understand that you have reconsidered my proposal for the vineyard?'

'I have.' The Duque pushed a document across the desk. 'I think you'll find all is in order.'

Rafael stepped forward and picked up the papers.

'I suppose I will be the first of many who will negotiate with you now you have married into a title. You did well to choose Cora Derwent—I doubt anyone else would have had you. Kaitlin wouldn't have given you the time of day.'

'I'm sorry. I'm not sure I understand.'

Chill, Rafael. No doubt he wants to goad you.

'Come, come. You are using her—I know that and so do you. Does she believe you love her? Or does she *know* that all you want is acceptance into the upper echelons of society? I'm not criticising you—I applaud your acumen. You picked the less attractive, mousy one—the one who wouldn't say boo to the proverbial goose. Excellent choice. You can manipulate Cora and no doubt school her into accepting your infidelities, accepting being used with good grace. Her family have used her for years. So, as I said, you did well to choose such malleable material. It has certainly won you this vineyard. I can at least know that one day my land will go to a child with Derwent blood in its veins.'

Bile rose in his throat. Don Carlos, Duque de Aiza, the grandfather he loathed, was *applauding* him for his use of Cora, and the idea of his grandfather's approval turned his stomach. The way he spoke of Cora, of the woman he loved, made anger pulse in his veins.

Loved.

Rafael reached out a hand to steady himself against the dark wood of the desk.

Loved.

The idea impacted on him in all its inevitability—the knowledge was absolute and true. He *loved* his wife, and to use her was an impossibility.

So many thoughts freewheeled in his brain…a plethora of emotions twisted his guts. It was imperative that he got out of this godforsaken office, away from this bitter, envenomed man.

'I've changed my mind.'

'Excuse me?'

'I've changed my mind.'

Rafael barely recognised the croak of his own voice. The shocked disbelief on Don Carlos's face should have caused him satisfaction, but his brain was too busy imploding.

'I no longer wish to buy your vineyard.'

With that Rafael swivelled and left the office, barely registering the *swoosh* of the lift doors or its descent, or his arrival on the pavements of the city.

'I'll walk,' he told his driver.

Perhaps the air would clear his head and show him that this epiphany had been no more than illusion. How had it happened? How had Cora wriggled right under every single one of his defences? Though perhaps a better question would be how could he undo the damage—push her out so he could re-barricade his heart?

Panic set his head awhirl and he increased his stride. Love was not for him—he would *not* give Cora that power over him. So somehow he had to purge himself of this unwanted emotion. Yet there was a part of him that wanted to shout it from the rooftops—run straight to Cora and tell her. *Fool.* Was this how his mother had felt about Ramon Aiza—this heady, out of control, terrifying sensation? Even maybe the way Ramon had once felt for Emma? This so-called love that led to tragedy.

Well, he would withstand it—as his parents must have wished *they* had had the strength to do. His feet pounded the pavement. Love made you weak, and he would not succumb to its pervasive power.

* * *

Cora paced—she now knew that the lounge of Rafael's Madrid apartment was fifteen paces by seventeen. Also that it *was* possible to eat her own weight in chocolate.

Where was Rafael? Surely his meeting with Don Carlos couldn't have taken this long?

Her nails dug into her palms. What if he hadn't got the vineyard—what if it was some sort of underhand ploy by the Duque? In which case she could almost taste Rafael's rage and—worse—his humiliation. Cora didn't know why this vineyard mattered so much, but she suspected it was wrapped up in a desire to prove something to Don Carlos. So if that man had hurt Rafael in any way, Cora would... She wasn't sure what she'd do, but it would involve marching down to his office to give him a piece of her mind.

The idea stopped her in her tracks—she, timid, gauche Cora Derwent, was able to envisage bearding Don Carlos in his lair in defence of Rafael. Maybe she should have offered to attend the meeting—to emphasise their togetherness.

The sadness that she had tried so hard to ignore all day descended in an unstoppable wave. Sadness that last night had been the grand finale of their marriage contract. That there could be no more togetherness. But the night had given her memories, an experience that she would treasure for ever.

The click of his key in the door caused her to spin as the noise of his feet on the marble floor of the hall told of his arrival.

There was a pause, and then the door opened and Rafael stood in the arch. For a second she was sure something was wrong. There was a set to his features, a slight pallor under the Mediterranean hue. Then his lips turned up into a smile.

'How did it go?'

'Don Carlos agreed to sell the vineyard to me.' There was a curious flatness to his voice, though his smile widened.

'That is fantastic. You must be thrilled.' Yet she could feel her forehead scrunching into a frown of disquiet.

As if sensing it, he shrugged. 'I am—but an hour in that man's company makes me want to boil myself in disinfectant.'

'You need never see him again. The main thing is that you've got what you wanted. Don't let Don Carlos spoil it—not after all the effort you put in.'

'You're right.' He pushed himself off the doorjamb in one lithe movement and headed towards his laptop. 'And the same goes for you. I'll transfer the final balance now and then you're free. Free to return home.' His dark head was angled so he could see the screen, his expression hidden. 'Free to discharge your debt and win back your job.'

She watched as his dextrous fingers flew over the keyboard and panic assailed her. Because those words that should have been magical had left her cold. Instead of anticipation at her return to the Derwent fold she felt emptiness, a precipitate sense of loss. Because she didn't want to leave Rafael.

No. Please, no.

There was no way she could have fallen for Rafael Martinez—that was unacceptable.

Rafael did not want her love. He'd wanted her title, and now that commodity was used up he would be ready to move on to the next opportunity. It was the way he lived his life—free and uncluttered—and she had nothing to offer against that. She could never be enough for him, just as she had never been enough for her parents. She would *not* love him—would not allow herself to.

'Cora?'

And yet as she turned to face him the words strained to

be released, telling her to throw dignity to the wind and tell him the truth. But sudden fear paralysed her vocal cords. How could she bear rejection from him?

Rafael Martinez was out of her league—on a different playing field altogether. He was a man whose father had abandoned him in the cruellest way possible, whose mother had died after the waste of a decade mourning her lost love. Little wonder the idea of love was anathema to him. Maybe one day he'd meet a woman capable of making him change his mind, but she wasn't that woman. Rafael needed someone who could match his extraordinary energy, his love of life—someone who could leash his power. A beautiful, attractive, strong woman. Not her.

They had a deal and she would not renege on it. Any more than on the deal she had made with herself. To play by his rules and leave with her pride intact. With her memories of her time with him unsullied.

His expression was shuttered, though for an instant she thought concern lit the darkness of his eyes. *Pull it together.* If there was ever a time to resurrect cool, aloof Cora it was now.

'Sorry. I was miles away. I'm all packed—I just need to sort a flight.'

'Whenever you're ready. The money is in your account.'

There was nothing in his tone to indicate that he felt any regret, even a hint of sadness at this ending. If anything she had the impression he couldn't wait to be shot of her. And why not? *Get with it.* This was how Rafael Martinez rocked and rolled—he was a playboy, after all, and he'd never once tried to make her believe otherwise.

'Thank you. I'm glad this deal has worked out for us both.'

He rose from the desk and her breath caught in her throat—if he so much as touched her hand she would unravel, and right now it was imperative that she left before her pride cracked along with her heart.

Stepping backwards, she managed, 'Before I go we'd better get the story straight on our break-up.'

'I'll issue a statement—something along the lines of, "It is with sadness that Lady Cora Derwent and Rafael Martinez announce that their marriage is unsustainable. Once the romantic whirlwind wore off the couple realised that in fact they have very little in common and have decided to call it a day. The split is entirely amicable and they wish each other well."'

Unsustainable. Very little in common. Each word was like an individual bullet to her heart.

'Perfect. So now that's sorted I'll be on my way.'

No matter if she had to camp overnight, waiting for a flight, it would be better than remaining here. Digging deep, she pulled a smile to her lips, forced back tears of pain and humiliation.

'Thanks for everything. I hope life brings you many more opportunities.'

A strange self-mocking smile twisted his lips, but then he stepped forward and his expression morphed, and for a heartbeat he looked like *her* Rafael.

'Thank you. And *I* hope your parents start to appreciate and love you the way you deserve to be loved.'

His arms closed around her in a final hug so bittersweet her very soul ached.

CHAPTER SIXTEEN

It was an ache that persisted throughout her journey back to England, where the plane descended through grey, gloomy, rain-laden skies. A miserable train journey later and Cora braced herself as she approached Derwent Manor, gazing at the imposing pile of bricks and stone, the landscaped curve of the gardens, and trying and failing to feel even a flicker of pride or happiness at her heritage.

There was little point in putting off the inevitable, and despite her yearning to go and find Poppy and Prue she made her way to the library to find her parents.

The Duchess looked up from the table, where she sat surrounded by piles of photograph albums.

'Cora. What are *you* doing here?' Irritation sparked in her emerald eyes. 'We're having a dinner for Prince Frederick and Kaitlin and a few others. In fact I was just looking for some photos of Kaitlin as a child to show Frederick. It really is not a good time for you to be here—I don't want this dinner to go wrong, and I certainly don't need the Prince to remember our connection with Rafael Martinez.'

'You don't need to worry about that.' Cora blinked back tears. 'The marriage is officially over.'

Her parents exchanged glances and then the Duke gave a crack of laughter. 'Well, that's a record—even for you, Cora.'

'But no matter,' his wife said. 'The prenup still stands, and that's what matters.'

'Really?' Cora stared at them, realising that they weren't going to ask her how she was—didn't care about the abject misery her expression held.

'Really.' Her father rolled his eyes. 'The man is an oik—low-born, base scum who grew up in squalor. You've besmirched our name with that marriage, but that will be compensated for if it benefits the family coffers. Given the amount your stupidity with that journalist cost, I assume you're planning to hand over the cash?'

Expectant silence filled the air, and for a heartbeat the habit of Cora's lifetime nearly kicked in. *This* was why she had married Rafael—for this moment, the moment when she handed over the money, paid off her debt. Approval would dawn in her mother's emerald-green eyes, and a genuine smile would curl her father's lips. A true Derwent wouldn't hesitate—would hand over Rafael's money and feel good.

Yuck! There was no way she could do it. Her nails clenched into her palms as she looked at her parents and felt as if she was truly seeing them for the first time. Perhaps this was what love did to you—true love.

An icy rage possessed her, gave her courage. 'No. I'm not planning on handing over the cash. Rafael Martinez is worth a hundred Derwents and I'd be proud to stay married to him. I love him. Love doesn't depend on someone's birth or blood, or what they look like, or how socially acceptable they are. It depends on their inner worth. In which case, forget a hundred—Rafael is worth a *thousand* Derwents. Either way, I don't see why he should line the Derwent coffers. So I plan to give his money back. As for my stupidity—I fully acknowledge that and I will pay you back what I can, *when* I can. That I promise.'

The Duchess rose to her feet and Cora forced herself

to remain still, not to back off at the look of incandescent rage on her mother's face.

'I always knew you weren't a true Derwent. From the moment of your birth I knew you must be some throwback, some—'

'Stop!'

Cora spun round, realised she hadn't even heard the library door open to admit Kaitlin.

'Enough.'

Her sister stepped forward to stand by her side, her skin leeched of colour.

'Cora is my twin—she is as true a Derwent as I am. So please stop this *now*. Cora is your daughter and—'

The Duke shook his head. 'And *as* our daughter she needs to behave the way our daughter should.'

Cora turned to her sister and smiled, truly touched that for the first time ever Kaitlin had jumped off the fence and offered support. 'It's OK, Kait.' Stepping away from her sister, she approached her parents. 'I'm sorry that you feel my actions are wrong, but I am behaving in the way that feels right to *me*. In a way that makes me feel good about myself. I'll be in touch.'

With that she turned and headed for the library door, aware that Kaitlin was close behind her.

'Where will you go?' her sister asked, once they had exited the Manor.

'I'm not sure yet. Somewhere I can take Poppy or Prue.'

A welcome numbness seemed to have settled over her, blanketing her from consideration of her actions. The spur that had driven her for so long no longer drove her and she felt only emptiness, an abyss made worse by the pain of wanting Rafael. The instinctive temptation to go to him for sanctuary nigh on overwhelmed her even as she recognised the sheer stupidity of that thought.

Rafael Martinez did not want her.

Kaitlin's beautiful face creased into a frown of concern. 'Take my car. Do you need money or…?'

'I'll be fine, Kait. I promise. Now, you'd better go and get ready for Prince Frederick and that dinner. There's no point making Mum and Dad even angrier.'

There was a pause, and then Kaitlin pulled her into an awkward hug before she headed back to the Manor.

Two months later

Cora approached Ethan and Ruby Caversham's London house. *Right.* The same rules applied as had applied for the past eight weeks. No matter what, she would *not* ask about Rafael. This lunch was supposed to be a pleasant social event with two people who had proved to be true friends. Friends who had given her sanctuary in Cornwall until press interest in her marriage break-up had died down and then given her a job at the Caversham Foundation in London.

Best of all, they had asked no questions. Or at least they hadn't until now. But there had been a certain something in Ruby's tone when she'd issued the lunch invitation that had made Cora suspect a hidden agenda. So here she was, hovering outside whilst considering retreat.

The front door opened and Ruby came out. 'Cora. I am *so* glad you're here. Ethan, you can stand down…' she called over her shoulder. 'Operation Kidnap Cora is no longer necessary.'

A genuine smile tipped her lips, though envy panged as Ethan came out and looped an easy arm round his wife's waist.

'Welcome, Cora. And many thanks for all you're doing at the office.'

'You're very welcome.'

'No more talk about work, Ethan Caversham!' Ruby

ordered in a severe tone totally alleviated by the look of adoration she cast on her husband. 'Come on in, Cora.'

Cora followed the Cavershams down the spacious book-lined hall and into a lounge that oozed an air of comfort and cosiness, with its overstuffed sofas, soft cushions, bean bags and bright paintings.

'This is gorgeous.'

'Thank you.' Ruby's sapphire eyes sparkled. 'Ethan and I want it to feel like a home. Its early days yet, but hope-fully, if one day we get accepted as adopters, I want to have the homiest home imaginable. And in the meantime some of those teens we're helping come round sometimes—it's really lovely. I mean, they pretend it's no big deal but it is. A lot of them live in residential homes and we want them to have somewhere else to go. In fact we're going to con-vert the basement into a teen den.'

Cora felt warmth and admiration touch her—Ruby *cared*, and so did Ethan. They worked together to bring good into others' lives, worked at something they both be-lieved in and felt passionate about.

'But enough of us,' Ruby said. 'What I really want to know is how *you* are? Not workwise, but how *you* are.'

'Fine…'

If you didn't count the number of minutes in the day she wasted on Rafael Martinez, remembering the way his genuine smile lit his eyes, his tendency to scrub his hand down his face when he was annoyed, his scent, his…

Ruby's dark blue eyes met hers. 'Really?'

'Of course.'

After all, once she got over Rafael she *would* be fine—she'd probably also be grey-haired and in her dotage, but hey-ho.

'I've got started on my plans for setting up a dog rescue centre too. Thank you both so much for that brainstorm-ing session—it really helped.'

Cora felt a fizz of excitement at the thought of her project. She'd thought it all through. Her determination to pay her parents back hadn't diminished, but if she could set up the charity in such a way as to earn a salary from it, and supplement that with dog-walking and maybe some part-time work for the Cavershams, she truly believed she could do it.

'Any time,' Ethan said as he paced the room.

Ruby glanced at her watch with a small frown and cast a glance at Ethan that clearly constituted some sort of telepathic conversation. 'Ethan, could you check the lunch? It should be nearly ready. Cora and I will just chill in here.'

Ethan hesitated, rubbing the back of his neck as he eyed his wife. 'Rube…'

There was a warning note to his voice that caused his wife to shake her head at him.

'It's OK, Ethan. I know what I'm doing.'

Cora frowned, watching as Ethan exited the room. 'Ruby, what is going on? Is there a problem? Ethan only paces when he's uncomfortable about something.'

The dark-haired woman sat back and exhaled, blowing her fringe off her forehead. 'There isn't a problem as such. Or at least I *hope* it's not a problem.'

'What is it?'

'Rafael will be here soon. He's asked us to arrange this because he doesn't want to risk any press attention. Or at least that's what he said. I think he was worried that if he asked you directly you'd refuse. That's why he didn't want us to tell you. But that doesn't seem fair to you.'

Cora could barely register the meaning of Ruby's words—all she could focus on was the fact that Rafael's arrival was imminent. The idea made her feel alive, filled her with excitement and fear and panic and joy.

The doorbell pealed and Ruby's sapphire gaze met hers. 'What do you want me to do? Do you want to see him?'

Indecisiveness added itself to the mix. Could she bear to see him? Could she bear not to?

'Yes... No...I don't know. I mean...did he say *why* he wants to see me?'

Ruby shook her head. 'He was very unforthcoming, despite my best efforts.'

'Then there's only one way to find out. I'll see him.'

Ruby nodded and then headed for the door. Cora rose to her feet and gripped the back of the chair for support, her fingers squishing into the soft material as she tried to calm the rocketing of her pulse.

The door opened and her heart stopped, started, skittered and eventually settled on a rhythm that threatened to rattle her ribcage.

'Rafael,' she said.

Rafael paused on the threshold, brought to a halt by the sheer impact of seeing Cora. He absorbed the beauty of her face, the glory of the red hair that cascaded to her shoulders, observed the smudges under her turquoise eyes, her extra slenderness accentuated by the simple dark green T-shirt and denim cut-offs she wore.

It took all his self-control not to stride forward and pull her into his arms. *Cool it, Martinez.* There was wariness in her expression, and the last thing he wanted was to spook her.

Then her gaze dropped from his as she spotted Dottie by his side. Her lips formed a circle of surprise before curving up into a smile as the large sandy-coloured dog trotted forward, sniffed Cora's out-turned hands, then sat in front of her and pawed her leg with a gentle stroke. Without reservation Cora sank to her haunches and the big dog rolled over for a tummy-rub, head lolling in sheer appreciation.

He stepped forward as Ruby and Ethan entered the room. 'Right,' Ruby said. 'We'll leave you two to it. If you want lunch it's in the kitchen. Boeuf Bourgignon, wild rice and salad, and a bottle of Martinez plonk.'

Cora gave Dottie one last pat and rose to her feet. 'Thank you,' she said, with a touch of doubt in her voice—presumably as to what she was thanking them *for*.

As Ethan walked past he clapped Rafael on the shoulder. 'Good luck, mate—and don't blow it,' he murmured.

Easy for Ethan to say.

Once the Cavershams had departed silence descended. Rafael's thoughts were scrambled. His guts seethed with nerves and his legendary charm seemed to have legged it to faraway places.

'So…' Cora retreated back behind the dark red armchair. 'You took Dottie in?'

'Yes.' *Gold star for conversational ability, Martinez.*

'That's great. How's it working out?' She glanced down to where Dottie was crashed out at his feet. 'Not that I need to ask. It seems clear she has bonded.'

A sudden smile lit her face, then vanished, and he knew why—saw the concern in her eyes.

'I've bonded too. I would never have taken Dottie if it wasn't for ever.'

He could see the doubt etched in the crease of her forehead and he could hardly blame her. His remembered words on the subject of lifestyle and commitment swooped in to bite him royally on the behind.

'Cora. I promise. Dottie is a part of my life now.'

Until now he'd never understood how people could bond so completely with an animal. But from the moment he had picked Dottie up from Sally Anne he'd not once regretted it. This enormous soppy dog was full of a capacity to love, and Rafael had little doubt that she would guard him with her life if necessary. Full of character and independence, she had settled into his villa in La Rioja, loving the freedom of the local fields. Yet she also roamed the vineyard at his heel. Equally, she seemed to have adapted to his London home and in truth…

'I couldn't imagine life without her.'

For a long moment Cora studied his expression. Then, as if satisfied by whatever she'd read, she gave a small nod. 'Good.' Her eyes narrowed and her knuckles whitened on the back of the chair. 'So why are you here?'

'I needed to see you…to tell you…' *I love you.* 'I didn't buy the Aiza vineyard.'

Jeez. What was the matter with him? *Fear.* He was terrified to tell her how he felt in case she ran screaming from the room—in case he lost her for ever.

Her forehead scrunched into that quintessentially Cora frown and his fingers itched to smooth the creases.

'You didn't buy it? But you said… You… Why on earth not?'

'I couldn't do it. I stood in Don Carlos's office and he offered me his admiration for my marriage, for using you to get a foothold into the higher echelons of society—using you to gain his vineyard and future deals. And I couldn't do it. I couldn't use you like that.'

Her turquoise eyes widened and she shook her head. 'Why not? I know how much that vineyard meant to you.'

'Not as much as you do.'

All the fear had gone now. Whatever the outcome for himself, he wanted her to know he loved her.

'I love you, Cora. With all my heart and soul.'

Her face was illuminated—and then the frown returned. 'But…that doesn't make sense. I thought you didn't *do* love. I thought you couldn't wait to be shot of me.'

'I definitely do love.'

He met her gaze full-on, hoped she could see the sincerity and love that blazed inside him.

'I think I've loved you since I took you to La Rioja and saw through to the *real* Cora Derwent. The beautiful, passionate woman who sees good in people. The incredibly generous woman who cares and who has the most astounding capacity to love. I love you, Cora, and I don't want you to *ever* doubt that. Because I never will. You've changed me. I always swore I'd avoid love because I saw it as something that weakened you, gave someone else power over you, held you back from living life.'

'And now?'

'Now I know it doesn't have to be like that. I will still want to seize opportunities and live life to the full, but now I want to do that with you by my side. Now I see that love can make you a better person, give you strength and compassion, and that with love comes trust. Trust that you can work through the hard times, knowledge that being together is a million times better than being apart. You make me whole, Cora, and I love every hair on your head and every molecule of your being. I love your smile, and the way you scrunch your forehead up when you're thinking. I love being with you. And all I want is to wake up beside you every day for the rest of my life. I *love* you. You've made me see the world differently. Does that make sense?'

'Completely. Because I love you too. More than anything.'

Two strides brought him to the red armchair and she walked round it and straight into his arms. Elation and joy bubbled inside him—Cora loved him.

'Loving you has changed the way I see the world too. I believed you couldn't love a person like me—not when there are so many beautiful, talented women in the world. Because my parents made me believe that that's how love works. They loved Kaitlin and Gabe because of their looks and their talents—they couldn't love me because I wasn't beautiful or talented. But now I know love *doesn't* work like that. I love you because you're *you*, and these past two months I've missed you. I've missed your voice, our con-

versations, the way you make me feel alive, your touch...
I've missed *you*. *Everything* about you—your stubborn-
ness, your ability to seize the moment, the way you know
how to have fun but also care so deeply.'

Her beautiful smile curved her lips, lit her eyes with
joy.

'So I love you because you're you, and you love me because I'm me.'

'I couldn't have put it better myself. You've made me
a better person, Cora. Do you remember I told you about
my father?'

'Of course I remember.'

'What I didn't tell you was his identity. My father is
Ramon de Guzman, and my grandfather—the man who
terrorised my mother with his goons—is Don Carlos,
Duque de Aiza.'

Her lips parted in a small gasp. 'So *that's* why you
wanted the vineyard?'

'Yes. It felt fair on some level that some Aiza land
should come to *me*, and I knew that Don Carlos would
be horrified that his land had ended up in his illegitimate
grandson's hands. I dreamt of his face when I told him
who I was, showed him my success. Stood over him and
watched him realise that I held the power to plunge his
house into scandal. I savoured the idea of producing the
first batch of Martinez wine on his vineyard—I would
have named it "Lady Emma".'

Anger crossed Cora's beautiful features. 'He would have
deserved all that.'

'Yes, but in the past months I've come to realise I don't
want revenge any more. I don't want to torment my enemies. Because you were right to say that vengeance and
justice are two different things. If I avenged myself on Don
Carlos others would be affected. I would effectively block
Juanita and Alvaro from my life—and they are my half-

siblings. Then there's my father... My mother wanted me to forgive him so I decided to write to him.'

As he recounted the story to Cora he relived it himself. Ramon de Guzman had written back to request a meeting, and days later he had arrived at Rafael's Madrid apartment. He had entered his study and stood for a moment in the doorway. The sense of how surreal it had felt as they had faced each other was impossible to describe. Memories had flooded back and Rafael had been able to see a glimpse of the man his father had once been, to see bits of himself in the aquiline features and dark eyes, as his father spoke.

'Rafael. I have come to...to apologise. To you and to the memory of your mother. I did love her, with all my heart, and I have never loved another since. I loved you too. But I wasn't strong enough to stand up for that love and deny my duty.

'When my father told me he had arranged a marriage for me, to a woman of noble blood, I did try to refuse. In the end I told him about your mother and you. He explained to me the impossibility of marriage to your mother, convinced me that to marry her would be to wrong my family name, my heritage. He promised me that if I agreed never to see you both again he would sort everything out honourably. You would be provided for, given a house, an education, an allowance—you and your mother would want for nothing. And, God forgive me, I agreed.

'Until I got your letter I believed all had happened as he'd said. I should have known, I should have tried to find you, but I knew that if I saw your mother again I would be lost. How could I have that on my conscience? My poor wife...she has already endured a cold, loveless marriage. And my children, Alvaro and Juanita—I had to think of them too.'

Ramon Aiza had looked at him with a plea in his eyes.

'Now I know what really happened I am in your hands. I will acknowledge you to the world if that is what you wish.'

'*Is* that what you want?' Cora asked now.

'No. I can't see the point in wreaking that kind of pain on all and sundry. I told Ramon that I would like Alvaro and Juanita to know of my existence, and that if they wish to meet with me I would like that.'

Cora squeezed his hand. 'I think you did the right thing—what your mother would have wished. But I'm so sorry that you went through all that alone. I wish I could have been there for you.'

'It sounds mad, but in a way you were. I carried your image in my mind and in my heart.' He reached into his pocket. 'But now I want more than that. I want to spend the rest of my life with the real flesh and blood you.' As he pulled the jeweller's box from his pocket he sank to one knee and looked up at her. 'Will you marry me for real, Cora Derwent?'

'Yes, Rafael Martinez, I will. Yes, with all my heart.'

He slipped the ring onto her finger and saw her face light up as she gazed down at the blue turquoise set in gold. Not a diamond in sight. Because now he understood their connotations for her, so he had chosen a rare form of turquoise to match her eyes—a ring designed and chosen with love, not for show.

'It's beautiful,' she breathed as he rose to his feet. 'I am honoured to wear it.'

One final qualm assailed him. 'But your parents…they won't be happy about this.'

'That's up to them. You told me that I changed you for the better—well, you have done the same for me. Loving you gave me the strength to stand up to my parents, because I realised I didn't want to win their approval at the cost of losing my self-respect. I can't sacrifice my life or my principles to gain their love. If they love me they have to love the real Cora. And if they decide to disown me because I marry you then so be it. It's their loss. I love you and you love me.'

And now the joy remained on her face, illuminating it with a glow of such happiness that it was impossible to doubt her sincerity.

'And I want us to feel good about that love and proclaim it to the world. I won't do what Ramon did and let my family's misguided notions dictate my happiness. Or yours.' Stepping into the warm circle of his arms, she smiled up at him. 'I want to live my life to the very fullest, with you by my side.'

Happiness banded his chest, and as he kissed her Rafael Martinez took the greatest opportunity of all—to love and be loved in return.

EPILOGUE

CORA WATCHED THE shadow and light from the September sun dapple the villa floor, inhaled the heavy harvest scent as it wafted through the open windows from the nearby vineyard.

'How do I look this time?' she asked Kaitlin.

'Stunning. This dress is perfect.'

Cora had to agree—she adored the dress she had chosen for the renewal of their wedding vows. Long and flowing, it fell in pools of white round her feet, whilst the transparent neckline with its pretty floral pattern round her shoulders gave it a fairytale touch.

'But it's not only the dress, Sis. It's you. You glow with happiness.'

'That's what love does,' Cora said. 'I seem to radiate joy.'

Every morning she woke up with her heart full of wonder and thanks as she reached out to feel the solid strength of her husband next to her.

Then she saw her sister's expression, heavy with despair. 'Kait, what's wrong?'

'Nothing. I'm fine.'

'No, you're not.'

Cora had seen more of her sister in the past months than she had since their childhood. Kaitlin had given both public and private support to her decision to remain married to Rafael, and had helped win her parents' grudging acceptance of the union—though they had declined to attend this simple renewal ceremony.

'Tell me what's wrong, Kait. Maybe I can help. Is it Prince Frederick?'

Kaitlin pressed her lips together. 'Please don't worry—I will sort it out. Really, I will. And if I need help I'll come to you. I promise.'

'I'll hold you to that. But, Kait, don't marry Frederick unless you love him.'

Her sister shook her head. 'Come on. Now isn't the time.'

Cora nodded and led the way out to the vineyard. She beamed at the scattering of guests. There was Juanita, who had welcomed the advent of Rafael into her life, and Ethan and Ruby, on the cusp of parenthood—they had been approved as adopters just the previous week. And there stood Gabe, whom Kaitlin had managed to track down—though he refused to discuss where he'd been or why, or what he'd been doing—arms folded, his hazel eyes watchful. María and Tomás stood arm in arm and the three dogs—Dottie, Prue and Poppy—lay at their feet, their coats gleaming in the Spanish sunshine.

And most important of all there was Rafael—her rock, her partner and her soulmate.

Her heart skipped as she walked towards him without hesitation, saw his smile light his face with happiness. As she reached him and he took her hands in his she knew that their love would endure the test of time, and she looked forward with all her heart and soul to spending the rest of her life with this wonderful man—this time each word of their vows would resonate with truth and love.

* * * * *

"James Bravo, you may kiss your bride."

Addie was looking up into his dark-fringed blue eyes, already feeling that she'd pretty much hit the jackpot as far as temporary husbands went.

And then James slowly smiled at her and she realized that it was actually happening: they were about to share their first kiss.

James said her name softly, in that wonderful smooth, deep voice of his that sent little thrills of excitement pulsing all through her.

She said, "James," low and sweet, just for him. And she thought of the last three nights, of the two of them together in the hotel room bed. Of waking up each morning cuddled up close to him, of one or the other of them gently, reluctantly pulling away…

Okay, maybe it wasn't a *real* marriage. And it would be over as soon as her grandfather was back on his feet.

So what? It was probably as close to a real marriage as she was ever going to get.

* * *

The Bravos of Justice Creek:
Where bold hearts collide
under Western skies

JAMES BRAVO'S
SHOTGUN BRIDE

BY
CHRISTINE RIMMER

MILLS &
BOON®

First Published in Great Britain 2016
By Mills & Boon, an imprint of HarperCollins*Publishers*
1 London Bridge Street, London, SE1 9GF

© 2016 Christine Rimmer

ISBN: 978-0-263-91985-1

23-0516

Our policy is to use papers that are natural, renewable and recyclable products and made from wood grown in sustainable forests. The logging and manufacturing processes conform to the legal environmental regulations of the country of origin.

Printed and bound in Spain
by CPI, Barcelona

Christine Rimmer came to her profession the long way around. She tried everything from acting to teaching to telephone sales. Now she's finally found work that suits her perfectly. She insists she never had a problem keeping a job— she was merely gaining "life experience" for her future as a novelist. Christine lives with her family in Oregon. Visit her at www.christinerimmer.com.

For Anita Hayes,
crafter, great cook and world's
most attentive raiser of chickens.
You make me laugh and touch my heart.
This one's for you, Anitabug.

Chapter One

Waking up tied to a chair is bad.

But waking up tied to a chair staring down the deadly single barrel of old Levi Kenwright's pump-action shotgun?

So. Much. Worse.

James Bravo stifled a groan. Not only did it appear he was about to eat serious lead, but he had the mother of all headaches. Surely Levi didn't really intend to shoot him. James shook his head, hoping to clear it.

Still a little fuzzy. And still hurt, too. And Levi still had that shotgun trained right on him.

The old man wasn't at his best. His wiry white hair looked as if he'd combed it with a cattle prod and his craggy face seemed kind of pale—except for two spots of color, burning red, cresting his cheekbones. Sweat shone on his wrinkled throat and darkened the underarms of his worn checked shirt.

His aim, however?

Way too steady. Levi grunted as he sighted down the barrel. "Good. You're awake. I was beginnin' to worry I'd hit you a mite hard."

James winced, blinked in another failed attempt to ease his pounding head and cast a careful glance around him. Judging by the lack of windows, the knotty pine paneling, the faint smell of cool earth and the stairs leading upward along the far wall, Levi had brought him to a basement. Was it the basement of the house at Red Hill Ranch, where Levi lived with his way too damn attractive granddaughter Addie?

Probably.

On the battered pasteboard side table a few feet away, James spotted his phone, his wallet and his keys. So even if he managed to get his hand into his pocket, there was no phone in there to use to call for help.

And just how in hell had all of this happened?

James remembered standing on the porch of his nearly finished new house ten miles outside his hometown of Justice Creek, Colorado. It was a cool and sunny March afternoon. He'd been gazing off toward the big weathered barn at Red Hill, hoping that Addie would soon ride by on one of those horses she boarded and trained.

The crazy old coot must have come up on him from behind.

Cautiously, James inquired, "Er, Mr. Kenwright?"

"No need for formalities, son," Levi replied downright pleasantly as he continued to point the shotgun at James. "We're gonna be family. I want you to call me Levi."

Had the old man just said they were going to be… family? James's head hurt too much for him to even try to get a handle on that one. "Levi it is, then."

A wry little chortle escaped the wild-haired old man. "That's better."

Better? Better would be if Levi put down the gun and untied him immediately. But James didn't say that. For the time being, he would say nothing that might rile his captor. A riled Levi could suddenly decide to fire that shotgun. That would be good and bad. Good, because James would no longer have a headache. Bad, because he wouldn't have a head, either.

"Levi, do you mind if I ask you something?"

"You go right ahead, son."

"Why am I tied to a chair in the basement of your house?"

Another chortle. And then, very slowly, Levi lowered the shotgun. James drew a cautious breath of relief as Levi replied, "Good question. And one I am sure you will know the answer to if you just give it a little more thought."

James closed his eyes. He thought. But thinking gave him nothing, except to make his head pound harder. "Sorry, but I honestly have no idea why you're doing this to me."

"Well, then." Levi backed three steps, sank into the battered leather easy chair behind him and laid the shotgun across his knees. "Allow me to explain."

"Wonderful. Thank you."

"Think nothin' of it—I know you know my granddaughter Addison."

"Of course I know Addie." Was she somehow involved in this? Why? He'd done nothing to cause her to make her grandfather hit him on the head, drag him to Red Hill and tie him to a chair.

Had he?

"Means everything to me, that girl," Levi said. "She

and her big sister, Carmen, are what I got that matters in this world—well, them and my great-grandkids, Tammy and Ian, and their dad, Devin. A fine lad, Devin. Like you, he needed a little convincing. But once he understood the situation, he stepped right up. Same as you're gonna do—and where was I?"

"Uh, Addie and the rest of your family mean everything to you?"

"Right. Family, son. Family is everything. So you can imagine my concern when I recently discovered that Addie's in the *family* way." *Addie pregnant?* Could that be true? Levi went right on. "Naturally, I want my new great-grandbaby to have two parents. That's the old-fashioned way, which is to say, it is God's way. And that means it's the *best* way. And of course, I know very well that *you* are my new great-grandbaby's daddy. So I'm just helping things along a little here, just nudging you down the path known as doing the right thing."

James cleared his throat. Carefully. "Hold on a minute…"

"Yeah?"

James had a strong suspicion that there was a lump on the back of his head where Levi had hit him. The lump throbbed. It felt like a big lump, a lump that was growing bigger as he tried to make sense of what Addie's crazy grandpa said to him. "Did you just say that Addie's having my baby?"

Holding the shotgun between his two gnarled fists, looking weary as a traveler at the end of a very long road, Levi rose to his feet again. "Your baby needs a daddy, son. And my Addie needs a husband." He raised the gun and aimed the damn thing at James's aching head once more. "So tell me, is the path becoming clearer now?"

James had never had sex with Addie. Never kissed her, never done more than brush a touch against her hand.

True, he would very much have liked to do any number of things to Addie. But he hadn't. So if Addie had a little one on the way, he wasn't the man responsible.

And that he wasn't really pissed him off.

But James's jealousy of some mystery man who got a whole lot luckier than he ever had was not the issue here.

The issue was that Levi had kidnapped the wrong guy.

Not that James had any intention of setting the old codger straight. Not at the moment, anyway. James had more sense than to argue with a man who'd already cold-cocked him, abducted him and tied him to a chair.

Yeah. Levi meant business, all right. And it was looking more and more likely that the old guy had a screw loose. James was a lawyer by profession. He'd dealt with more than one screwball client in his career. Arguing with a nutcase had never gotten him anywhere.

So instead of insisting he'd never laid a hand on Addie, James announced with all the sincerity he could muster, "Levi, the right thing is exactly what I want to do."

"Glad to hear it, son."

"Great, then. If you'll just untie—"

"Not. Quite. Yet." Levi shook his head, but at least he lowered the gun again.

Keeping it cool, James breathed slowly and carefully. "All righty, Levi. When, exactly, *do* you plan to untie me?"

"Soon as I'm absolutely certain you're not gonna pull any tricks on me. Soon as I know I can count on you to…" Levi's sentence died unfinished as a door slammed shut upstairs. The old man gasped. His rheumy eyes widened as footsteps echoed from above.

Addie. James's heart leaped as his head pounded harder. Had to be Addie.

And it was. "PawPaw!" she hollered, the sound far

away, muffled, not coming from whatever room was directly overhead. "Where are you?"

James and Levi both stared at the ceiling, tracking the path of her quick, firm footsteps on the floor above as those footsteps came closer.

And closer…

They passed right overhead.

The basement door squeaked as it opened. James couldn't see that door, not from where he was tied in the middle of the basement floor. But he heard Addie crystal clear now as she called down the stairs, "PawPaw?"

"Don't you come down here!" Levi glared at James and waved the shotgun threateningly for silence. "I'll be up in a minute!"

The door only creaked wider, followed by more creaking: footsteps on the stairs. A pair of tan boots appeared, descending, bringing with them shapely legs in a snug pair of faded jeans. "What are you up to down here?" The curvy top half of Addie came into view, including those beautiful breasts of hers in a tight T-shirt and all that softly curling ginger hair. About then, she turned and caught sight of James. Big golden-brown eyes went wide in surprise. "What the…?" She stumbled. A frantic screech escaped her as her booted feet flew out. She windmilled her arms.

"Addie!" James and Levi shouted their useless warnings simultaneously.

But then, with another cry, she grabbed the iron stair rail and righted herself just in time to keep from tumbling the rest of the way to the concrete floor.

"Get hold of yourself, girl," old Levi grumbled as she made it down the last step and sagged against the railing. "A woman in your condition has got to be careful."

Those baby-doll lips of hers flattened in a scowl and

two bright spots of color flared high on her round cheeks as she put a hand to her stomach and tried to catch her breath. "PawPaw, you're scaring me to death. Put down that gun and untie James immediately."

Levi lowered the gun, but he didn't put it down. "Now, Addie honey." His tone had turned coaxing. "I can't untie him right yet. First, James and I need to come to a clear understanding."

"An understanding of what?" Addie drew herself up, stuck out her pretty, round chin and glared daggers at Levi, who stared back at her sheepishly but didn't answer. He must have known she would figure it out—and she did. Her eyes went wide again as she put it together. "Have you lost your mind? I told you. James is not the guy."

Levi granted her a patient, disbelieving look—and explained to James, "Morning sickness. That's how I knew. Just like her grandma, her mom and her big sister, too. Morning sickness early and often. Then I found that little stick she used to take the test. I put it all together, yes, I did. Levi Kenwright is no fool."

Addie made a growling sound. She actually seemed to vibrate with frustration. "You had no right, PawPaw, none, to go snooping through my bathroom wastebasket. I told you what I think of that. That is just wrong. And now to *kidnap* poor James, too? What is the *matter* with you?"

"Nothing is the matter with me," Levi huffed. "I'm fixing things for you and James here, just like I fixed them for Carmen and Devin."

James decided he couldn't be hearing this right. Surely Levi wasn't implying that he'd kidnapped Carmen's husband, too?

Addie shrieked again, this time in fury. Waving her arms as she went, she started pacing back and forth across the big rag rug that anchored the makeshift basement living area. "How can I *talk* to you? You are impossible. You know very well that it was *wrong* of you to kidnap Devin."

Levi just stood there, cradling his shotgun, looking smug. "Worked, didn't it? Eight years later, he and Carmen and the kids are just as happy as bugs in a basket."

Addie stopped stock-still beside the ancient portable TV on its rickety stand. She sucked air like a bull about to charge. "I can't *talk* to you. I want to *kill* you." She planted her fists on her hips and commanded, "Untie James right this minute."

Levi didn't budge. "Now, Addie honey, don't get yourself all worked up. James has told me the truth, accepted his responsibility to you and the baby and promised to do the right thing."

Addie gasped in outrage and whipped her head around to glare at James. "You told him *what*?"

Oh, great. As if all this was his fault? He suggested mildly, "Given the situation, arguing with your grandfather didn't seem like a good idea."

"I don't... I can't..." Addie sputtered, furious, glancing back and forth between him and the old man. And then she pinned her grandfather with another baleful glare. "Of course James *confessed*. What choice did he have? You held a shotgun to his head."

Levi blustered, "He confessed because it's true and we both know that it is."

"No. No, it is *not* true. James is not my baby's daddy. How many ways can I say it? How in the hell am I going to get through to you?"

Levi made a humphing sound and flung out an arm in James's direction. "If not him, then who?"

By then, Addie's plump cheeks were beet red with

fury and frustration. She drew in a slow, hard breath. "Fine. All right. It is none of your business until I'm ready to tell you and you ought to know that. But if you just *have* to know, it's Brandon. Brandon is my baby's father."

Levi blinked three times in rapid succession. And then he let out a mocking cackle of a laugh. "Brandon Hall?"

James fully understood Levi's disbelief. A local poor boy made good who'd designed supersuccessful video games for a living, Brandon Hall was never all that hale and hearty. Recently, he'd died of cancer, having been bedridden for months before he passed on. It seemed pretty unlikely that Brandon had been in any condition to father a child—not in the last few months, anyway. And Addie's stomach was still flat. She couldn't be that far along. Uh-uh. James didn't buy Addie's story any more than Levi did.

"Yes," Addie insisted tightly. "Brandon *is* the dad."

"I may be old, but I'm not senile," Levi reminded her. "There is no way that Brandon Hall could've done what needed doing to put you in this predicament, Addison Anne, and you know that as well as I do."

Addie fumed some more. "You are so thickheaded. Honestly, I cannot talk to you…" She turned to James and spoke softly, gently. Soothingly, even. "I am so sorry, James, for what my grandpa has done." She gave him the big eyes. God, she was cute. "Are you hurt?"

He nodded, wincing. "He got the jump on me, whacked me on the back of the head, hard, out at my new place. Knocked me out cold. I'm not sure how long I was unconscious, but when I woke up, I was here."

She hissed in a breath and whirled to pin her grandfather with another accusing glare.

Levi played it off. "He's fine. Hardheaded. All the Bravos are. Everybody knows that."

"You *hit* him, Grandpa." She threw out a hand in James's direction. "You *hurt* him. And you have restrained him against his will." Levi started to speak. "Shush," she commanded. "Do not say another word to me. I can't even look at you right now." She turned back to James. "I really am so, so sorry…" James sat very still and tried his best to look appropriately noble and wounded. She came closer. "Can I…take a peek, see how bad it is?"

"Sure." He turned his head so she could see.

And then she was right there, bending over him, smelling of sunshine and clean hay and something else, something purely womanly, wonderfully sweet. "Oh!" she cried. "It's a big bump. And you're *bleeding*…"

"I'm all right," he said. It was the truth. The pain and the pounding had lessened in the past few minutes. And the closer Addie got, the better he felt. "And there's not *that* much blood—is there?"

"No, just a dribble of it. But blood is blood and that's not good."

He turned and met her enormous eyes. "I'll be all right. I'm sure I will."

She drew back. He wished she wouldn't. It was harder to smell her now she'd moved away. "I don't know what to say, James. I feel horrible about this. We need to patch you up immediately…"

"Don't untie him!" shouted Levi.

Addie just waved a hand in the old guy's direction and kept those big eyes on James. "Of course I will untie you."

"No!" Levi hollered.

She ignored him and spoke directly to James. "I will

untie you right now if you'll only promise me not to call the police on my crazy old granddad."

"I'm not crazy!" Levi huffed. "I'm not crazy and he's the dad—and you are not, under any circumstances, to untie him yet."

"Grandpa, he is *not* the dad. Brandon's the dad."

"No."

"Yeah—and if you just *have* to have all the gory details, Brandon was my lifelong friend." She choked a little then, emotion welling.

Levi only groaned in impatient disgust. "I know he was your friend. I also know that's *all* he was to you— nothing like you and lover boy here. Come on, Addie honey. I wasn't born yesterday. I've seen the way this man looks at you, the way he's been chasin' after you— and though I know you've been trying to pretend nothing's going on, it's plain as the nose on my face that you are just as gone on him as he is on you."

"She is?" James barely kept himself from grinning like a fool.

But no one was looking at him anyway. Levi kept arguing, "James is the daddy, no doubt about it. And, Addie girl, you need to quit telling your old PawPaw lies and admit the truth so that we can move on and fix what doesn't need to be broken."

"I am not lying," she cried. "Brandon was my best friend in the whole world and he grew up in foster care, with no family, with nothing."

"Stop tellin' me things I already know."

"What I am telling you is that he wanted a child, someone to carry on a little piece of him when he was gone. Before he got too sick, he took steps. He had his sperm frozen…" Addie sniffed. Her big eyes brimmed. She blinked furiously, but it was no good. She couldn't hold back her tears. They overflowed and ran down her cheeks. "And then he asked me if just maybe I would do that for him, if I would have his child so that something would be left of him in this world when he was nothing but ashes scattered on the cold ground…"

By then James was so caught up in the story he'd pretty much forgotten his own predicament. Everyone in Justice Creek knew that Addie Kenwright and Brandon Hall had been best friends from childhood. People said that, near the end, she'd spent every spare moment at Brandon's bedside. As the dead man had no one else, Addie had been the one to arrange the funeral service. She and Levi and her sister, Carmen, and Carmen's husband, Devin, had sat together in the front pew, all the family that Brandon had.

James asked her gently, "So, then, it was artificial insemination?"

Addie sniffed, swiped the tears with the back of her hand and nodded. "We tried three times. What's that they say? The third time's the charm? Well, it was. But Brandon died the day after the third time. He died not even knowing that he was going to be a dad."

James realized he was in awe of Addie Kenwright and her willingness to have a baby for her dying friend.

Levi, however, refused to accept that he'd kidnapped the wrong man. "That's the most ridiculous bunch of bull I've ever heard. And I'm seventy-eight years old, Addie Anne, so you'd better believe I've heard some tall tales in my lifetime."

Addie only swiped more tears away and moved to stand behind James again. He glanced over his shoulder at her. She met his eyes and said softly, "I just hope you'll be kind, that you'll take pity on an old man who never meant to hurt anyone."

"I will," he vowed quietly. "I do."

"Thank you." Her cool hands swift and capable, she began working at the knots Levi had used to bind him.

Levi let out another shout. "No!" He started waving the shotgun again. "Don't you do that, Addie Anne. Don't you dare. Under no circumstances can James be untied until I am absolutely certain that he's ready to do the right thing!"

Addie said nothing. She kept working the knots as Levi kept shouting, "Stop! Stop this instant!" He ran in circles, the gun held high.

Just as the ropes binding James went slack, Levi let out a strange, strangled cry. He clapped his hand to his chest—and let go of the shotgun.

The gun hit the floor. An ungodly explosion followed and a foot-wide hole bloomed in the ceiling. Addie screamed. Ears ringing, James jumped from the chair. Sheetrock, wood framing and kitchen flooring rained down.

And Levi, his face gone a scary shade of purple, keeled over on his back gasping and moaning, clutching his chest in a desperate, gnarled fist.

"PawPaw!" Addie cried and ran to him. She dropped to her knees at his side.

Levi gasped and groaned and clutched his chest even harder. "Shouldn't've...untied him..."

"Oh, dear God." She cast a quick, frantic glance in James's direction. "Call an ambulance. Please..."

James grabbed his phone off the side table and called 911.

Chapter Two

Once he got help on the line, James gave his phone to Addie so she could talk to the dispatcher directly. He scooped up his keys and wallet and stuck them in his pocket. And then he waited, ready to help in any way he might be needed.

Addie pulled his phone away from her ear. "You can go."

He didn't budge. "Later. What can I do?"

She listened on the phone again as Levi lay there groaning. "Yes," she said. "All right, yes." She made soothing sounds at Levi. Then she looked at James again. "If you could maybe go up and get a pillow from his bed. His room's off the front entry on the main floor. And get the aspirin from the medicine cabinet in the bathroom there?"

He was already on his way up the stairs. He found the pillow and the aspirin and ran them back down to her.

"Thank you," she said. "And really. We're okay. You just go ahead and go."

Levi was clearly very far from okay. James pretended he hadn't heard her and eased the pillow under Levi's head.

Addie gave the old man an aspirin. "Put it under your tongue and let it dissolve there." Levi grumbled out a few curse words, but he did what Addie told him to do. Addie shot another glance at James. "I mean it. Go on and get out of here."

Again, he ignored her. Not that he blamed her for wanting him to go, after all that had happened. But no way was he leaving her alone right now. What if Levi didn't make it? James would never forgive himself for running off and deserting them at a time like this, with Addie scared to death and Levi just lying there, sweating and moaning and clutching his chest as he tried to answer the questions that Addie relayed to him from the dispatcher.

At the last minute, as the ambulance siren wailed in the yard, James glanced up at the hole in the ceiling. He looked down at the rope abandoned on the rug at the base of the chair and the shotgun that had landed in front of the TV. All that was going to look pretty strange.

He couldn't do much about the hole, but he did grab the shotgun. He ejected the remaining shells and gathered them up, including the spent casing, which he found right out in the open in front of the sofa. He put the gun and the shells in the closet under the stairs and tossed the rope in there, too. The straight chair, he moved to a spot against the wall.

"Thank you," Addie said. He glanced over and saw she was watching him.

He shrugged. "There's still the hole in the ceiling. But don't worry. It'll be fine."

"Hope so."

"Just a little accident, that's all."

She pressed those fine lips together, her eyes full of fear for her grandpa. "Would you go up and show them down here?"

"You bet." He ran up the stairs and greeted the med techs. "Roberta," he said. "Sal." They were local people and he'd known them all his life.

Sal asked, "Where is he?"

"In the basement. This way…"

Roberta and Sal were pros. In no time, they had Levi on a stretcher, an oxygen mask on his face and an IV in his arm. James helped them get Levi up the stairs. As they put him in the ambulance, Addie ran back inside to grab her purse and lock up. Her sweet-natured chocolate Labrador retriever, Moose, followed after her, whining with concern. Addie told the dog to stay. With another worried whine, Moose trotted to the porch and dropped to his haunches. Addie climbed in the back of the ambulance with her grandfather and Roberta.

Sal went around and got in behind the wheel. James trailed after him.

"Who blew the hole in the kitchen floor?" Sal asked out the open driver's window as he started the engine.

"Levi was cleaning his shotgun."

Sal just shook his head. "You've got blood on your collar."

"It's nothing. You taking him to Justice Creek General?"

With a nod, Sal put it in gear.

A moment later, James stood there alone in the dirt yard a few feet from Levi's pre-WWII green Ford pickup, which had no doubt been used to kidnap him. Overhead, the sun beamed down. Not a cloud in the sky. It wasn't at all the kind of day a man expected to be kidnapped on.

Gently, he probed the goose egg on the back of his head. It was going to be fine. *He* was going to be fine.

Levi, though?

Hard to say.

And what about Addie, all on her own at Justice Creek General, waiting to hear if her granddad would make it or not? At a time like this, a woman should have family around her. Her half sister, Carmen, would come from Wyoming. But how long would it take for Carmen to arrive?

He just didn't like to think of Addie sitting in a hospital waiting room all alone.

As the ambulance disappeared around the first turn in the long driveway that led to the road, James took off toward the barn.

A couple of the horses Addie boarded watched him with mild interest as he jumped the fence into the horse pasture and ran until he got to the fence on the far side. He jumped that, too, and kept on running. Fifteen minutes after leaving Addie's front yard, he reached his quad cab, which was parked in front of his nearly finished new house. He had a bad cramp in his side and he had to walk in circles catching his breath, now and then bending over, sucking in air like a drowning man.

There was blood on his tan boots—not much, just a few drops. He pictured old Levi, hitting him on the head and then dragging him to that green Ford truck of his—and not only to the truck, but then out of the truck, into the house at Red Hill and down to the basement. No wonder the old fool had a heart attack.

As soon as his breath evened out a little, James dug his keys from his pocket and got in his quad cab. He checked his shirt collar in the sunscreen mirror. The blood wasn't that bad and the bump hardly hurt at all anymore.

He started the pickup and peeled out of there.

* * *

Addie needed to throw up. She needed to do that way too much lately. Right now, however, was not a convenient time. She sat in the molded plastic chair in the ER waiting room and pressed her hands over her mouth as she resolutely willed the contents of her stomach to stay down.

She had James's phone in her purse. In her frantic scramble to get in the ambulance with Levi, she hadn't thought to give the phone back. And then she'd clutched it like a lifeline all the way to the hospital. She'd only stuck it in her purse to free her hands when the reception clerk had given her all those forms to fill out.

Addie sucked in a slow breath and let it out even slower. *Oh, dear Lord, please. Let PawPaw pull through this and let me not throw up now.* Everything had happened way too fast. Her mind—and her poor stomach—was still struggling to catch up.

Her own cell phone was in her purse, too. She'd barely remembered to grab it off the front hall table before racing out the door. She needed to get it out and call Carmen in Laramie. But the nurse had said Levi wouldn't be in the ER for long. They would evaluate his condition and move him over to cardiac care for the next step. Addie was kind of waiting to find out what, exactly, the next step might be so that she could share it with her sister when she broke the terrifying news.

A door opened across the room. The doctor she'd talked to earlier emerged and came toward her.

Addie jumped to her feet, swallowed hard to keep from vomiting all over her boots and demanded, "My grandfather. Is he…?" Somehow she couldn't quite make herself ask the whole dangerous question.

"He's all right for now." The doctor, a tall, thin woman

with straight brown hair, spoke to her soothingly. "We've done a series of X-rays and given him medications to stabilize him."

"Stabilize him," Addie repeated idiotically. "Is that good? That's good, right?"

"Yes. But his X-rays show that he's got more than one artery blocked. He's going to need emergency open-heart surgery. We want to airlift him to Denver, to St. Anne's Memorial. It's a Level-One trauma center and they will be fully equipped to give him the specialized care that he needs."

Her head spun. Denver. Open-heart surgery. How could this be happening? From the moment she'd caught sight of James Bravo tied to a chair in the basement at Red Hill, nothing had seemed real. "But…he's never been sick a day in his life."

The doctor spoke gently, "It happens like this sometimes. That's why they call heart disease the silent killer. Too often, you only know you've got a problem when you have a heart attack—but I promise we're doing everything we can to get him the best care there is. You got him here quickly and that's a large part of the battle. His chances are good."

Good. His chances were good. Was the doctor just saying that or was it really true? Addie sucked in air slowly and ordered her queasy stomach to settle down. "Can I see my grandfather, please?"

"Of course you can. This way."

In the curtained-off cubicle, Addie kissed Levi's pale, wrinkled cheek and smoothed his wiry white hair and whispered, as much to reassure herself as to comfort him,

"PawPaw, I promise you, everything is going to be fine. You'll be on the mend before you know it."

Levi only groaned and demanded in a rough whisper, "Where's James?"

That made her long to start yelling at him again. But he looked so small and shrunken lying there, hooked up to an IV and a bunch of machines that monitored every breath he took, every beat of his overstressed heart. Yelling at him would have to wait until he was better.

Because he *would* get better. He *had* to get better. The alternative was simply unthinkable.

Right now nothing could be allowed to upset him. So she lied through her teeth. "James is out in front waiting to hear how you're doing."

"Good." Levi barely mouthed the word. "Good…" And then, with a long, tired sigh, he shut his eyes.

Addie bent close to him. "I love you, PawPaw." She kissed him and had to close her mind against the flood of tender images. Her mom had died having her and she'd never known her dad. All her memories of growing up, he was there for her, and for Carmen. He was their mom and their dad, all rolled into one cantankerous, dependable, annoyingly lovable package.

She could not—*would* not—lose him now.

A nurse pushed back the curtain and announced, "The critical-care helicopter has arrived. We need to get your grandfather on his way now."

"Can I ride with him?"

The nurse explained gently that there just wasn't room.

About then, Addie realized her pickup was back at the ranch. She'd have to call someone to give her a ride home so she could get herself to Denver. And what about the horses? She had to find someone to look after them at least until tomorrow. And she still really needed to call Carmen immediately.

She thanked the nurse, kissed her grandpa one more time and hustled back out to the waiting room, where the clerk had more paperwork waiting for her to fill out. She took the clipboard the clerk passed her through the reception window, reclaimed her seat and got to work filling in the blanks and signing her name repeatedly, simultaneously praying that Levi was going to pull through.

At least they had the best health coverage money could buy now. Brandon had seen to that months ago. When she agreed to have the baby, he'd set up a fund that would pay thirty years' worth of premiums for her and the child. At the time, she'd argued that she had Affordable Care and that would be plenty. But he'd insisted that she should have the very best—and that the fund would be set up to cover Levi, too, and any children she ever had.

"Everybody gets sick at some point," Brandon had reminded her softly, a hard truth that he knew all too intimately. "Everybody needs health care at some point. When that happens for you, for the baby or for Levi, you don't need to be worrying about how to pay your share of the hospital bill."

Thank God for Brandon.

Tears searing the back of her throat, Addie signed the last form, got up and passed the clipboard through the window to the clerk. The clerk handed back a couple of forms and her insurance card. She jammed all that in her purse and was pulling out her phone to call her half sister when James Bravo pushed through the emergency room doors.

He came right for her, so big and solid and capable-looking, still wearing the same jeans and chambray shirt with blood on the collar that he'd been wearing when she found him tied up in the basement an hour before. Those blue eyes with the dark rims around the iris were full of concern. "How're you holding up?"

She wanted to lean on him, to have him put his big arms around her and promise her that everything would work out fine. But what gave her the right to go leaning on him? She didn't get it. It was…something he did to her. As if he were a magnet and she were a paper clip. Every time she saw the guy, she felt like just…falling into him, plastering herself against him. She didn't understand it, felt nothing but suspicious of it, of her own powerful attraction to him.

And what made it all even worse was that she seemed to feel he was magnetized to her, too.

Addie didn't have time for indulging in the feelings he stirred in her. She completely distrusted feelings like those and she knew she was right to distrust them. Really, why shouldn't she reject all that craziness that happened between men and women?

Her dad ran off, vanished before she was born, never to be seen or heard from again, just as her sister's dad had done before that, leaving their mother single, pregnant and brokenhearted both times—or so her grandpa always said. Addie had never been able to ask her mom about it. Hannah Kenwright had died giving her life.

So yeah, Addie was cynical about romantic love. And every time she'd tried it, she'd grown only more cynical. Yes, all right. Love had worked out fine for her sister. Still, Addie didn't trust it. To her, romance and all that just seemed like a really stupid and dangerous thing.

And it wasn't as if she hadn't given it her best shot. Three times. In high school and then again when she was twenty-one and finally with a bull rider she'd met at the county rodeo. Her high school love had married someone else and her second forever guy had dumped her flat. The bull rider had dumped her, too, the morning after their first night together. For her, same as for her mother, love had not lasted.

And now she had a baby on the way. And her grandfather to care for. And Red Hill and her horses and a side business she loved. It was enough. She didn't need the human magnet that was James Bravo, thank you very much.

He asked again if she was okay.

"I'm fine," she lied and plastered on a smile. "It's all taken care of. Before he died, Brandon saw to it that we have the kind of insurance that covers everything, no deductibles and no co-pays. So money is no worry. Everything is going to be okay."

He didn't buy that lie. She could see that in those gorgeous eyes of his. But he didn't call her on it. He only asked, "How's Levi?"

"They have him stabilized, they said, and they're flying him to St. Anne's Memorial in Denver for surgery." She dropped her phone in her purse yet again and pulled his out. It was one of those fancy android phones with all the bells and whistles. "I'm sorry. I forgot to give this back to you." She shoved it at him.

He took it. "No problem."

"Thank you. For everything, up to and including *not* having my granddad thrown in jail."

A smile twitched at the corner of his handsome mouth. "You're welcome."

She was just trying to figure out how to tell him gently to get lost, when he continued, "So you need to get to Denver? Come on, I'll drive you."

And then, with no warning, he touched her.

He wrapped his big, warm fingers around her bare

arm right below the short sleeve of her T-shirt, causing a sudden hot havoc of sensation, like little fireworks exploding in a line, up to her shoulder, across to the base of her throat and then straight down to the center of her.

She stood stock-still, gaping up at him, thinking, *Just tell him that you'll manage. Just tell him to let go and leave.*

"Let me drive you." He said it low. Intensely. As if he knew what she was thinking and wouldn't give up until he'd gone and changed her mind.

She demanded, "Don't you have to be in court or something?"

He looked kind of amused—but in a serious and determined way. "Not today. Let me take you to Denver."

She longed to refuse again. But the truth was she needed to get to St. Anne's, and she needed to get there fast. As soon as PawPaw was safely through his surgery, she could figure out the rest.

James watched her face. He still held her arm and he smelled way too good. A little dusty, a little sweaty, with a faint hint of some manly aftershave still lingering even after all her grandpa had put him through. He demanded, "Have you called Carmen?"

"Not yet."

"So it's best to let me take you. You can make all the calls you need to make while we're on the road."

Ten minutes later, they were flying along the state highway on the way to I-25. She called Carmen.

At the sound of her sister's voice, the damn tears started spurting again. "Carm?" she squeaked, all tight and wobbly, both at once.

And Carmen knew instantly that something was wrong. "Omigod, honey, what's happened?"

James reached over in front of her and dropped open the glove box. He pulled out a box of tissues. Was there anything the man wasn't ready for? She whipped out a tissue and dabbed at her eyes. He put the box back and withdrew his big, hard arm.

"Addie Anne. Honey, are you still there?"

"I'm here. I'm okay. It's PawPaw."

"Oh, no. Is he—"

"He had a heart attack, but he's still alive." *At least, he was half an hour ago.* She explained about the helicopter to St. Anne's and the emergency surgery that would happen there.

"But…a heart attack? How…?"

Addie squeezed her eyes shut as she pictured James tied to that chair, Levi yelling and waving his shotgun, the hole he'd blown in the basement ceiling. "Long story." Dear Lord. Was it ever! And Carmen didn't know about the baby yet, either. "I'll fill you in on everything later, promise. But…do you think you can come?"

"Of course I'll come."

Relief flooded through Addie. Times like this, a girl needed her big sister's hand to hold. "I'm so glad."

"I'll be there as soon as I can. St. Anne's, you said?"

"Yeah. I've got nothing but the name of the hospital at this point."

"Don't worry. I'll find you. I can get family leave from work and figure it all out with Devin, see if his mom can come and stay with the kids." Devin's mother had moved to Laramie after her husband died. She'd wanted to be closer to her grandkids. "I'll get everything arranged as fast as I can and then meet you there. Call my cell if…" Carmen faltered and then finished weakly, "If there's any other news."

"I will. Love you, Carm."

"Love you, too…"

They said goodbye. Addie disconnected the call and sagged against the passenger window. Too much was happening. Losing Brandon followed by constant morning sickness had been more than enough for her to handle. She had simply not been prepared to deal with her crazy grandpa kidnapping James Bravo and then having a heart attack on top of the rest. Pressing a hand against her roiling belly, she dabbed at her eyes and willed James's fancy quad cab to get there superfast.

At the hospital, they were sent straight to the surgery wing, where her grandpa was being prepped for bypass surgery. Addie dealt with yet more forms. James took a seat in the waiting room and Addie went in with the surgeon to look at images of Levi's heart and listen to a description of the surgery to come.

James was waiting when she emerged. She knew the sweetest rush of gratitude, just to have him there. He was practically a stranger—or at least, no more than a casual friend—and she needed to remember that. Still, it meant so much to have someone waiting when she left the surgeon and his pictures of her grandpa's blocked-up arteries. It meant the world to her not to have to do this alone.

At the sight of her, he got up and came for her. "Addie," he said. "You're dead white. You need to sit down."

"I can't… I don't…" What was wrong with her words? Why wouldn't they organize themselves into actual sentences?

"Come on now." He reached out and drew her close, into his height and hardness and warmth. "It's going to be all right." She let herself sag against his solid strength. It felt way too good there, pressed tight to his side, his big arm banded around her.

But then her poor stomach started churning again. And this time, she couldn't swallow hard enough or breathe slowly enough to settle it down. With a sharp cry, she pushed James away and ran for the ladies' room.

At least it wasn't far, a quick sprint across the waiting room. She shoved through the door and made for the first stall, knocking the stall door inward with the flat of her hand, flinging back the seat and bracing her palms on her thighs just in time. Everything started coming up as her long hair fell forward, getting in the way. She grabbed for it, trying to shove it back and keep her purse from dropping off her shoulder and spilling all over the floor, too.

And then, suddenly, there was James again, right there in the stall with her, gently gathering her hair and smoothing it back out of the way. God. How humiliating. And this *was* the ladies' room. He shouldn't even be in here.

"It's okay, take it easy. You're okay, okay…" He kept saying that, "You're okay," over and over in that deep, velvety voice of his. She didn't feel okay, not in the least. But she was in no position to argue the point, with all her attention focused on the grim job of ejecting what was left of her lunch.

She gagged for what seemed like such a long, awful time. But then, finally, when there was nothing left inside her poor belly, the retching slowed and stopped. Panting, trying to even out her breathing, she waited to make sure there would be no surprises.

"Better?" he asked, still in that low, gentle, comforting voice.

Addie groaned and nodded. "Would you…?" *Sentences. Whole sentences.* "Go. I'll be all right. Just…go on out. I'll be there in a minute."

"You're sure?"

"Yeah. Uh, thank you. I'm sure." She flushed away the mess and straightened with care, clutching her shoulder bag closer, physically unable to face him right then.

She felt him back from the stall, the warmth and size of him retreating. He said, "I'll be right outside, if you need anything."

"Thank you." She stared, unblinking, at the tan wall above the toilet, willing him to go.

And at last, he did. She heard the door open and shut and instantly released the breath she hadn't realized she'd been holding.

Slowly, with another long sigh, she turned to confront the empty space behind her. On rubbery legs, she went to the sink and rinsed her face and her mouth. At least there were Tic Tacs in her purse. She ate four of them, sucking on them madly, grateful beyond measure for their sharp, minty taste. She brushed her hair and checked her T-shirt for spills. Really, she looked terrible, hollow-eyed and pasty-faced. But at least her stomach had stopped churning now that it was empty.

Note to self: Never eat again—and get out there and tell poor James that you are fine and he can go.

Smoothing her hair one last time and settling her purse strap firmly on her shoulder, she returned to the waiting room.

He was sitting across the room in the row of padded chairs, busy on his fancy phone. She got maybe two steps in his direction before he glanced up and saw her. He jumped to his feet, his handsome, square-jawed face so serious, his beautiful eyes darkened with concern.

For her.

Okay, he really was a good person. And he shouldn't be so concerned about her. He should find himself a nice woman, one who didn't have all her issues, one who believed in true love and forever. Clearly, the guy deserved a woman like that.

She marched right up to him and aimed her chin high. "You have been…amazing. I can't thank you enough for everything. And my sister will be here before you know it, so there isn't any need for you to—"

"Stop." He actually put up a hand. And then he took her by the arm again, causing all those strange, heated sensations to pulse along her skin. "Sit down before you fall down." He took her other arm, too, and then he turned her and carefully guided her down into the chair where he'd been sitting. The chair was warm from his body, and that felt both enormously comforting—and way too intimate, somehow.

Once he had her in the chair, he just stayed there, bent over her, his big hands gripping the chair arms, kind of holding her there, his face with its manly sprouting of five-o'clock shadow so close she could see the faint, white ridge of an old scar on the underside of his chin. It was a tiny scar, and she wondered where he might have gotten it.

She stared up at him, miserable, wishing for a little more gumption when she needed it. "It's not right that you have to be here. It's not fair, after…everything. Given the…situation. James, I'm taking total advantage of you and I hate that."

"You're not. Stop saying you are. I'm here because I want to be here."

She laughed. It was a sad laugh, almost like a sob. "Having a great time, are you?"

"Wonderful."

"Ha!"

He let go of the chair arms and rose to his height. "And you'll feel better if you eat something."

"Oh, no." She pressed a hand to her belly, which still ached a little from the aftermath of losing everything that had been in it, including what felt like a good portion of her stomach lining. "Uh-uh. What I need is never, ever to eat again."

"A little hot tea and some soda crackers. You should be able to keep that down. Then later, I'll get you some soup."

She glared up at him. "What I really hate…"

"Tell me."

"…is that tea and soda crackers sound kind of good."

His fine mouth twitched at the corners. "Sugar?"

"Yes, please. Two packets."

"Don't budge from that chair. I'll be right back."

Addie drank her tea and ate four packets of soda crackers. She felt better after that, and she told James so. He nodded approvingly as he munched on the turkey sandwich he'd brought back from the cafeteria along with her tea and crackers.

Actually, his sandwich looked kind of good, too. She tried not to stare at it longingly.

But the man missed nothing. He chuckled and held out the other half to her.

She should have refused it. It wasn't right to take the guy's food. He was probably starving. She knew *she* was. And just to prove it, her stomach rumbled.

"Take it," he said, those blue eyes all twinkly and teasing. "I know where to get more."

She did take it. Ate it all, too. And felt a whole lot better once she did.

A few minutes after she'd demolished half his sandwich, her cell rang. It was Carm, who said that her mother-in-law was staying with the kids and she and Devin were on the way.

"A couple of hours and we're there," Carmen promised. "How's PawPaw?"

"In surgery, which is going to take at least three hours from what the surgeon said. When you get here, they'll still be operating on him."

"Anything you need?"

She longed for a toothbrush. And she still needed to find someone to take care of Moose and the horses back at the ranch. But she could call her neighbors herself. And she didn't want her sister wasting her time stopping at a drugstore. "Just you. Just get here as fast as you can." Carmen promised she would do exactly that and they said goodbye.

Addie got to work trying to find someone to look after the livestock. But the Fitzgeralds, who had twenty acres bordering Red Hill, were off visiting relatives in Southern California. And Grant Newsome, Levi's longtime friend, had put his house and acreage up for sale and gone to Florida to live near his oldest daughter and her family.

She was trying to figure out who else she might try when James suggested, "How about Walker McKellan? He and his wife, my cousin Rory, would be happy to help. They're not that far from Red Hill." Walker and Rory lived at Walker's guest ranch, the Bar N, which was maybe eight miles from the Red Hill ranch house.

Addie knew Walker, but not that well. He'd been more than a decade ahead of her in school. And Rory was an actual princess from some tiny country in Europe. Addie had met her just once and been impressed with how friendly and down-to-earth she was. "I hardly know them and I'm sure they're busy and don't have time to—"

"Stop," James said again, in the same flat, dismissive

tone he'd used on her when she tried to tell him to go. "*I* know them. And I know they'll want to help. I'm calling them." He had his phone out and ready.

"*You* stop," she insisted, strongly enough that he quit scrolling through his contacts and looked at her with great patience. She added, "I *said* that I hardly know them and it doesn't seem right to take advantage of them."

"It's not taking advantage. It's just asking for help. And there's nothing wrong with asking for help now and then, Addie."

She didn't really have a comeback ready for that one, so she settled for glaring daggers at him.

He gentled his tone. "Look. You'd do the same for them in a heartbeat, wouldn't you?"

"Of course I would, but—"

"So someday they'll need you. And you'll be there. And that's good."

By then, she didn't know why she'd even tried to argue with him. "I bet you could sell an Eskimo a refrigerator," she grumbled.

He shrugged. "Hey, with the way weather patterns are changing, an Eskimo might need one. Ah. Here we go." He punched in the call.

Ten minutes later, she'd talked to both Walker and Rory and they were set to tend to the animals for as long as she needed them to. Walker said he'd take Moose back to the Bar-N. He even insisted she give him the phone numbers of the owners of the horses she boarded. He said he would call them personally and let them know what was happening, reassure them that their animals were being cared for and that if they needed anything, he would see that they got it.

Addie thanked Walker profusely.

He said essentially what James had said. "We should have joined forces years ago for times like this."

When she hung up, she handed James back his phone. "I think I'm running out of ways to thank you."

He didn't miss a beat. "You can thank me by eating the soup I'm going to go get for you now. They have chicken noodle or New England clam chowder."

"No clams. Please."

"Chicken noodle it is, then."

She dug in her purse for her wallet. But he was already up and headed for the elevators.

When he returned with the soup, he also brought sandwiches. Two of them—one roast beef, one ham, both with chips.

She took the soup and tried to give him a ten. He waved it away. She should insist he take the money, but so far, insisting wasn't getting her anywhere with him.

So fine, then. She ate every last drop of that soup and half of his ham sandwich, too. Unfortunately, once the food was gone, there was nothing else to do but sit there and try to read the magazines strewn about the waiting room tables, try *not* to watch the second hand crawling around the face of the clock on the far wall, try not to think too hard about what might be happening down the long hallway beyond the automatic double doors.

Carmen and Devin arrived at a little after nine. Addie ran to her sister. Carmen grabbed her and they hugged each other tight. Then Carmen took her by the shoulders and held her a little away. Carmen was taller and thinner than Addie and her hair was dark brown, her eyes a warm hazel.

"Any news?" her sister asked.

Addie pressed her lips together and shook her head.

"We're still waiting to hear. I'm hoping it won't be too long now."

Devin, tall and lean with light blond hair, said, "Levi's tough as old boots. He'll pull through and be driving us all crazy again in no time."

Addie turned to her brother-in-law. "I know you're right." He hugged her, too. "I can't even tell you how glad I am you're both here." She wrapped an arm around each of them and turned for the row of chairs several feet away where James, on his feet now, was waiting.

Carmen leaned close and whispered, "Isn't that one of the Bravo brothers?"

Addie stifled a tired sigh. "It's James."

"The lawyer, right, second of Sondra's two sons?"

Addie nodded. "He was, um, there when PawPaw had the heart attack. He's been wonderful," she whispered back grimly, reminded again of all the news she needed to share with her sister. "I can't get him to leave."

"I heard that," James said wryly. "Carmen, Devin. How have you been?" He held out his big hand.

Devin took it first, and then Carmen. Carmen said how grateful she was for his help. She assured him he could go now.

He just shook his head. "I can't go now. I wouldn't feel right. At least not until Levi's through surgery."

Carmen shot Addie a look and then turned to him again. "You and our grandfather are…friends?"

"Well, we've kind of formed a bond, I think you might say."

Now Carmen glanced at Devin, who shrugged, then back to James and finally at Addie. "Okay. What is going on?"

Addie groaned. "Got a month, I'll tell you everything."

"I'm here and I'm listening," Carmen replied.

Addie hardly knew where to start.

James got up. "I could use some coffee. Anybody else?"

Carmen piped right up. "I'll take some." She elbowed her husband. "Dev will go with you."

"Uh. I will?" When Carmen elbowed him again, Devin caught on. "Sure. Great idea."

"Tea?" Addie asked James, and then got uncomfortable all over again thinking how easily she'd started to depend on him.

"You got it—and maybe Devin and I will hang around the cafeteria for a while." He gave her a look—one thick, dark eyebrow raised.

And she took his meaning. "Go ahead. Tell him," she said. "Tell him everything you know. Believe me, he won't be surprised."

"My God," murmured Carmen. "What *is* going on?" For that, she got another bewildered shrug from her husband.

James asked, "You sure?"

Addie nodded. "He has to know eventually anyway."

So the men left. And Carmen said, "Okay. Tell me everything."

Addie told all—from how she'd agreed to have Brandon's baby, to the fact that she was now pregnant with said baby, to Levi snooping in her trash and finding the test stick and then kidnapping James just the way he'd done to Devin eight years ago. Carmen sat there with her mouth hanging open, as Addie went on to describe finding James and Levi in the basement and the shotgun going off, blowing a hole in the ceiling while Levi had a heart attack.

Finally, when the totally out-there story was told,

Carmen hugged her again and told her she loved her and could hardly believe she was going to be an auntie.

Then came the questions. "If Brandon's the father, why did PawPaw kidnap James?"

"He won't believe it's Brandon. He claims he's seen the way James and I look at each other and he just knows there's been a lot more than looking going on."

Carmen was silent. Too silent.

Addie was forced to demand, "What is all this *silence* about, Carm?"

"Well, now, honey. I did see the way you and James looked at each other just now…"

"What are you talking about? I swear to you, James Bravo has never done more than shake my hand—at least not until today, when he put his arm around me to comfort me, held my hair while I threw up and then made me sit down when I tried to get him to leave."

"But that's just it, see?"

"No, I don't see."

"He seems very devoted. And I saw the blood on his collar."

"I told you, PawPaw knocked him out, tied him to a chair in the basement and put a shotgun to his head. Because you know PawPaw. He thinks we live in some Wild West romance novel where it's perfectly okay to hold a man at gunpoint in order to convince him to 'do the right thing.'" She said that with air quotes.

Carm snickered and then quickly switched to a more sober expression. "And yet, even after all the abuse PawPaw heaped on the poor guy, James drives you to Denver and holds your hair while you hurl? He knows you're having another man's baby, but he brings you food and tea and insists he has to stay with you to make sure that your crazy old grandpa makes it through surgery?"

"Carm, it's not like that. It's just that he's a good guy."

"Beyond stellar, apparently."

"Really, I hardly know him. We...well, we talk now and then."

A sideways look from Carmen. "You talk."

"Yeah. He's bought land that borders Red Hill and he's building a house there. I go by there a lot, working with the horses, you know?"

"Right..."

"Quit looking at me like that. Sometimes I stop is all. We visit. We talk about life and stuff—in general, I mean. Nothing all that personal." Well, okay. Once, James had told her about his ex-wife. But as a rule, they kept it casual. She added, "And now and then, he drops by the ranch house. We sit out under the stars and chat."

"Chat," Carmen repeated, as though the simple word held a bunch of other meanings that Addie wasn't admitting to.

"Yeah." Addie straightened her shoulders. "Chat. Just chat. And that's it. That's all. I've never gone out with him. It's casual and it's only conversation and you couldn't even really call us friends."

Carmen patted her hand. "I'm only saying I'm not surprised that PawPaw jumped to conclusions."

Addie batted off her sister's touch. "It is Brandon's baby. I have never even kissed James Bravo."

Carmen put up both hands. "Okay, okay. I believe you."

"Oh, gee. Thanks a bunch." Addie pressed a hand to her stomach, which had started churning again.

Carmen hooked an arm around her shoulders and drew her close. "And I don't want you upset." She stroked Addie's hair. It felt really good. Carmen was only two years older, but Addie had always looked up to her. When you grow up without a mom, a good big sister really helps. Carmen chided, "It's bad for the baby, for you to get so upset."

"No kidding." Grudgingly, Addie leaned her head on her big sister's shoulder.

"Just breathe and relax. We're going to get through this. PawPaw is going to be fine—and here come the guys."

Addie glanced up and saw that James and Devin had just come around the corner from the elevators. "I don't like the way you say *the guys*. Like James is suddenly part of the family."

"Honey, stop overreacting. It's only going to make you want to throw up."

Well, okay. That was true. And Carmen was right. They just needed to stay calm and support each other. There'd been more than enough drama today to last Addie a lifetime.

So she focused on speaking softly, on being grateful—for her sister and Devin. And yes, for James, too. He'd made a horrible time a lot less awful and she needed to remember how much she owed him.

She drank her tea and ate the toast James had brought her. Strangely enough, she'd kept more food down in the past few hours than she had in days. Yet another reason to be grateful to James.

When she finished her tea and toast, she realized she was completely exhausted. She leaned her head back against the wall behind her and closed her eyes just for a minute.

The next thing she knew, James was rubbing her arm, stroking her hair, whispering in her ear, "Addie, wake up. The doctor's coming…"

With a sharp cry she sat bolt upright—and realized she'd been sound asleep, her head on James's broad shoulder. The big clock on the far wall showed that over an hour had passed since she leaned back and closed her eyes.

And James was right.

Levi's surgeon had emerged from the long hallway between the double doors and was coming right for them.

Chapter Three

They all popped to their feet at once—James, Addie, Carmen and Devin. And then they waited in a horrible, breath-held silence until the doctor, still in surgical scrubs with a matching cap on his head and a mask hanging around his neck, reached them and started speaking.

Addie watched his mouth move and tried to listen to what he was saying, but her heart was beating so damn loud and her blood made a whooshing sound as it spurted through her body and the words were really hard to understand.

But then Carm said, "Oh, thank God."

And Addie put it together: he'd made it. PawPaw had survived the surgery.

Forty-five minutes later, they all proceeded to a new waiting room, this one adjacent to the Cardiac Surgery

Intensive Care Unit, which was five floors up from surgery and in another wing.

A nurse came out and led Addie and Carmen through automatic doors and down a hall to one of those rooms full of curtained cubicles. In this room, all the curtains were drawn back. There were twenty beds, two rows of ten, half of them with patients in them. Nurses, doctors and technicians moved between the beds and back and forth from the group of desks that formed a command center in the middle of the room. The nurse led them to the left side of the room, the third bed from the door. Addie clutched for Carm's hand and when she got it, she held on tight.

Levi lay on the hospital bed with a tube down his throat and another in his nose. There were tubes and wires hooked to his chest, and more of them disappearing under the blankets. And there was an IV in the back of his hand and another in the crook of his arm. Both arms were strapped to the bed; Addie assumed that was to keep him from pulling out any of the complicated apparatus that hooked him up to the various machines. There was a ventilator by the bed. It wheezed softly as it pushed air in through the tube in his mouth.

He looked terrible, every line in his craggy face dug in deeper than before. But he did open his eyes briefly. It seemed he saw them, recognized them. But then a second later, his eyelids drooped shut. Together, still clutching each other's hands, Addie and Carm moved closer, up to the head of the bed. Gently, so lightly, Addie dared to touch his pale forehead below the blue cap that covered his hair.

He groaned and opened his eyes again.

Carm touched his wiry upper arm at a rare spot where no tube or needle was stuck. "I'm here, PawPaw. We're both here. You made it through your surgery and you're going to get well."

"We love you," said Addie, biting back tears. "We love you so much."

His red-rimmed blue eyes tracked—from Addie, to Carmen, back to Addie again. And then he tried to speak. "Aiff. Air aiff?"

Carm said, "Shh, don't try to talk now. The tube's in the way."

But he wouldn't shush. "Aiff? Ear? Aiff?" He tried to lift an arm, found it pinned to the bed and groaned in frustration.

Addie stroked his brow. "Shh, PawPaw. Don't. You'll only hurt your throat."

The nurse who'd brought them in approached again. Addie and Carmen stepped back and the nurse bent close to Levi. "Easy, now, Levi. It's okay. We'll find out what you want and get it for you. I've got a pencil and a paper…" She pulled a small tablet and a pencil out of her pocket.

He nodded, making a harsh gargling sound around the tube.

"Is he left-handed?" she asked.

Carm said, "No, right-handed."

The nurse eased the tablet under his right hand and wrapped his scarred, knotted old fingers around the pencil. He gripped it and scratched at the paper.

When he stopped, the nurse asked, "Is that it?"

Levi grunted a yes.

The nurse took the tablet and read, "Jane? You want to see Jane?"

Another grunt accompanied by a head shake.

Addie knew. "James," she said bleakly. "You want James."

More grunting, but this time with a nod. Her grandpa stared right at her, daring her to produce the man he demanded to see.

She turned away—and there was Carm, looking all innocent, giving a little "what can you do about it?" shrug.

"Fine," Addie said and tried not to sound as fed up as she felt. "I'll get him."

Levi grunted again. To Addie, the sound was way too triumphant.

The nurse took her out and waited by the double doors.

Devin and James jumped to their feet again at the sight of her. She marched up to James, blew out a breath of pure frustration and said, "I'm sorry. He's asking to see you."

"Uh. Sure."

"I hate to ask you to go in there."

"I don't mind. Honestly, I don't."

"It only encourages him in his ridiculous delusions."

James held her eyes steadily. "Addie. Right now we just want him happy and calm, right?"

"Yeah. But what if you weren't here?"

"But I am here."

And you shouldn't be. But she didn't say that out loud. Because he'd been a lifesaver and she was so grateful to him it made an ache down in the heart of her. She turned to Devin. "Don't be hurt that PawPaw didn't ask for you. You know he thinks the world of you."

"I'm not hurt." Dev seemed to mean it. "I'm just glad he's pulled through the surgery all right." He clapped James on the shoulder. "Good luck, man."

James made a low noise in his throat that could have meant anything and fell in beside Addie as she marched back to where the nurse waited to lead them through the double doors.

In CSICU, Carm stood by the bed holding Levi's hand. His eyes were shut. But he must have heard their footsteps, because, with obvious effort, he opened them again and focused instantly in on James.

"Levi," James said mildly. "See? I'm right here and I'm going nowhere." Addie gasped and shot him a sharp look, but he kept his gaze on Levi as he softly added, "Rest now."

Levi blinked a couple of times, as if to reassure himself that his old eyes and his drugged mind weren't playing any tricks on him. Then, with a low, rough sound of pure satisfaction, he closed his eyes and didn't open them again, though the three of them stood there for several more minutes. Finally, the nurse bustled over and whispered that it was time to go. They would be allowed back in for brief visits—no more than two of them at a time, please—for as long as Levi stayed in intensive care.

They filed back out to the waiting room, where Carmen went straight to Devin. She sagged against him. He gathered her in and stroked her hair as Addie told herself she was not, under any circumstances, going to sidle up close to James and hope that he might wrap those big arms around her.

James said, "I've got a room at the Marriott down the street. I figure we can take turns using it. For showers, naps, whatever."

Carm beamed at him from her husband's arms. "Great idea. Addie should go first. She looks dead on her feet."

Addie sent her sister a quelling glance and asked James, "When did you have time to get a room at the Marriott?"

All twinkly blue eyes and easy charm, he coaxed, "Come on, don't look so suspicious. I made a phone call when you two went in to see Levi. The Marriott had rooms available—you know, being a hotel and all? So I got us one."

He'd done way more than she should have let him do and she needed to put an end to it. Immediately. "We have to talk."

He frowned. "Now, Addie—"

"Go ahead," said Carm with a shooing motion. "You two work it out. We'll be right here."

Addie so didn't like the way Carm had shooed her—as if she and James had had some lovers' spat they needed to resolve. But she could deal with her sister later. Now she and James had to get a few things straight.

She whirled and marched across the waiting room to a grouping of chairs along the other wall. When she got there, she dropped into one.

James took his sweet time following, but finally he sat down next to her. "What's the problem now?"

She turned and met his beautiful eyes and said sincerely, "It's enough—no, it's too much, all you've done. And I thank you so much for everything. But my grandfather's out of surgery now. You said yourself that you were only staying to see that he made it through all right. Well, he has. And Carm and Devin are here, to help me. You don't need to stay anymore."

He studied her face for several nerve-racking seconds. Then he shook his head. "I've reconsidered."

Somehow she made herself ask him quietly, "Reconsidered what?"

"Levi wants me here. And he needs to have what he wants—at least until he's out of the woods."

"But he *is* out of the woods."

"Addie. He's almost eighty. He's just been through major surgery. You know you want him relaxed and focused on getting well. You don't want anything preying on his mind."

Okay, that was true. She didn't want PawPaw upset. But sometimes, well, people just didn't get things the way they wanted them. "I can't help it if he insists on lying to himself." She blew out a hard breath. "Uh-uh. He needs to accept that he's got it all wrong and get past his totally out-there assumption that you are the father of my baby. As long as you're here, that's not going to happen. As long as you're here, he can tell himself his crazy-ass plan to marry us at gunpoint is working the same as it worked when he pulled it on Dev and Carmen."

"So what if he tells himself his plan is working?"

She was gaping again. She'd been doing way too much of that recently. "What do you mean, so what? His plan is *not* working. It's never going to work. You are not my baby's daddy and PawPaw needs to learn to accept that."

"And he will. When he's ready. But he's not ready now. All I'm saying is let me help. Let him believe what he needs to believe until he's back on his feet."

God. He was not only big and strong and kind and helpful, with that killer smile and those damn twinkly eyes. He not only looked good and smelled way too manly and tempting. He was also so calm and logical. And what he said actually seemed to make a bizarre kind of sense.

And she was so darn tired. She kept thinking of that room he'd taken at the Marriott. Of a shower and clean sheets and a few hours of much-needed sleep.

He leaned closer, filling her tipped-over world with his strength and his steadiness. "Come on, Addie." His deep, smooth voice washed through her, so soothing, making her want to lean into him, to curl into a ball and cuddle up close. "Let me help you. I *want* to help you."

"Why?"

The question seemed to hang in the charged air between them.

And then he actually answered it. "I like it, helping you. I honestly do. I like Levi and I want him to get well."

"Even after what he did to you?"

James chuckled. "He's a determined old guy. I admire that. I'm not crazy about his methods, but his intentions are good."

She almost laughed. "What's that they say about good intentions paving the road to hell?"

"Addie, lighten up."

"You shouldn't make excuses for him."

"I'm not. And it's not really all that complicated, or it doesn't have to be. I'll just hang around for a few days, help out however I can, until your grandfather's better."

"Define *better*."

He dodged right on by that one. "Can't we just play that by ear, see how he does?"

"I don't…get what *you* get out of this. I really don't. It's not fair to you, to take advantage of you this way."

His square jaw hardened. "Didn't we already clear up the whole 'taking advantage' question when you finally let Walker and Rory help you out with the animals? No one is taking advantage of me. I'm doing what I want to do. And that is to be here and help out however I can. I *like* helping out."

She really needed just to say it outright and she knew that she did. "You do get that you and me, that's never going to happen, right? I've got a whole lot to deal with in my life right now, and a man is the last thing I need."

He leaned even closer. Every nerve in her body went on red alert. "I do get that, Addie. Yes." Something deep inside her ached with loss when he said that. Which was absurd. It was a simple fact and they needed to be on the same page about it. And then he smiled, so slow and sweet and tender. "Nothing is going to happen. Not unless you ask me real nice."

Warmth slithered through her, followed immediately by annoyance. "Oh, very funny."

"Was I funny?" he teased. "I didn't *mean* to be funny…"

"This isn't a joke."

"And I wasn't joking." His voice was so serious. His eyes were not.

She decided she'd better just let it go. "Good, then. Hold that thought. And…well, you need to remember that I'm *pregnant*, James." She thought of Brandon then, with a sharp ache of loss. Brandon, too thin, too pale, the light fading from his green eyes. She made herself put it right out there, blunt as you please. "I'm pregnant with my dead best friend's baby."

"I am very clear on that." He took her hand. His was so warm and big and strong. It felt way too good and she should pull away.

But she didn't.

Across the waiting area, Carm was watching her, a sly smile on her face.

That did it. Addie tried to jerk free.

But James held on. "Hey."

"What?"

"I want to help and I think you could use the support. It doesn't have to mean anything more than that."

"But you know that it does. People…think we're together. My grandpa is still sure of that. And Carm thinks so, too, and so does Dev."

"So…?"

She did pull her hand from his then. "Do you need *everything* spelled out for you?"

He just wouldn't give up. "Look at me. In my eyes." The man was impossible.

She puffed out her cheeks with a hard breath. "I don't think that's such a good idea."

"Come on…"

"Fine." She met that gorgeous blue gaze. "What?"

"It's so simple. I want to be here and I don't expect anything from you. Can't you just take my word on that?"

Why not just let him stay?

He wanted to help and she liked having him here. She felt…safe and protected with him around. No, it couldn't go anywhere. And yeah, the way he hovered over her, taking care of her, gave her family the wrong idea. But if it made PawPaw happy right now, if it took a load off his mind when he needed to be focused on getting well…

How could that be bad, really? How could that possibly hurt?

She groused, "You're way too convincing."

He seemed amused. "You mentioned that before."

"Yeah, well, I'd hate to see you in court. You're probably responsible for a whole bunch of murderers getting off scot-free."

He gave her that smile of his, the one that warmed her up from her head to her toes and just about everywhere in between. "I'm in business and family law. Trusts and estates, real estate, asset protection. Not a single murderer ever got off because of me."

"I am so relieved to hear it."

He leaned closer. "So, then. Are you going to let me stay?"

She made a humphing sound. "Is there any way I can get rid of you?"

He pretended to think it over. "Nope. Give it up.

There's no way I'm leaving, not until I'm sure you don't need me anymore."

What if I never stop needing you? The crazy question just popped into her head.

And she quickly banished it. Because it really wasn't a question of need. Uh-uh. Not at all. She didn't need him. She didn't need any man. She could take care of herself and her coming baby just fine on her own. They'd get through this rough patch, get her grandfather back on his feet, and her life would go back to the way it had always been.

James didn't even wait for her to say he could stay, just went right on as though it was all settled—which, she supposed, it was. "I think your sister is right. You should get some rest. Let me take you to the hotel and get you settled in."

"I hate to leave Carm and Dev here to deal with everything on their—"

"Shh." He put a finger to her lips, so lightly, causing a bunch of silly butterflies to start flapping their wings low in her belly. "You'll be right down the street. Carmen can call you if there's any news."

Addie gave in and confessed, "I am kind of tired…"

He took her hand again. "Come on. You'll be rested and back here at the hospital before you know it."

Ten minutes later, James accepted four key cards from the desk clerk and handed one to Addie.

She took it and looked down at it as though she wondered what to do with it. The woman was dead on her feet.

He took her arm. "Come on. Let's get you to the room."

She glanced up at him then, big bronze eyes rimmed

in shadows—and full of questions. "You're going up with me?"

"Just to see that you're all set. Then I'll head back to Justice Creek."

Her smooth forehead crinkled with a frown. "So… you're leaving, after all?" Did she look kind of hurt? After all that resistance, she really did want him to stay?

That pleased him, probably more than he should allow it to. "Addie, I'm coming right back. I'll just go home, grab a shower and toss a few things in a bag. I'll stop by Red Hill, too. If you give me a key and a list, I'll bring you anything you need."

She stared up at him for a long count of ten after he stopped speaking. Finally, she said, "That would be amazing, if you would do that." Her eyes were almost gold right then. He wished they might shine like that for him all the time—and he started pulling her toward the elevators before she could find something new to argue about. Then she asked, "Can we stop in the gift shop so I can get a toothbrush, please?"

He looked down into her upturned face and never wanted to look away. "The gift shop it is."

"This is a suite," she accused when he pushed the door inward and she saw there was a sitting room. "You didn't need to go and get a suite."

"Too late now." He pulled her in and shut the door. "Sorry, there are only two bedrooms. The presidential suite has three, but it's booked. I thought Carmen and Devin could take one and you and I can make it work with the other. I'll be going back and forth from home anyway." He waited for her to argue that no way she was sharing a room with him.

But instead she said, "I will pay the bill for this room." It wasn't a question.

"It's already handled. Don't worry about it."

"It's not right."

"Sure it is."

"But—"

He cut her off with a wave of his hand. "Let it go. Please."

She started to speak again, seemed to reconsider and then said, "I just don't have the energy to keep arguing about this."

"So don't."

At that, she gave a tired little chuckle. And then, shaking her head, she wandered into the living area and dropped onto the couch, plunking her purse and her gift shop bag on the wide, button-tucked gray ottoman in front of her. "I could sleep for a week." With a groan, she planted her face in her hands.

He sat down beside her, hooked an arm around her shoulders and pulled her close. She stiffened at first, but then she gave in, drooping against him the way she had done in the waiting room when she fell asleep during Levi's surgery. He really liked having her there, tucked in nice and cozy against his side, so he leaned back into the cushions, pulling her right along with him.

She sighed. "I meant what I said about you and me."

"That we're not happening?"

"Yeah. But still…"

He smoothed her hair. "Go ahead. I can take it."

She made a thoughtful sound low in her throat. "Well, I just can't believe your wife let you get away."

He resisted the urge to press a kiss to the crown of her head. "Addie. What a nice thing to say."

"I couldn't stop myself. You really are being completely wonderful."

"Happy to help." He was thinking of those evenings they'd sat talking on the front steps at the Red Hill ranch house. On one of those nights, a bitter cold one not long after Christmas, they'd sat outside in heavy jackets and warm gloves drinking hot chocolate that she'd whipped up for them. That night, he'd told her that he'd been married.

He and Vicki Kelley had tied the knot when he was just starting law school.

Vicki...

He'd been head over heels for Vicki. She was smokin' hot, a real firecracker in bed. She was also extremely possessive. And with rules. Lots and lots of rules.

Vicki didn't like his friends or his family. For the three years of their marriage, he did what Vicki wanted and avoided all the other people who mattered in his life. By the time it ended, he'd pretty much come to the conclusion that marriage wasn't worth it, that a man gave up too much when he tried to make a life with a woman. After Vicki, he'd never gotten anywhere near the altar again. He kept his relationships casual and fun. And when they stopped being one or the other, he would end it as quickly and gently as possible.

Addie sighed again. He stroked her arm and tried not to think too hard about what, exactly, he wanted from her.

That night when he'd told her about his marriage, he'd also said he would never get married again. She'd laughed and said she understood that. She was never getting married, period.

He'd said he didn't get it. Most everyone was willing to give marriage a try at least once, weren't they?

She said she'd had rotten luck with men and she just

didn't want to go there. He'd tried to coax more out of her on the subject. But that was all she would say.

Somehow, in the past few months, he was constantly thinking about her. About her smile and her thick strawberry hair, her round cheeks and curvy body. About the scent of her that was somehow just right, all sweet and sexy and fresh and feminine. About how she said what was on her mind. About how she behaved as though she liked him, but she'd always somehow made it so he never quite got a chance to ask her out. He should probably get smart and take a hint. Hadn't she just told him for the second time tonight that nothing would be happening between them?

And still he refused to believe her.

She was having Brandon Hall's baby. That ought to serve as something of a turnoff.

Nope. He was still hot for her. He hadn't been this attracted to a woman since Vicki.

And look how that turned out.

He said, "I thought I told you that by the end of it, my ex-wife didn't have much appreciation for my many sterling qualities."

Addie tipped her head back and gave him a tired smile. "You did tell me that. And I'm sorry it didn't work out."

"I'm pretty much over it. It was a long time ago." Reluctantly, he reminded her, "And I should get on the road."

She ducked free of his hold and sat forward, leaving his arms feeling empty without her. "You sure it's not too much, stopping by the ranch house?"

He pulled out his phone and brought up the memo app. "Just tell me what you want and where to find it."

After James left, Addie took a shower and brushed her teeth. In her bra and panties, she set the bedside clock to give her two hours of sleep and climbed between the soft white sheets. Not that she expected any sleeping to happen. She just knew she would end up lying there wide-awake, worrying about Levi.

The alarm went off what seemed like five minutes later. She whacked the off button to stop the noise and realized she'd conked right out and slept straight through.

Dragging herself to her feet, she trudged to the bathroom and splashed water on her face. Then she combed her hair, pulled on her clothes and returned to the hospital.

Carmen said that they'd just been in to see him. "They took out the breathing tube, so he's breathing on his own."

"He asked about James again," Devin reported in a wary tone.

"He said he wanted to talk to James," Carmen added gingerly.

"Talk to James about what?" Addie demanded and tried not to sound hostile. It wasn't Carm's fault that their grandfather had a screw loose when it came to James.

Carmen winced. "About the, um, wedding."

Chapter Four

A low noise rose from Addie's throat. She realized as she made it that it sounded a whole lot like a growl. "What wedding? There's no wedding."

Carm put on her innocent face. "Ahem, well, apparently, PawPaw thinks that you and James are getting married."

Addie drew three slow breaths through her nose and then said with quiet reasonableness, "PawPaw has it all wrong."

"Well, we know that," said Carmen. "We're only telling you what *he* said—and where *is* James, by the way?"

"He went home to pick up a few things."

"But he's coming back?"

"Carm. You are altogether too concerned about what James Bravo is doing."

"Well, I like him. He's a great guy and at a time like this, it's good to have someone like him around. Is that so wrong?"

Dev jumped right to Carm's defense, wrapping an arm around her, pressing a husbandly kiss at her temple. "I like him, too. The man is solid."

Addie looked from Dev to Carm and back to Dev again. "You both get that none of this is his problem, right? You get that he's only helping out from the goodness of his heart. And why he could find any goodness there for PawPaw, I haven't a clue. Not after what PawPaw did to him. James owes us nothing. Get that? Not. A. Thing."

Carmen sniffed. "Sheesh, Addie Anne. Defensive much?"

"I just need to make that stubborn old man see the light, that's all."

"Not right this minute, you don't," Carmen argued. "Right this minute, he doesn't need anything upsetting him. He needs to rest and get better."

Addie got that. She did. She just hated the idea of allowing their grandfather to continue in his delusion that James was the father of her baby. Worse, he was completely locked in to the idea that James's imagined paternity automatically meant she and James needed to be married.

It was so stupid. *Earth to PawPaw. The 1950s called and they would like their rigid moral standards back.*

And how was her standing here arguing about it with her sister and brother-in-law going to help PawPaw see the light?

It wasn't.

She gave them the key to the suite, explained that the unused bedroom was theirs and told them to go get some rest.

Once they were gone, she used the phone on the wall by the double doors to check with the nurses' station.

They said Levi was resting and, yes, she could come in and sit by his bed.

She spent an hour in there, just watching him sleep. He looked so sick and frail. It broke her heart to see him that way.

But then he opened his eyes and the first word out of his mouth was a raspy "James?"

She bent closer to him. "Shh, now," she whispered, way too aware of the other patients trying to sleep nearby, of the other patients' relatives, sitting quietly in the dark. "Rest, PawPaw. Get your strength back."

"Where is he?"

"It doesn't matter. He's got nothing to do with you."

"I want to talk to him."

"Shh. You'll wake the other patients."

He grabbed her hand, his grip surprisingly strong, given that he'd just been through open-heart surgery. "You get him in here." The machines hooked up to him started making insistent beeping noises as the fluorescent green rows of wavy patterns leaped and dipped across the heart monitor screen over the bed.

"He's not here." She jerked her hand free of his grip. "PawPaw, settle down."

Two nurses hustled over. One bent over Levi as the other spoke softly to Addie, "He's going to be fine. Come on with me."

Out in the waiting room, the nurse reassured her that they would give her grandfather something to relax him. She wanted to know what had agitated him.

Addie gave a hopeless shrug. "I don't even know where to start."

"Whatever you can tell us will help us to help him."

She gave in and told the nurse that she was pregnant and her grandfather refused to accept who the father was but had fixated on someone else and was determined to make her the wrong guy's shotgun bride. "In the, um, figurative sense, of course," she hastened to add and felt her silly cheeks flaming at the lie.

"Of course," the nurse repeated. Because it was the twenty-first century and everybody knew that there were no *real* shotgun brides anymore.

"My grandfather wants to talk to the guy he *thinks* is the father. He's just sure he can get the poor man to give in and marry me—even though I've told him repeatedly that he's got it all wrong. And that's not even taking into account the fact that I have no intention of marrying anyone."

The nurse listened patiently and then suggested, "Maybe the best thing is to leave him to us for the night. We'll keep him calm and make sure he gets the rest he needs."

What could she do but agree? "Okay. But I'll be right here in the waiting room—either me or my sister."

The nurse reassured her that she would be notified immediately if there was any change in Levi's condition. And then she said that she was sure everything would work out and Levi would soon come to accept that he needed to stop upsetting himself and focus on his recovery.

Addie fervently hoped that the nurse had it right.

The nurse returned to ICU and Addie went over and dropped into a chair. Her phone, which she'd set on vibrate, buzzed from the outer pocket of her purse.

It was James. "I'm on my way. About twenty minutes out. Where are you?"

Her silly heart leaped. She really shouldn't be so overjoyed just to hear his voice, to know he was coming, that he would be here soon. "I'm at the hospital."

"Did you get any rest at all?"

"I did, yes." She forced a little brightness into her tone. "Two whole hours. I was out like a light. I got back here to the hospital about an hour and a half ago and sent Carmen and Dev back to the hotel."

"How's your grandfather doing?"

"He's fine. They've got him resting comfortably." It wasn't a lie, exactly. The nurse had promised they would quiet him down. "You should go straight to the hotel. Get a little sleep."

"I'll see you in a few minutes."

"Did you hear what I said, James?"

"Every word." He sounded amused, which annoyed her no end. "Gotta go. See you in a few."

"James?"

But he'd already hung up.

James came around the corner from the bank of elevators and saw Addie alone in the CSICU waiting room reading a paperback book.

He hung back for a moment and just looked at her. She had her elbows on the chair arms, her bright head bent to the page, legs crossed, one booted foot bouncing a little. He smiled at the sight.

That was the thing about Addie. Most times, just the sight of her made the day—or in this case, the middle of the night—seem a whole light brighter.

As he stood there and grinned, she suddenly looked up and caught sight of him. Those big eyes softened—but only for a second. Then she pursed up her mouth at him. Because he'd been watching her unawares? Because he hadn't followed her instructions and gone to the hotel?

Who knew?

And it didn't matter. Whatever her mood, he liked to look at her.

He went and claimed the chair next to her. "Good book?"

"Yeah, as a matter of fact." She flashed him the battered cover, which showed a passionately embracing, nearly naked couple, both with seriously '80s hair. "I read it years ago. It was in my mother's stash of romances in the closet of her old room. Carm and I read them all."

"So…now you're reading it again?"

She shrugged. "I found this copy under that chair against the far wall. Just the sight of it made me smile. It's about this teacher who takes a job in North Dakota in the early 1900s. She meets this grouchy farmer. They're always bickering. It's funny. And sweet. Made me cry, too. And right about now, I'm grateful for anything that takes my mind off my burning desire to strangle my grandfather."

Apparently, something had happened with Levi. Why wasn't he surprised? "Come on, whatever he did, it can't be that bad. He's barely out of surgery. He doesn't have the strength to make trouble."

She slanted him a glance—and then muttered, "You'd be surprised. He's so unbelievably stubborn. He gets some crazy idea in his head and he won't give it up no matter what."

James waited for her to get more specific. When she didn't, he asked, "And this crazy idea he won't give up is…?"

She bit her soft lower lip and shook her head. "Take a wild guess."

Guessing wasn't necessary. "He still thinks I'm the baby's father and he wants us married now or sooner."

"It is so wrong on so many levels."

"Hey." He waited until she turned her head and met his eyes. "How about if, tomorrow, when he's feeling better, I try to talk to him?"

Her round cheeks went bright red. "Are you kidding? That's what he wants. To get you in there and beat up on you. He's just so certain you're going to see the light and say you'll marry me—as if I'm waiting around in a white dress for you to finally agree to make an honest woman of me." She shook her head some more. "Uh-uh. No way are you going in there and dealing with him. He's going to have to wake up and face reality. That's all there is to it."

The next day, when Levi refused to start drinking clear liquids until he'd spoken with James, Addie tried to hold firm.

But they all ganged up on her. The nurses said that if James was willing to quietly discuss the matter with Levi, it could be helpful. Surely he might as well try to make the old man see reason. Carm and Dev agreed with the nurses. Why shouldn't James try? What could it hurt? Maybe James could get through to him. *Somebody* had to.

Addie said, "Oh, please. You know him. When he's like this, there is no way to get through to him. He's locked in to what he's so sure is right. He will do anything—*anything*—to accomplish his goal. It's a sickness, when he gets like this. And trying to talk to him, to humor him, to get him to see things differently? None of that will work. We just need to hold firm."

And then James said, all calm and noble and gratingly sure of himself and his charm and his talent for making people do things *his* way, "I would like to try."

Addie elbowed him in the side when he said that. "I

told you. Weren't you listening? You trying to reason with him will only make him surer that if he keeps pushing, we're going to give in."

"Oh, come on, Addie Anne," Carm pleaded. "At least James can *try*."

"No," Addie said again.

But they wouldn't listen. Ten minutes later, James went through the double doors.

Addie had to hand it to him. He stayed in there a long time. But when he finally came out, she could tell right away from the look on his face that the conversation had only made things worse.

"At least I got him to drink some broth and eat a little Jell-O," he said sheepishly when she and Carm and Dev surrounded him and asked what had happened.

But Addie wasn't reassured. She looked James straight in the eye—and his gaze kind of slid to the side. "Okay. You'd better tell me now. What did you do, James?"

He sank to a chair. "He's just so relentless. And he looks so sick and I...well, I couldn't stand it, all right? I hated to see him like that."

Addie demanded for the second time, "What did you *do*?"

James braced his elbows on his knees and put his head in his hands. "I ended up promising him I would talk to you."

Glances were flying. Carm looked at Addie. Addie looked at Dev. Dev shrugged in confusion and frowned at James.

Addie's stomach lurched alarmingly. "You told him you'd *talk* to me?"

James looked absolutely miserable. "Yeah. I, well, that was how I got him to drink the broth."

Somehow she kept her voice even and reasonable as she inquired, "Talk to me about what?"

"Er, the wedding?"

Dead silence. Then Dev said, "Man. Seriously?"

Addie pressed a hand to her churning belly and asked very softly, "What wedding?"

James dropped his hands between his spread knees, sagged back in the chair and groaned at the ceiling. "*Our* wedding."

That did it for Addie. "I'll be right back." She clapped her hand over her mouth and ran for the ladies' room.

"Addie?" Carm called from behind her, close on her heels.

Addie didn't turn. She didn't dare. She knocked the door wide with the heel of her hand and made for the stall.

Addie needed him. James leaped to his feet. He started to follow after the women.

Devin grabbed his arm. "Hold on, man. Let Carm take care of her. She'll be okay."

James knew Dev was right. He collapsed into the chair again. "It seemed like a good idea at the time, you know? Just to humor him…"

Dev took the chair next to him. "So you told Levi the baby was yours?"

"Hell, no!" He said it way too loud. A couple of old ladies waiting together in the chairs across the room stopped whispering and glared at him. "Sorry," he said. They glared a few seconds more for good measure and went back to their low conversation.

Dev clapped him on the shoulder. "No offense, dude. Just trying to understand what's going on here."

James leaned his head against the wall. It pressed on

the bump back there—the one Levi had made when he coldcocked him the day before. He winced and sat forward, bracing his forearms on his knees. "Maybe we'd just better wait until Addie and Carmen get back."

Dev grunted. "Yeah. No point in going through it all twice."

"Thanks," James said wearily. His phone vibrated. He took it out and checked it. The emails were piling up and he needed to call the office.

Later.

He and Dev waited in a grim yet companionable silence until Addie and Carmen emerged from the ladies' room.

James asked, "You okay?" when Addie sat down next to him. Carmen took the chair on Devin's other side.

"I'm okay," Addie said. "Tell us the rest."

He worried that she really ought to eat something. "Maybe you should have some soda crackers or something?"

"James, just tell us what happened."

He speared his fingers through his hair. "What can I say? I tried."

She actually bumped him with her shoulder, a reassuring little nudge that somehow made him feel better about everything. And then she said, "I know you tried. We all do. We also know PawPaw. He has a sort of fixation with situations like this. He lost our grandma June when our mother was just five."

Carmen said, "And our mom, well, she just seemed born to heartbreak. She fell in love with two men and both of them ran off, leaving her behind—and pregnant, both times."

Addie went on, "Both times, our grandpa went looking for those men. Both times, he planned to make sure those fathers-to-be did the right thing. But he never found either of them. Then our mother died having me and Paw-Paw raised us on his own."

"We had a happy childhood," said Carmen softly. "PawPaw saw to that."

Devin said, "You heard how he came after me?"

James nodded. "Levi mentioned something about that yesterday." *While he had me at gunpoint.*

Devin explained, "We'd had a fight, me and Carm, and I'd gone off to Laramie to start my life over again."

Carmen said, "I was too proud to tell him that I was pregnant. I'm ashamed to say I lied to PawPaw and told him that Devin had turned his back on me and the baby."

"I would never do that," said Dev.

"I know you wouldn't," Carmen answered tenderly.

Dev went on. "That time, Levi knew where to look. He got in that ancient green pickup and drove to Laramie. He got the jump on me, kidnapped me at gunpoint, tied me up and drove me back to Colorado."

Carmen chuckled. "Where I promptly went ballistic that my insane old grandpa had kidnapped poor Devin. But then Devin was so glad to see me and I'd missed him so much. I cried and confessed about the baby. And Dev said of course he wanted our baby and he wanted *me*, too." Carmen and Devin shared a long, intimate glance. And Carmen said, "So PawPaw put away his shotgun and Dev and I got married and I moved to Laramie with him."

"And since then they've been busy, having their babies and living happily ever after," said Addie fondly. Then her voice turned harder. "And to this day, PawPaw prides himself on doing what *had to be done*—his words, not mine—so that Carmen and Dev could find the love and

CHRISTINE RIMMER   73

happiness they so richly deserve. The way he looks at it, he and his shotgun made everything right."

"Wow," said James. "I guess he figures it worked before, so why not try it again?"

"Exactly." Addie bumped his shoulder again. "Go on. Tell us the rest. What happened when you talked to him just now?"

"It was like talking to a wall."

"I'll bet."

"I tried to make him see that he should listen to you. That it *is* Brandon's baby and not mine, that it *couldn't* be mine, that I never even managed to get you to go out with me, let alone…well, you know."

A soft smile curved her plump lips. A soft smile just for him. He thought how he'd never even gotten a kiss from her, of how much he'd like to have one. Even after all the months she'd kept him at arm's length, even now that he knew she was having Brandon Hall's baby.

There was just something about her. She made the world feel fresh. Brand-new. He'd had more fun taking care of her and helping out with her crazy-ass grandpa over the past twenty-four hours than he'd had in years.

He'd meant what he'd told her. He *liked* helping out— when the one he was helping out was her.

She prompted, "We're listening."

He went ahead and told them. "I knew I wasn't getting through to him, but I kept talking to him, nice and quiet and low, trying to get him to admit he had it all wrong. I kept reminding him that he needed to focus on getting well, that he should listen to his nurses. I said that all of us only want to help him get back on his feet. He mostly just lay there with his eyes shut, now and then opening them and glaring at me like he didn't believe a word I was saying. Finally, I just thought, well, if I could get him to take some liquids, at least, that would be something. I started pushing for that, coaxing him, you know? Telling him to try just a few spoonfuls of broth..."

"And then?"

"Out of nowhere, after several minutes of deathly silence, just as I was about to give up and slink out, he spoke again. He agreed he might have some broth if I would be reasonable."

Carmen made a low, knowing sound in her throat.

Dev said, "Uh-oh."

Addie groaned. "You thought *you* were working *him*." She let out a frustrated cry. "I can't believe you let him do that to you. You should know better."

He couldn't deny it. "Yes, I should. I really should."

"After the way you've worked me in the last twenty-four hours," she scolded, "to get me to let you stay, to coax me to eat, to convince me to keep that suite that is way more than we need and way more than I should ever allow you to—"

James put up a hand. "Do you want to hear the rest of the story?"

She made a humphing sound. "Yes. Go ahead." She glared as hard as Levi had.

He conceded the point. "You're right, okay?"

"Of course I'm right."

"Your granddad puts me to shame when it comes to manipulation. And I have to say, he can be damn charming when he wants to be." Carmen, Addie and Dev all nodded. James frowned. "Where was I? Oh, yeah. So he asked me if I would be reasonable. I said of course I was reasonable. He let me feed him a spoonful of broth, and then another spoonful, and I was feeling like I was really making some progress at last. A couple of the nurses caught my eye and nodded in approval that I was getting nourishment down him. He ate all the broth. I felt like a million bucks and I wanted him to try the Jell-O and…"

Dev clapped him on the shoulder, a gesture of support and understanding.

James said, "I don't know how it happened. Somehow I became totally invested in getting him to eat just a little bit more. And then, quietly, in a ragged but kindly tone of voice, he asked me if I would just try to talk to you, if I would only try to convince you to go ahead and marry me. I don't know. I had that spoonful of Jell-O right up to his mouth and…I agreed. I just said yeah, that I would do that. And he smiled and I smiled and then he took the spoon out of my hand and ate the rest of the Jell-O himself."

There was a silence. Then Carmen sighed.

And Addie said, "That is just not right and you know it's not, James. You've set us back in getting through to him. You realize that, don't you?"

He gave a hopeless shrug. "I'm sorry. I know I blew it."

Carmen hurried to reassure him, "But it's good he ate the broth and the Jell-O." Dev made a low noise of agreement.

Addie shot them each a baleful glance and demanded, "So after he ate the Jell-O, did you at least make it clear that you knew he was playing you? Did you at least say that you shouldn't have agreed to do what he asked, because the baby is not your baby and you and I are *not* getting married?"

He stared at her, at her soft, plump lips and her round cheeks and her golden eyes, which gazed back at him reproachfully. All he wanted to do was reach out, curl his hand around the back of her soft neck and pull her close. She was altogether too independent and she needed someone to lean on.

Those plump lips thinned in annoyance. At him. "James. I have asked you a question."

He made himself answer her. "He ate the Jell-O and he had this pleased gleam in his eyes and… I don't know. I just couldn't stand to disappoint him."

"You are telling me that you didn't even take back your promise to try to convince me to marry you?"

"Yeah," he said bleakly. "That's what I'm telling you."

"Well, that does it," she announced. "You're not getting near him again."

An hour later, Addie went back in to deal with Levi herself. She told him what James hadn't managed to say, what she'd *already* told her grandfather more than once before—that she and James were not getting married and the baby was not James's baby and Levi needed to forget about all that and focus on getting well.

Levi turned his head away. He pretended not to hear her.

And three days later, when he should have been in a regular hospital room and getting close to getting the okay to go home, he was still in CSICU.

Could a man *will* himself not to get better?

Apparently, Levi was doing just that.

He wouldn't eat—or not much, anyway. Just enough to keep the nurses from sticking a feeding tube down his throat. But not really enough to get better.

Instead, he got weaker. He suffered a minor incision-area infection and then another on his leg, where they'd harvested the vein for the bypass grafts. His blood counts refused to return to anything approaching normal. He had shortness of breath and he claimed he was too weak to get up and try to walk a step or two. And when the respiratory therapist worked with him, he put in zero effort to do the exercises she gave him.

He should be improving, the nurses said. But he seemed to have lost the will to get better. They feared pneumonia would be next if he didn't start working to clear his lungs, if he didn't start making an effort to sit up and then walk.

All of them—the nurses, his doctors, Addie, Carmen, Devin and James—they all knew exactly what he was doing. He was betting his own life, scaring them all to death in the interest of getting what he wanted most: Addie and James married.

It was so wrong. Wrong and deluded, dangerous and terrifying. Addie was worried sick and furious, simultaneously and constantly.

Finally, on Monday, a full week after Levi's heart attack and surgery, Addie had James drive her back home. She needed a vehicle and she wanted to check on Red Hill. They set out nice and early, so that James could have the whole day to catch up on his work. He dropped her off at the ranch at a little after eight and headed for the county courthouse. She would take her own pickup back to Denver.

Thanks to Walker and Rory McKellan, everything was in order at the ranch. The horses were all groomed and sleek and healthy. They greeted her with happy chuffing sounds and eagerly munched the carrots she offered them. She couldn't resist saddling her own gray mare, Tildy, and indulging in a long, relaxing ride. Her garden didn't need much care this early in the season, but she spent some time digging in it, getting the rows ready for planting.

At the house, she averted her eyes every time she

walked past the ragged hole in the kitchen floor. She would have to take care of that. But not today.

She went through the mail that had piled up in the past week and separated out the bills she needed to pay, sticking them in her shoulder bag to deal with later. She tried not to think how far behind she was getting on her little side business of making scarecrows on order and for sale on Etsy. Red Hill wasn't a working ranch, really, and it hadn't been since her grandpa was a boy. Over the years, the Kenwrights had sold off the land little by little. Now there were two hundred and fifty acres left, a barn, stables, the large, rambling main house and a foreman's cottage. Addie did whatever she had to do in order to make ends meet. Like boarding horses, growing most of the produce they ate and making cute scarecrows for sale.

She had some new orders, for a bride, groom and baby scarecrow family. For a Raggedy Andy scarecrow and a ballerina, too. Plus, she had shipments of clothes and straw and other supplies that had been delivered in her absence, signed for by Walker or Rory and left in the barn. She checked them over to see what had come. It was one in the afternoon by then. And being behind on her scarecrows wasn't the priority.

Getting PawPaw to see the light, give up his crazy plan to get her married to James and instead focus on his recovery: that was the priority.

And that was another reason she'd had James bring her home.

Addie went upstairs to the back bedroom she used as her office. In the file cabinet there, she found the paperwork from the sperm bank where Brandon had stored the sperm that had made their baby. She took the file, gathered a few fresh changes of clothes from her bedroom closet and ran back downstairs. Five minutes later, she was out the door and behind the wheel of her trusty pickup, headed back to Denver.

After reluctantly leaving Addie on her own at Red Hill, James drove to the county seat forty miles from Justice Creek. He spent the morning at the courthouse, handling legal matters for various clients. Then he drove back toward Justice Creek, stopping at the Sylvan Inn a few miles outside town, where he joined his half sister, Nell, his half brothers, Garrett and Quinn, and Quinn's wife, Chloe, for lunch.

Together, Garrett and Nell ran Bravo Construction. Quinn, who owned a fitness center in town, had recently started buying houses to flip. His wife, Chloe, an interior designer, would draw up the plans to redesign the dated interiors. Then Garrett and Nell would bring in their crews and start knocking out walls. Once the renovation was complete, Chloe would stage the rooms with furniture and attractive accessories before they put the house up for sale.

James liked all of his siblings and half siblings. They'd had some rough patches growing up, natural resentments created because their father, Franklin Bravo, refused to choose between his wife, Sondra—who gave him four children, James included—and Willow, his mistress, who gave him five more, including Garrett, Quinn and Nell. Over a decade ago, when James's mother died, Frank had promptly married Willow and moved her into the mansion he'd originally built for Sondra. Now Frank was gone, too. Willow lived alone in the house that had once belonged to her rival.

James and his siblings and half siblings were fine with how things had turned out. The years had mellowed everyone. They all tried to show up for the major events: weddings, births, christenings, whatever. James enjoyed having such a big, close-knit family.

He also liked doing business with his brothers and sisters. He'd not only had Bravo Construction build his new house, but put money into Nell and Garrett's company, and he was planning to buy some commercial real estate and then have Chloe, Garrett and Nell fix it up before he put it back on the market. Quinn had expressed an interest in going in with him on that.

It was a good lunch, James thought. Productive. They talked business, kicking around ideas as to which properties might be right for them.

They'd all heard about Levi's heart attack, about how Walker and Rory were looking after the Red Hill livestock and babysitting Addie's dog while Levi was in the hospital. James admitted that he'd been there when the heart attack happened, but he kept the details to himself.

Nell said, "Heard you've been spending a lot of time with the Kenwrights in Denver."

He played it off. "Just helping them out a little when things are tough, that's all. Levi's not recovering as fast he should."

They all expressed their sympathy and offered to pitch in if there was any way they might be needed.

Nell kept after him. "I was at your new house installing the kitchen cabinets a couple of weeks ago, remember?"

He knew exactly where she was going and accepted the inevitable with a shrug. "I remember."

His half sister, who was the beauty of the family with killer curves and a face that brought to mind the sultry singer Lana Del Rey, flipped a hank of thick auburn hair back over her shoulder and reminded him, "Addie stopped by that day."

"She stopped to say hi, that's all."

"I've got eyes, Jamie. You've got a soft spot for Addie Kenwright."

James didn't deny it. Why should he? He did have a soft spot for Addie. And he hoped she was managing all right, whatever she just *had* to do at Red Hill.

He thought of the hole Levi had blown in the kitchen floor and almost asked Garrett and Nell to take care of it. They could get the key from Walker and do the work while the house was empty.

But he knew he'd better discuss it with Addie before he set anything up. She could get testy when he took care of her business without consulting her first. Plus, Nell was bound to ask who'd made that hole and how. He supposed he could tell them what he'd told Sal, the med tech—that Levi had been cleaning his shotgun.

But no. Better not to go there until he'd had a word with Addie about it.

They finished up the meal at a little before two and walked out to the parking lot together, climbing into their separate vehicles, everyone headed back to town. James led the way out of the lot onto the highway, with the others falling in behind him. His plan was to return to the office, where he would catch up with clients, go over his calendar with his secretary and deal with any correspondence that had piled up since he last came in on Friday. Then at five, he would be on his way to Denver again.

It was a nice, sunny day and he drove with the windows down—which meant he smelled the smoke long before he had a clue what might be on fire. Also, he heard the sirens wailing in the distance, to the northeast.

Calder and Bravo, Attorneys-at-Law, had offices on West Central, but he could see the black smoke billowing skyward to the east. His pulse ratcheted up several notches. Damned if it didn't look as though the fire was right there in town.

So he went east on Central, toward the smoke and the sirens. A glance in his rearview mirror showed him that Quinn and Chloe, Garrett and Nell had made the same choice.

Four long blocks later, past most of the shops and businesses that lined Central Street, he saw that the building his sister Elise owned jointly with her best friend, Tracy Winham, was on fire.

The gorgeous old brick structure had three shops on the bottom floor: a jewelry store, a gift shop and Bravo Catering, which Elise and Tracy owned and ran. Tracy and Elise also each had a large apartment on the upper two floors.

Or they used to. Judging by the extent of the fire, the building would end up a complete loss.

The firefighters were on it, though, hoses rolled out, dousing the blaze that had engulfed all three floors. Flames licked out of every window and the smoke, thick and black, turned the blue sky murky gray.

He spotted Elise and Tracy on the sidewalk, well away from the fire. They had their arms around each other as they watched both their homes and their business go up in smoke. In the arm that wasn't wrapped tight around her best friend, Elise clutched her big orange cat, Mr. Wiggles.

James's other full sister, Clara, stood with them, as did his other half sister, Jody. He recognized the owner of the jewelry store and the couple who ran the gift shop and dared to hope that everyone had gotten out safely. Plus, he saw neither flames nor smoke coming from the structures to either side. So far at least, they'd kept the fire from spreading to any other buildings.

He drove on past the fire, past the two fire trucks and

the huddled knots of people on the sidewalk. When he spotted an empty space, he eased his pickup in at the curb. He shoved open his door and hit the pavement at a run, headed back to his sisters and Tracy. Garrett, Nell, Quinn and Chloe followed on his heels.

James was half a block from the fire when it happened.

With a sound like the final gasp of some great, dying beast, the roof of the burning building collapsed inward, sending a river of sparks and live ash shooting up toward the afternoon sky.

Chapter Five

At the hospital in Denver, with the file she'd taken from her office nook at Red Hill under her arm, Addie went straight in to see her grandfather.

He opened his eyes when she said his name.

She took his glasses from the table by the bed and gently put them on his pasty, puffy face. And then she showed him the papers that proved she had been artificially inseminated with Brandon Hall's sperm.

"PawPaw, come on," she whispered fervently. "Face the truth, please. For Carm's and my sake. For Dev and your grandkids, for the sake of everyone who loves you so much. Let it go. Move on. Let yourself get well."

She didn't even know she was crying until he reached up a shaking, wrinkled, bruised-up hand with an IV taped to the back of it and, lightly as moth wings, brushed at the tears that trailed down her cheeks. The touch lasted only a second or two. Then his hand plopped to his side and he let out a soft little sigh, as though just that small effort had thoroughly exhausted him.

She pleaded again. "Please, PawPaw. Please don't do this. I'm not my mother all those years ago, sitting around pining for men who did me wrong. I'm not Carm, letting her pride keep her from telling Dev that he was going to be a dad. PawPaw, won't you just open your eyes and see that I'm having this baby because I *want* this baby? I swear on my life, it *is* Brandon's baby. I got pregnant on purpose and I don't need a man to make things right for me. Things *are* right. Or they would be, if you would only stop this craziness and start trying to get well…" She let her voice trail off and waited for him to say something, *anything*.

But he gave her only silence.

She tried again. "And as for James, you just don't get it. It's not what you think. He's a good guy, that's all. He's a…a friend, you know? He's just trying to help out. I swear to you I've never even kissed that man, let alone *slept* with him. He really, truly is not the dad and my baby is not his problem."

Levi spoke then, his wrinkled lips moving, his stale breath coming out in a rattling little puff.

Hope rising that maybe, just maybe, she'd finally gotten through to him, she leaned closer. "What, PawPaw? Tell me, please. What?"

And he spoke again, just loud enough, finally, that she could make out the words. "Marry James. I'll get well."

Addie gasped in hurt and outrage. "I can't believe you're doing this. Risking your own life to try to force me to do something that is completely my own business, something you have no say in whatsoever. You… you need to stop this ridiculousness right this minute. I…I can't… I don't…" God. She'd run out of words. She sucked in a hard breath and demanded, "What is the *matter* with you? Have you heard a single thing I said to you just now?"

"I heard you. All of it." The words came out raspy and ragged, as if all of him were dry inside, as if he were nothing but a bunch of sticks and brown, crumpled leaves rubbing together in a cold, uncaring wind. And then he said it again. "Marry James."

That did it. She straightened, whirled on her heel and got out fast. If she hadn't, she would have vomited right there on the floor by her dying grandpa's bed.

Carm took one look at her and grabbed her arm. "How long since you ate something?"

"Don't talk to me about eating. I am never going to eat again."

"Oh, great. Turning suicidal, just like PawPaw. And remember, you'll be starving yourself *and* your innocent child."

"Sometimes he makes me just want to scream. Scream and scream and never stop."

Carm locked eyes with Dev. "We're going to the cafeteria."

Dev nodded. "Keep your phone close. I'll call if they need you up here."

Carm wrapped an arm around Addie's shoulders. "This way. Don't argue."

By the time they got down to the basement, Addie no longer felt as if the top of her head was about to blow off from all the fury spinning and popping inside her. Her stomach had settled marginally. And she did know that she needed to eat. She took a tray and got in line behind Carmen.

Once they'd paid the cashier, they got a table by the row

of narrow windows that looked out on a pretty, landscaped walkway where, owing to the cafeteria being mostly underground, the view was of the bottom halves of well-trimmed bushes and people's legs going by.

Carm waited for her to eat a few crackers and sip up a couple of spoonfuls of vegetable soup before asking, "Okay, what was that about?"

Addie had set the file folder on the empty chair beside her. She passed it to Carmen. "I showed him proof that the baby is Brandon's."

Carmen gave the papers inside a quick glance and handed them back. "Didn't help, huh?"

"He actually said right out loud to me that if I married James, he would get well."

Carmen dropped the French fry she'd been about to put in her mouth. "Get outta Dodge."

"God's truth. He did."

"Incredible. I mean, we all knew that was what he was doing."

"Right. But at least until now, we could tell ourselves it wasn't a conscious choice, that he was just so depressed over the failure of his wrong and completely insane shotgun wedding plans, he couldn't focus on getting better."

"But now we know it's much worse." Carmen picked up a triangle of club sandwich, ate a bite and chewed slowly. When she swallowed, she said, "I don't even want to say it out loud."

"Not saying it won't make it any less true."

So her sister went ahead and said it. "He's doing this to himself, risking his own life on purpose."

"Carm. What am I going to do?"

Carmen set the sandwich down and drank a little cranberry juice. "Don't make me tell you. Please."

Addie whispered, "I really think he might not make it if I don't do what he wants."

Carmen whispered back, "At this point, honey, he might not make it anyway."

"Oh, dear God." Addie felt the tears clogging her throat again. "No wonder all I want to do lately is cry and throw up."

Carm reached across the table. Addie met her halfway. They clutched hands and stared into each other's eyes.

Finally, Carm gulped and said what Addie couldn't stop herself from thinking. "I know James would do it if you asked him to."

Addie shut her eyes and drew a slow, steadying breath. "It's just…you know, so wrong to put that on him. He's a good guy and he's been nothing but wonderful about all this. PawPaw knocked him out cold, dragged him to Red Hill, tied him to a chair and threatened him with the business end of his Mossberg Maverick 88. And yet here he is, right beside us, helping out in any way he can, sticking by us through everything. I don't get it."

"Oh, yeah, you do. He's not only a great guy. He's wild for you, Addie Anne."

Addie's throat clutched and her cheeks grew warm. "Oh, you don't know that."

"Yeah. I do. And you want *him*, too. You *could* look at it as taking a chance on love for once."

"I *have* taken chances on love. None of them ended well."

"You took chances on the wrong guys. Look at me and Dev. Things do work out between men and women, you know?"

"Can we not get all down in the weeds about love and romance right now, please?"

"You need to talk about this with James. When's he coming back?"

"I don't know. After he's done at his office, I guess." She cast a desperate, pleading glance at the ceiling. "Dear sweet Lord, I cannot ask such a thing of him."

"Yeah, you can. And you'd better do it as soon as possible. The longer you put it off, the harder it's going to be for PawPaw to pull himself back from the brink of death."

Once they'd eaten, they went back upstairs, where Devin had no news.

Carm took the situation in hand. "Go to the hotel. Try to get a little rest. And call James. Tell him you're in the suite and you want him to meet you there. That'll give you two some privacy for the big discussion."

Addie looked to Dev, who had no idea yet what they were talking about. But Dev was a wonderfully well-trained husband. He just gave her an encouraging smile and went back to playing World of Warcraft on his phone. "The big discussion?" she scoffed. "Carm, I didn't say I would do it. I don't know if I *can* do it."

Carm just looked at her. It was all she had to do. Addie knew what her sister was thinking: *What choice have you got?*

Addie autodialed James as she walked into the suite.

He didn't answer. It was almost four by then and she assumed he must be busy at the office. She left a short message asking him to call her back.

And then she filled up the jetted tub in the luxurious bathroom off the bedroom she and James were sharing—meaning, really, that they took turns crashing in it. She took a long bath, keeping the phone close so she could snatch it right up when he called her back.

But half an hour later, he hadn't called and her skin had started feeling pruney. She got out, toweled off and slathered on the lotion. Once she was dressed again, she debated giving him another call.

But somehow that seemed wrong and way too needy—which, to be brutally honest, was exactly how things stood. She needed him to marry her, and that was all wrong.

Plus, what about her pride?

She knew the answer. Her pride had to go. She was headed straight for the pride-free zone, about to beg a man to marry her in order to keep her pigheaded, self-destructive grandfather from killing himself.

She called James again. Again, there was no answer. She left another message. "Sorry to bother you, really. But if you could just call me as soon as you get this? Please, James. I…need to talk to you." She hung up feeling like the wimpiest, most pitiful creature the world had ever known.

James stayed right there on the street with the family as Elise's building continued to burn.

Once his sister's former home and place of business was nothing more than a soggy, smoking pile of charred bricks, Elise, Tracy and the other shop owners were interviewed by the deputy fire marshal. The gift shop owners confessed that they kept a hot plate in the back of the store. One of them might have left it on by accident. And then they'd both stepped out to run an errand, leaving the shop empty until the flames had already taken hold. Also, when the deputy marshal leaned on them a little, the couple admitted that they'd taken the batteries out of the smoke alarms in the shop because they kept going off whenever anyone wanted to enjoy a smoke.

Elise, already at her wit's end after losing everything but the shirt on her back, burst into tears when she learned all that. She clung to Tracy and to her increasingly agitated cat.

James represented Elise and Tracy. He'd helped them work out the lease, which clearly stated that there was no smoking in the building. Not to mention, Colorado was a smoke-free state. If your business was open to the public, you weren't allowed to smoke in it. As to the fire alarms, it was illegal to disable them. James could see a lawsuit in the works. That was never fun—not for the plaintiff *or* the defendant.

Once the interviews with the deputy marshal were over, Clara asked everyone to come to her house a couple of blocks away. James went along in case there might be some way he could help out. Everyone was worried about Tracy. She'd lost both her parents in a fire. She seemed practically catatonic after living through another disastrous blaze. Elise kept her close and Tracy clung to her.

At Clara's house, Elise finally let go of her big orange cat. Mr. Wiggles promptly took off down the front hall and detoured into the first room with an open door, the master bedroom.

Clara waved a hand. "It's all right. Poor guy needs a little time to himself after all the excitement. He'll probably just hide under the bed, and that's fine with me."

Clara and her housekeeper and babysitter, Mrs. Scruggs, got to work making coffee and scouring the cupboards for snacks to share. Jody and Nell hovered close to Elise and Tracy, ready to get them whatever they needed.

James volunteered to call Elise and Tracy's insurance agent for them, but when he reached for his phone, it wasn't in his pocket. He must have left it in the truck.

Clara told him to use the house phone, which he did. The agent, Bob Karnes, said he'd be right over.

Bob was as good as his word. He showed up half an hour later, got the information he needed to get started on the claim and promised Elise and Tracy he would speed up the process as much as he possibly could.

When Bob left, it was a quarter of five. James couldn't help wondering how things were going in Denver. Addie must be back at the hospital by now. He was getting antsy to check in on Levi's condition, see how Addie was doing and make sure she took some time to eat.

But he knew she got tired of him hovering over her. He told himself nothing that important was going to happen in the next few hours. He'd see Addie and check on Levi's progress as soon as he could get back to Denver.

And right now he had more to do in Justice Creek.

He got Clara aside and gave her the keys to his condo in town. "Give these to Elise when they start trying to decide where to go tonight," he said. "She and Tracy and the cat can have it for as long as they need a place. I'm spending my nights in Denver for the next several days, at least. And my new house is almost ready anyway."

Clara hugged him. "You're the best big brother we ever had."

He grunted and tipped his head toward their brother Darius, who'd just shown up a short time before to see if there was anything he could do to help. "You mean, other than Dare," he teased.

Clara nodded. "Right. You're *both* the best."

He kissed her cheek, went over and gave Elise and Tracy each a last hug and then left for his office. When he got in the quad cab, he didn't see his phone in the console where he usually left it. Had he gone and lost the damn thing? That would be a pain in the ass. It was brand-new, had all the bells and whistles, a boatload of memory, and had cost a lot more than any sane man should pay for a phone.

He went to his office and worked for an hour and a half, eating takeout his secretary, Louise, had ordered for him as he plowed through correspondence, dealing only with the issues that couldn't wait another day. He almost called Addie before he left the building but decided to just get on the road instead.

He was halfway to Denver and it was just after eight when he heard his phone ringing. The sound was coming from under the seat, where it must have fallen at some point during the day. He was on the interstate by then. But he had his GPS connected to the phone for hands-free calling. The earpiece was right there in the cup holder, so he stuck it in his ear and turned on the GPS.

Nothing. At some point, he'd probably switched off the phone's Bluetooth connection. Technology. Never worked when you needed it. There was nowhere safe to pull over, so he just kept driving. But whoever had called left a message, because the phone buzzed at intervals to let him know he had voice mail.

As the intermittent buzzing kept happening, he remembered that he'd heard it before and tuned it out, what with thinking about Elise and Tracy, wondering how Addie was managing, and trying to figure out what he absolutely had to deal with before he could head for Denver again.

Now the buzzing worried the hell out of him. Was Levi okay? Did Elise need something at the condo?

Finally, he couldn't take it anymore. He turned off at the next exit, pulled into a convenience store parking lot and felt under the seat until he finally had the phone. There were four calls from Addie. There was also a text from her asking him to call her as soon as possible. Addie never texted. Her phone was ancient and texting with it took forever. And he had voice mail waiting. She must have left voice messages, too.

Four calls, voice mail and a text. That couldn't be good. He autodialed her.

She answered on the first ring, which freaked him out in itself. Addie never had her phone just waiting in her hand. Not unless there was some kind of emergency going on. "James?" she asked, too softly, then louder and a little bit frantic. "James?"

He couldn't explain himself fast enough. "I'm sorry. It's been an insane day. I had no idea you'd been calling. I lost track of my phone. It was under the seat and I…" Damn. He was babbling like a fool. "Addie, what's happened? Is Levi…?"

"He's okay," she said. "I mean, you know, not good, but still, um, with us."

"What is it? What can I do?"

"Oh, James…" A tiny, muffled sniffle.

"Addie, are you crying?"

Another barely audible sniff. "No. No, of course not. I just thought…"

"You thought what?" He tried to keep his voice even and gentle, in spite of the fact that she was freaking him out.

She sniffed again. "It doesn't matter."

"Addie, that's not true. You can tell me. I'm listening."

"Fine," she said sharply. "I thought, well, that maybe you were just getting tired of me taking advantage of you. I thought maybe you were pissed off because I kept calling and you wanted me to stop bugging you. I thought—"

"Addie."

"What?"

"I'm sorry I didn't call you. I misplaced my phone and there was a lot going on and I was hurrying to get back to you. And *I* didn't want to bug *you*."

She didn't say anything for several seconds. Then, grudgingly, "You never minded bugging me before."

That made him smile. "Hmm. Good point. I guess I decided to give you a break from me at exactly the wrong time."

"Yes. Well, I guess you did."

"You sound better."

"Better? What are you talking about? I'm perfectly fine."

He couldn't help grinning. "Yep. Almost like your old self, all snap and vinegar."

"Gee, thanks," she said. He just knew she was rolling her eyes. "And where are you now, anyway?"

"At a convenience store about forty-five minutes from the hospital. I finally heard the phone buzzing under the seat, so I stopped and fished it out. Are you at the hospital?"

"No. I'm at the hotel. Would you, um, come straight here to the suite? I really need to talk to you."

This didn't sound good. "Addie, what's going on?"

"Can you just come here, please? Directly here? I'll tell you everything, but I need to do it face-to-face."

"Okay, now you've got me seriously worried."

"James, will you just come to the hotel and *talk* to me, please?"

"Okay." Whatever had gone wrong—and he had a feeling it was pretty bad—he needed to be there to help her with it. "Forty-five minutes, tops, and I'm there. I'll turn on the Bluetooth so if you need me again, I can take it while I'm driving."

"The Bluetooth?" she echoed, as though she had no idea what he was talking about.

"I'm just saying, if you call again, I'll be here. I'll answer."

"Just come straight to the hotel."

"I'm on my way."

He made it in thirty-five minutes, pushing his speed the whole way. Luck was with him and no state trooper pulled him over.

At twenty of nine, he was sticking his key card in the slot. Addie must have heard him at the door. She was waiting in the little entry area, barefoot, wearing a Harley-Davidson T-shirt and plaid pajama bottoms, when he came through the door.

"James." She had her hands against her soft lips, and her eyes were all misty. As though he was the best thing she'd seen all day.

"Addie," he said in a whisper, because it felt so damn good to have her looking at him like that.

And then she ran to him, as if he were her guy, as though all she wanted was to feel his arms around her. He grabbed on tight, picked her up and swung her around. Damn, she felt good, soft in all the right places, her full breasts against his chest, her hair warm and silky against his cheek, the scent of her so sweet.

When he set her down, she gazed up at him, all round cheeks, plump lips and red-rimmed golden eyes. He wanted to kiss her more than he wanted to draw his next breath.

But before he could swoop down and claim that tempting mouth for the very first time, she grabbed his hand from behind her back, whirled around and pulled him into the living area.

"Did you eat?" she demanded as she pushed him down on the sofa and then sat next to him.

"I did." He wanted her closer. So he dropped his briefcase beside the couch, hooked his arm around her waist and tucked her into his side.

"James!" she groused. But she didn't pull away. On the contrary, she leaned her head on his shoulder with a sigh.

Whatever bad thing had happened, it had made her reach out to him. He could feel downright grateful for that. He pulled her even closer and stroked her thick, soft hair. "The important question is, did *you* eat?"

"I did. I had lunch with Carm at the hospital. And I had room-service dinner."

"Excellent."

She gave a long, slow sigh. "You said your day was crazy…?"

He put a finger under her chin and tipped it up so she would look at him. "Stuff happened, but it's as sorted out as it's going to get for tonight. I'll tell you all about it later."

"No. Please. Tell me now."

"Addie, what is going on?"

"I need time to build up to what I have to say, okay? And I've been sitting here half the afternoon and into the evening thinking of all the ways I've taken advantage of you, all the ways I haven't *appreciated* you. Thinking that you didn't call me back because you were finally fed up with me and that I totally understood why you would feel that way."

"You're beating yourself up for nothing. You know that, right? You've got it all wrong and I already told you why I didn't call you back."

"I know. But I think it's time I started appreciating you more."

He suppressed a chuckle. "Okay. If you just *have* to."

"I do, as a matter of fact," she replied with great dignity. "And part of appreciating you is listening to how *your* day went. So just tell me what happened in Justice Creek, please."

"You really want to hear about it?" Actually, that she did was kind of gratifying.

"I do. Yes."

So he gave in and told her about the fire. "The building's a total loss," he added at the end. "Elise and Tracy will be staying at my condo for a while."

"Your poor sister. And poor Tracy…"

"Nobody died and they have insurance. Elise even got her cat out safely. It could have been worse."

"Yeah. But to lose your home, all your personal belongings *and* your business on the same day. That's gotta hurt."

"They'll be okay. We'll all pitch in to make sure of that—and now it's your turn. Tell me whatever it is that's so hard to say."

"I don't know how to…" She ran out of steam before she even got going. Her big eyes filled with tears again. "Crap." She pulled free of his arms and dashed the moisture away. "I am not going to cry anymore. I'm not, and that's final."

He wanted to grab her close again, to demand that she tell him right now what had her so upset. But he did neither. He just waited, let her find her own way to it.

And finally, she said, "I thought that if I showed Paw-Paw the documents that proved I really did have intra-uterine insemination with Brandon's sperm, he might finally see the light and admit that Brandon's the baby's dad. So when I was at the ranch, I got the paperwork they gave me at the sperm bank and the bill from the doctor I used. Then when I got back to the hospital, I took them in to PawPaw."

"Did it work?"

She threw up both hands. "Are you kidding? He's made up his mind and no mere facts are going to change it for him."

"I have to say I'm not really surprised."

She hummed low in her throat. "Yeah, well. It was a shot. And the way he blew me off wasn't the worst of it. James, he looks so horrible. I worry he's not going to make it. They're all worried—the nurses, the doctors, Carm and Dev. Every day, he gets weaker. He simply refuses to get well. And today, he told me… He whispered to me…"

James took her hand. She didn't attempt to pull away when he twined his fingers with her smaller ones. "Go on."

And at last, she got down to it. "He said, and I quote, 'Marry James. I'll get well.'" With a soft cry, she yanked her fingers free of his grip and raked them back through her tumbled hair. "I mean, I know it might be too late anyway. He looks *really* bad. It scares me that even if he tries, it's not going to do any good. But I…"

He couldn't stand to watch her suffer as she danced around the real question. "Addie."

"Lord in heaven." She sagged against him and he wrapped his arms around her again. "You know what I'm leading up to here, right?" She whispered the question.

He felt the warmth of her breath against his shoulder and he gathered her just a little bit closer. "I do. And Levi is one tough old bird. I'm thinking if he says he'll get well, there's a better than fifty-fifty chance he can make that happen."

"Still, he could die anyway."

"I don't think he will. But if I'm wrong, he would die believing that he'd done everything he could to see you cared for and protected."

"We both know that's just deluded."

"Yeah, well. Deluded or not, if we got married, he would still die happy."

"It feels so wrong to ask this of you."

"Hey." He waited until she tipped her head up and looked at him. "You haven't even asked yet and I'm already saying yes. Let's get married, Addie. Let's do it right away."

"I just keep thinking about what you said that night you told me about your ex-wife. You never planned to get married again."

"I also said that I was slowly realizing that never is a long, long time."

"Still…" She shook her head. "I hate doing this to you."

"You're not *doing* anything to me. Once, I planned never to get married again. But plans change and I'm going to get married *now*. To you. If you'll have me."

Her soft mouth trembled. "Yes, I will. Definitely. And thank you." She said it prayerfully.

"You're welcome." Trying to lighten the heavy mood, he teased, "Wait a minute. Was I too easy? Do you think I should probably be playing at least a little hard to get?"

"Oh, you…" She fake-punched him in the side and then cuddled back in close once more. "Just until he's better. And then we can, you know, get an annulment."

"However you want it." He rubbed his chin across the crown of her head.

She pulled away. He let her go reluctantly and she retreated to her side of the couch. "I've been thinking about it all afternoon," she said, "about how it would go if you agreed. If he does start recovering, the marriage will have to last for a couple of months—six weeks at the least. He needs time to get well enough that he can't just give up again and start fading away as soon as he finds out we called it off."

"Two months. It's a deal."

"We would have to live together and share a room for that time. I mean, he has to believe that it's the real thing, that we're really trying to make it work. When they let him out of the hospital, I would want you to move in with me at Red Hill. He'll want to be there. And I'll want to be with him."

"I get that. Living at Red Hill for two months is fine with me."

She made a sound midway between a chuckle and a sob. "I kind of think we're crazy to do this."

He didn't. "It's not the least crazy to be doing whatever you have to do to keep an old man you love alive."

She watched him so solemnly. "That's fine for me. He raised Carm and me on his own and he seemed to love doing it. I have a thousand precious, golden memories, all made because of him. Him rocking me, singing 'Down in the Valley' off-key to comfort me, when I was really small and had the flu. Him pushing me on the tire swing out behind the house. Teaching me to ride. Teaching me to drive…

"He gave us a happy childhood, James. I owe him everything. I can't stand for him to die when it's really not his time. I'm so angry at him now. I need him to live for years and years more so I can have time to forgive him for every wrong choice he's made since he conked you on the head a week ago."

"As I said, you love him. And I understand why you love him. Makes complete sense to me."

She chewed nervously on that soft lower lip of hers. "But *you*, on the other hand…"

"Hey, come on. I actually like Levi. And if this will

allow him to focus on getting well, I'm happy to do it." She still gazed at him with doubting eyes. He chided, "Look at yourself. Trying to talk me out of what I've already agreed to do."

She thought about that, tipping her head to the side, her thick, wavy hair tumbling down her arm, shining in the lamplight. "That wouldn't be so smart, would it?"

He shook his head slowly. "Let it be, Addie. We're doing it. We'll get the license first thing tomorrow, and then we'll go tell Levi that if he wants us married, we damn well expect him to stop all this idiocy and live." He didn't like the tortured expression on her face. "You still look worried."

"He's just so…weak, you know?"

"Damn it, Addie. Are you saying you don't think he'll last until tomorrow?"

She shuddered. "No. No, of course not. I called Carm an hour ago. She said there was no change."

He made the decision for her then. "Put some clothes on. We'll go and tell him right now."

"It's late…"

"In this case, Addie, I'm sure the nurses will let us in to see him."

Chapter Six

Twenty minutes later, Addie stood by Levi's bed in CSICU, with James at her side. The night staff had accepted their promise to keep things quiet and a nurse had pulled the privacy curtain shut around them—for their sake and for the sake of the other patients in the unit. The machines that kept track of her grandfather's slow slide toward a too-early end whooshed and beeped very softly around them and the green light from the heart monitor cast a cold glow across the bed.

Levi seemed to be sleeping.

But he opened his eyes when she bent close to kiss his forehead and smooth his dry white hair. "PawPaw," she whispered. As his eyes widened, she stood to her height and reached for James's hand.

His fingers closed around hers, warm and strong. So steady.

Levi blinked several times in rapid succession. The

sounds from the heart monitor sped up—but thankfully not enough to trigger an alarm.

James spoke then. "We came to tell you that Addie and I are getting married."

Addie said, "Tomorrow, we'll get the license."

Her grandfather shut his eyes. A slow sigh escaped him. "Good."

Addie wanted to grab on to him and hold him so he could never, ever slip away from her. She also wanted to shake him and shout at him for being such a stubborn and totally misguided old fool. But she did none of those things. She said, "As soon as you're moved to a regular room, we'll arrange for a pastor and get married right there."

"In my room?" A raspy, thin whisper.

"Yes. As soon as you're well enough to leave ICU."

He let out a dry, crackling sound. It took her a moment to realize it was a chuckle. "Namin' your terms, are you, Addie Anne?"

The truth was, if he didn't improve, they'd ask the nurses if they could get married right here in CSICU. It was all a big bluff. She and James had already agreed that her grandfather was going to get what he wanted. Even if it turned out to be nothing more than the answer to a dying man's last wish—or, in Levi's case, his last demand.

She said, "I am making you a promise, PawPaw. James and I *are* getting married. In your hospital room, as soon as you're out of CSICU."

Carm and Dev jumped to their feet when Addie and James came through the double doors.

Carm asked, "Well?"

"It's done," said Addie. "We told him. And I swear, he almost seems better already."

"Oh, I hope so." Carm grabbed her and hugged her. Then she took her by the shoulders and held her a little away. "I think we all need to go to the hotel and try to get some rest. I'll ask one of the nurses to call if there's any change."

Nobody argued. They were all beat. It was only a block to the hotel, and all three of their vehicles were in the hotel lot, so they walked. Outside, it was snowing. A springtime snow, light and wet, the kind that would be gone without a trace come morning. They wrapped their winter jackets tighter around them and hustled along at a brisk pace.

In the suite, Carm and Dev said good-night and went straight to their room.

James started to offer, "I can take the—"

"Don't even go there," she said wearily. "We're getting married, remember?"

"I just didn't want you to think I was taking advantage of you." He said it lightly, but she knew that he meant it.

She led the way to the bedroom and waited in the open doorway, shaking her head at him. "You're such a gentleman, James."

He crossed the room and dropped to the end of the bed. "A gentleman, huh? That sounds really boring."

"It's not." She shut the door and sagged back against it. "Not in the least."

He arched a thick eyebrow. "Which side do you want?"

Easy. "The one closer to the bathroom?"

"You got it." He crossed one foot over his knee and tugged off a boot. "Put on your pajamas. Let's get some sleep."

"Yes, dear." She dragged herself upright, grabbed the

Harley T-shirt and flannel jammie bottoms off the bedside chair and headed for the bathroom to change.

When she came back out, he took his turn, emerging in a pair of track pants and a dark blue T-shirt, brushing past her on the way to his side of the bed, trailing the minty scent of toothpaste.

They slid in under the covers and reached out simultaneously to turn off their bedside lamps.

"Good night, Addie."

"Night, James." She turned over on her side, closed her eyes and dropped off to sleep in an instant.

James woke to daylight, spooning Addie. And sporting wood. She smelled so good and felt so soft…

He could so easily get ideas.

Okay. He *had* ideas. Always had when it came to her. From that first day he met her, almost a year ago now, when he'd stood on the exact spot where he planned to build his dream house and she appeared in the distance on a gray mare. He'd watched her ride closer, liking what he saw. When she'd reached him, he'd introduced himself and asked her if she'd like a tour of his new house.

"What house?" She'd given him a look that was part wariness and part willingness to play his game.

"You're in the living room, you and your horse."

She swung down off the mare. He'd moved to help her, but she didn't need a man's help to dismount. Her booted feet were already on solid ground. "So it's an invisible house."

"It is now, but not for long."

She'd laughed at that. And then she'd listened intently, her hat down her back and her hair gleaming red-gold under the bright morning sun, as he showed her where each room would be.

In his arms now, she sighed but didn't stir. Was she still asleep? How awkward would it be if she woke up with him wrapped all around her?

He was seriously tempted to find out.

But then he thought about the day ahead of them, getting a license so they could proceed with their shotgun wedding. They were getting married to keep her crazy grandpa alive. Thinking about that kind of ruined the mood.

Very carefully, he pulled his arm from the sweet inward curve of her waist and eased himself back so their bodies were no longer touching.

Addie lay very still, her eyes closed, letting James think she was still sleeping as he slid away and out of the bed. He tiptoed around the end of it and she heard him go into the bathroom and slowly, quietly shut the door.

It had felt good. Right. To wake up with his body pressed to hers. As though that was how it *should* be, the two of them waking up together in the same bed.

Addie groaned, grabbed her pillow out from under her head and plunked it down on top of her face. They were going to spend the next two months or so in the same bed.

And she really needed not to be thinking how amazing it might be to simply let nature take its course.

But already she *was* thinking it.

She put her hand on her flat belly, thought about her tiny little tadpole of a baby swimming around in there. Having a baby without having any of the fun that *made* babies. How fair was that?

She groaned again, pressed the pillow down harder and told herself that no way was she planning to try to seduce James.

And that made her yank the pillow away and plunk

it down on top of the covers and press her hand to her mouth to keep from laughing out loud. She was totally losing it. All the stress and the worry of the past eight days had wrung the sanity clean out of her.

Because, dang it, if she was going to be married to a good, helpful, thoughtful, terrific and very hunky guy, well, why *shouldn't* she get all the benefits of being married to said guy? Even if the whole thing lasted for only eight weeks.

A marriage was a marriage, no matter how short.

James might be a total gentleman, but she really didn't think he'd take all that much seducing. They liked each other, had from the first. They *wanted* each other, even if she had spent the past several months trying to protect herself from the danger of falling for him and eventually finding out—as she always had before—that she'd fallen a lot harder and deeper than he had. She'd tried really hard to pretend she didn't feel the pull.

In the bathroom, she heard the shower start up. "Not going to do that," she said quietly to the ceiling. "Not going to make this situation any more complicated than it already is."

She frowned at the sound of her own voice. Did she sound the least convincing?

No, she did not.

James came out of the bathroom showered, shaved and fully dressed. Addie grabbed her clothes and traded places with him. When she came out, she found him on the couch in the living room, his laptop open on the coffee table in front of him.

He glanced up with a quick smile that did lovely things to all the most feminine parts of her. "I ordered room service. Should be here in fifteen minutes or so. Hope you can get some eggs down."

She realized she was starving. Strangely, when he was around, morning sickness tended to be less of a problem for her. "Eggs sound great." She glanced over and saw that the door to Carm and Dev's room stood open.

James caught the direction of her gaze. "They went back to the hospital."

Her heart rate spiked. "Is PawPaw okay?"

"Relax. There's no emergency. I told your sister we were getting the license first thing. She said that they would hold down the fort at the hospital while we took care of that. She promised to call you right away if there's anything you need to know about Levi."

"Sounds good."

He patted the sofa cushion. "Let me show you what I've found out."

She went and sat beside him. He smelled of soap and aftershave and she wanted to lean against him and have him wrap his arm around her. But then she saw what he'd pulled up on the laptop screen, and her stomach got a knot in it. "A marriage license form?"

"Colorado makes it easy. No blood tests. All you need is valid identification. We can go to the nearest clerk recorder's office—that's in Littleton, less than ten miles from here—and get the license on the spot. And we can make the process even faster if we fill out this form online before we go. Then we go to Littleton, we each produce ID, they bring up our completed form and the license is ours."

They were back at the hospital well before noon.

Addie ran to her sister. "How is he?"

"You won't believe this."

Her stomach turned over. "Oh, God. What now?"

Carm grabbed her and hugged her. "Hey. It's *good* news. He's sitting up. The nurses say he ate broth, a few diced, canned pears and a little bit of toast. He also participated fully for the first time in the session with the respiratory therapist. And he's asked that you and James go right in when you get here with the marriage license."

Levi was sitting up, wide-awake, when they went in. "Let me see it."

Addie longed to roll it into a tube and bop him on his obstinate head with it. But James handed it over.

Levi peered at it as though searching for flaws. But when he lifted his gaze to them, the blue eyes flashed with triumph. "Looks official to me. I'll be in a regular room by tomorrow—Thursday at the latest. Just see if I'm not. And Patty over there..." He gestured toward a nurse at the central nurses' station. She gave him a wink and a big smile. "Patty says they have pastors and priests on call to minister to the critically ill. She says it should be no problem getting a pastor to perform the ceremony in my regular room as soon as I get there."

"We looked into it already," Addie said defiantly. "In Colorado a couple can solemnize their own marriage. We thought we'd do that. It's as legal and binding as if you have a pastor or a judge do it."

"We're havin' none of that," snapped her grandfather. "I want a pastor and that means you're havin' one."

Oh, it was going to take a very long time for her to forgive him for all this. She considered calling him a very bad name. But then she felt James's fingers brushing the back of her hand. She grabbed on tight and said with quiet dignity, "All right, then. A pastor it is."

* * *

Two days later, at nine in the morning on Thursday, eleven days after Levi's heart attack, he was moved at last to his own hospital room. At two that afternoon, Addie and James stood in front of the smiling pastor at Levi's bedside.

James looked so handsome in his beautifully cut dark gray suit with an ice-blue tie. Addie wore a cream-colored lace dress that she and Carmen had bought at Nordstrom the day before. She carried a bouquet of bright Gerbera daisies. Okay, the marriage wouldn't last forever. But she and James had agreed they wanted to look their best when they stood up in front of the pastor.

Devin, who fooled around with photography in his spare time, had gone home Wednesday to check on things in Laramie. He'd brought back one of his digital cameras so he could take pictures of the simple bedside wedding.

Addie tried not to think how sad she would be later, when the two-month marriage was over, to look at the photos of her and James holding hands and repeating their vows. It might bring a tear or two, to see herself clutching her bright daisies, dressed in lace, facing the tall, broad-shouldered man she'd married—but was destined not to keep.

Did it surprise her when James produced a ring? Not really. They hadn't talked about getting one, but he'd spent the day before in Justice Creek, checking on his sister Elise and her friend, and catching up on work. At some point in his busy day, he'd taken time to choose a ring for her.

How like him to think of it—and then to make it happen.

It was a beauty, too. With a double halo of diamonds circling the wonderfully sparkly round central stone and channel-cut stones along the band. He slipped it on first and then the matching wedding band.

She knew he'd spent way too much on it and she almost whispered that he shouldn't have. But it was so beautiful. Why not simply be grateful and enjoy the moment? "Oh, James. And it's a perfect fit. How did you manage that?"

"I asked Carmen your ring size. She took a guess."

"She guessed right. I love it. I do."

The pastor cleared his throat.

Addie giggled. "Oh. Sorry. Carry on."

With a solemn nod, the minister instructed, "James Bravo, you may kiss your bride."

Addie was already looking up into his dark-fringed blue eyes, already feeling that she'd pretty much hit the jackpot as far as temporary husbands went.

And then James slowly smiled at her and she realized that it was actually happening: they were about to share their first kiss.

She stuck out her daisy bouquet and Carm took the hint and whipped it free of her hand.

James said her name, "Addie," softly, in that wonderful smooth, deep voice of his that sent little thrills of excitement pulsing all through her.

She said, "James," low and sweet, just for him. And she thought of the past three nights, of the two of them together in the hotel room bed. Of waking up each morning cuddled up close to him, of one or the other of them gently, reluctantly pulling away...

Okay, maybe it wasn't a *real* marriage. And it would be over as soon as her grandfather was back on his feet.

So what? It was probably as close to a real marriage as she was ever going to get. Her luck really stank when it came to love and forever. She had her mother's special talent for getting it wrong.

But "so what?" to all that, too. She had *this*, didn't she—a certain magic, a certain undeniable attraction to James? She'd spent months denying that attraction. Where had that gotten her?

No place fun, that was for sure.

And now, as he smiled down at her about to kiss her for the very first time, she made her decision.

If James agreed, tonight would be *their* night, a *real* wedding night. When morning came, neither of them would feel that they had to pull away.

So what if they weren't forever? Right now felt wonderful. Right now felt right. And if they *had* to be married for her crazy grandfather's sake, well, why shouldn't she and James enjoy the full range of benefits getting married was supposed to bring?

Addie lifted her face to James. His mouth still curving in that tender, sexy smile, he lowered his dark head to hers.

Chapter Seven

Jame's's lips brushed Addie's, so lightly, a caress and a question both at once. *More?* that kiss seemed to ask.

Longing moved within her. Heat flared across her skin.

Oh, yes, definitely. More.

With a sigh, she put her hands on the fine fabric of his suit, over the strong, hard contours of his deep chest. And then she slid them up to wrap around his neck.

He gathered her closer, his big arms tight around her. He smelled so good and he felt even better. And he tasted like a promise of good things to come.

She parted her lips under his and tasted him more deeply. *Yes*, she thought happily.

Or maybe she'd actually *said* it, maybe she'd kind of breathed the word into his beautiful, oh-so-kissable mouth. Because he lifted away a little and opened his eyes.

And the way that he looked at her…

Definitely. *Tonight*.

They could be as married as they wanted to be when they were alone. It might mess things up for an annulment and they'd end up having to get a divorce.

So what? Divorce or annulment, the end was the end.

He dipped his head to kiss her again and she waited expectantly, her mouth tipped up. But then her grandpa gave a thoroughly annoying raspy little chuckle. Totally wrecked the mood.

James heard that chuckle and arched an eyebrow at her. Reminded all over again of how angry she was at Levi, she pulled a face. He stepped back.

Carm and Dev moved in with hugs and congratulations.

After the pastor left, they all hung around in Levi's room.

James was thoroughly enjoying himself. Why shouldn't he be happy? He'd gotten a first kiss out of Addie. It made him grin to think that he'd had to marry her to get it.

Carmen went out briefly and came back with a cart on which sat a three-tiered wedding cake decked out in frosting flowers. It even had the bride and groom figures at the top beneath a miniature flower-bedecked arch.

Addie laughed. "A cake? You actually went out and ordered a cake?"

"Yes, I did," Carmen replied proudly. "There's a bakery just down the street."

Addie's face betrayed the conflict inside her. James understood. She didn't want to give her grandfather the satisfaction of having a good time at the wedding the old coot had forced on her.

But she *was* having a good time. Her very kissable mouth kept trying to pull into a smile, and that dimple kept tucking itself into her sweet, round left cheek.

In the end, her good nature won out over her anger with Levi. She threw her arms around Carmen and planted a loud kiss on her cheek. "You are the best sister I ever had."

"You bet I am—now get over here, the two of you, and cut this cake. Dev, get the camera ready."

James and Addie mugged for the camera and fed each other the cake and then cut the whole thing into slices so that everyone—the nurses, the clerks, the candy stripers, everyone—could have a slice if they wanted one.

Carmen tried to stop them when they started cutting up the top tier. "You're supposed to freeze that for your first anniversary."

Levi, who was looking healthier by the second and way too pleased with himself, piped up with "Good thinkin'."

Addie ignored her grandfather. Instead, she sidled up close to her sister and whispered something in her ear. James had no trouble guessing what. Something along the lines of *What first anniversary?*

Whatever she said, Carmen pretended to pout. "Just getting into the spirit of things."

"Right." Addie pulled off the little bride and groom and their plastic floral arch, licked the frosting off the base, plunked them down on a paper plate and got busy cutting up the top tier.

The cake was rich and white, with a jam and custard center. Everybody at the nurses' station and up and down the hall wanted some. By the time they were through, there was nothing left but crumbs.

Eventually, at a little after four, the nurses shooed them out so they could look after Levi and make sure he got up and walked around a bit. They all—Addie, Carmen,

Dev and James—decided they were starving, even after all that cake.

So the four of them went out for dinner. James drove. He took them to his favorite steak house downtown, which was just opening its doors for the dinner crowd. James passed the maître d' a fifty and they got a cozy table in a quiet corner. He ordered champagne.

Dev raised a laughing toast. "To the healing power of marriage."

They all laughed at that, even Addie. Marriage—his and Addie's—did seem to be damn good for Levi's health.

Actually, Addie seemed downright happy. James was glad. He'd half expected her to endure their hasty wedding and the aftermath with a grim expression and possibly a couple of quick trips to the ladies' room, because the stress of this whole situation tended to bring on her morning sickness.

But no. She was taking it in stride.

And that kiss—the one that sealed their destined-to-be-short-lived vows, the first kiss he'd ever shared with her?

She'd really gotten into that kiss. The way she'd gazed up at him before and after, well, that look had been something he wouldn't soon forget.

That look had him wondering if tonight was going to be a *real* wedding night.

Was that just wishful thinking?

He hoped not. He'd waited a long time to get Addie in bed—and now that he'd gotten her there the past three nights, well, could anyone blame him for fantasizing about how fine it would be to do more than just sleep with her?

But whatever happened when they were alone together

later, getting married to Addie, even temporarily, was a lot of fun. She might get him even hotter than Vicki did—but that was the only similarity he could find between his first and second wives.

Addie had a big heart. And when she wasn't seething in fury at her grandfather, she was funny and open and easy to be with. She never tried to control him or tell him what to do the way Vicki used to—well, except for the day of Levi's heart attack, when she had been constantly trying to send him on his way.

She really didn't seem to want to get rid of him anymore. He decided to take that as a positive sign.

When they were ready to leave the restaurant, he had to practically wrestle Devin to claim the check. But he pulled rank, being the groom and all. He paid the tab and they returned to the hospital, where they all went in to see Levi one more time that night.

Addie's granddad was cheerful and talkative. He had some color in his cheeks again. James smiled at the sound of that cackling laugh of his. If James's marrying Addie had done that for the old miscreant, it was more than worth it as far as James was concerned.

Levi said that the day had been one of the best of his life. "Because my girls are both married at last, I got two great-grandkids and another on the way. And it looks like I'll live, after all."

Addie got kind of quiet then. James knew, by the way she pressed her lips together and avoided looking at Levi directly, that she remained angry with him for what he'd made her do.

And Levi, being Levi, just couldn't leave it alone. "Addie Anne, stop lookin' like you sucked a giant lemon and give your old PawPaw a hug."

Silence. The old man and the pretty woman in the white lace dress stared each other down.

Carmen cleared her throat. "Go on, Addie. Give him a hug."

Addie made a scoffing noise, but then she did step up closer to Levi's bed, pressed her round cheek to his wrinkled one and then kissed him on the forehead. "I love you, PawPaw," she said in a whisper as grim as her expression.

For once, Levi had sense enough to leave it at that.

At a little after eight, Carmen insisted that the newlyweds should go back to the hotel. "Dev and I will be along eventually—don't wait up, though. I'm not sure how late we'll be."

Devin frowned. "I was kind of thinking we might— Ouch!" He sent Carmen a wounded glance. James couldn't be sure, because he and Addie were on the other side of Levi's bed from Addie's sister and Devin, but it appeared that Carmen had kicked him to get his attention. Devin coughed into his fist and added, "You know what? Forget what I was thinking. You two go ahead."

James waited for Addie to object—and for Levi to make some joking comment that would get Addie angry all over again.

But Addie just said, "Good idea. James, you ready to go?" She held out her hand. James took it happily. How long had he waited for her to reach for his hand?

Too long.

She bent to the bed and gave her grandfather one last kiss.

The old man looked over her bright head and directly at James. "Proud to have you in the family, son." He seemed completely sincere.

James felt a stab of guilt that they weren't giving Levi the marriage he'd bargained for. But really, why feel guilty for disappointing a master manipulator? James tamped down the self-reproach and answered, "Thanks, Levi. I'm a lucky, lucky man."

Addie laughed. It was a carefree sound. James drank it in, loving it, loving that she held his hand as tightly as he held hers. "Let's go." She pulled him through the door and out into the hallway.

It was snowing again, but he'd left the quad cab in the underground hospital lot, so they took it back to the hotel.

In their room, she ushered him ahead, shut and locked the door and followed him over to the side of the turned-back bed. She caught his hand and then gazed up at him, her cheeks flushed the prettiest pink.

He dared to reach out and cradle her face with his free hand. Her scent teased him—flowery, a little tart, wonderfully sweet. "You're a beautiful bride."

She sighed. Her breath smelled like apples, like the cinnamon tea she'd had after dinner. "We shared our first kiss today." She said it softly, almost shyly.

He couldn't help smiling. He rubbed the back of his fingers along the silky side of her neck. That brought another sigh. He was becoming more and more certain that tonight would be a night he would never forget—the kind of night he'd given up on ever having with her. "I knew I would love the taste of your mouth. And I do."

She trembled a little. "I...well, I always told myself that I was never going to kiss you."

"I'm so glad you changed your mind." He traced the line of her thick red-gold hair, where it fell along her plump cheek.

"I don't know. It never seemed safe to kiss you."

"Because I'm such a dangerous guy?" He ran his index

finger down the slope of her pert little nose, loving the way it turned up at the tip. The texture of her skin pleased him immensely, so soft, so smooth, just begging for his touch.

Those amber eyes looked enormous right then. Huge and shining, staring up at him. "You are dangerous to me."

"We should talk about that."

"Maybe someday—and it's not that I haven't wanted to kiss you. I have wanted to. So much. For such a very long time."

"We have a lot of missed kisses to make up for."

She shocked him by agreeing. "We do. And I have a question."

"Shoot."

"There's a tiny white scar." With a finger she brushed the tip of his chin. "Here. How did you get it?"

"School-yard brawl with my half brother Quinn," he said. "We had issues, back then, in the family, what with my father essentially having two wives—my mother, Sondra, and Quinn's mom, Willow."

Addie nodded. "That must have been hard on you— all of you." She didn't ask him to explain any of it, and he wasn't surprised. Pretty much everyone in Justice Creek had heard the old story.

He said, "When we were kids, we resented each other, and we took sides. My mom's kids against Willow's kids."

"Even though what your parents did wasn't their children's fault?"

"We had to get older and wiser to figure that out. In the meantime, when we were kids, sometimes we boys argued with our fists."

"But you all get along now?"

"Yeah, we do. I like my family a lot."

"I'm glad. Family matters."

"It certainly does." He traced the perfect shape of her ear and then caught her earlobe and rubbed it gently between his thumb and forefinger. She wore pearl studs, and the single pearl felt so hard and smooth against his thumb, in contrast to the velvety texture of her skin. He let himself imagine touching her all over, tracing every curve, pressing his lips to her most secret places.

Making her moan for him.

Making her beg.

She started to say something.

He interrupted her. "Kiss me again. Do it right now."

She caught her lower lip between her small, straight teeth. "I want to kiss you. I want to do *more* than kiss you."

"I'm up for that." Oh, yes, he was. Already. Just from the feel of her skin and the look in her eyes and the shy, sexy way she called him dangerous.

"It's just that I…well, I didn't plan ahead." Her cheeks, already flushed, went deep red. "No condoms. And yeah, I'm already pregnant. But babies aren't the only thing that should be considered. I believe in safe sex—I mean, if a person is going to have sex. I just, well, I didn't realize how I would feel now, alone with you, you know? How much I would want us to have a real wedding night, after that wedding kiss, after standing up beside you in front of that pastor, after all of it, everything you've done, James. All the ways you've been about the best guy I've ever known."

Her words made an ache in the center of his chest to match the one growing beneath his fly. He pressed his hand to her cheek. Burning hot with her blush. Beautiful. "I bought some yesterday."

Impossible, but her eyes got even wider. "You did?"

"After I bought the ring, I stopped in at a Walgreens. I didn't really think it would happen. But I knew I'd be an idiot not to be ready if it did."

She actually giggled. "I guess that makes me an idiot."

"No way. How could you plan ahead? You only made up your mind about this today."

"See?" She pointed her finger at the tip of his nose. "That. You are always doing that. Saying just the right thing when you really don't have to."

He caught her pointing finger and kissed the tip of it. "I guess I should just accept my own wonderfulness."

"Yes, you should—and if you bought them, where are they?"

He pressed his lips to the back of her hand. "In my briefcase."

"Go get them."

"You sure you'll be all right if I leave you here alone?"

She leaned up, brushed a kiss against his jaw and whispered, "You should hurry. I'm very impatient."

He swooped to catch her mouth and succeeded, if only briefly. "Don't move."

"I won't. Go."

His soft briefcase was braced against the wall by the door. He went to it, unzipped the center pocket, took out the box and brought it right back to her, dropping it on the nightstand and reaching for her.

She laughed and stepped back. "Not so fast."

"Bossy woman."

A slow, naughty smile. "Take off your jacket."

He did, tossing it onto the bedside chair. "My turn."

She looked at him from under the fringe of dark eyelashes. "We're taking turns?"

"It's only fair. Take off that dress."

Now she fluttered those eyelashes at him. "I might need help with the zipper."

"Turn around."

She did, showing him her back, smoothing her hair out of his way. Stepping right up, he took that zipper down and then couldn't resist pressing his mouth to the sweet bump at the top of her spine, causing her to suck in a sharp breath that proved all over again she was every bit as into this as he was. She pulled her arms free of the snug lace sleeves.

"Don't," he said.

She stopped. "Don't what?"

"I want to see you."

She faced him again. "Like this?" At his nod, she took the dress down to her waist and then wiggled it off over her hips. It dropped around her ankles. She bent and scooped it up.

"Give it to me." She handed it over and he dropped it on top of his jacket.

Now she stood before him in her shoes and white satin bra and lacy panties. And nothing else. Except for her earrings, a thin gold necklace and a lacy blue garter. She must have noted the direction of his gaze, because she pointed at the garter. "Something blue. I bought it when I bought the dress—which makes the dress something new." She touched the delicate gold chain around her neck. "I borrowed this from Carmen. And the pearl earrings are Carm's, too. They're also old. They were my grandmother's."

He reminded himself that they were married only because Levi had forced them into it, that she was having another guy's baby and they'd agreed that they'd be together for only two months. Still, he was an old-fashioned guy at heart. It pleased him no end to think of her finding a way to observe a few wedding traditions.

"It's my turn, James." That adorable dimple tucked itself into her soft cheek.

"Don't rush me." He took his time admiring her, from the top of her strawberry head to the tips of her high-heeled shoes. So curvy and strong. "Perfect in every way."

"Thank you. And at this rate, we'll be getting un-dressed all night long."

That didn't sound like a bad idea to him at all. "What next?" he asked with real enthusiasm.

"Your shoes and socks and tie *and* your shirt."

He didn't argue, just jumped on one foot and then the other, getting rid of his shoes and socks. Off went the tie to join the clothes already on the chair. A minute later, the shirt landed there, too. "Shoes," he instructed.

She took them off and ordered, "Belt and pants."

He got rid of those and remarked with a groan, "Now I'm getting eager."

Her gaze wandered down to the front of his boxer briefs, and her smile brightened the dim corners of the lamp-lit room. "I can see that."

He commanded, "Bra, panties, garter."

"I will be naked," she warned and shook a finger at him.

"Looking forward to that."

Swiftly, with deft, no-nonsense movements that left his mouth dry and his body yearning, she reached be-hind her and undid the bra clasp, slipping the straps off her pretty shoulders and tossing the bit of satin at the chair. Damn. Her breasts were so pretty, round and full, tipped in soft pink the same color as her lips. Had his mouth gone dry a moment ago? No more. Now he was practically drooling. She slid down her panties, taking the garter with them, and kicked both away.

That did it. He couldn't live another second without having his hands on her. "Come here." He reached for her.

She danced back, giggling. "Boxer briefs."

He didn't argue, just eased them over the part of him that was aching to get to her and shoved them off and away. "Come here."

She put her hands to her red cheeks. "Oh, James. You are handsome all over."

"I said, come here."

"And you keep calling *me* bossy." She took off the gold chain and the earrings and set them on the nightstand. "There."

He couldn't wait another second to get his hands on her, so he grabbed for her. That time, she let him catch her. Hauling her close, he pressed his mouth to her temple and breathed in the wonderful, sweet scent of her hair, drank in the feel of her silky skin pressing all along the front of him. Nothing had ever felt so good as Addie naked in his arms.

She wrapped her arms around him, held him as hard and tight as he was holding her. And she whispered, her breath warm against his shoulder, "I don't care what happens, how it all ends up. Because tonight I'm just…so glad. Glad that we're right here, right now, you and me…"

He captured her chin and tipped her face up. Lowering his mouth to hers, he kissed her deeply as he guided her down to the bed.

She went willingly, clinging to his shoulders, her tongue meeting his, wrapping around it, eager and shy at once.

He stroked a hand down the center of her. So much to touch. He could never, ever get enough.

But damned if he wasn't determined to try. He captured one sweet, round breast, teasing it, rubbing the pink nipple between his thumb and forefinger, drinking in her moan as she lifted her body up for him, offering him everything he'd thought never to hold.

He kept on kissing her as his touch strayed lower, into the hollow just under her rib cage, her skin softer than ever there. And down, over her belly all the way to the neatly trimmed dark gold curls at the juncture of her strong thighs.

She cried out when he parted her. He dipped a finger into her slick heat. He drank her cry as he touched her, stroking her, loving the way her body moved for him, the way she lifted into his touch.

He wanted to taste her everywhere. So he let his mouth follow the path his hands had blazed, down and down. Gently, he guided her, lifting one sleek leg and easing under it, until he could settle between her open thighs.

"James?" she asked, a little nervously. "James, are you sure you want to…?"

"Shh," he said. "I do, yes. I do…"

With a sigh, she surrendered.

And he kissed the sweet feminine heart of her. She tasted just right, salty and musky, so slick and so wet. He took his time with her, driving her higher, until she clutched his head and called his name as she went over.

After that, well, yeah, he was eager, hurting even, to plunge into her softness. But some things in life should be done right. This, his first time with Addie?

This fell cleanly into the "do it right" category.

He kissed his way back up her body, turned her to face him and gathered her tightly to him, with both of them on their sides. She reached down between them and wrapped her fingers around him.

"You do that, no telling what will happen," he warned in a growl.

She pressed a sweet, hot kiss to the base of his throat, sticking out her naughty tongue and licking up the sweat that clung to his skin. "I love this, touching you. I've waited way too long to do this."

He groaned in approval—and then couldn't resist razzing her a little. "Why *did* you wait so long?"

"I've had enough man trouble in my life. I was determined not to go there again." She wrapped her fingers tighter around him.

Tight enough she made him groan again. He breathed carefully through his nose and cradled her cheek in his palm. "What do you mean, exactly, by man trouble? You never say."

She tried to look away. "Never mind."

He eased his thumb beneath her chin, holding her sweet face in place, waiting until she looked at him again. Then he said, "Whoever it was, just tell me. I'll bust his face in for you."

She made a disapproving sound. "Really? Seriously? You want to talk about that now?" And then she stroked that hand of hers up and down the length of him, holding on wonderfully tight as she did it.

What were they talking about? He forgot. He forgot everything but her name. "Addie..."

"Shh." She slowed her hand, rubbing, rotating her grip as she caressed him. It was pure agony, but in such a good way.

In the end, he had to grab her wrist and hold her still. "This first time, I want to be with you. I want to be in you..."

She pressed her lips to his throat, to his jaw, and finally she took his mouth, spearing her hot little tongue in, making him groan deep and hard, and then pulling back enough to gaze into his eyes as she continued to stroke him with that determined, clever hand. "However you want it, James, that's how it will be."

"I love it when you pretend to be obedient."

"As long as we're clear that it's only pretend." She kissed him again.

He felt her smile against his mouth and advised, "So, then, in the interest of my not losing it too soon, I think you should maybe let go of me…"

She made a low, purring sort of sound deep in her throat. "Not a chance." And then she gave him a cruel, hard little squeeze that brought another groan up from the deepest part of him. "But I'll be careful not to push you too far."

He gritted his teeth, it felt so good. "You have no idea how close I am to losing it."

"But you won't lose it, will you?"

He never ought to argue with her. It never got him anywhere. With another groan, he reached across her beautiful, naked body and snatched the box off the nightstand. One-handed, he flipped back the lid and whipped out what they needed. "Help."

She took pity on him, letting go of his aching hardness and taking the box from him. She set it back on the nightstand and then took the still-wrapped condom. "Lie back. I've got this."

With a shaky sigh, he rolled to his back.

She unwrapped the condom and carefully rolled it down over him. "There," she said with a pleased little smile.

"Addie." He reached up and clasped her shoulders.

She met his eyes with the softest little smile. "What?"

"Ride me."

For once, she didn't argue, just swung one of those muscled horsewoman's thighs across his hips, lifted herself up onto her knees above him and then reached down to put him right where she wanted him.

"Addie," he whispered, dying a little in the best kind of way. "At last."

She really was something. He'd waited so long for this, to see her like this, bare and open to him, lost in her pleasure. On her knees above him, golden eyes watching him, baby-doll lips parted, her breath coming shallow and fast, she lowered her body down to him, taking him, all of him, in a sweet, perfect glide.

Tight. Hot. Wet.

So exactly what he wanted, so completely right.

"James?" A sweet flush suffused the soft skin above her breasts. With a moan, she came down to him, her body curving over him, settling against his chest, her hair falling forward, brushing his throat, sliding like ribbons of satin along his arms. "Oh, James. Oh, my goodness…"

He gathered her close. Never in his life had he been anywhere sweeter than buried in Addie on their wedding night. "There's no one like you, Addie. No one in the whole world…"

"It's good," she whispered. "James, it's so good with you…"

And then she was kissing him, her mouth wet and open over his, her hair so silky and warm all around him, her body taking him, holding him, owning him, so good and deep.

Making him crazy in the best kind of way.

He groaned her name. She gave his back to him.

And then he slid his hands down and took hold of her fine, round bottom. He surged up into her.

She shouted his name then, out good and loud. And then she was riding him, hard and fast, racing to the finish. He held on and went with it, with her, as he felt her body tightening, reaching...

And then it happened, both of them going still, not even breathing. Until she cried out again—and unraveled around him, her inner muscles contracting, releasing and then clutching him tight once more.

That did it. He couldn't hold out a single second longer.

He rolled, taking her with him, claiming the top position. Another cry escaped her, a softer cry. And yet somehow a wilder one, too.

She lifted her legs and wrapped them around him.

By then, he was gone, lost in her, lost in the searing heat that set the air on fire between them, in the connection they shared that she'd denied for so long.

But not tonight. Tonight she had no denials. Tonight she belonged to him. At last.

James and Addie. Like this.

The way he'd always dreamed they might be.

He buried his face against her throat and gave himself up to her, pushing hard into her, so far gone in her that nothing else existed. There was only Addie, holding him. Addie, whispering naughty, sexy things.

Addie, moaning his name again as the world spun away.

Chapter Eight

"A home nurse?" Levi sucked in a breath of pure outrage and then groaned because it hurt his incision. Addie could almost feel sorry for him. Except that, as usual, he was being a major pain in the butt. "Don't be ridiculous," he barked. "I don't need a nurse and we don't need to go wasting good money on one—and, son…" He turned to James with another groan of pain. "Do you have to hit every damn bump in the highway? You're killing me here."

"Sorry," James answered mildly. "I'll watch that."

Levi groaned yet again and shifted uncomfortably, pulling on the seat belt to loosen it up a little.

It was exactly a week since Addie had married James. They were on their way home to Red Hill at last—James, Levi and Addie in James's roomy quad cab. Levi had the passenger seat, where they'd thought he'd be the most comfortable, and Addie had taken a seat in back.

Somewhere on the highway not too far behind them, Carmen followed in Addie's old pickup. Dev had returned to Laramie a few days before.

James caught Addie's eye in the rearview mirror. Was that an "I told you so" look he was giving her? It certainly appeared to be. He'd thought they should tell her grandfather about the nurse sooner. She'd vetoed that. Levi wasn't going to like it, no matter when they told him, so she'd decided to do it during the ride home, thus limiting at least the duration of the fit he was bound to pitch over the idea of paying a professional to help with his recovery.

Addie narrowed her eyes at her temporary husband to signal that she had this handled; she knew what she was doing. She told her grandfather, "It's not going to cost us anything. We have the best insurance money can buy, thanks to Brandon—you remember Brandon, PawPaw? My sadly departed best friend and the father of my baby? Brandon wanted us to have really good insurance for the baby's sake and also because when something terrible happens to someone you love, the last thing you need is to be stewing over how to pay for high-quality care."

Levi exchanged a glance with James. They'd been doing that a lot in the past few days, silently communicating their manly thoughts, whatever the heck those were. Sometimes she found it kind of sweet that they got along so well.

Right now she wanted to tell them both to knock it off.

Levi blew right on by her pointed remarks about Brandon and the baby and insisted, "I can take care of myself."

"But a trained nurse can take care of you even better. And that's what you're getting. You're getting the best care."

"You just tell that nurse not to come."

"She's already moved in at Red Hill."

Levi made a sputtering noise followed by more grunts of pain.

Addie said, "Her name is Lola Dorset. She's a retired RN. She will see that you take your meds and eat right. She will supervise your exercises, all of them, strength, cardio *and* breathing. She'll get you out walking but not let you overdo it. She'll be helping you bathe and making sure you take proper care of your incision sites."

"My incision sites are doing just fine, thank you. And no strange woman is going to be giving me baths."

Addie suppressed a sigh. "Strange women—and men—bathed you in the hospital there at first when you refused to start getting well. You weren't complaining about it then. And Lola is only there to help. Whatever you can manage for yourself, fine. But she will be ready to push you when you need it, to offer encouragement, too. She'll be all about you for the next six weeks, at least—with a little help from a relief nurse two days a week and evenings whenever Lola wants time to herself. You need someone who's all about you right now, and we were lucky to get Lola. She only takes a few jobs a year now. And when she chooses to work, she doesn't mind living in. As a matter of fact, James found her for you."

Her grandfather scowled in James's direction and accused, "So you're in on this, too?"

James gave an easy shrug and evaded the question. "Lola looked after my great-aunt Agnes when Agnes had hip surgery two years ago."

Addie added, "Lola is about as good as it gets for home nursing care, PawPaw. You should be grateful that she's going to be looking after you."

"*Grateful* is not the word that comes to mind," grumbled Levi. "*Unnecessary.* That's the word for your precious

Lola. How many ways do I have to say it? We don't need her. You and Carmen can—"

Addie cut him off. "Carm has a life, in case you didn't notice. And she needs to get back to it today. Both she and Dev have used up their family leave. She misses her kids—and she misses her husband, too, now he had to go home and get back to work."

"Humph," her grandfather said. "You and me and James will manage just fine."

"No. No, we will not. James has an office he needs to go to now and then. And I have a mountain of scarecrow orders to catch up on. I also have the horses to look after, not to mention all the chores you won't be doing for a while yet. It's a critical time in your recovery and you need a professional to help you make the most of it. Lola Dorset will be seeing to it that you get exactly what you need."

Silence from the front seat. Apparently, she'd actually managed to overrule all of his objections.

Did she feel like a bully? Oh, well, maybe a little. But sometimes, with her grandfather, bullying was the only way to go.

James caught her eye in the mirror. She scowled at him defiantly. For her sour face, he gave her a wink.

The guy was a prize. No doubt about it. Supportive, smart, funny and kind. Also easy on the eyes and amazing in bed. Every day it got a little harder to remember not to let herself get too attached.

Lola, a trim woman with chin-length silvery hair and excellent posture, was waiting on the front porch when they drove up. Two days ago, when Addie had met her here at the house to give her a set of keys and show her around, the nurse had asked what the family would prefer her to wear. Addie had advised comfortable street clothes. So today, Lola wore new-looking jeans, white running shoes and a long-sleeved Henley shirt.

Addie's dog, Moose, sat at the nurse's feet. Walker McKellan had dropped him off just that morning. The dog ran to greet them, but the nurse stayed where she was.

With a glad cry, Addie shoved open the backseat door. "Moosey boy, I've missed you so much."

The sweet chocolate Lab bounced up on his hind legs with excitement and let out a bark, then remembered his manners and dropped to sitting position. A shudder of pure happiness wiggled through him and he whined for her to get down there and say hi.

Addie jumped from the cab and dropped to a knee. "That's my good boy…" She threw her arms around him, breathed in his dusty doggy smell and let him swipe his wet tongue across her cheek. "We're home," she whispered gratefully into his short brown coat. "Home at last…"

James got out and came around to her. When Moose gave him a whine of greeting, he patted the dog on the head.

Levi pushed open his door. "Ah. It's good to be home." He sounded happy, too, in spite of the recent battle over Lola and whatever pain the ride home had caused him. Addie's heart lifted to hear him sound so cheerful. Then he muttered, "That her?" and tipped his wiry white head in Lola's direction.

Lola must have heard him. She came down the steps. "Yes, Mr. Kenwright. I'm Lola, your nurse." That silvery hair really shone in the sunlight. She gave him a cool smile as she strode confidently toward him.

He already had the seat belt undone and he swung

his legs out. Addie stifled a nervous cry for him to be careful.

James simply stepped into position so that Levi could brace an arm on his shoulder to ease his way down. It was gracefully done, with zero fanfare. Just the way her grandfather liked it. "Thanks, son."

"Anytime." James reached into the cab and pulled out the cane they'd bought him a few days before. "Here you go."

Levi took it with a nod and leaned on it gratefully.

Lola marched right up to him and slipped her hand around his free arm. "Walk me inside, will you? Let me show you how we've set things up."

"Take it slow," he replied, sounding perfectly content—as if he hadn't just given Addie all kinds of grief for hiring the woman. "Some fool doctor cut my chest open two weeks ago and I'm not as spry as I used to be."

Lola laughed. It was an easy, throaty sound. "One step at a time."

Levi actually smiled. "That's the way you do it." Slowly, the two of them started for the house. "You call me Levi," Addie heard him say when they were almost to the steps.

"Levi it is."

James, who was standing right behind Addie, put his big hands on her hips and whispered in her ear, "I told you she was something else."

"Amazing. She's got a real talent with grumpy old men."

"And with bossy old women, too. Have you met my great-aunt Agnes? She can be difficult, to put it mildly, but she took to Lola on sight." He pressed a kiss into her hair.

She started to lean back against him, because then

he would wrap his arms around her and that always felt wonderful. But right then, Carm rolled into the yard and stopped the pickup a few feet from James's quad cab. Reluctantly, Addie suggested, "We should get our suitcases inside so Carm can be on her way back to Laramie."

He made a sound of agreement and let go of her waist. They turned together to get the bags that waited under the camper shell.

He handed her the one that belonged to Levi. "I'll take your suitcase and mine upstairs."

She thought about sharing her bedroom with him for the next several weeks and liked the idea way more than she probably should. It was altogether too much fun playing newlyweds with James. "We're the big room at the front. Turn left at the top of the stairs, left again at the end of that hall and it's the only door on your left. I'll get up there this afternoon and clear you out some drawers and closet space. You can put your stuff away this evening."

He held her gaze, a lovely, intimate look that sent hot little sparks dancing across the surface of her skin. "Sounds like a plan."

Way back in the day, when Levi had married Addie's grandmother June, he'd bumped out walls and added on a master suite for his new bride. The large bedroom, bath and walk-in closet were on the ground floor off the central hall. Now, all these years later, the suite was a godsend for Levi's recovery. He wouldn't be stuck upstairs most of the time, or have to make a temporary bedroom of one of the downstairs living areas.

Addie had given Lola the upstairs bedroom that faced the backyard. It was closest to the stairs. The nurse had brought handheld monitors—a two-way system. Not only could she hear if Levi needed her, but she could communicate with him, find out what he needed without having to run down to his room first.

Also, they'd replaced Levi's old four-poster with a fully adjustable recliner bed that would not only be more comfortable, but would be easier for him to get in and out of, too. When Addie carried his suitcase in there, Lola had him on the bed and was showing him how to work the controller.

"I like this bed," he was saying as he raised himself slowly to a sitting position. "I could get used to this."

"It's a nice one," Lola agreed. "I think you'll be very comfortable."

About then, Levi spotted Addie. "I took a peek in the kitchen. Who fixed the floor?"

Addie set down the suitcase in the corner by the door to deal with later. "James's brother Garrett sent some people over." James had asked her the morning after their wedding if it was all right to hire Garrett to fix the floor—and to install up-to-code grab bars for Levi in the master bath while he was at it. Addie had given the go-ahead. She'd also insisted that she wanted the bill sent to her. So far, that bill had failed to materialize. She made a mental note to remind James that she would pay for both the floor repair and the bath railings, thank you very much.

"Looks good," the old man said cheerfully. "I like the new tile." As though it had been some everyday home improvement project. He gave Lola a distinctly cheeky grin. "I had a little accident cleaning my shotgun."

Lola was sympathetic. "That must have been scary."

Addie couldn't resist grumbling, "You have no idea," as she left them alone.

Back out in front, Moose trailed after her down the

steps. She found the back of the quad cab still open. Only Carmen's suitcase and overnight bag remained inside. They'd already agreed that James would drive Carm into town, where she could pick up a rental car and head for home. Addie closed up the back and turned for the house as James came down the front steps.

"Everything's in," he said. "I like those two dormer windows in your bedroom, with those cozy window seats."

She nodded. "That used to be Carm's room when we were kids. I got it when she married Dev. Hated to see her go—but loved getting her room."

He came closer and guided a few strands of hair out of her eyes. She gazed up at him, thinking how good it felt to be close to him, how great they got along. More than once in the past few days, she almost forgot that by the end of May, they wouldn't be married anymore. "Where's Carm?"

"I think she's saying goodbye to your grandfather." With a sweet brush of his finger, he traced her eyebrows and then the shape of her nose, thrilling her with those simple, silly caresses, and then slid his warm fingers back under her hair to cradle the nape of her neck.

"What are you up to now?" She tried to sound suspicious, but somehow it came out all breathless and hopeful.

"I'm off to work for the rest of the day. Any reason I shouldn't kiss my wife goodbye?"

"No reason at all." She lifted her lips to him and he settled his wonderful mouth over hers.

Time and reality faded off into nothing. There was only the two of them in that hazy, hot, beautiful place they went to whenever they touched.

Oh, she had a mad and crazy crush on him. She kept trying to remember all the reasons they shouldn't get too close, all the ways love and romance never had worked out for her.

But somehow, when he touched her, when he kissed her, whenever he was near, she forgot her bad track record with the male gender, forgot how, after the last time two years ago with Donnie Jacobs, who had sworn that he loved her and wanted forever with her one night and then told her the next night that they were through, she'd finally accepted that romance was just a bad idea for her. She took love way too seriously and she always ended up with her heart cut to ribbons.

She and James should probably talk about that, about how they had to watch themselves, not let things get too intense. They both needed to remember that this wasn't forever.

But then again, just because *she* kept forgetting that this wasn't the real thing, that didn't mean *he* was having any problem keeping his grip on reality.

And please. Did they *really* need to go there, to talk about all the reasons they shouldn't let themselves get carried away?

Why make everything heavy and grim? Why not just enjoy themselves for the time they had together? Too soon, it would be over and she would be big as a house with the baby. And then she'd be a mom, with a newborn to care for. Beautiful, sexy nights like the ones she shared with James right now would be pretty hard to come by.

Why shouldn't they wring every drop of pleasure out of this marriage PawPaw had forced on them? Why not think of it as a fabulous, smokin'-hot fling, and leave it at that?

"What is it with you two? Like a couple of newly-weds," Carmen teased. Somehow she'd come all the way down the front steps and out to the quad cab without Addie noticing.

James broke the kiss, but he didn't let go of her. He wrapped an arm around her waist and drew her close to his side. "Don't know what it is about this woman. Can't seem to keep my hands off her."

"I noticed." Carm held out her arms. "Gotta go."

Addie slipped free of James's embrace to hug her sister goodbye. "I'm so sorry you had to stay so long, but I'm so glad you came. And Dev, too. Give him my love, and tell the kids that Auntie Addie will see them soon."

"I will." Carm stepped back. "You need us, you call. Don't you dare hesitate."

"I won't."

Carm looked toward the ranch house. "I have a feeling PawPaw's going to be okay now."

"Me, too."

"And I really like Lola. She's smart and funny and she won't take any crap off him."

Addie grinned at that. "I think you're right."

Carm turned to James. "Ready?"

He pulled open the front passenger door and Carmen got in. "I'll be back by six or so," he promised, those blue eyes warm as a summer sky. "You want me to bring takeout?"

She shook her head. "I bought groceries Tuesday when I got Lola settled in. We're having roast chicken, baked sweet potatoes and green salad, totally heart healthy for PawPaw's sake."

He hooked his hand around her neck again and pulled her close for another kiss. "You are an ideal granddaughter."

"Tell PawPaw that."

"I have. And you just might be the perfect wife."

"Call me amazing. Go right ahead."

"Amazing." He whispered it. The sound reached out and touched her in all her most hungry, sensitive places.

She kissed him. It started out as a light, brushing caress. But it just felt so good. With a sigh, she wrapped her arms around his neck and deepened the contact.

Inside the quad cab, Carm tapped on the passenger window. *Knock it off,* she mouthed. *Let's go.*

James kissed her once more, quick and sweet, for good measure, then went around and climbed up behind the wheel.

Addie stood waving, Moose at her side, until the pickup rounded the first curve on the way to the highway.

Then she turned to her dog. "Lots to do." Moose tipped his head to the side and whined in doggy under-standing. "Come on. We'll clear some dresser and closet space for James first. Then we'll catch up with the horses until it's time to get dinner going. If we're lucky, we may even have a little time to get out to the shed and get going on the orders." She needed to get to work on the garden, too. The window had arrived for planting broccoli, cab-bage, cauliflower, peppers and tomatoes. She would start them in her little greenhouse out by her work shed. But that wouldn't be happening today or tomorrow. Maybe next week, if she was lucky.

Moose gazed up at her with those big brown eyes of his, listening intently, as though he couldn't wait for the next pearl of wisdom to drop from her lips.

She asked, "So, what do you think, Moosey?"

He took his cue and gave her a bark of encouragement.

She scratched his wide forehead. "Well, all right. Let's get after it, then."

Panting happily, he followed her back into the house.

"I still haven't seen the bill for the floor repair and the bath railings," Addie complained that evening.

James didn't answer her. He didn't plan to give her that bill.

They were in her upstairs bedroom. He'd brought more clothes from the condo and he was putting them away.

"James. Stop pretending you didn't hear me."

Tucking a stack of T-shirts in next to his boxer briefs, he shut the drawer and returned to the suitcase spread open on the bed next to his adorable short-term wife.

She caught his arm as he reached for a stack of sweaters. "I want that bill."

Grabbing her hand, he straightened and yanked her up into his waiting embrace.

"Stop that." She struggled, but not very hard.

He held her lightly. "Don't worry about that bill. I already paid for it and Garrett gave me a great deal." He tried to kiss her.

But she pressed her hands against his chest, craned back away from him and glared. "It is so wrong for you to pay to fix the hole that my grandfather made while he had you tied to a chair."

"It's not wrong if I want to do it. And I do want to do it. I'm over all that with the chair and the shotgun."

"You shouldn't be. I'm certainly not."

"Addie." He said it softly, coaxing her.

Stubborn as always, she looked away. But then she looked back. He could tell she was trying not to smile. "Oh, all right. What?"

"Let it go." He put on his most appealing expression. He hoped. "Please."

She kept trying to pretend she wasn't looking at him— but then couldn't seem to resist shooting him quick glances. "Let what go? The bill or what PawPaw did to you?"

"Both—and while you're at it, stop pushing me away."

She relaxed her arms, slid her hands up and clasped his shoulders. "Fine. I'm not pushing you away."

"Better. Let me pay for the repairs."

"It still seems—"

"Shh. Don't say anything more—except for yes."

"The insurance will pay for the grab bars if I can just send them the itemized bill."

"Well, all right, then. I'll get a separate bill from Garrett for the railings, you send it in and then when they pay you, you give me that check."

"But the floor... That had to be expensive."

"Let it go, Addie. Let me help a little. I'm living here with you rent free."

"Because I asked you to."

"I like it here."

"That's right." She widened her big eyes in pretend horror. "You poor man. As soon as you leave here you'll be forced to go live in that big, beautiful new house of yours."

He didn't want to think about leaving her yet. After all, he was just moving in. "You didn't even let me help pay for the groceries."

"You'll figure out a way to do that," she grumbled. "I know how you are."

"Let it go. Accept a few good things when they come your way. Say thank you. And then move on."

Her mouth got softer. So did those big eyes. "Thank you."

"You're welcome."

"You are so good to me—and to PawPaw."

"Only because I like you." He dared to reach out and trace the sweet curve of her cheek. She let him do it, a very good sign. He whispered, "Both of you. A lot." He tugged on her earlobe. "Especially you…"

She sighed then. And this time, when he bent to claim her lips, she didn't back away.

Eventually, with great reluctance, he let her go to finish putting his clothes away. She helped him hang his shirts, slacks and jackets in the closet.

Once that was done, he took her hand and pulled her over to one of the dormers and then down with him onto the window seat. Outside, the sun had just set, leaving a last gleam of daylight along the rims of the mountains.

She asked, "Did you see Elise when you stopped by to get your clothes?"

"I did. She and Tracy have agreed to stay at the condo for a while. But already, they're talking about finding new apartments. That's Elise for you. Too damn independent."

"There's nothing wrong with independence," she informed him smartly.

He grinned. "How did I know you were going to say that?"

And then she grew thoughtful. "I've been trying to think of what I could do to help. They don't by any chance need horses boarded, yummy fresh vegetables come summer or a free scarecrow?"

He tugged on a silky strawberry curl. "I'll tell Elise you offered—or you could tell her yourself. She'll be at our party."

She was gazing out at the sunset—but at the words *our party*, she whipped her head around to pin him with a look. "What are you up to now and which party is that?"

He caught her hand again. "It's like this. My sister Clara came to my office today. She's reserved the upstairs room at McKellan's for a week from Saturday night." Walker's brother, Ryan, owned and ran the popular Irish-style bar.

"They're all a little annoyed with me for getting married out of the blue."

Shadows filled those golden eyes. "You know, they're right. We should have told them."

"There wasn't a lot of time to send out wedding announcements. And they'll get over their annoyance. Especially if they can welcome you to the family with an after-the-fact wedding reception."

"Oh, James. What are they going to say when we suddenly separate in May?"

He lifted her fingers and kissed them, one by one. "Let's ford that river when we get to it."

"I feel guilty, you know? Like we'd be celebrating under false pretenses."

"Don't."

"But, James, I—"

"Just come to the party with me and have a good time. That's all you have to do. Clara says it'll be low-key. Nothing fancy or anything. They want to get together with you, welcome you to the family, celebrate a little, that's all. They're not going to judge us later because it didn't work out."

"Is that what you'll tell them? That it didn't work out?"

Now *he* was feeling a little annoyed. "I don't really know yet what I'll tell them. Do I need to know right this minute?"

"Well, of course not. I just mean…"

"What, Addie? What exactly do you mean?"

She slanted him a sideways look. "Am I upsetting you?"

"No," he firmly lied.

A big sigh escaped her. "It's so nice of them to do this." She sounded sincere—and also as though she might actually be about to say yes.

He'd been dreading this conversation all afternoon, had just known it would be hell trying to convince her. But she seemed at least to be considering the idea. He breathed a cautious sigh of relief and pushed for an affirmative. "So that's a yes? You'll come?"

A frown crinkled the space between her smooth eyebrows. "You would have to tell them no presents. You'd have to make it very clear. I can't stand the thought of them giving us toasters and nice glassware and who knows what all, and then feeling like I should send it all back when we're not together anymore."

He really wished she'd quit talking about when it was over. After all, it had barely begun. But he knew he had to let that go for now and concentrate on the goal of getting her to say yes to the party. "No presents. Not a single one. I'll get Clara's promise on that." He mimed an *X* on his chest. "Cross my heart."

And that was when she leaned close and kissed him, sweet as you please. "All right. Yes, I would love it if your family gave us a party."

Chapter Nine

The dress was cinnamon-colored, fitted close on top, gently skimming her hips and widening out to a flirty hem that came to just above her knees. Addie had sexy black heels to go with it and she felt like a million bucks as she turned to check out the back in the cheval mirror that had once been her grandmother's.

James, dressed in good jeans and a black dress shirt, whistled at her from the bedside chair. "Beautiful. Just beautiful."

She smoothed a hand down her still-flat belly. "I'm glad I get to wear it at least once before my stomach's out to here." She turned to him. "Thank you." She'd been working like crazy, trying to catch up on her orders, take care of the horses and get the early vegetables started in the greenhouse. They'd argued when he insisted she take an afternoon off last week. But as usual, he kept after her until she agreed to go. She was glad that he'd talked her into it. They'd had a great time in Denver, where he bought her both the dress and the shoes and then taken her out for Italian food. "Seems like I'm always saying thank you to you."

He got up and came to her, causing her breath to catch and her tummy to fill with small winged creatures. "I like you smiling and grateful." He tipped up her chin and looked at her as if he was considering eating her right up—something she really wouldn't mind in the least. "Scratch that. I like you any way I can get you."

"You are so easy to please."

"I can see how you might think that, because everything you do pleases me." He brushed his lips across hers. The man smelled like heaven—minty soap and a hint of aftershave. Too soon, he stepped back. "If I keep kissing you, I'll only want to take that dress right off you again."

"And we'll never make it to our party."

"Then my family will *really* be annoyed with me."

"Can't have that." She grabbed her clutch from the low bureau.

Downstairs, they stopped in the master suite to say good-night to her grandfather.

"Get over here, Addie Anne," Levi demanded from his fancy recliner bed. She held back a snappy reply and went to him. "Give your old granddad a kiss." Obediently, she bent down and kissed his cheek. When she straightened, he gave her a nod of approval. "You do look mighty fine."

"Thank you, PawPaw." She said it sweetly, thinking how much she loved him—even if she was still angry with him for all the wrong things he'd done. Moose got up from his bed by the bureau and came over to give her a sniff. She scratched his head. He licked her hand and then wandered over to get attention from James.

"Lola should be here to see you," Levi grumbled. The nurse had the weekend off—her first days off since she'd started taking care of Levi.

"Lola has a right to days off now and then," Addie chided.

"I know. But I've gotten used to her and I don't like it when she's not here." As a matter of fact, he already seemed to consider the nurse a part of the family.

Daniel, the relief nurse, rose from the chair in the corner and suggested briskly, "You need to keep busy. Let's take another walk around the house." He meant that literally. Every couple of hours, her grandfather got up and made a circuit of the ground floor. Lola insisted he take those walks religiously. And Daniel did, too. Moose would trail after them, wagging his tail.

Levi grunted. "The next torture session begins." He waved a hand. "Go on, you two. Have fun. Stay out late. Addie, no drinking. You have my future great-grandson to consider, after all."

McKellan's, on Marmot Drive in the heart of Justice Creek, took up most of the block between West Central and Elk Street. It had lots of windows and blue awnings that shaded outdoor tables in the summer months.

The pub was always busy. This Saturday night, it was packed downstairs, not a single seat available at the long mahogany bar, every table in use. A crowd waited near the hostess stand, everyone eager to get a seat.

James waved at the hostess and they went on past, weaving their way through the crowd to the open stairway that led to the party room on the second floor.

Clara, James's sister, was waiting for them at the top. A pretty brunette in her early thirties, Clara grabbed her brother in a hug. "There you are. Congratulations, James."

He beamed. "I am one lucky man and that is no lie." He said it as though he meant it. Addie tamped down the guilt that they weren't what they seemed to be and focused on being grateful for all he'd given her, for every day and night they shared.

Clara turned to her. "What a beautiful bride. Welcome to the family, Addie." She held out her arms and Addie went into them. Clara said softly, for her ears alone, "Thank you for making my brother a happy man."

Addie pulled back and met Clara's warm dark eyes. "I'm sorry we didn't even give you a heads-up. My grandfather was so sick. We were afraid he wouldn't make it…"

"No apologies necessary," Clara insisted. Then she asked hopefully, "But he's doing well now?"

"Much better, yes. Thank you."

By then, they were surrounded by Bravos. Addie got lots of hugs and a very warm welcome from each of James's siblings and half siblings. And from his cousin Rory McKellan and her husband, Walker, as well.

Rory grabbed Addie's hand and pulled her over to the upstairs bar. Addie ordered a club soda with lime and thanked Rory for taking such good care of her dog and her horses.

Best of all, when she offered scarecrows and fresh vegetables as a sort of thank-you gift, Rory said she would love a scarecrow. Rory's garden at the Bar N was fenced, but that didn't keep the occasional hungry crow away from the corn. "Plus," she added with a musical laugh, "scarecrows are hot right now, aren't they?"

"Very," Addie agreed. "And that's why I need to make you one. All you have to do is describe to me the scarecrow of your dreams."

"How about a lady scarecrow?" Rory asked. "With a big straw hat and an old-school gingham dress?"

"You want it country, you mean?"

Rory nodded. "Oh, yes, I do."

"I can so do country. I'll drop it by as soon as it's finished. A week, maybe. Two at the most…"

In the corner, a DJ was hard at work over a pair of turntables. Dance music filled the brick-walled party room. Addie got only one sip from her club soda before James was grabbing her hand and pulling her out onto the small square of dance floor. They danced several fast ones in a row. When there was finally a slow one, he pulled her close and they swayed in place, other couples pressing close.

"Hungry?" he asked her when the slow song was through.

"Of course." The past week or so, her morning sickness seemed to have vanished. Now she was hungry all the time.

He led her to the buffet table set up along the wall across from the stairs. They each loaded a plate and found seats at a table with his sister Elise and Elise's best friend, Tracy Winham.

Both women asked after Addie's grandfather and teased James because he'd finally settled down when everyone in the family had begun to wonder if he ever would. The two women tried to keep it light and easy, but Addie saw they were both under stress in the aftermath of the fire that had taken pretty much everything they owned. There were lines of strain on Elise's face and a faraway look in Tracy's eyes.

James asked what they planned to do about their catering business.

Elise replied, "As soon as the insurance pays off, we'll be looking for a new space so we can reopen."

Tracy jumped up as if someone had pinched her. "I could use another drink." And she made a beeline for the bar.

Elise, shoulders drooping, watched Tracy go with a bewildered expression on her face. Then she turned to James. "I don't want you to worry. We'll be out of your hair by the first of May."

He reached out and clasped her shoulder. "What did I tell you? I don't need the condo. Stay as long as you want to."

Elise's eyes turned steely as she hitched up her chin. "You've been a lifesaver. And we'll find our own place by May first." She bent close and kissed his cheek, a quick kiss—and final. Then she got up and followed after Tracy.

James leaned close to Addie. "Elise has always been way too proud for her own good."

It seemed to Addie that there was more going on with Elise and her friend than too much pride and a burned-down building. She said, "It must be awful, losing everything that way."

Before James could answer, Clara and her husband, Dalton Ames, president of Ames Bank and Trust, claimed the chairs Tracy and Elise had just abandoned. The four of them sat together for a while, talking casually about Clara and Dalton's eleven-month-old daughter, Kiera, about Levi's improving health and how much he liked his nurse Lola. As it turned out, Clara had been the one to hire Lola after Great-aunt Agnes's hip surgery.

James said, "I think Levi's got a crush on Lola."

Clara laughed. "I think *I've* got a crush on Lola. She's amazing."

Addie agreed. "What's not to love? She's a dream with my grandfather. She knows when to push him and when to indulge him. Without her, I'm pretty sure I would have strangled him by now."

Dalton said wryly, "So I guess that makes her a life-saver in more ways than one."

By then, Addie had cleaned her plate. James asked her if she wanted to make another run on the buffet.

"Maybe later." She excused herself to find the ladies' room.

The small one upstairs was in use, so she went down to the main floor to try that one.

Triumph! She got in and found an empty stall just in time. Once that was handled, she washed her hands, ran a quick comb through her hair and hurried to rejoin the party upstairs.

She was almost to the stairs when a voice she knew too well said, "Addie Kenwright. Well, what do you know?"

Her stomach lurched. *Keep going. Don't even glance back.*

But then again, why run away from him? Why give him the satisfaction of thinking he mattered that much? He didn't. Not anymore, anyway. He was just proof, and that was all that he was. Proof that she didn't have what it took to make a real and lasting relationship with a man.

She stopped, spun on her pretty black high heel and gave Donnie Jacobs a big, fat smile. "Hello, Donnie."

He wore dress Wranglers and a shiny trophy buckle on his heavily tooled belt. "You are looking very hot, Addie Anne." He tipped his black Resistol at her and whistled slow and low.

She couldn't believe this. He was such a jerk. How could she ever have imagined herself in love with him? "Really, Donnie. I'm not the least interested, so don't even start." She forced a brittle smile. "You have a nice night now."

"Hold on a minute, babe." He grabbed her wrist. "Don't be mean now, sweet Addie. We both know you've missed me…" About then, he spotted her wedding ring. "Whoa, what's this?"

"Let her go. Do it now." *James.* He was coming down the stairs toward them, moving fast.

Addie whipped her hand free. "That's my husband, James," she said to Donnie with a lot more pleasure than she should have let herself feel. "He doesn't look too happy. You'd better get lost."

Donnie made a low sound—a kind of worried sound. He was lean and fit. But James was bigger. And the expression on James's face said he did not appreciate anyone manhandling his bride.

James came right to Addie. He wrapped his arm around her. "You okay?"

She looked up into his handsome face and wished with her whole heart that she could keep him all the way past May and into forever. But she couldn't keep him. She didn't have whatever it took to make forever work. And she *would* remember that this time. "I am fine. This is Donnie Jacobs. He was just leaving."

Donnie tipped his hat so fast, he almost dropped it. "Uh. Congratulations, man. I, er, hope you'll be very happy."

James just looked at him. He didn't say a word.

Donnie muttered, "Addie. You take care." And then he was turning, striding away.

James pulled her closer, pressed a kiss into her hair. "You want me to have a private talk with him?"

"I do not. But thank you for offering."

"It would be my pleasure."

She held his gaze. "No. I mean it."

"What did he do?"

She glanced up to the top of the stairs where one of his half sisters, the gorgeous one, Nell, leaned on the railing gazing down at them. "It's not the time or the place. Let's go back to the party."

He smoothed her hair, ran a finger down the side of her neck, a caress that reminded her acutely of how much she loved it every time he touched her. "You sure you're all right?"

She went on tiptoe and kissed him. "I am just fine, I promise you. Especially now that you're here."

James waited most of the night to ask her about Donnie Jacobs.

When they finally climbed into bed at quarter of three, he went for it. "So, what's the story with the douche bag in the black hat?"

Instead of answering, she rolled over good and close to him. He gathered her closer still. She wore tiny panties and a silky bit of nothing on top. He wanted to get them off her.

But he wanted her to talk to him more. "Addie?"

"Mmm?" She pressed a kiss against his shoulder.

"Remember what I told you about Vicki? About how I came out of that marriage sure I was never getting married again?"

"I remember. James, it's clear to me that your first wife was a piece of work. All those rules. You must have felt like you were living in a prison. And she didn't like your family. I mean, what's not to like about your family? That was just wrong of her, to try to keep you away from everyone you care about."

He ran his hand down her arm, loving the silky feel

of her skin, thinking he would never get enough of having his hands on her. "By the time it was over, I was pretty messed up."

"And I am not the least surprised."

"My point is it took me several years after the divorce to start figuring out that every woman isn't Vicki. Is it possible you have some idea that every guy is like that Donnie guy?"

She sighed and pushed away from him.

"Get back here," he whispered. She resisted, but only for a second. Then she let him draw her close once more. He rolled to his back. Restless, she tried to roll away from him. He kept his arm around her. Finally, she settled her head on his chest. The silence stretched out. He kissed the top of her head. "Talk to me."

She lifted up enough to meet his eyes. "Well, the truth is my track record is just not good. I'm like my mother. She never could find a man to love her and stay with her. I'm not... I don't know how to explain it. It's like I've got a part missing. The part that knows how to be in a relationship. Every time I finally give in and take a chance on a guy, he changes and can't wait to get away from me. Somehow I always end up with a broken heart."

"So you're saying that guy tonight broke your heart?"

"He's not the only one."

James waited for her to elaborate. When she didn't, he prompted, "Who else, then?"

There was more sighing. Over on the rug by the door, Moose's tags clinked together as he rolled over in his sleep. Addie rested her arm on James's chest and then braced her chin on it. "You'll think I'm such a loser."

He shook his head at her. "Those fools who hurt you, *they're* the losers."

She smiled then, a sad little smile. "My high school

boyfriend, Eddie Bolanger, and I were supposed to get married. He bought me a ring and we started planning the wedding. And then Eddie went out on me. I should have thrown his ring in his face. But no, I tried to understand, tried to talk with him about why he would do that to me, to *us*. He said he did it because I was too clingy and needy and he couldn't take it anymore. He dumped me."

"Bastard." He lifted his head off the pillow and pressed a kiss to the center of her forehead.

"I sure thought so. Then he married the girl he dumped me for."

"SOB. No doubt about it."

"I swore off men forever."

"Forever is a long, long time."

"Yeah, I know. And swearing off men didn't work anyway."

"Did you seriously think that it would?"

She made a cute little humphing sound and then went on. "For a while, it was fine. I hung with Brandon and my high school girlfriends in my free time and stayed away from temptation."

"But...?"

"Randy Pettier happened. I met him the night I turned twenty-one. Brandon and I went to Alicia's to celebrate." Alicia's was a roadhouse out on the state highway about five miles from town. "Randy tended bar at Alicia's. He gave me free birthday drinks and told me I was the girl of his dreams. I resisted falling for him for months. Brandon tried to warn me that I was doing it all over again, losing my heart to some guy who would only hurt me. But I kept going back to Alicia's and Randy kept coming on to me. One night I kissed him. And then I did more than kiss him. We lasted a little over a month, Randy and me. I was just gone on him, so sure that I'd found true love at last. Finally, one night at his place, I told him that I loved him. He didn't say it back. A week later, he decided he was tired of Colorado. He said he needed to 'move on.' He packed up his pickup and left. Never saw him again."

"Good riddance."

"True. But I didn't see that then. I cried myself to sleep night after night. Finally, I pulled it together and reaffirmed my vow never to fall in love again."

"And then you met that Donnie character?"

"Yeah. Donnie's a cowboy. He works the local ranches, wherever he can find a job. And he loves the rodeo."

"I noticed the prize buckle."

"He means for people to notice it. He competes across several events. Including bull riding. That's where I first saw him. Riding a bull at the Justice Creek Summer Daze Rodeo. The guy is at his best with seventeen hundred pounds of bucking beef between his legs."

James laughed. "I take it you were impressed."

"Yes, I was. And I saw him in the beer garden later and he asked me to dance. For once, I showed a little backbone and said no. But then, suddenly, Donnie was everywhere. He got work on the Fitzgerald place. It borders Red Hill. And then PawPaw hired him to mend fences. Just seemed like I couldn't turn around without finding Donnie standing right in front of me. Over a period of about a year, I weakened. He asked me out a bunch of times before I ever said yes. But then I did say yes. Yes to dinner and a movie. Yes to spending every Friday night with him.

"I kissed him and fooled around with him. But somehow I kept myself from ending up in bed with him—or I did, until I finally decided that he was different and I needed to stop being so skittish and take a chance on him. One night he cooked me dinner out at this little cabin he was renting about ten miles from here. After dinner, we sat on the step and looked at the stars. He took my hand and gazed in my eyes and said he was in love with me. That did it. I confessed I loved him, too. We spent the night together…" Her voice trailed off. She laid her head down on his chest again.

James stroked her hair, rubbed a hand down her back. The room was way too quiet.

Finally, she drew in a slow, shaky breath. "In the morning, he cooked me breakfast. Then I drove back home with the radio on full blast, singing along to one corny country love song after another. I was so happy, James. I thought it had finally happened, that I'd found true love at last."

He rubbed her shoulder, ran his hand down the silky skin of her arm until he reached her hand and could weave his fingers with hers. "But…?"

"After that night, he stopped calling me and he never once answered the phone when I called him. I left him message after message. He never returned a one. I never ran into him out riding anymore. I tried to find him at the cabin. It was empty. If he was working for any of my neighbors, I never knew about it. By then it was summer again. So I went to the Summer Daze Rodeo and followed him to the beer garden between events. I walked right up to him and asked him what had happened, what went wrong. He said he'd never meant for things to get so serious and that we needed to take a break from each other for a while, start seeing other people."

James squeezed her hand. "I really should have decked that jerk."

"No, you shouldn't have. You were wonderful and calm just like you always are. He took one look at you and knew he couldn't take you. So he turned tail and ran. Totally worked for me."

"So that was it, then, with him, when you found him in the beer garden and he said he wanted to see other people?"

"Yep. Tonight's the first time I've set eyes on him since then. And if I never see his smug face again, it'll be way too soon."

James completely understood now why she'd kept him at a distance for all those months before Levi stepped in with his shotgun. She had no faith in her own judgment when it came to men. "So, then, after the bull rider...?"

"I swore off men for the third and final time—well, except for you."

He almost started to feel hopeful.

Until she continued. "But you are a special circumstance. I mean, if we *have* to be married until PawPaw recovers, at least we deserve a little fun in the bargain."

James said nothing. He was trying to figure out why he felt hurt. They *were* having fun. It was nothing like with Vicki. He was loving every minute of being Addie's short-term husband. Days, he looked forward to coming home to her. And the nights? Well, he and Vicki had had a lot of problems, but sex wasn't one of them. In fact, he'd never found a woman to match his ex in bed.

Until Addie. And Addie was so much more than just amazing in bed. She was also sweet and funny and tender. And she could be tough if you messed with her. He liked that about her, too. Her toughness and her sharp tongue kept things edgy and interesting. He was an easygoing guy at heart and he needed the kind of woman who kept him on his toes.

And maybe that was his problem here.

She'd figured out what she wanted in her life, had a

baby on the way and no inclination to try again long-term with any guy. When Levi had threatened to give up and die if she didn't marry James, she'd done what she had to do. And then turned right around and made the best of the situation. The way she saw it, they were simply enjoying themselves for as long as the marriage needed to last.

But for him it was different. Somewhere in the past few weeks, he'd gone way beyond just having a great time playing house with her. At first, he'd only tried not to think about it ending.

And now?

Now he loved it so much with her, he thought about the end all the time. Dreaded it. Hated it.

The bald truth was that he never wanted it to end. He wanted to keep on being Addie's husband for the rest of their lives.

Chapter Ten

The days were zipping by much too fast, Addie thought. Her marriage would be over in no time.

And James wasn't making it easy to think about letting him go. He was too good to her. Sometimes she wondered how she'd ever gotten along without him.

Which was downright ridiculous. She'd made it twenty-six years, after all, without depending on any man—well, except for her grandfather, when she was small. She could take care of herself and her coming baby just fine on her own.

Still, it was lovely having James around. He just had a natural tendency to pick up any slack, to help out whenever or wherever he might be needed.

Most mornings, he got up before dawn with her and helped her with the horses. He said that, growing up, he'd spent a lot of time out at the McKellans' ranch with Walker and his brother, Ryan, so he'd learned early to ride and to take care of horses. He claimed it made him feel useful to help her feed and groom them.

And the afternoons he got home early from town, he would show up at the shed where she made her scarecrows. He would haul in the bales of straw she needed for stuffing, or go digging through the boxes of old clothes she kept handy, trying to find the shirt she wanted or the perfect hat.

Sometimes she would look at him and feel that warm, expanding sensation inside her chest. She knew that feeling, the one that in the past had led inevitably to her saying *I love you.*

Well, she wouldn't say it this time. Those three little words were a great big jinx for her and her poor heart. She just needed *not* to say them and things would be fine.

Levi was doing really well. He grumbled and griped, but Lola just smiled and made him do his exercises and eat the heart-healthy foods Addie cooked.

Little by little, Lola had reduced his pain meds. He complained that his chest bone was killing him. That every breath he took, every time he coughed, every breathing exercise she put him through, every workout session—all of it was agony. She replied that agony was part of getting well and the pain meds only delayed the process, not to mention the dangers of addiction and constipation.

Addie and James both tried not to laugh when Lola got to the part about constipation. Levi would always get huffy and mutter that he damn well didn't want to talk about his bowels.

And Lola would come right back with "And we don't *have* to talk about your bowels, because we have your pain medication under control."

"What's this *we*, woman? *I've* got nothin' under control. *You're* the one who runs everything around here."

"Which is as it should be because I am your nurse, hired to see that you take care of yourself."

"I don't want to argue with you. It makes my chest hurt."

"Then stop. And come with me. We'll take a walk around the house…"

And he would mutter and swear, but he would get up from his fancy bed and take that walk with her, Moose falling in behind them, wagging his tail as they went.

Two weeks after the engagement party at McKellan's, Addie and James took Rory's new scarecrow out to the Bar N. Addie had gone all out with a blue denim jumper over a floral-patterned blouse. The flour-sack face had blue eyes, puckered red lips and pink cheeks with freckles. From yellow yarn, Addie had fashioned a wig with a long braid down the back. She'd added a wide straw hat with a big silk peony stuck in the band. As a final touch, she'd looped several long strands of fake pearls around the broomstick neck.

Rory loved it. They put it up in her garden and she said it was about the cutest scarecrow she'd ever seen.

The day was warm and sunny. Addie had packed lunch for four and suggested a picnic. Rory and Walker said they were in. So they tacked up four of the Bar N horses and set out toward the mountains, following the trails on the edge of the national forest. Eventually, they chose a spot in a sunny meadow just starting to green up now that the snow had melted. They spread their blanket and shared lunch.

Rory really was a great person, Addie thought, not the least pretentious. You'd never peg her as a princess if you didn't already know that she was the youngest daughter of the sovereign princess of Montedoro.

The Bravo-Calabrettis were not strictly royal, Rory explained. They were princes, and that meant they claimed a throne but not a crown.

To be royal, somehow, there had to be a crown involved. Addie didn't really get all that and said so.

Rory laughed. "Most people don't. Go ahead. Call us royal if you must." She went on to describe a little of what it had been like to grow up in the world-famous Prince's Palace perched high on a hill overlooking the Mediterranean Sea.

That following Monday, the last one in April, Addie got a package from Carmen in the mail. Dev had printed up the pictures of Addie and James's wedding. Carm had mounted them in an old-fashioned wedding album. Addie turned back the fancy padded white cover and there she was with James, both of them in their wedding best, holding hands by Levi's hospital bed in front of the pastor. Just the sight of that first picture tore her heart in two. Tears clogged her throat and a choked sob escaped her.

No. She was not going to break down crying like some hopeless romantic fool.

She slammed that cover shut and carried it straight upstairs, where she stuck it in the hall linen closet under a stack of towels. If she looked at even one more picture of her and James's wedding day, she knew she'd end up bawling like a baby.

Time was passing way too quickly. In less than a week, it would be May. In two weeks or so, Lola would be leaving. Levi's health improved daily. He took long walks outside now, him and Lola and Moose. It wouldn't be long before he had no more need for a nurse.

And her marriage to James? They'd agreed it would last two months. As of now, they were more than halfway there. Before they knew it, she would have to let him go.

The next day, when she went grocery shopping in town, she bought a pretty Hallmark thank-you card. She scribbled a little note inside to Dev and Carm, saying how great PawPaw was doing and how much she loved the wedding album—no, she did not mention that she'd glanced at only the first picture and then stuck the thing away in the linen closet to keep herself from collapsing in a crying jag. Some things her sister and her brother-in-law just didn't need to know.

Three days later, she got the certificate of marriage in the mail. She carried it right upstairs, stuck it in the wedding album and then hid the album back in the stack of towels in the dark. Yes, it was foolish to get so emotional over some pictures and a marriage license. And she felt a little guilty that she didn't mention either to James. He would probably need the license to file for their divorce. And he might get a kick out of seeing the pictures.

Too bad. She just couldn't bear to have to deal with those pictures. And the sight of the marriage license made her heart hurt.

Carm called a little later that day, before James got home from the office. Addie was able to thank her sister again for the album without worrying that James might hear what she said and ask questions later.

"You sound weepy," Carm said. She'd always had an annoying way of knowing when Addie got the blues.

"Uh-uh," Addie replied. "I'm not weepy in the least."

"Is it James?"

"Didn't I just say there's nothing wrong?"

"Yeah, and you're lying. Is it about James?"

"James is the best there is." He really was. "I'm crazy about him and he treats me like a queen." All true, if not the whole story.

Carm bought it. "Oh, honey. I'm so glad your marriage

is going so well. See? I told you that there really are good guys out there, that you just hadn't found the one for you yet. And now you know what I was talking about. You're a good match, you and James."

More guilt on her shoulders. She'd never exactly told Carm that she and James had agreed to stay together for a set period of time.

And she really didn't feel up to discussing it now. Yes, putting it off was cowardly of her. Too bad. She'd do it later, after James had moved out. "James and I are getting along great." That part was true, at least.

"PawPaw making you miserable?"

"Nope. He's getting better every day. His chest still hurts and he complains about it constantly, but that's to be expected. Lola takes good care of him and he adores her. When she's not here, he has Daniel to look after him. I hardly have to do a thing."

"Hormones, then, right? Don't you have an ultrasound coming up?"

Addie ignored the first question and went with the second. "I do. A week from tomorrow, as a matter of fact."

"Feeling okay physically?"

"Carm, will you give it up? I mean it. I'm fine."

They talked a little longer, about how good business was at Dev's sporting goods store, about how Addie's niece and nephew, Tammy and Ian, were both doing well at school. After that, Addie said goodbye and ran to Levi's room to tell him that Carm was on the phone. He picked up his bedroom extension and Addie returned to the kitchen, where she got to work on dinner.

Faintly, from the master suite, she heard her grandfather's chortling laugh. The sound cheered her. He really was getting well and her life was back on track.

It wouldn't be easy, giving up James. But for now, she

would just keep moving forward and try not to dwell on what the future would bring.

James got home half an hour later. He came straight to the kitchen, where she was putting zucchini, tomatoes and onions on to steam.

"There you are." He slid one arm around her waist and smoothed her hair out of his way with his free hand. Heaven, the heat and strength of him at her back, the feel of that hard arm wrapped around her. Then he bent close and kissed the side of her neck. He whispered, "You are the most delicious woman." And then he nibbled a line of kisses downward toward the crook of her shoulder, setting off lovely flares of sensation as he went.

She put all her dark thoughts of losing him away and let out a low laugh. "Delicious, am I?"

"Yes, you are."

A silly giggle escaped her. "Don't ruin your dinner now."

"How about if I just make *you* my dinner?" He turned her around. She put her hands against his broad chest, looked up into those dark-rimmed blue eyes and couldn't help wishing that things could be different, that their marriage could be what Carm and PawPaw believed it to be: real and lasting, true and strong.

It could be, chided a voice her head. *Possibly. If you'll just step up and ask for it. If you'll only put your heart on the line one more time.*

Oh, she wanted to do that so bad that she could taste the longing on her tongue, a sweet taste, but bitter, too.

Because she *had* stepped up before. And encountered only heartbreak every time.

But James…

James is different, nothing like the others.

He bent close and kissed her.

Yes. Perfect. Nobody kissed the way James kissed.

But hadn't she thought the same of Eddie's kisses, back in high school? And Randy's and Donnie's, too?

Wasn't she, really, something of a love junkie? She got addicted so easily, and then she crashed and burned.

He kissed her again. She could have stood there in that kitchen and kissed him for hours. Or better yet, grabbed his hand and led him upstairs, where they could lock themselves in her bedroom and do more than just kissing.

But PawPaw needed his low-fat, nutritious dinner. And the vegetables weren't going to steam themselves.

She kissed him once more and said, "Have a beer and let me get this dinner on."

He took a cold one from the fridge and set the table for the four of them. "I talked to Elise today," he said as he set the plates around.

"How's she doing?"

"Great, she says. I don't know if I believe her. She told me that she and Tracy had a long heart-to-heart." He went to the flatware drawer and counted out the knives and forks and spoons, then carried the silverware to the table and started setting it out at each place. "Tracy said she's never been happy in the catering business. She wants to go into the master's program in molecular biology at the University of Washington."

"Whoa." Addie put on her oven mitts and checked the pork roast. Done. Careful not to spill the drippings, she eased the roasting pan onto the top of the stove, shut the oven door and turned it off. "Molecular biology? Tracy? Where'd that come from?"

"Tracy's always been something of a science whiz. But she and Elise are pretty much joined at the hip, and have been since they were in diapers. My mother and Tracy's mother were best friends. Tracy was eleven when her mom and dad died. She moved in with us. She and Elise were constantly together, a unit, closer than twins. Elise leads, Tracy follows."

"Not anymore, apparently."

"Elise says she wants Tracy to be happy and that she's fine reopening Bravo Catering on her own."

Fine. It was a word Addie had been using way too much lately. *I'm fine* and *it's all fine,* when really it wasn't. *She* wasn't. In reality, she was spinning in circles emotionally, longing to tell James what was in her heart, knowing from hard experience that telling a guy how she felt about him was a bad, bad idea.

He said, "Elise and Tracy have both found apartments. It's official—they're moving out of the condo on the first of May. I don't really get that, why they had to scramble to get new places. I told them they could have the condo for as long as they wanted."

"I know." She set the mitts on the counter. "You did what you could. But you know how it goes. People do what they feel they have to do."

He'd finished setting the table. He picked up his beer, took a sip, set it down at his place and went to her at the stove. "So, how was your day?"

"Uneventful." *Except that our marriage certificate came and I hid it in the closet with the wedding album you will never see. And then I lied to Carm and told her that everything was just fine.*

Some hint of her uncertainty and heartache must have shown in her face. He frowned down at her. "You okay?"

She smiled up at him as though she hadn't a care in the world. "I am fine."

His frown disappeared. "You certainly are." He bent close for another quick kiss, after which she sent him to tell Levi and Lola that dinner would be ready in ten.

* * *

Addie was sitting on the front step, her arm around Moose, when James got home from the office the next day. He knew instantly from the haunted look in her amber eyes that something had happened.

He got out and went to her. "What is it? What's wrong?"

"Sit with me?"

He dropped to the step next to her. Moose got up from her other side, went around and plopped down next to him.

He scratched the dog behind the ears and asked again, "What's the matter, Addie Anne?"

She leaned her head on his shoulder. "I got a call from Brandon's lawyer in Denver a couple of hours ago. He wants me to come to his office on Monday at ten. He wouldn't tell me what it's about, just said he'd explain everything then." A small groan escaped her. "Why is it that bill collectors and lawyers and doctors with bad news always get in touch on Friday afternoon to let you know about scary stuff you can do nothing about over the weekend?"

He smoothed a hand down her hair. "Just consider this…"

"What?"

"Could be that it's good news."

"James, he called on *Friday* afternoon. Didn't I just explain to you that no good calls come in on Friday afternoon?"

He hooked his arm around her hip and snugged her up nice and close. She'd been working with her scarecrows. She smelled sweetly of the fabric softener she used on the flour sacks she stuffed to make the scarecrow heads. "I'll drive you."

She sucked in a sharp breath and looked up at him, big eyes soft and grateful. "Would you?"

"Try to talk me out of it." He brushed a kiss between her eyebrows.

"I don't know why I'm so nervous. I mean, how bad can it be? I did kind of worry that maybe there was some problem with the insurance."

He remembered that Brandon Hall had set the Kenwrights up with a trust to pay hefty health insurance bills for the next several decades. He shook his head. "If there was an insurance issue, you'd hear either from the insurance company denying a claim or from the hospital letting you know that they haven't been paid."

"I got the first statement. It all looks good—the bills are enormous, but all of PawPaw's care is being covered, including Lola, who is totally worth the big bucks she's getting."

"So, then, don't worry. Whatever it is, we're going to find out on Monday. Maybe Brandon left you something more than the insurance."

"No. He left it all to a foundation he established to help kids like he used to be, kids with acute medical conditions growing up in foster care."

"Hey." He wrapped his arm around her neck and used his thumb to tip up her chin. "Do not—" he pressed a kiss on those plump lips "—worry."

Her smile was like the sun slipping out from behind a dark cloud. "I won't. Now that you're coming with me, I'll feel like I have a lawyer of my own."

"Because you do." And he kissed her again, but slowly that time, savoring the taste of her, loving the way her breath hitched and she wrapped her arms around his neck and slid her fingers up into his hair.

When he lifted his head, she looked up at him with eyes full of stars. "Thanks."

"For what?"

"For working so hard to convince me that everything will be all right."

"It will be." One way or another, he would make sure of that. She got up and held down her hand. He took it and stood. "What's for dinner?"

"Leftovers. Let's go in. I'll cut up the salad and you can set the table."

James made sure Addie arrived at the lawyer's office at five minutes of ten on Monday morning.

A secretary ushered them into a small conference room, where a blue folder waited with Addie's name on it. James pulled back the chair for her and she sat, her hands in her lap, looking down at the folder as though she feared it might bite.

James took the chair beside her and leaned close. He was just about to have a look in that folder to see what this was all about when Brandon's attorney appeared in the doorway.

"Good morning."

"David," Addie said with a nod. She introduced James. He reached across and shook hands with the other lawyer, whose last name was Pearson. Pearson sat down, too. He had a blue folder of his own.

Addie shifted nervously. James leaned into her and rested his arm on the back of her chair. She sent him a wobbly smile and then faced the other lawyer. "Okay, David. Will you please tell me now what this is about?"

Pearson opened his folder. James reached over and opened the one in front of Addie. It was Brandon Hall's will.

Brandon's lawyer explained, "I'm sorry to have made this such a mystery, but Brandon wanted it that way."

Addie sent James another glance, confusion in her eyes. Then she asked Pearson, "But why?"

"A week before his death, Brandon sent for me."

"Because…?"

"He said he wanted a change to his will and he didn't want you to know about it until three full months had passed after his death."

"Three months. That would've been Saturday," Addie said softly, wonderingly. "He died three months ago this past Saturday."

"That's right."

She made a frustrated sound. "I just don't get it."

James leaned even closer and gave her arm a reassuring squeeze. "Let him explain."

She gulped and sighed. "Sorry, David. Go on."

Pearson said, "Brandon told me that he wanted you provided for, but the most you were willing to accept from him was the health insurance trust he arranged for you and your family and any children you might have. He said that every time he tried to tell you he was leaving you a large monetary bequest as well, you became upset and said absolutely not."

"The insurance fund alone is so generous," she insisted. "More than enough. I let him talk me into that. I refused to accept more until we knew for certain that there was going to be a baby. And then he died suddenly. We had thought he had at least a few months left…"

David Pearson asked gently, "So there is a child?"

"I'm pregnant, yes."

He looked from Addie to James and back to Addie again. "Brandon Hall's child?"

Addie let out a laugh that sounded a lot like a sob. "It's a long story. But yes, I'm having Brandon's baby. And James and I got married a little over a month ago."

Pearson said, "It's unfortunate that Brandon didn't live to know he would be a father. But the child's existence has no effect on the will in front of you. The bequest is to *you*, Addie. Brandon Hall was adamant that you should be provided for, child or no. The document before you takes care of that. He told me he knew that you would be upset enough at his death. He didn't want to have you confronted right away with the fact that he'd left you a large sum of money, which you had insisted you didn't want. His wish was to give you time after his death to grieve and accept his passing before springing this bequest on you."

Addie bent her head. "Oh, this is just so…Brandon." Tears clogged her voice, frustration, too. And love. She really had loved Brandon Hall. James sucked in a slow breath and reminded himself that he would not be jealous of a dead man who had only wanted to make sure she was taken care of after he was gone.

Pearson said, "If you'll turn to page five, you'll see that the bequest is a generous one and that the inheritance taxes are already paid." When Addie just sat there staring at the open folder, James turned the pages for her.

At the sight of all those zeroes, Addie cried, "Oh, James…" She groped for his hand. He gave it and she held on tight. "Is this really happening?"

"Yes, it is," said Brandon's lawyer. David Pearson was smiling.

Addie said, "I think I maybe need to pinch myself." She turned those big golden eyes on James. "Sometimes I…" She gulped. "Oh, it's silly. Never mind."

"It's all right," he coaxed. "Go ahead. You can say it."

"Well, especially since PawPaw's heart attack, I've been so worried about all that could go wrong."

"I know…" He gave her hand a squeeze.

"We've always managed all right, PawPaw and me. We really have. But the hard truth is that we're getting by month to month. There's not a whole lot left over for emergencies. Even knowing that we had the cost of Paw-Paw's medical care covered, I still worried constantly the whole time he was in the hospital. I kept telling myself not to freak out about all the orders I wasn't filling, about owners moving their horses elsewhere because I wasn't there to take care of them."

"I know," he said again, though there'd been no need for her to worry. Saintly Brandon Hall wasn't the only one who would see to it that she was taken care of no matter what. Whatever happened in the end between him and Addie, *he* would have made certain that she and Levi and the baby had everything they needed to get by.

And wait a minute...

What exactly was he feeling here?

Pissed off.

Yeah. That was it. He felt pissed off—angry at a dead man who'd done nothing but see to the future well-being of someone he cared about.

That was pretty damn small of him.

And it got worse. He was not only pissed off at Brandon Hall's generosity; he'd actually been counting on Addie's sketchy finances, at least a little, hadn't he? He'd been counting on all he could offer her that she didn't have, counting on her needing to turn to him for help whenever things got tight.

He hadn't admitted that to himself until right now because he'd never needed to admit it. Until right now, it had only been a simple fact: she didn't have a lot of money and he had plenty and of course he would help her in any way he could.

But now the truth came way too clear.

She wasn't going to need James to take care of her. Brandon Hall had left her enough that she could take care of herself and her family in style. As of today, Addie could say goodbye to worrying about how to make ends meet.

Thanks to Brandon Hall and his millions, she would never want for anything again.

Chapter Eleven

Addie left the lawyer's office with her copy of Brandon's will and a check so big she felt kind of faint every time she looked at it. She sat in the passenger seat of James's quad cab clutching the blue folder with the check paper-clipped inside it and wondered if this was all just a dream.

"Let's stop for lunch and celebrate," James offered before he started up the truck.

"I couldn't eat a bite. Not until this check is safely in my bank."

"Straight to the bank, then?"

"Um, yes, if that's all right? It's Ames Bank and Trust." Of which Dalton Ames, Clara's husband, just happened to be president.

"Dalton's bank." James echoed her thoughts.

"Yes. And I would like to go to my own branch, the

one in Justice Creek. It's been our bank since PawPaw was young."

"That's a lot of money…"

"Oh, no kidding." She thought of all those zeros again and tried not to hyperventilate. "So what? You have a suggestion?"

He nodded. "Why don't you let me call Dalton and he can tell us if it's better to go to the main branch here in Denver for this—kind of give the bank a heads-up?"

"That's a good idea." She gave him a grateful smile. "Yes, please. Call Dalton."

He used the car's speakerphone to make the call. As it turned out, Dalton Ames was right there in Denver that day. He said he would meet them at the main branch.

James drove them over there and Clara's husband took them into his fancy office and personally put her giant check into savings for her. It didn't take long. Dalton promised she'd have access to her money within a few days. She left with a handful of pamphlets offering her various investment opportunities.

When they were back in the quad cab, she said, "Now. Let me take *you* to lunch. Pick the place. Money is no object."

"Big spender, huh?" he teased.

"Oh, you bet. Steak? How about steak?"

"I know just the place."

He took her to the legendary Buckhorn Exchange, where the red walls were covered in mounted big game, the tables had old-timey checked cloths and you could get not only prime aged beef, but also buffalo, elk and alligator tail. The Buckhorn Exchange had fabulous steaks and double-chocolate rocky road brownies for dessert and for the first time in her life, she didn't even blink when she got a look at the check, just handed over her credit card and added a generous tip.

On the way home, she started thinking about all those investment brochures from the bank. "James?"

"Hmm?"

"You told me once that you do asset protection."

"That's right. I'm in business and family law."

"But I mean…that money I just put in the bank is one wonkin' asset."

"It certainly is."

She glanced over at him. He was watching the road, his profile looking sterner, more serious than usual. "What's the matter?"

He turned and gave her a quick, warm smile before focusing on his driving again. "Not a thing."

Did she believe him? It seemed something had been bothering him. She decided not to pressure him and returned to the subject at hand. "Ahem. Will you help me to figure out the smart things to do with all the money? Will you be my lawyer for real? Advise me, you know, so I don't mess up and lose it all?"

He laughed then, a low, sexy sound that made her want to reach out and touch him—run her fingers up into his thick hair and wrap a possessive hand around the nape of his neck. "Addie, you're much too frugal to go throwing your money away."

"But you hear about it all the time. How people who don't have much get a windfall and they go kind of crazy and it's all gone in the blink of an eye."

He looked her way again, his blue gaze steady. Calm. Oh, she did love that about him. That calm at the center of him, like a cool blue pond in some secret mountain glen. It always reassured her, made her feel that no matter how rough things could get, with James around, it would all work out in the end.

Don't leave me, she thought and tried not to let her yearning show on her face. *Don't ever go.*

But of course, he would go. And she would *let* him go. Gracefully. Without making any big scenes.

"We'll talk about it," he said and put his attention back on the road. "Discuss possible investments and your comfort level with risk."

"Risk?" She wrinkled up her nose at the word. "James, I don't like risk."

"Well, then, it will be pretty simple. Savings accounts, savings bonds, CDs, the kinds of investments that are very secure but pay small dividends."

"I don't need big dividends and I like that word, *secure*."

"Okay, then. You can take your time about it. No need to rush into anything."

"There is one thing I keep thinking about."

"Say it."

"Well, I'm at three months now, with the baby. Riding horses from the second trimester on can be dangerous. So I'm thinking maybe it's time I hired someone to help with the animals and to handle some of the chores around Red Hill."

"Addie Anne, you could get yourself an army of hired hands."

She grinned at him. "No, really. I think for now just one will do."

He drove her back to the ranch, dropped her off and then went on into town to check in at his office. Moose came running out to greet her. She dropped to a crouch and hugged him good and tight and whispered, "Oh, Moosey. We're rich. Do you believe it?" The dog panted and wagged his tail as though the happy news pleased him no end. "Come on. Let's go tell PawPaw."

But when she went inside and knocked on Levi's door, he called out in his grouchiest voice, "Is the house on fire?"

"No, PawPaw. I just want to—"

"I don't care what you want, Addie Anne. *I* want to be left alone."

"Well, fine. Be like that." She'd tell the old meanie the big news later. As she turned from the door, it opened and Lola came out, closing it quietly behind her.

Addie asked, "What's put a bug in his butt, anyway?"

Lola's composed smile did not reach her eyes. "I told him this morning that Friday will be my last day taking care of him. He's doing so well, Addie. Even his chest has finally stopped hurting. He can walk a good distance at a steady clip." Addie knew Lola was right. Over the weekend, he'd helped her out in the garden. He'd been managing light chores for over a week now. "He's eating well and off the pain meds," said Lola. "He really doesn't need a nurse anymore."

Levi's bad attitude suddenly made perfect sense. "He's upset that you're leaving."

"He's become…somewhat attached, that's all."

Addie wanted to hug the older woman—and why shouldn't she? She reached out. Lola didn't turn away. She stepped forward and for a moment they held on tight. Addie felt the tears itching at the back of her throat. It was stacking up to be a pretty emotional day. "You know, I think I've become attached, too. I don't want you to go, either."

Lola gave a shrug, the movement both sad and resigned. "I'll miss you both. *And* that handsome husband of yours." Moose, at Addie's feet, let out a whine. Lola patted his head. "And you, too, Moosey. I'll miss you, too." She met Addie's eyes again. "But that's the nature of my job. Just when I feel as though I'm part of the family, it's time to move on."

Levi refused to come out of his room for the rest of the day. When James got home, Addie told him that Lola was leaving at the end of the week and that Levi was angry about it.

They put the dinner on the table and then she had James go in and tell Levi and Lola that the food was ready. Addie expected her grandfather to go right on sulking, to refuse to come to dinner like a naughty five-year-old.

But he came to the table.

Too bad that when he got there, he made them all wish he'd just stayed in his room. He was awful. He ignored his meal. Folding his arms across his chest, he glared at Lola.

Lola was amazing about it. She smiled sweetly back at him and appeared to enjoy her trout, green beans and salad enormously. Addie guessed it was all an act, but still. She admired the nurse all the more for not giving her grandfather the satisfaction of knowing he was getting to her.

Finally, when all that surly glaring didn't work, Levi took his rudeness to a whole new level. "Give me that sweet smile all you want to, Lo, I know you're scared." *Lo?* PawPaw called Lola *Lo?* That was kind of…intimate. Addie zipped a glance at James. He looked as bewildered as she felt. Levi went on. "You aren't really the heartless bitch you keep pretending to be."

Addie gasped. "PawPaw. What is the *matter* with you?"

Before he could answer, Lola let out a cry, jumped to

her feet and threw down her napkin. "That does it, Lee. That simply takes the cake."

Addie whipped her head toward James again and mouthed, *Lee?* Wide-eyed, James shook his head, his surprise a match for hers.

PawPaw stared up at Lola, a hot smirk on his thin lips. "What? Don't tell me. For once you're actually going to admit how you feel?"

Lola sucked in a hard breath. And then, her face flaming red, all her usual cool composure fled, she cried, "You petulant, spoiled old fool. I could…could… Oh, you just make me want to throw back my head and shout this house down!" And with that, she turned and fled through the family room.

"Lo! Lo, you get back here!" Levi jumped to his feet, fast as he ever had before his heart attack. He took right off after her.

Addie asked James, "What is going on?"

"Hell if I know."

They got up simultaneously and trailed after Levi and Lola.

From down the short hall to the master suite, Addie heard Lola cry, "No! No, Levi, this is wrong. It's so unprofessional…"

And her grandfather came right back with "You're done, remember? You're not my nurse anymore."

"But I—"

"Shh, Lo. It's all right. I know I've been an ass. But I couldn't make you listen."

"Lee, I can't—"

"Yeah. Yeah, you can. Please don't fight it anymore. I love you, sweetheart. And I promise you, we're gonna make it work, gonna find the happiness we both deserve. Lo, it's gonna be all right…"

Another soft cry followed. And then there was silence.
Addie and James just gaped at each other.

About then, either Levi or Lola must have realized
they'd left the bedroom door open. Somebody gave it
a kick.

Addie startled as it slammed. "Well," she said softly.
"PawPaw and Lola. Should I have guessed?"

"Probably." James took her hand and led her back to
the breakfast nook table. They sat down and picked up
their forks again.

Addie ate a green bean. "I never did get around to telling him about the money." She sighed. "Maybe tomorrow."

James sipped from his beer. "He's looking pretty spry,
your grandfather. Bounced right up out of that chair and
chased right after her."

"Lola did say he doesn't need a nurse anymore."

James sent her one of those smiles that warmed her
inside and out. "He still needs Lola, though."

"Yep. I think he really does. And from what just happened, I'm guessing that maybe she needs him, too."

The next morning at breakfast Levi announced, "Lo
is no longer my nurse. I fired her." He reached for Lola's
hand. She gave it and he kissed the back of it. "She's not
my nurse, and she's not going anywhere."

Lola colored like a youngster. "We want to spend time
together."

"Lots of time," said Levi. "So she'll be staying here
at the ranch house with me."

Lola added, "And if I'm not here, he'll be coming to
stay at my house. But we'll also take time alone, too, so
we each get some space."

"Not too much damn space," Levi muttered.

And she chuckled. "No, darling. Not much space at

all." She said to Addie, "When you get older, you find you don't want to waste a minute that you might spend with the person who means the most to you."

Without stopping to think twice, Addie looked to James. His blue gaze was waiting. They shared a glance that felt so tender. So right.

The old folks were in love. And so was she. And she really, really wanted to speak of her love with James.

Yes, she had promised herself not to go there ever again. But some promises, well, didn't they just beg to be broken?

If her grandfather could find love again after so many lonely years, didn't that just prove that love was something you should never give up on?

Addie swallowed down the tears that always seemed to be so near the surface lately. She said, "I'm so happy for you two," and she meant it with all her heart.

James nodded in agreement and Levi and Lola beamed with happiness.

That evening at dinner, Addie finally told her grandfather of the visit to Brandon's lawyer and the enormous sum of money Brandon had settled on her.

Levi didn't seem the least surprised. "I knew he was filthy rich, that boy—and don't get prickly, Addie Anne. I mean 'filthy rich' in the nicest way possible."

"Oh, PawPaw," she chided.

The wrinkles in Levi's brow deepened. "But I thought you said you refused to take any of his money."

"He left it to me anyway."

Her grandfather said very gently, "Well. God rest his soul."

Addie was sorely tempted at that moment to bring up the baby again, to try to get her grandfather to admit, at last, that she hadn't lied, that Brandon *was* the baby's father and her grandfather had kidnapped an innocent man—and then forced her and James to marry by threatening to let himself die.

But why ruin a really good moment with accusations and anger? James claimed he was over it.

And PawPaw was almost eighty. He'd survived a massive heart attack and found true love again at last.

Let him have his illusion that James was her baby's father. In this case, she doubted that the truth would set anyone free.

A little later as she and James were clearing the table, a rolling boom of thunder sounded outside.

"Storm coming," she said.

James set down the two plates he'd carried to the counter and moved to stand behind her. He wrapped his arms around her.

He was brushing a lovely line of kisses down the side of her throat when thunder rolled again and she warned, "Don't tempt me."

"I live to tempt you…" He kissed the words against her skin.

She turned her head back over her shoulder and they shared a swift, hot little kiss. "I have to hurry, get my sleeping bag and get out to the stables."

He frowned at her, confused. "Because…?"

"You know Dodger?"

"That big bay gelding, you mean?"

"That's the one. He goes wild when there's a thunderstorm. Weather report said it might storm, so I put him in a stall for the night just to be safe. If I leave him in the pasture, he's been known to jump the fence and run off. But I need to get out there and make sure he doesn't hurt himself kicking at the stall."

"I thought you were going to hire someone to help you with the horses."

"I have. I called around and found a dependable man who's worked for us before, but he can't start till next Monday, so I'm on my own tonight."

Out the breakfast nook window, lightning flashed, followed by a rolling boom of thunder. She kissed him one more time and then made for the mudroom. "Just leave all that," she said over her shoulder of the half-cleared table. "I'll deal with it in the morning."

He followed and stood in the doorway to the kitchen as she grabbed her hooded canvas jacket off the peg by the back door. "You'll be sleeping out there tonight?"

"Probably." She grabbed some wrinkled apples from the bin under the mudroom sink and stuffed them in her jacket pockets.

He said, "I'll finish clearing off and be with you in ten minutes."

The idea delighted her, but it was only fair to warn him, "You'll be a lot more comfortable upstairs in bed."

"Uh-uh. Where you are. That's where I want to be."

Addie stopped by the storage shed and got two sleeping bags. It was starting to rain as she ran for the stables. Slipping in through the outside door, she tossed the sleeping bags in the corner.

Dodger gave a snort, followed by a nervous whinny of greeting. She went to his stall and spoke to him soothingly. He snorted twice more but seemed to settle a bit.

"Good boy, good boy." She fed him two of the apples as the rain came down harder, drumming on the rafters overhead.

Dodger let her pet him and whisper to him.

When it seemed safe to leave him for a minute, she went

to unlatch the doors that led into the pasture, pushing them open just wide enough that she could look out. Through the veil of the rain, she could see the other horses huddled in the run-in shed, an open-sided structure that provided shelter during bad weather. They should be all right.

As she pulled the doors shut again, lightning blazed and thunder roared. Dodger neighed and kicked the stall door, hard. She went back to try to soothe him, waiting till he danced around to face the stall door again, then getting hold of the halter she'd left on him just for this purpose.

He kept rearing back, trying to jerk free. But she held on and blew in his nostrils and petted his fine, long forehead with its pretty white blaze. "Shh, it's okay. You're okay now, boy…"

She'd just gotten him settled when the thunder roared again. With a squeal, he pulled free and started kicking the stable wall behind him, tossing his head so she couldn't catch the harness.

And then there was James beside her, his hair wet from the rain, wearing his heavy quilted jacket. He had the extra height and longer arms to catch the harness again.

Addie caught the other side. Together, they whispered soothing words until Dodger finally settled once more.

The rain drummed harder on the roof. Addie heard Moose whine. Still holding her side of Dodger's harness, she glanced over to see the dog sitting by the sleeping bags, tongue lolling, expression hopeful.

James stroked Dodger's muzzle and followed her glance. "He came out of Levi's room looking for you, so I brought him along."

More thunder.

They both focused on the horse again, holding on,

petting him, whispering that he was safe, that everything was okay.

The rain kept on coming down. But after fifteen minutes had passed with no more claps of thunder, Dodger seemed calm enough that she gave him another apple for being such a good boy. Then she and James went to spread some clean straw on the floor and lay out their sleeping bags.

James had brought a couple of blankets and two pillows. They used the sleeping bags as a bed and the blankets to cover them.

"Very cozy," he said, when they lay together on their mattress of straw, with Moose stretched out contentedly beside them.

She had her head on James's chest and her hand on his heart, with his strong arm around her, her very favorite place to be. "You showed up at just the right moment."

He pressed his lips to her hair. "We make a good team."

Her heart did something impossible inside her chest. "Yeah," she agreed in barely a whisper. She tipped her head back to smile at him. "We really do." *And I love you so much and I'm terrified to tell you that—scared to death that when I do, everything will go wrong.*

He bent a little closer. "Addie, I—"

She pressed a finger to his lips, her stomach going hollow with fear—of what he might ask of her, of the things he might say that she might answer in kind. Last night, seeing her grandfather and Lola all dewy-eyed, in love as two teenagers and admitting it openly, anything had seemed possible. Last night, for a little while, she'd actually believed that she could say her love out loud to James and it would all work out.

But right now, as he looked at her with tender intentions, right now, with the moment upon her…

Uh-uh. No.

These things never worked out for her. She couldn't bear to go there again and have it all go bad. She didn't even want to think about it.

Not tonight, anyway.

"Don't talk," she whispered. "Just kiss me."

"Addie." He said it tenderly—and reproachfully, too. "We can't go on forever without—"

She cut him off. "Kiss me, James."

He shook his head, but then he did give in. Their lips met. He gathered her close.

Outside, the rain poured down. Moose gave a big yawn. In his stall, Dodger shifted with a low sound very much like a sigh.

James pushed at her jacket. She let him take it away and then helped him get rid of his. It didn't take long to shed all their clothes. James pulled the blankets over them.

He laid his big, warm hand on her belly. "You're a little bit rounder here, I think…"

It was true. She had a tiny baby bump now, though it was nowhere near big enough to show under her clothes. Laughing, she elbowed him in the side. "James Bravo, are you calling me fat?"

"I'm calling you beautiful." And then he kissed her again.

It was so sweet and right, just the two of them, the rain drumming overhead, making love, saying things with their bodies that she could never quite bring herself to put into words.

Addie told herself that was okay. It wasn't that she would never tell him. It was only that she wasn't ready yet, to say it, to find out if this time really was as different as it seemed to be. She had two weeks yet until their two-month marriage ended. Surely by then she would find a way to say that she loved him and wished with all her heart that he might stay.

Thursday, Levi spent the night at Lola's house in town.

Friday morning, it was just Addie and James at the ranch house. They got up before dawn, as always, and tended to the horses. Back inside, he cooked them breakfast and she set the table.

When they sat down, he asked her what she had planned for the day. She told him about the orders she needed to work on, the weeds she needed to pull in the garden and that she had her second ultrasound at Justice Creek General at one.

He gazed across at her so steadily and she had that scary, wonderful feeling that he could see right down inside her heart. And then he asked in a worried tone, "Is something wrong, then? With you? With the baby?"

"No. Honestly. This is an optional ultrasound for me. More and more doctors are advising that women have them at eleven to thirteen weeks. There's really no indication that ultrasounds hurt the baby or the mother. It's totally noninvasive. It uses sound waves and not radiation. And at thirteen weeks, they can check for issues like Down syndrome and other genetic disorders." He'd gone from worried-looking to slightly alarmed, so she added, "James. It's okay, I promise you. I have no reason to believe the baby has any of those things. I just think it's a good idea, to check everything that can be checked. Plus, I might be able to find out if it's a boy or a girl—that's not real likely this early, but it's possible."

"It's at one, you said?"

"That's right."

"I want to be with you. I'll meet you there."

James wasn't sure, exactly, why he wanted to be with Addie for the ultrasound.

He just felt that he should be there, that he wanted to see those shadowy sonogram images, see for himself the tiny person inside Addie that had somehow changed everything. Because of the baby, Levi had kidnapped him. Everything, really, had started from there. If not for that awful day when Levi had his heart attack, James doubted he'd ever have had a chance with Addie.

Sometimes he still doubted that he really had a chance. She was scared to go all the way with her feelings. She'd been hurt more than once revealing her heart and she wasn't eager to try that again.

James got that. He did. He kept trying to figure out how to talk about forever with her.

But he hadn't managed it yet. Something always held him back. He wasn't sure exactly what. Maybe the way she still guarded her heart. When he held her and made love to her, she gave herself completely. But somehow she made it so that the moment was never right to talk about where they might go from here. He didn't want to ruin what they had by pushing too fast.

For the ultrasound, Addie lay on a padded exam table in a darkened room. The technician, whose name was Kate, slid the gel-smeared probe in slow, exploratory circles over her bare belly.

James stood beside Addie, across from Kate and her keyboard and the sonogram screen. On the screen, the images flickered and changed. They heard the baby's heartbeat, a hundred and sixty beats per minute.

And then, for a second, a glimmer of a shape that

might have been a human form. Slowly, as Kate worked the probe, the image came a little clearer. James could make out separate body parts beyond the overlarge head. He saw tiny arms, hands, fingers—even toes. Kate said the baby was only three inches long, that fingerprints were starting to form, that reflexes had begun to develop, that the baby could hiccup and yawn and swallow, that the kidneys were just beginning to function.

"Did you want to know the sex?" she asked.

Addie said, "Yes."

Kate slid the probe around in a slowly narrowing circle. "See that? He's not shy."

A boy, then? James thought maybe he saw something that just might have been a penis, but then it was gone. "You just said 'he.' So it's a boy?"

Kate the technician answered with a firm "Yes."

"A boy," Addie repeated with a happy little sigh.

James stared at the tiny figure floating inside Addie, watched the little guy flex his transparent fingers, wiggle his miniature feet. Brandon Hall's baby.

But somehow, strangely, *his* baby, too.

Was he out of line, to think that?

He didn't see how.

With Brandon gone, the little guy could use a dad.

I can do this, he found himself thinking. *I can be this baby's dad.*

He not only *could*, but he *wanted* to. Like a warm and welcoming light going on inside that shadowed room, as he watched the thirteen-week-old baby on the flickering ultrasound screen, everything changed again, the same as it had changed the day Levi tied him to a chair.

That barely formed baby had James seeing with perfect clarity that he had no more need to be jealous of Brandon Hall and his money. Brandon had loved Addie.

Brandon had done all he could to protect her, to take care of her after he was gone. And Addie had loved Brandon, too. But not *that* way, not the way she could love James if she would only let herself. Addie needed *him*, James, no matter how afraid she was to claim him.

And this tiny baby? This baby needed him, too.

And all that was just fine with James. Because he needed both of them.

Now if he could only make Addie believe that he did.

James waited for the right moment to tell her that he loved being married to her—he loved *her*, damn it. That he wanted to be a dad to the baby she'd made with Brandon Hall. He wanted the life *they* had made together. He wanted it all with her until death did them part, which he expected to be a long, long time from now.

Unfortunately, that moment never came. Somehow she always found a way to silence him before he even started talking. She did it so cleverly, with a sweet kiss, or a deft change of subject—or the sudden absolute necessity to be off and doing something in another room.

The new hand, Rudy Jeffries, came to work on Monday. He brought two of his own horses and a single-wide house trailer to live in until Addie could get the foreman's cottage across from the main house fixed up for him. Tuesday, Addie had a plumber and an electrician out to add hookups for the trailer on a pretty grassy space not far from the barn.

That night, she told James how good it felt, to whip out her checkbook and pay for what was needed without batting an eye. Wednesday, she called Nell to get Bravo Construction out to tell her how much it would cost to make the needed repairs to the foreman's cottage and some upgrades to the house, as well.

The following Monday, when she got the formal estimate from Nell, she freaked out a little. The total for everything she wanted done was well over fifty thousand.

That night in bed after they made slow love, James held her and soothed her and reminded her that she was rich now. He teased, "Fifty K is chump change."

She got all prickly. "I do not like throwing money away, James."

"You'll like it less when the foreman's cottage caves in from neglect. Plus, it's about time you got a new kitchen and an overhaul of that basement room."

She snuggled in closer. "You're right. I know you are…"

It seemed a perfect moment to bring up their future. "Addie Anne, I—"

She lifted herself right up and put a finger to his lips. "Sorry, but I really have to pee. Be right back." And she jumped from the bed, scooped her short robe off the bed-side chair and disappeared into the bathroom.

No way was he waiting even one more day to talk about the future. According to the original agreement they'd made, their supposed two-month marriage ended on Thursday. He had a feeling if he just let things go without insisting they talk about it, they could wander on into the future together without ever saying the words that meant so much.

But he didn't want it like that between them. He wanted her to know how he felt, what he wanted with her, how precious she was to him. He wanted to tell her that he would like to be a father to the baby, to say all the words that mattered so much when two people de-cided to make one life together. He also wanted to hear those words coming back to him out of her sweet, plump mouth.

He turned on the lamp, propped his pillow against the headboard and sat up to wait for her.

Took her a good ten minutes to return. She hovered out of the circle of the lamp's light, her big eyes wary, arms wrapped around herself as though for comfort. Even through the shadows he could see her quick mind working. She didn't want to ask him why he'd turned the light on, because he just might tell her that he wanted to talk. Then she'd have to invent some new excuse to shut him up.

He broke the silence. "Come back to bed, Addie Anne."

She started chewing that sweet lower lip. "Oh, James…"

"We have to talk about it." He patted the empty space beside him.

"Please." The distress in her voice was way too evident and she hadn't come any closer. "We have a few more days. Can't we just enjoy them?"

He didn't like the sound of that at all. But this time, he was getting the damn words out no matter what she did to stop him. "We can have forever and you know it."

"James—"

"No. You're not going to stop me. Not this time. I love you and I want to stay with you. I want the baby, too. I want it all with you, Addie. I don't want it to end and there is absolutely no reason that it has to end. We're married and we can stay that way. I want that. And I want you to tell me that you want it, too." Yeah, all right. As declarations of love went, it lacked finesse. But still. He'd meant every word and he hoped, at least, that his sincerity came through.

She shifted from one foot to the other, let her arms drop to her sides and then rewrapped them around herself. But she didn't come to him. She stayed in the shadows. "I'm just… You're such a good man. I… You're everything, James. But I'm not going to say it. Saying it never works for me. Saying it only makes everything go bad."

"Will you listen to yourself? You know that's not true."

"I just... I *can't*, James. I'm not going to say it. It's not going to happen."

He had a really bad feeling. A feeling that she meant it, that she never would say it, never would let herself get past what Donnie Jacobs, Eddie Bolanger and Randy Pettier had done to her heart. "You're smarter than this, Addie. And I'm not like any of those jerks who messed you over."

"I know you're not. You're good and true. But it's like a jinx for me, you know? I say it, and everything goes wrong."

"That's not going to happen with me, with *us*."

"I'm sorry." She did take a step closer then, into the pool of light cast by the lamp. He held his breath as she raised both hands—and then let them drop to her sides. "No, I just can't. I really can't."

He kind of wanted to break something. But he tried another tack instead. "So, then, what's going to happen? How do you see this playing out? Are you thinking that on Thursday, I'm just going to pack my stuff and move out?"

She shut her eyes. "I don't know. The truth is I don't want to think about it. I *never* want to think about it."

He held out his hand. "Come here."

She did look at him then. And she let out a hard, shaky sigh. "I feel like such a complete loser. I mean, I'm a woman. Women are supposed to be good at all this, at dealing with emotions, expressing their feelings..."

"Come here."

At last, she came. She even put her slim, work-roughened hand in his and let him pull her onto the bed beside him.

"Take off the robe."

She pulled the tie. It fell open.

He pushed it off one shoulder and then let go of her hand in order to ease it all the way off. "Lift up." She lifted up from the mattress enough that he could get the robe out from under her. He tossed it onto the chair a few feet away. She looked so beautiful and so sad, sitting there naked, unable to let herself say what he wanted most to hear. He held up the covers and she slid beneath them. He settled them over her and pulled her into his arms.

"I'm sorry," she whispered against his heart.

He stroked a hand down her hair, cupped the velvety curve of her shoulder. "Be warned. I'm saying it again. I love you. That's *my* choice, to love you. I chased you for all those months before Levi took the situation in hand and made it so I could catch you—at least for a while. In all those months before your grandfather came after me with his shotgun, I never had a prayer with you, did I?"

"I just couldn't." Her voice was so small, he almost didn't hear it. "I just never know what I'm doing when it comes to—" she had to swallow before she could say it "—love. I always mess it up."

"You haven't messed a damn thing up. But you haven't had a chance to choose, either, have you—not when it comes to you and me?"

She tipped her head back. Those amber eyes met his. "What are you getting at?"

"That *I* chose *you* the first time you rode that gray mare past my new house."

"Oh, that's just crazy."

"Maybe. But it's also the truth. I saw that ginger hair

escaping out from under your hat, shining in the sun, saw the perfect, curvy shape of you astride that pretty horse. And then you stopped and you smiled at me. We started talking. By the time you rode away that day, my heart went with you."

Her eyes shone brighter, the shine of tears. One escaped and trailed down her round cheek. "Oh, just look at me. Crying." She sniffed. "I'm not only a loser, I'm a wuss, a complete wuss."

"No, you're not." He brushed at the wetness with his thumb. "And I don't want to make you cry, Addie Anne. But I do want you to have your chance to make *your* choice, a choice you make not because I won't stop chasing you and not because your grandfather threatens to die unless you marry me—die like Brandon did. And your mom, too. That was so cruel of Levi to do that to you."

She pressed her lips together hard, wrapped her fingers around his upper arm and held on too tight. "You are planning something, James. I know you are and already I don't like it, whatever it is." He kissed the tip of her upturned nose—and she accused, "You *are* leaving me, aren't you?"

"I'm moving to my new house, that's all. I'm moving there loving you with all of my heart. And I will be there, waiting, hoping that you decide it's safe to believe—in me and in you and in the life we can have together."

"It's what I said," she whispered again, that plump lower lip trembling. "Dress it up however you want, make it sound like you're doing me a favor. You. Are. Leaving."

"What matters is I love you. And yes, on Thursday, I'm moving to my new house, where I will be waiting, praying every damn day that passes that you will give yourself a chance to trust me, that you will come and get me. That you will make *your* choice to take me as your husband for the rest of our lives."

Chapter Twelve

Addie longed to beg him to stay.

But she didn't. She knew he was nothing like Eddie or Randy or Donnie, knew that he really did care for her, knew that what she had with him was deeper, truer and more real than anything she'd had with any man before.

Still, she shed that one tear right when he told her he would go—and after that, well, something went numb in her.

She didn't want him to go, but of course he *would* go. She'd known that all along, now, hadn't she?

At least this time she hadn't made a fool of herself. He'd even said he loved her and somehow she'd managed not to say it back. That had always been her brilliant plan if any man ever said those three little words to her again: not to say them back.

So she'd followed through with the plan.

And it didn't feel so brilliant, after all. Truth was, it

felt even worse than declaring her love and ending up with a stomped-on heart. It seemed to her by then that something really had gotten broken inside her. She'd lost that special, sacred part of a person that knew how to love and be loved in return.

Would she ever be mended?

She just didn't know.

The morning James left, he hugged her and kissed her and whispered, "Take care of yourself, Addie Anne." She stared up at him, wordless, until he dropped his cherishing arms and stepped back.

"Bye, James," she managed at last.

PawPaw came out on the porch right then. Addie waited for him to throw a fit. After all, the shotgun marriage he'd threatened to die for was ending so easily, with James walking away and Addie planning simply to stand there and watch as he drove off and left her.

Levi offered his hand to James. They shook and Levi pulled James close to pound his other hand on James's broad back. "Don't be a stranger," said Levi gruffly, as though James had just dropped in for a visit and now he was heading off back to his own life.

Well, and maybe that was exactly what was happening here.

Tell him you love him. Beg him to stay, pleaded the lovesick fool within.

But she wasn't going to do that.

And on second thought, she wasn't standing there on the porch to see James drive away, either. She slipped past her grandfather and went into the house, shutting the door quietly behind her.

Inside, she waited for Levi to come stomping back in and read her the riot act for letting James go.

Didn't happen. PawPaw came in. He asked gently, "You all right?"

"No, I am not and I don't want to talk about it."

"Fair enough." He headed for the kitchen. Addie trailed along behind him, not sure what to do with herself. He went straight to Lola, who stood at the sink loading the dishwasher after their breakfast. He wrapped his wiry old arms around her and kissed her neck.

That did it.

Addie whirled around and left the room. The last thing she needed right at that moment was to see a pair of happy lovers kissing on each other.

She went out to the stables, but there wasn't much to do there. Rudy was conscientious and good at his job. So after hanging on the pasture fence and petting the horses that came to say hi, she went on to her work shed and spent the morning stuffing flour-sack heads, painting faces on them and assembling the outfits for her next several orders.

That day passed. And the next one. The weekend dragged by. Three times, she started to take off her wedding and engagement ring set. She should have given them to James before he left Thursday morning. But she hadn't even let herself think of such a thing then.

And now, well, she couldn't bear to do it. So she just went on wearing them, telling herself that eventually she would have to take them off and return them to him.

It hurt so much—the vast emptiness of her own bed at night, the space at the table that didn't have him in it, the words she needed to say to him that he wasn't there to hear.

And his touch. And his kiss. And the scent of his aftershave.

How long would it take her to get over James Bravo? She really, really needed to stop asking herself that.

Monday, Nell Bravo came with a crew to start fixing up the foreman's cottage. Nell was well-known in her family for speaking her mind. Addie worried that James's half sister might demand to know what had gone wrong with her and James. But Nell only gave her a big hug and asked her a few questions about the teardown and went to work with her crew.

Another week dragged by. That following Monday, the final one in May, Addie drove into town for groceries. She stopped at the bank and arranged with the branch manager to put some of her money from Brandon into CDs, which were safe and low risk. Because she didn't do well with risk. Not when it came to money.

Or her heart, apparently.

Once that was done, she considered the amount left in her savings account. She'd hardly made a dent in it. So she transferred another fifty thousand into her checking account. She went home and sent money to the Wounded Warrior Project, the ASPCA, UNICEF, the Salvation Army and the family shelter in town.

She felt a little better after giving some of her windfall to people who needed it and she decided she would make a habit of giving regularly.

But did writing those checks help her get over James? Not one bit.

Two more weeks went by. She talked to her sister twice on the phone. Carmen didn't like it that James had moved out, but when Addie asked her to leave the subject alone, Carm didn't argue, either.

Addie met Rory in town for lunch. Rory asked how she was doing. Addie said she was managing all right. Rory offered to listen if Addie had needed to talk. Addie thanked her and said she would think about it. They left it at that.

The days ran together. Addie worked on her orders, approved of the progress Nell and her crew were making on the cottage and started thinking about more stuff that could stand doing around Red Hill. She hired another hand to work three days a week. He would mend fences, help Rudy when needed and clear brush to keep the danger down in fire season.

Addie's stomach grew rounder. She wished James were there to put his big hand on it and smile at her in that special, tender way that only he did. She ached to drive by his house and see how he was doing.

But she stopped herself. What would she say to him? Nothing would do for him but *I love you* and she was too much of a coward to ever say those words again.

The second week of June, she had her eighteen-week ultrasound and missed James desperately all through it. He would have loved to see the baby now. The little boy had grown to five and a half inches. Addie watched him kick, roll and flex his arms, activities she'd already felt him doing in the past couple of weeks.

She couldn't button her jeans anymore. So the next week, on Friday, she went into town and bought actual maternity clothes. She was putting them away in her closet and bureau when she heard footsteps along the upper hall.

PawPaw appeared in the doorway to her room. "Addie Anne, we need to have us a talk."

Whatever he had to say, she didn't want to hear it.

She still hadn't forgiven him for kidnapping James and causing his own heart attack—and then forcing her and James to the altar by refusing to get well.

"Please," he said, his eyes, the faded blue of worn denim, so sad.

She went over, plopped to the edge of the bed and gestured at the bedside chair. "Have a seat."

He came into the room and eased himself down into the chair. "How you feelin'?"

Except for my hopeless broken heart? "Fine, Paw-Paw. Truly."

"Good. You look good—except for that sad face you're wearing all the time."

She asked him wearily, "What is it you wanted to talk about?"

He folded his gnarled hands and twiddled his ancient thumbs. Finally, he came out with it. "I know that my new great-grandson is Brandon Hall's baby. I knew since that day in the hospital when you brought me all those damn papers from that sperm bank and your doctor."

Addie sat very still for a second or two. And then she accused, way too softly, "You knew and yet you *still* wouldn't get better until James and I got married?"

The white head dipped once in confirmation. "I knew he loved you and I knew you would never give him a chance to make you happy. Not unless somebody took the matter in hand. So I did what I had to do. But I know that what I did was wrong and I'm thinking you're never going to forgive me. I could live with that, with you hating your old PawPaw for the rest of my days. Except that now you've sent James away. Now you haven't got love and you're mad at me, too."

"Serves you right," she muttered. "And at least out of the wrong you did, you found Lola. I'm glad for that."

"Lo is my miracle and I thank the good Lord daily for the gift of her love. But what about *your* miracle, Addie?" When she only swallowed hard and looked away, he said, "James and I had a long talk, before he left."

"I'd wondered about that," she said to the far wall. "I figured something had gone down between you two when you just let him go with a handshake and a pat on the back."

Levi grunted. "He made me admit how wrong I was to threaten to die on you unless you married him. He made me see that you blame yourself for your mother's death—though that was not in any way your fault—and then you also lost Brandon. And the men you loved before, well, they weren't worthy of you. So you had been hurt again and again. And I piled more hurt on you. It was a very bad thing I did, to blackmail you with the threat of dying on you. I only made everything worse for you, harder for you, when I did that, only battered your heart around all over again."

She looked at him then. How could she help it? The hard knot of anger within her at him? It was melting away like an icicle in the morning sun. "You know I forgive you. You're everything to me, PawPaw."

"I'm old, is what I am. And I won't be around for all that long."

That numbness inside her—where had it gone? Her heart ached. Tears welled. She gulped them down hard. "Please don't say that."

His smile was the sweetest she'd ever seen. "Don't be afraid. I'm not planning to go *that* soon."

"Good."

"Addie, I want you to have your true love before I go. I would do a whole lot of wrong all over again, God forgive me, if you would just go to James and tell him what's in your heart for him. If you would just bring him home to Red Hill, where he belongs."

"Oh, PawPaw. What if he's changed his mind by now?"

Levi gazed at her patiently. "I promise you he hasn't—and that's not to make light of your fear. Lovers do leave and the people who mean the most someday will die. But in the meantime, when you find the one for you, you need to grab hold, Addie."

She saw the truth suddenly. "I fulfilled my own fear, didn't I? I *made* him leave."

"But the good news is he loves you."

"He…he did say he would be waiting."

"So, then, you only need to master the fear in you. Master the fear, go after him. And once you get him, hold on tight."

The next morning was Saturday. James woke up again in his dream house.

In the month since he'd left Addie, he'd furnished the place just the way he liked it, with comfortable and attractive high-quality furniture in the neutral colors he preferred. He liked the way the kitchen faced the mountains and the back deck was wide and welcoming, with an outdoor kitchen to rival the one inside.

It was all exactly as he'd dreamed it would be.

And he hated it.

Because Addie wasn't in it with him. Because it wasn't the house at Red Hill.

Was he losing hope that she would come for him?

Maybe. A little.

Was he considering saying to hell with giving her the time to make her choice and just going after her? So what if he was? If she was going to make the *wrong* choice, well, where was the good in that?

Those were the questions that chased themselves around in his brain constantly now. The only thing that kept him from going after her was the promise he'd made her: to let her do her own choosing in her own time.

First thing, he made coffee with his brand-new pod machine and he carried a full cup out to the front porch as he did every morning, to sit on the step and stare off toward Red Hill and tell himself that today was the day Addie Anne would finally appear on his doorstep to tell him she loved him and wanted him to come home.

She wasn't out there.

But his heart did a forward roll in his chest anyway.

Because a scarecrow in a business suit sat on the front porch swing, his arm around a lady scarecrow in denim overalls, with a roundness at her waistline that could only mean the lady scarecrow was about to have a little pile of straw. The husband scarecrow had a white picture album in his lap.

James set his coffee on the little table by the swing and picked up the album. Inside the front cover was his and Addie's marriage certificate, complete with the seal of the Arapahoe County Clerk. Legal and binding. He smiled to himself at the thought and turned the next page and then the next, taking his time, thumbing through the pictures of him and Addie on their wedding day.

They both looked so happy. As though the wedding really was the real thing and what they both wanted.

Because they *had* been happy. And it had been exactly what *he* wanted, at least.

And the scarecrows in the porch swing had him thinking she was finally admitting that she wanted it, too.

Carefully, he set the album back down in the lap of the scarecrow. He picked up his coffee and took a sip of his favorite morning blend. His knees felt a little wobbly—with hope and anticipation, with the thrill of knowing she had to be somewhere nearby. He went to the front steps and sat down. The coffee sloshed in his cup; his damn hand was shaking. Carefully, he set the cup beside him, up against the porch post, where he knew it wouldn't spill.

Only then did he dare to say her name. "Addie."

For endless seconds there was nothing. And then he heard her footsteps, light and quick as ever, coming around the corner from the side deck.

There was plenty of room on the step beside him. She dropped into the empty space, filling it with everything that mattered in the world.

His vision fogged over with unmanly tears. He didn't dare to look at her. "Addie," he whispered, as if it were the only word he knew.

She took his hand. Nothing had ever meant so much as that—her hand in his, guiding his palm to rest on her belly.

"Rounder," he said, his voice a sandpaper rasp.

"James, I…" She seemed unable to go on. But then she did. "I got here an hour ago, set out the scarecrows and then couldn't quite manage to knock on your door. I've been sitting in a chair on the side deck, trying to get up the nerve to face you. I'm such a wimp…"

"No, you're not."

"Yeah, I am."

He couldn't stand anymore not to see her face. Slowly, he turned his head. "Where's your horse?"

"I drove the pickup, left it around that bend in your driveway." She pointed toward a clump of ponderosa pines not far from the house. "It seemed so important, that you see the scarecrows first. And the wedding album. Carm sent it about two months ago. I stuck it under some towels in the upstairs hall closet, hid it from you."

"And from yourself?"

A little hum of agreement escaped her. She stared off toward the pines and confessed, "I hid the marriage license, too. That was silly, huh? Like hiding what we really are to each other would make it so I never had to tell you what I'm so afraid to say."

"You can do it," he said gently. "I know you can."

She turned her head to gaze at him again. Her golden eyes shone and her soft mouth trembled. And then, at last, she gave him the words he'd waited so long to hear. "I…don't like my life without you. I miss you so much, it hurts. I…well, I *have* made my choice and my choice is *you*, James. I want you to come back to me, please. I want you as my husband and a second father to my baby. I want us to have *more* babies—I mean, if you want that, too…"

"You bet I do."

"I…I love you, James." A small cry escaped her. "There. I said it." She squeezed her eyes shut, quivered out another breath—and opened her eyes again. "You're still here."

He felt the welcoming smile break across his face. "Damn it, Addie. I was getting worried." He couldn't wait a second longer. He reached for her.

"James." She melted against him with another, happier cry.

"Addie, Addie..." He buried his face in the crook of her neck and breathed in the yearned-for scent of her. "I love you. Only you. Always."

She held on so tight. "I love you, too. I love you, love you, love you, I do."

He took that sweet mouth of hers then, in a kiss he would never forget for as long as he lived. A kiss of reunion, a kiss that promised she would take him with her, home to Red Hill.

A kiss that said she was ready at last to take a chance on forever.

With him.

After the kiss, he got up. She rose beside him. He took her hand and led her into the house. He showed her the rooms and the back deck and the outside kitchen.

And the master bedroom, too. They spent an hour in there, celebrating their reunion. It was by far the happiest he'd ever been in that king-size bed.

Afterward, they dressed slowly, stealing kisses as they buttoned up and pulled on their boots, laughing together like a couple of kids.

"This house is beautiful," she said once they had all their clothes back on and sat on the bed side by side.

"I think we can get a good price for it," he replied with satisfaction.

"But...do you want to live here? I would be happy to live here. It's such a fine house and it's right next to Red Hill."

He lifted her hand and kissed the back of it. "It was my dream house."

"I know. And I mean it. Let's live here. As long as we're together, I'm happy wherever we are."

"No."

"Are you sure?"

"Yes. Dreams change, Addie Anne. I don't want to live here anymore. We belong at Red Hill. I want us to raise our family there." He pulled her close for another sweet, endless kiss. When he lifted his head, he said, "Give me five minutes. I'll pack up a few things and we'll go home."

* * * * *

MILLS & BOON®

Cherish™

EXPERIENCE THE ULTIMATE RUSH OF FALLING IN LOVE

0516/23

MILLS & BOON®

Mills & Boon have been at the heart of romance since 1908... and while the fashions may have changed, one thing remains the same: from pulse-pounding passion to the gentlest caress, we're always known how to bring romance alive.

Now, we're delighted to present you with these irresistible illustrations, inspired by the vintage glamour of our covers. So indulge your wildest dreams and unleash your imagination as we present the most iconic Mills & Boon moments of the last century.

Visit **www.millsandboon.co.uk/ArtofRomance** to order yours!

MILLS & BOON®

Why shop at millsandboon.co.uk?

Each year, thousands of romance readers find their perfect read at millsandboon.co.uk. That's because we're passionate about bringing you the very best romantic fiction. Here are some of the advantages of shopping at www.millsandboon.co.uk:

* **Get new books first**—you'll be able to buy your favourite books one month before they hit the shops

* **Get exclusive discounts**—you'll also be able to buy our specially created monthly collections, with up to 50% off the RRP

* **Find your favourite authors**—latest news, interviews and new releases for all your favourite authors and series on our website, plus ideas for what to try next

* **Join in**—once you've bought your favourite books, don't forget to register with us to rate, review and join in the discussions

Visit **www.millsandboon.co.uk**
for all this and more today!